Praise for *New York Times* bestselling author Karen White

"There is a rhythm to the writing of Karen White. It has a pace, a beat, a cadence that is all its own."   —Jackie K. Cooper, The Huffington Post

"White captures the true essence of Charleston by intertwining the sights and smells of the historic town with an enchanting story filled with ghostly spirits, love, and forgiveness . . . a once-in-a-lifetime series."   —Fresh Fiction

"White's dizzying carousel of a plot keeps those pages turning, so much so that the book can [be]—and should be—finished in one afternoon, interrupted only by a glass of sweet iced tea."   —Oprah.com

"An intriguing and romantic family drama."   —*Booklist*

"A story as intricate and sturdy as a sweetgrass basket, with the fresh, magnetic voices of its headstrong characters."   —ArtsATL

"A read that plumbs the depth of humanity, of life and death and tragedy and perseverance. . . . White is adept at writing page-turners."
                                                       —*The Herald-Sun* (NC)

"This is storytelling of the highest order: the kind of book that leaves you both deeply satisfied and aching for more."
   —Beatriz Williams, *New York Times* bestselling author of *Tiny Little Thing*

"Readers will find White's prose an uplifting experience, as she is a truly gifted storyteller."   —*Las Vegas Review-Journal*

Other Titles
by Karen White

The Color of Light

Learning to Breathe

Pieces of the Heart

The Memory of Water

The Lost Hours

On Folly Beach

Falling Home

The Beach Trees

Sea Change

After the Rain

The Time Between

A Long Time Gone

The Sound of Glass

The Forgotten Room
(cowritten with Beatriz Williams and Lauren Willig)

Flight Patterns

Spinning the Moon

The Night the Lights Went Out

Dreams of Falling

The Tradd Street Series

The House on Tradd Street

The Girl on Legare Street

The Strangers on Montagu Street

Return to Tradd Street

THE GUESTS ON SOUTH BATTERY

KAREN WHITE

Berkley

New York

BERKLEY

An imprint of Penguin Random House LLC

375 Hudson Street, New York, New York 10014

ISBN: 9780399584701

The Library of Congress cataloged the hardcover edition of this title as follows:

Names: White, Karen (Karen S.) author.
Title: The guests on South Battery/Karen White.
Description: First Edition. | New York: Berkley, 2017. | Series: Tradd Street; 5
Identifiers: LCCN 2016032087 (print) | LCCN 2016038647 (ebook) |
ISBN 9780451475237 (hardback) | ISBN 9780698193000 (ebook)
Subjects: LCSH: Women real estate agents—Fiction. | Women psychics—Fiction. |
Haunted houses—Fiction. | Historic buildings—South Carolina—Charleston—
Fiction. | Charleston (S.C.)—Fiction. | BISAC: FICTION/Contemporary Women. |
FICTION/Ghost. | FICTION/Mystery & Detective/Women Sleuths. |
GSAFD: Ghost stories.
Classification: LCC PS3623.H5776 G84 2017 (print) | LCC PS3623.H5776 (ebook) |
DDC 813/.6—dc23
LC record available at https://lccn.loc.gov/2016032087

Berkley hardcover edition / January 2017
Berkley trade paperback edition / August 2018

Printed in the United States of America
1   3   5   7   9   10   8   6   4   2

Cover art by Stephen Magsig
Cover design by Rita Frangie
Book design by Alissa Theodor

To Meghan,
who loves Charleston as much as I do

Acknowledgments

Thank you to the City of Charleston and its lovely inhabitants, both living and gone, who have inspired this series.

CHAPTER 1

There is no escaping the dead. On the slender peninsula that is Charleston, we cannot help being surrounded by them, packed as they are into ancient cemeteries behind ornate iron fencing. Beneath our streets. And under our homes and parking garages. Land is at a premium here, and it was inevitable that over the course of time the living and the dead would eventually rub elbows. Most residents of the Holy City are blissfully unaware of its former citizens who have passed on but whose names and homes we share and whose presence lingers still. Others, like me, are not so lucky.

It's one of the reasons why I've always been such a light sleeper. Even before I became the owner of a needy, money-sucking historic home on Tradd Street, and then the mother of twins, I always slept half awake, anticipating a cold hand on my shoulder or a shadow by the window. For years I'd learned how to ignore them, to pretend I'd felt only a draft, had seen only a shift in the light as morning nudged the night. But that's the thing with pretending. It doesn't make them go away.

Which is why when the shrill of the telephone jerked me fully awake I was already reaching for the nightstand to answer it before I remembered that we no longer kept a house phone in our bedroom.

Sitting straight up in bed, I stared at my nightstand, where my cell phone lay, its face glowing with an unexpected blue light, the ring tone not my usual "Mamma Mia" but identical to the tone of the now-defunct landline handset.

Fumbling to pick it up before it woke my sleeping companions, I slid my thumb across the screen and answered, "Hello?"

A distant, hollow sound, like a small rock being dropped into a deep well, echoed in my ear.

"Hello?" I said again. "Grandmother?" She'd been dead since I was a little girl, but it wouldn't have been the first time she'd called me since then. Yet I knew it wasn't her. When she called I always had a sense of peace and well-being. Of love and protection. Not the feeling of unseen insects crawling over my scalp. And somewhere, in that deep dark space at the other end of the line, was the sound of groaning nails and something being pried loose, and a tinny note, almost indecipherable, vibrating in the empty air.

I pulled the phone from my ear and hit END, noticing the local 843 area code but not recognizing the number. Placing the phone back on the nightstand, I looked at the video monitor, which showed my ten-month-old twins sleeping peacefully in their nursery down the hall, then turned to Jack. I was met with the wet nose and large eyes of my dog, General Lee. I'd inherited him along with the house and housekeeper, Mrs. Houlihan.

Despite my protestations that I didn't like dogs, I now found myself the owner of three. Even in his advanced years, General Lee had proven himself quite virile and had fathered a litter of puppies, two of which had been given to us as a wedding present the previous year. With the addition of a husband, two babies, and a stepdaughter, I barely recognized my life anymore and had to pinch myself on more than one occasion to make me believe it was true.

Which is why the phone call unnerved me more than it should have. The restless dead had left me alone for almost a year. It had been a blissful period when I'd begun to settle into my life as a new wife and mother without the distraction of spirits needing me for something. I'd even begun to hope that the dead had forgotten about me.

General Lee crawled on top of my pillow, above my head, allowing me to see Jack's face in the soft glow of the monitor. I still couldn't believe that he was my husband. That the irritating, opinionated, overly charming, and irresistible bestselling author Jack Trenholm was my husband and the father of my children. He was still irritating and opinionated, especially where I was concerned, but that somehow added to his attraction.

"Good morning, beautiful," he slurred, his voice thick with sleep. He reached over and pulled me toward him, spoon position, and I melted into his warmth. His lips found my neck, and the rest of my skin seemed to jump to attention, hoping to be next in line. "Who was that on the phone?"

"Hmm?" I said, forgetting what the word "phone" meant.

"The phone. It rang. Was it important?"

"Hmm," I repeated, the sound coming from deep in my throat. I'd already started to turn in his arms, my hands sliding up his chest, any phone call long since forgotten.

"Because I was wondering if it was your boss, checking to see if you were still planning on coming in today. Before your maternity leave, you were always there by seven on Mondays."

My eyes flew wide-open, his words the equivalent of ice-cold water thrown on my head. I jerked up in bed, receiving an unhappy groan from General Lee, and picked up my phone again. Five after seven. I looked across the room, where I'd set three different alarm clocks, all the old-fashioned wind-up kind, just in case the electricity went out in the middle of the night and my phone battery died.

I stared at them for a long moment before Jack sighed. "You really should keep your glasses nearby. I've seen you wearing them often enough that it wouldn't be a shock." He sat up so he could see better. "That's odd. It looks like they're all stopped at ten minutes past four."

I leaped from the bed, not really registering what he'd just said. It was my first day back after nearly a year away on extended maternity leave. It was supposed to have been only until the babies were three months old, but our inability to find a nanny who would stay longer than two weeks had proven not only baffling but problematic.

I ran to the bathroom and turned on the shower, then retreated to my closet, where I had laid out my outfit—complete with shoes and accessories—the night before. I threw off my nightgown, a slinky silk thing Jack had bought for me that didn't resemble the old high-necked flannel gowns of my single days, folded it neatly on my dressing table bench, and jumped in the shower.

Five minutes later I was brushing my teeth while simultaneously buttoning a blouse that didn't want to be buttoned and zipping up a skirt with an equally reluctant zipper. I stared at my reflection in the full-length mirror, too horrified by what I saw to allow my gaze to linger very long. I could hope that everybody in the office had gone blind and wouldn't notice my unfastened blouse and skirt, or I'd have to find something else to wear.

I carefully rinsed off my toothbrush head and handle and replaced it on the holder—only two tries to get it standing up perfectly straight—before marching back into the closet. "Damn dry cleaners," I muttered as I tried on outfit after outfit. I had no idea to whom Mrs. Houlihan was taking my clothes to be cleaned, but it needed to stop immediately or I'd be reduced to wearing my maternity clothes. The ones with elastic seams and stretchy fabrics.

When I finally emerged into the bedroom, I wore an A-line dress my mother had purchased for me around the fifth month of my pregnancy. The way it hugged my chest and nothing else and its pretty green hue that turned the color of my hazel eyes to something more exotic, like jungle leaves, were its only assets. I hobbled in my five-inch Manolo stilettos, my toes folding in on themselves, and wondered how my shoes had managed to shrink along with my clothes. Maybe there was something in the air in the newly renovated closet, something my best friend, Dr. Sophie Wallen-Arasi, professor of historic preservation at the College of Charleston, might know about. She was the one who had supervised its historically conscious construction, along with the never-ending number of renovations and preservation projects in my house on Tradd Street.

Like the recent roof replacement, which still had me dreaming of renting a bulldozer and being done with all of it. I had never liked old houses, mostly because of the restless dead who hated to leave them. And now that I owned one, and could even grudgingly admit that I occasionally experienced fond feelings toward it, I often found myself torn between thoughts of hugging that rare slab of Adams mantel and of accidentally throwing a flaming torch through a downstairs window.

I paused by the bed, where General Lee was now spooning with Jack. Jack opened his eyes, those beautiful blue eyes that both twins had inherited along with his black hair and dimples—I'd apparently been just an incubator—and I felt my knees soften. I wondered how long we had to be married before that would stop.

I picked up my phone and checked the time—eight o'clock. On the monitor, I watched as Sarah began to fret, right on time, in her pink canopy–draped crib. She was more reliable than the bells of St. Michael's for telling time, especially when it came to her feeding schedule. Her brother, JJ—for Jack Junior—continued to sleep peacefully in his own crib, flat on his back, with all four limbs spread out like a little starfish. No matter what position we placed him in to sleep, he always ended up like that. Just like his father.

"I got this," Jack said, reaching up to kiss me, his lips lingering on mine and making me regret my decision to get out of bed.

"I know. It's just . . . well, I've been with them since they were born."

"So have I. There's nothing to worry about."

I bit my lip. "I have their charts in the nursery and in the kitchen. Don't forget to write down all their bowel movements, including descriptions, as well as what they eat and how much. And I've laid out their outfits in their room, including spares in case anything gets dirty. If they need a third, their hangers are color-coded, so it's easy to match different pants with tops."

Jack stared up at me for a moment. "Sweetheart, don't take this the wrong way, but do you think the reason we haven't been able to hold on to a nanny is that things might be a little too . . . regulated?"

I straightened. "Of course not. Children do best when they're on a schedule and live in an organized environment. It's not my fault that I seem to know more about child-rearing than some of these so-called nannies. We'll try a new agency with more stringent qualifications. I just need to ask around, because I think I've already tried the ones that were recommended to us."

"You might need to go out of state." A corner of his lips turned up, and for a moment I thought he might be joking.

"That's a good idea. I'll make some calls this afternoon."

Sarah started to fret in earnest, while JJ continued to be oblivious. Jack was already out of bed and padding toward the door. "I know it's hard, but you probably shouldn't go in to see them—it might rile you up more than them. You'll see them when you get home, and I'll Skype with you at lunchtime. We'll be fine. I'm just working on revisions my editor wanted for my book, and I can do that while watching two little babies. I mean, how hard can it be?"

It was my turn to stare at him. "My mom said to call if you needed *anything*, and I'm just a phone call away as well. Sophie said to call her if you got stuck, but between you and me, I'd use her as a last resort. Last time I called she mentioned a baby massage while listening to whale music." I gave in to an involuntary shudder.

He walked back to me and gave me a long, deep kiss, one that left me not caring that I had to repair my lipstick. "We'll be fine. Now go."

His firm hand steered me toward the stairs as he headed to the nursery, briefly brushing my rear end before he let go. "And I just might have a surprise for you when you get home."

His eyes definitely held *that look* and it took all my strength reserves to continue down the stairs.

Halfway down, Nola's bedroom door opened and she peered out, a puppy in each arm—appropriately named Porgy and Bess—as she waved a front paw of each dog. "Say bye-bye, Mommy. Have a great first day back at work. Bring us back some kibble."

Nola, Jack's daughter whose surprise appearance after her mother's death a few years before had taken a bit of an adjustment, was one of life's unexpected gifts—and I never thought I'd be saying that about any teenager. A sophomore now at Ashley Hall, she was quirky, smart, an accomplished songwriter, and as much my daughter now as Jack's. Like all his children, she was his spitting image, right down to the dimple in her chin. I'd come to the conclusion long ago that Jack's genes were simply bullies in the conception department. She was a vegan (most of the time), and my self-appointed nutrition guru who liked to slip in tofu and quinoa on Mrs. Houlihan's shopping list in place of creamed spinach and fried okra, but I loved her anyway.

"Thanks, Nola. Good luck on your French test. Alston's mother is driving the morning and afternoon carpools today, so you can spend the time going over your flash cards."

"Yes, Melanie," she said, rolling her eyes.

I heard Mrs. Houlihan in the kitchen and tiptoed toward the front door to avoid her. Sophie had detected wood rot in one of the kitchen windows and had it removed so it could be restored and then reinstalled. That had been six weeks ago, prompting me to suggest replacing all the windows with new, vinyl ones, knowing it was only a matter of time before the remaining ones would start going soft around the sills and leaking water. Sophie, a new mother herself, had clutched at her heart and had to sit down, looking at me as if I'd just kicked a puppy. I'd let the suggestion drop. But I was tired of listening to Mrs. Houlihan complain about how dark it was in the kitchen with a boarded-up window, and how it was impossible for her to continue to work in such conditions.

I pulled on my coat before opening the front door, then shut it silently behind me. I drew up short at the sight of a van parked at the curb, HARD ROCK FOUNDATIONS painted on the side, and my father's car behind it. My father, with whom I'd recently reconciled, had made it his mission to restore my Loutrel Briggs garden to its former glory.

He'd done such a good job that both his remarriage to my mother as well as my own wedding had been held beneath the ancient oak tree in the back garden surrounded by roses and tea olives.

But that didn't explain why he and Rich Kobylt, my plumber, foundation repair technician, general handyman, and even erstwhile counselor, would be there so early in the morning. I remembered my conversation with my father the previous evening, his asking me when I planned to leave for work. As if he'd been secretly scheduling something with Rich Kobylt that he didn't want me to know about.

Probably because Rich's presence upset me. Not because of his penchant for low-slung and overly revealing pants, or even the sound of fluttering dollar bills and the ringing of a cash register I usually heard right after he showed up on my doorstep. His presence upset me because Rich had the uncanny ability to uncover things that I'd preferred not to deal with. Like foundation cracks and crumbling chimney bricks. And buried skeletons.

I looked with longing at the carriage house, where my Volvo station wagon was parked next to Jack's minivan, wanting nothing more than to pretend that I had no idea I had visitors and head into work as planned. But I was an adult now. The wife and mother of three. I was supposed to be brave.

Mentally girding my loins, I headed down the recently rebricked pathway to the rear garden, past the silent swing hanging from the oak tree, and the fountain, recently relieved of two skeletons, burbling in the chill winter air. I stopped when I reached the back corner of the house. I must have made a noise, because both my father and Rich turned to look at me.

They were standing in the rear garden, where the famous Louisa roses had been blooming for almost a century. But where there had once been rosebushes there was now only a deep, circular indentation on the ground.

My father took a step toward me, as if trying to block my view. "Sweet pea—I thought you'd be at work."

I frowned at him, then directed my attention toward Rich, quickly averting my eyes when I saw he was squatting at the edge of the indentation, his back to me. "What's happened?"

Thankfully, Rich stood. "Good mornin', Miz Middleton—I mean Miz Trenholm." His cheeks flushed. "I think with all this rain we've been having, this part of the yard sank. Looks like there might be some kind of structure underneath." He squatted to look more closely into the fissure and I turned my head. There are just some things you can't unsee.

"A structure?" I waited for him to say the word "cemetery." I'd seen *Poltergeist*, after all. And it wasn't as if that sort of thing hadn't happened before in Charleston. The recent construction of the new Gaillard Auditorium had unearthed a number of graves that had been there since the Colonial era.

"I'm sure it's nothing, sweet pea," my father said as he took another step toward me. I made the mistake of meeting his eyes, and knew he was also thinking about the anonymous letter that had been sent into the *Post and Courier* and printed right after the twins were born by intrepid reporter and staff writer Suzy Dorf. Something about more bodies to be found on my property.

I hadn't realized until now that I'd been holding my breath ever since, waiting for just this moment, and knowing that even though I claimed to be done with spirits and the dead, they would never be done with me.

I sidestepped them both to stand near the deep indentation that looked like a navel in my garden, old bricks now visible through the soggy earth and ruined rosebushes. My phone began to ring again, the old-fashioned telephone ring that didn't exist on my phone. I ended the call, then turned off my phone, knowing I'd hear only empty space if I answered it. Somehow this chasm in my garden and the phone call were related. And the clocks in my bedroom, all stopped at the same time. I didn't know how, but I suspected that I'd eventually find out whether I wanted to or not. There was no such thing as coincidence, according to Jack. And when my phone began to ring again, I had the sinking feeling that he was right.

CHAPTER 2

Despite the cold January air and shoes that felt like vises, I decided to walk the few short blocks to Henderson House Realty on Broad Street. I had hopes that the bright blue sky and the sun that shone valiantly despite the frigid temperature might clear my head. By the time I reached my old standby, Ruth's Bakery, my head was clear of all thoughts, but only because my feet were screaming at me, overriding any coherent thinking.

I smiled with surprise at Ruth, who shoved a folded-over bag and foam cup across the counter, just like old times. "How did you know I was starting back at work today?"

She smiled, her gold tooth winking at me. "That sweet girl, Nola, just called me. She's so thoughtful and caring, isn't she?" Ruth's hand patted the bag, and I felt my heart sink.

"Nola?" I asked, staring in horror at the bag, knowing it wouldn't contain my favorite cream-filled chocolate-covered doughnuts. "What's in the bag? Dirt and cardboard or grass and tree moss?" I wasn't completely joking. During my pregnancy, both Nola and Sophie had done their best to sabotage my food choices just because my ankles had been a little bit swollen. And Ruth had been a willing participant in their subterfuge.

Ruth threw back her head and laughed, her dark eyes shining as if I'd just made a joke. "No, ma'am. This is my new spinach and goat cheese in a chickpea flour wrap. Your friend Sophie gave me the recipe and I said I'd try it. Not that I'd eat it myself, but I figured being a businesswoman I should cater to my health-conscious customers, too."

"Of which I'm not one," I said. "I'm one of your taste-conscious customers—don't forget about us." I indicated the cup. "Is there at least lots of whipped cream and sugar in that?"

She made a face. "In green tea? No. Just good-for-you tea. Still nice and hot."

"I'm sorry you went to all that trouble, but I'd like my usual, please." I looked at her hopefully.

Instead of taking back the bag and cup, she let her gaze wander down the length of my maternity dress. "You sure about that?"

I stuck out an ankle, back to its trim prepregnancy size. "See? No more swollen ankles! I can eat what I like now."

Still, she didn't move. I caught sight of the clock on the wall behind her. Not having time to argue, I grabbed the bag and cup and slid a few bills across the counter. "Fine. But tomorrow, I'd like to go back to our regularly scheduled program. Don't make me turn to Glazed Gourmet Donuts on King. It's out of my way, but I need my doughnuts in the morning and can't be responsible for my actions if I'm deprived of them."

Ruth stopped smiling and I realized that my voice had risen an octave. Without breaking eye contact, she reached over and grabbed a single sugar packet and placed it on top of my cup. "Sounds like somebody's having withdrawal. Tomorrow we'll try half a packet."

I narrowed my eyes. "We'll see about that." I made my way to the door.

"You bring those sweet babies in, you hear? I'm sure they're getting so big. And with that Mr. Trenholm as their daddy, I just can't imagine how beautiful they must be."

I was torn between a mother's pride over her babies and resentment over how everybody completely overlooked the fact that I was the one who had not only carried the babies for nine months, but also given birth to them.

I backed out of the door. "Well, then. Maybe we can come to some sort of a deal."

She raised a dark eyebrow, and I did the same before turning around and letting the door close behind me.

I hobbled the few blocks to my office, my blistered feet almost completely numb by the time I opened the door into the reception area with its tasteful leather furniture and pineapple motif evident in the lamps, art, and throw pillows—all in an attempt to appear "old Charleston."

"May I help you?" said a voice from behind the reception desk.

I stared at the stranger. She had a mop of dark, curly hair and bright green eyes. She was one of those older women whose age was impossible to determine because of a lifelong avoidance of the sun and an expensive skin care regimen. A brilliantly colored enamel dragonfly pin sat gracefully on the lapel of her pale blue jacket. "Where's Joyce?"

"She's moved to Scotland to immerse herself in her knitting. Wanted to be closer to the source, she said. She trained me for about a month and now I'm going solo while I study for my real estate license. I'm Mary Thompson, but everybody calls me Jolly." She beamed and I noticed her sparkling earrings that matched her pin, with no golf motif in sight. I still missed Nancy Flaherty, my favorite receptionist who'd been here before Joyce, but she'd followed her love of golf and Tiger Woods and moved to Florida.

"Oh," I said. "It's nice to meet you." I hadn't expected a big welcome-back celebration, but a familiar face would have been nice. Especially since I was in the middle of an alarming sugar low. "I'm Melanie Middleton—I mean Trenholm." I still wasn't used to saying that. "I'm back from maternity leave."

The woman's smile broadened. "Oh, yes. I've heard all about you." She paused, leaving me to try to guess what she'd heard. "You used to be the number-one salesperson here. We have a new leaderboard now—it's no longer a chalkboard. Do you think I'll need to have a nameplate made with your name on it? Lots of competition for that number-one spot, and you've been gone awhile."

Maybe it was my blistered feet, my lack of sugar and caffeine, or the absence of my babies, but I was sure I was about to cry.

Jolly smiled sympathetically. "It's always hard coming back." She brightened. "I guess word has got around that you're back, though." She slid three pink message slips toward me. "These came in this morning—and there's someone waiting for you in your office."

"For me?"

Jolly nodded. "She's a walk-in, but she asked for you by name. I told her I wasn't sure when you'd be in—Mr. Henderson said you're usually here much earlier—but she said she didn't mind waiting." She slid a clip-board around to face her. "I made her sign in. She said her name is Jayne Smith—Jayne with a Y—and she's relocating here from Alabama."

"Alabama," I repeated. It had been so long since I'd shown homes to anyone that I was searching through my fuzzy head for what I was supposed to do next. And where Alabama was. I'd hoped to have the first week to get my bearings again, but the thought of a prospective client did manage to stir my adrenaline a bit.

"Yes," said Jolly. "And, Melanie? May I call you Melanie?"

"Of course."

She pulled out a notebook with a photograph of an alligator glued to the front cover, and opened it. Very carefully, she picked up her pencil and crossed off the first two items on a very long list. I peered at the notebook and, reading upside down, read, *Give Melanie her telephone messages. Let her know a client is waiting in her office.* I'd started to read the third item, *Find recipe for . . .*

Jolly slammed the notebook shut. With a guilty smile, she said, "I'm a habitual list maker. Pay me no mind."

I found myself relaxing for the first time that morning. "I think we'll get along just fine, Jolly." I turned toward the corridor that led to the small offices and cubicles of the various agents. I supposed I should have been grateful that Mr. Henderson had allowed me to keep my office, a perk to only the top-selling agents. I hoped that meant he was confident I'd be at the top of the leaderboard soon, assuming that I'd be given a name tag.

"Melanie?"

I paused and faced the new receptionist. "Yes, Jolly?"

"Since we're going to be working together, there's something you should know about me." She paused, her blue-painted fingernails playing with the dragonfly pin. "I'm a psychic. I do readings for people at fairs and festivals on the weekends, but since we're going to be coworkers, I'll give you a discount if you're interested in a reading. Just let me know."

My earlier optimism quickly evaporated. I wasn't exactly sure how I should respond, so I just smiled and nodded, then made my way back to my office.

Jayne—with a Y—had her back toward me when I reached the door. She faced the credenza, where she was carefully organizing my magazines and journals, making sure that each was spaced apart the same distance, and that the edges lined up in a perfect parallel to the edge of the furniture. I frowned. They might be out-of-date, considering I hadn't been into the office in a long time, but I always kept them tidy, organized by date, and with the title and issue of each volume clearly visible. And I'd left strict instructions that they weren't to be disturbed in my absence. I found it vaguely annoying that she'd mess with my magazines, and wondered if she might be nervous.

"Good morning," I said as I placed my bag and pink slips on the top of the desk.

The woman turned and smiled, then held out her hand to me. "Hello," she said, shaking my hand in a firm grasp. "I'm Jayne Smith." Her accent was definitely Southern, but not Charlestonian. Her hand felt bony, matching her thin wrists. And the rest of her body I noticed as I stepped back. The woman looked practically emaciated despite the fact that there were distinctive powdered sugar crumbs on her upper lip.

"Melanie Trenholm," I said, trying to ignore the crumbs, but wondering how I could let her know without any awkwardness. When I dropped my hand I surreptitiously flicked my index finger over my own lip. Her green eyes widened in understanding as she reached into her purse and, after removing several candy bar wrappers, found a napkin to wipe her mouth.

"I guess that's what I get for giving in to temptation," she said. "There's this wonderful bakery down the street—Ruth's Bakery, I think—and I could smell the doughnuts from the sidewalk. I've never been able to turn down sugar."

My own smile faltered as I thought about my ex-favorite bakery, imagining I could smell the sweet aroma of baking doughnuts. Feeling more than a little bit hurt, I reached for the paper bag from Ruth's and dropped it in the wastebasket, then resisted the urge to ask Jayne for her candy wrappers to throw away so I could bury my nose in them later.

I indicated for Jayne to take the seat in front of my desk while I sat down across from her. She was younger than me, early thirties, I thought, and her hair was blond—dyed—but her eyebrows were dark. She was attractive in an all-American way, with long legs and a wide smile. Despite her thinness, she had the kind of chest I'd always wanted yet had attained only when I was pregnant and nursing. Or wearing a padded bra. My breasts were still bigger than they had been, but had somehow managed to migrate to new positions on my chest since the children were born.

"I'm sorry to just drop in. I can reschedule if you have other appointments," Jayne said.

I was about to pretend to check my calendars when I paused. There was something oddly familiar about her smile, and the way the light through the office window lightened her eyes to a pale green.

"Have we met before?" I asked.

She shook her head. "Probably not. I've never been to Charleston before. Never been much farther than Birmingham before now, actually." She smiled again, but the light behind her eyes had dimmed somewhat. "I think I have one of those faces that look like a lot of other people's."

"That must be it," I said.

The sound of magazines slipping off the credenza and slapping against one another as they hit the floor had us both jumping from our chairs. Jayne quickly moved to pick them up, stacking them as neatly as they'd been before. "I must have put these too near the edge."

"Oh, okay." But they hadn't been. They had been five inches from the edge, and there was no way they could have slid on their own. I frowned. There was another presence in the room, someone I couldn't see and could barely feel. Not even a shadow, or a shimmer of light. I could tell that whoever it was *wanted* me to see them, but something was preventing me. I could almost see a curtain that had been pulled across my sixth sense, forcing me to use only the five senses everybody else had.

I sat down suddenly, confused and irritated. *I* wanted to call the shots regarding my inherited ability or disability—depending on how I was feeling about it at any given time—and something I couldn't understand was blocking me. I recalled how during my pregnancy my ability to see dead people had disappeared and how I'd found myself oddly missing it. I couldn't help wondering whether motherhood had somehow had the same effect. Maybe that was the reason I'd been undisturbed for so long. Maybe.

Jayne returned to her seat and smiled, but there was something different about her expression. Like a painting where the artist was still a few brushstrokes away from completion. "I'm looking for a Realtor. And when I was walking by the agency this morning, I felt compelled to stop. I saw your photo in the window and you looked . . ."

She paused, not sure I wanted to hear what she had to say. I was notoriously unphotogenic, as my driver's license photo could attest. I had visions of it pinned to a bulletin board in the DMV's break room as an example of their best work.

"Approachable," she finished. "Like you'd understand what it was I needed."

Feeling pleased and not a little relieved, I pulled out a notepad and pencil and regarded her. "So, what can I help you with?"

"I need to sell a house. And buy a new one."

"I only work in Charleston. So if you have a house in Birmingham to sell . . ."

She shook her head. "I've inherited a house, here in Charleston. It's an old house—I've walked by it a few times. I want to sell it and buy a new one."

I sat back, not completely understanding. "Have you been inside the house?"

"No. I don't need to. I don't like old houses as a rule, so there's no reason for me to go inside."

I stared at her. "You don't like old houses?"

"I don't like all that . . . history in a place. I want something fresh and new. Lots of metal and glass and stone."

"I see," I said, jotting down notes. I did see. I'd said those exact same words when I first inherited my house on Tradd Street and had said them often since, the most recent this very morning as I'd turned my back on my sunken garden and headed toward my car. "Where is your house located?"

"On South Battery Street. Right near the corner of Legare—the big white house with the portico and columns."

I thought for a moment. "The old Pinckney house?" I knew it, of course. I was on a first-name basis with just about every old house in Charleston either through a family connection or from my job as a Realtor specializing in historic real estate. "Button Pinckney was an acquaintance of my mine—a lovely woman. Was she a close relative?"

Jayne looked down at her hands as if embarrassed. "Actually, I'd never met her. And I didn't know until now that Caroline Pinckney had a nickname. I didn't even know of her existence until three weeks ago when her lawyers contacted me to let me know I'd inherited her estate."

Déjà vu. I had a flash of memory of me sitting in a lawyer's office not far from here as a lawyer explained to me that Nevin Vanderhorst, a man I'd met just once, had left me his crumbling house on Tradd Street that I neither wanted nor needed.

I was clenching the pencil so tightly that I had to place it on the pad of paper. I forced a smile. "Miss Pinckney was a friend of both my mother's and my mother-in-law's. They all went to school together at Ashley Hall." I thought for a moment. "As far as I recall, Button never married or had any children. There was an older brother, I believe, who died a few years back. I don't believe he had any children, either, although I'm pretty sure he was married at some point." I remembered, too, that there had been some sort of tragedy associated with the family, but I couldn't recall the details.

Jayne sighed. "Yes, well, you can't imagine my surprise to hear that I've inherited an old house from a complete stranger."

"Believe it or not, I actually can." I closed my mouth, unwilling to share my personal feelings toward old houses and the way the walls always seemed to be whispering. "Maybe your mother or father or some other family member might want to see it first before you make any decisions. Surely they'll have some idea as to why Miss Pinckney left her house to you."

Jayne went very still. "There's no one." She slowly raised her eyes to mine. "I don't have a family. I was raised in the foster care system and was never adopted."

"I'm sorry," I said. A disturbance in the air behind her made the space shimmer, like the shift in air pressure before a storm. I stared hard, trying to see what it was, but saw nothing. But I knew it was there, watching us. Listening. Wanting to be seen but unable to show itself. My gaze met Jayne's. She stared back at me unblinking, and again I felt as if we'd met before.

She continued. "I'm fine with it now—it was a long time ago. Maybe this inheritance is just karma for an unsettled childhood and I shouldn't question it too closely." She smiled brightly, and I almost believed her.

"Did the lawyer give any indication why Miss Pinckney chose you?"

"I did ask, but he said she didn't share any details or more information, even though he asked her repeatedly, anticipating, correctly, that

I'd have my own questions. He did say he'd done a little bit of research on his own but hadn't been able to discover anything."

There was something about this woman that I liked, that made me want to help her. Maybe it was because I remembered a time in my life when I'd felt like an abandoned orphan, navigating life all on my own. "My husband is a writer who writes books about the area and knows everybody in Charleston, living or dead. He has a real knack for finding unturned stones. If you'd like, I could ask him to help."

"Thank you—I'll think about it," she said. "I can't help wondering if finding out why would be a bit like looking a gift horse in the mouth."

I nodded, understanding her position more than she could imagine. "And you're sure you want to sell it?"

"Absolutely. Old houses don't appeal to me at all. They all have that . . . smell about them. Like decay and mildew and dust. That's why I'd like to take the money from the sale of the house and find something more modern and fresh. Preferably built within the last five years."

I nodded, thinking about my old condo in Mt. Pleasant, with its plain white walls and gleaming chrome and glass surfaces, where I'd lived before my unexpected inheritance and still thought fondly of from time to time. Usually directly after writing out another check to Rich Kobylt for a repair. "All right. But we'll have to go into the house to get a value. To see what kind of shape it's in and if it needs any imme-diate repairs before putting it on the market. Sadly, most of them do." I thought of Mr. Vanderhorst and his sad smile. *"It's like a piece of history you can hold in your hands."* I smiled at Jayne, trying to appear hopeful. "A good friend of mine—Dr. Sophie Wallen-Arasi—is a professor of historic preservation at the College of Charleston, and I know she'd love to come along and give us her professional opinion."

I could hear her swallow. "You can do that on your own, right? I wouldn't have to go inside, too, would I?"

"Not necessarily," I said, studying her. "But I think it would be a very good idea for you to see it for yourself. Who knows? Maybe you'll change your mind about selling. It's been known to happen."

"I won't," she said quickly. "So, ballpark—how much do you think the house could be worth? I'm not being mercenary or anything; it's just that I'll need to know how much I can spend on the new condo. I have no idea how long it will take to get a job here, so I won't be able to rely on a salary at first."

"To be honest, I have to go inside before I could make any determination. There are several houses on the same street that have sold in the low seven figures in the past few years, but there are also some that have sold for quite a bit less, mostly because of their condition. Buyers get them for a steal but then end up spending three or four times over the purchase price in restoration work. It would be in your best interest to get the highest selling price possible, which might mean doing some basic renovations before it hits the market."

She nodded slowly. "Well, that's a start anyway. And I've already made appointments with several agencies to start the job hunt. It's just a long process with background checks and all, and I really want the sale of the house behind me before I start working full-time. And I can't buy a new place until it sells."

I was busy writing down notes, including reminders to talk to Jack and my mother about Button Pinckney and her family, and their connection with Jayne Smith. "What is it that you do?" I asked absently.

"I'm a certified professional nanny."

The lead from my mechanical pencil snapped. "A nanny? Like, for small children?"

She laughed. "Are there any other kinds? But yes, a nanny for small children—and older ones, too. Some people find it odd that somebody raised without siblings would want to be a nanny, but I think that's why I am. I was in lots of foster families, and I always ended up taking care of the younger children. I guess even back then I knew that would be my only chance at having siblings—at least for a short time."

I placed the pencil down on my desk and leaned back in my chair. "What is your take on sleeping and feeding schedules for infants?"

"A definite must. Schedules are incredibly important to growing children. They need regular feeding and sleeping times."

"Family bed?"

"A bad idea."

"Bottles in the crib?"

"Never. Rots their teeth."

"Spanking?"

"Time-out chair is more effective."

"Cloth or disposable?"

"Disposable."

"Baby French lessons?"

"Ridiculous."

"Infant beauty pageants?"

Jayne sent me a sidewise glance. "Seriously? You don't seem the type."

I smiled. "I'm not—just checking." I pushed my chair back from the desk. "So, it just happens that I'm looking for a nanny for my ten-month-old twins. Their last one left rather suddenly and we're a bit desperate, I'm afraid. It seems as if we agree on many child-rearing issues. If you're interested, I'd love for you to come meet them and allow us to get to know each other better. Perhaps even make it a permanent thing if it all works out."

She practically beamed and I had to restrain myself from doing cartwheels around the room and giving myself fist bumps. "I'm definitely interested," she said.

"Good. I'll have to do a background check, of course."

"Absolutely. I can give you all the contact information from my agency in Birmingham, as well as references from my last three families. I think you'll be happy with my past performance."

I pulled out one of my business cards from the holder on my desk and handed it to her. I waited for her to say something about the multiple phone numbers, but instead she responded by sliding her own card across the desk toward me. I picked it up and saw that she had two cell phone numbers. I looked at her and smiled, feeling as if I had finally met a kindred spirit.

"Because you never know when one phone will stop working or has a dead battery," she explained.

"Exactly." My smile widened. "It's so nice to finally meet somebody who thinks ahead. Everybody else seems to only understand how to live in the minute."

Jayne stood, too. "I know, right? It can be annoying to be the only one prepared for the 'just in case' scenario." She reached her hand across the desk and we shook. "It's a pleasure meeting you. I'll get all my information together and bring it over later today so you can get started with my background check. And call me anytime to set up an appointment to meet your children and husband."

"And to go over and look at the Pinckney house. I'll check with Sophie about her availability and let you know."

Her smile dimmed. "All right. I guess the sooner we start, the sooner we can get it sold."

We said good-bye and I returned to my desk, spotting the pink slips Jolly had given me. Two were from my annoying cousin and Jack's ex-girlfriend, Rebecca, and one was from the journalist at the *Post and Courier*, Suzy Dorf, who had an abnormal interest in me and my house. Since I would have preferred to stick a knitting needle into my eyeball rather than speak with either of them, I folded each note up into tiny little squares, then placed them in the bottom of my trash can.

It was only when I picked up the phone to call Sophie that I realized the presence was gone, leaving only the fresh scent of rain as evidence that it had ever been there at all.

CHAPTER 3

Despite my battered and bruised feet, I nearly skipped home. It had been a long day, the bright spot being Skyping with Jack while he fed the babies their lunches of strained peas and pureed peaches. He'd still worn the T-shirt and pajama bottoms he'd slept in, but I refrained from commenting. I'd come to understand that writers had a few eccentricities I had to learn to live with. Not scheduling certain things like dressing in the morning or vetting one's sock and underwear drawer on a monthly basis were just a few of the quirks to which I was making an effort to adjust.

I couldn't wait to get home and kiss my babies and tell Jack that not only did I have a lead on a nanny, but I had three new clients—in addition to Jayne Smith—and six house showings already scheduled for the rest of the week. They'd all seen the ad I'd placed in the latest edition of *Charleston Magazine*, for which Nola had suggested including a picture of Jack and me, all three children, and the dogs in front of my Tradd Street house. She said it would make people believe that I knew what people meant when they said they were looking for a family home, and that I understood that historic homes were meant to be lived in.

I wasn't sure I believed all that, but if it helped me sell houses, so be it. During my downtime, in which I'd dealt with the prospect of losing my home, an angry ghost, a difficult pregnancy that included months of bed rest, and my undefined relationship with Jack, I'd lost out on two news-making sales in Charleston—the Chisholm-Alston Greek Revival purchased by a well-known international fashion designer and the old, dilapidated yet still magnificent Renaissance mansion known as Villa Margherita on South Battery. I'd cried for days after learning those homes had sold and I hadn't been the one to broker the deals. If anything, my anguish meant that my competitive spirit, dormant for so long, had reemerged kicking and screaming.

It was a good thing, considering we owed Nola for the money she'd given us to purchase the house when my ownership was contested. She was already a successful songwriter, having sold two songs to pop artist Jimmy Gordon and having one of them featured in an iPhone commercial, and she'd willingly given us the money, but neither Jack nor I would feel good about it until we paid her back in full with interest. Despite recent career setbacks, Jack had just signed a healthy two-book contract with his new publisher, but we were still trying to recover financially. Not to mention the fact that we owned an old house whose favorite hobby seemed to be hemorrhaging money.

My pace slowed as I neared my house, catching sight of not only Sophie's white Prius parked at the curb, but also Rich Kobylt's truck still in the same spot as I'd last seen it. This couldn't be good. I hadn't been able to reach Sophie when I tried earlier, and I wondered if she'd been avoiding speaking to me on the phone. She mistakenly believed that people would prefer bad news to be delivered in person. I didn't, simply because if there were no witnesses to me hearing the news, then I could pretend it never happened.

I stopped, considering retreating to the office, but I suddenly became aware of my feet—or what was left of them—and knew I couldn't. With a heavy sigh, I slipped off my shoes and limped the last hundred feet to the garden gate barefoot.

Sophie and Rich were standing by the indentation in my yard, now surrounded by yellow tape, along with a woman in her early twenties. Sophie spotted me and turned around with a huge smile. Her daughter, two months younger than my own babies, was worn in an outward-facing papoose, and gave me a single-toothed smile. She had dark, curly hair like her mother, big blue eyes like her father, Chad, and baby Birkenstocks over socks on her tiny feet. In my opinion, only babies looked good in Birkenstocks.

"Melanie!" Sophie said enthusiastically, making me immediately suspicious.

"Good to see you, Sophie. I've got to go change and check on the babies. . . ."

"Nice try. Nola and Jack are with the children." She looked down at my shoes dangling from my hand. "And you're almost undressed anyway. You know, if you wore Birkenstocks, your feet wouldn't hurt."

"But then I wouldn't have any self-respect." As I approached, a frigid wind blew across my face and lifted my hair, but I could see that no one else was affected. Ignoring it, I headed straight for Sophie and the baby. My new-mother status made me a magnet for small babies with soft skin and pudgy toes, and I gently squeezed the baby's plump cheek. "How is Blue Skye today?" I no longer cringed when I said her name, which was a good thing, since I saw her frequently. Still, I shortened it to Skye often enough that I hoped they'd stop expecting to hear "Blue" in front of it. There was only so much Bohemian I could take.

"I've been trying to reach you," I said to Sophie, studying the brightly colored tie-dyed kerchief that kept her curls at bay, and her similarly hued pants and T-shirt ensemble, all worn under a rainbow-striped parka opened at the front to accommodate the baby. I couldn't see much of the bundled baby except for her face and the tie-dyed knit hat and socks beneath her Birkenstocks, but I had the horrible feeling that they were wearing matching outfits.

Sophie smiled brightly, confirming my earlier suspicions. "Yes, well, I had two classes to teach today, and then Mr. Kobylt called. Seems like he's found something interesting in your backyard."

I waited for someone to say the words "dead body," my gaze moving from Sophie to Rich and to the young woman who kept staring at me as if she knew me.

Instead Sophie said, "I'd like you to meet my new research assistant, Meghan Black. She's a second-year in the historic preservation program at the college. Her thesis is on this very thing, so I knew she would be the right person to bring over to take a look."

I introduced myself to the grad student, distracted by the pearls around her neck, the pale green cardigan and khakis she wore, and the Kate Spade flats on her feet. Not the sort of thing one might wear to dig in the dirt. She had pretty brown eyes and long light brown hair she wore in a high ponytail, and had the same kind of enthusiasm Sophie had when surrounded by old things. I wondered absently how long it would take before she began wearing Birkenstocks, too, and how her mother might feel about that.

I focused on Sophie again. "What sort of thing?"

"An old cistern. Right here in the back of your property!" She sounded as if we'd just found Blackbeard's buried treasure.

"A cistern? As in an old water collector?"

"Exactly!" She beamed as if I were her favorite student. "This thing has been sitting here since probably before the house was built in 1848. I'm thinking it might even predate the Revolutionary War and was the cistern for a previous building on the site."

At the mention of something even older than my house being found in my backyard, I'd already begun to shake my head in denial before Meghan said, "From what we can already see, the bricks are mismatched and were probably taken from other structures. Could have been from outbuildings that were no longer used from here or different places. I've even seen a few cases where bricks were taken from cemeteries when they were moved to make way for new streets and buildings."

I froze at the word "cemeteries." That was the thing with old bricks. They weren't just sand and clay. They also contained the accumulated memories and the residual energy of the people who'd lived in their midst. These bricks had been buried in my backyard for more than 150 years and were now being bared to the light of day. I shuddered at the thought of what else might be waiting to be exposed.

"I promise you won't even know we're here," Sophie said, as if I'd already given permission to use my backyard as an archaeological dig. "Meghan and a few of my other grad students are so excited about excavating the cistern. It's not just the bricks we find fascinating. Usually things were tossed or dropped into cisterns over the years that can be a real thrill for historians like us."

I just stared back at her, not understanding the thrill at all. Because digging into the past usually meant unearthing a nasty ghost or two. I didn't relish dodging falling light fixtures or objects thrown across a room, especially now that there were two babies in the house.

I looked from her to Rich. "How long do you think it will take before I get my garden back? I'd hoped to have a big first birthday party for the twins out here in March."

Rich pulled up the waistband of his pants, only to let them droop again once he let go. "Filling it in won't be a problem—no more than a day or two to get it back the way it was. But I have to wait for Dr. Wallen-Arasi to finish first. Hate to think I'd be reburying some artifact if we don't give her enough time."

The instruction to go ahead and fill in the hole as soon as possible was on the tip of my tongue. I couldn't, of course. I wouldn't put it past Sophie and her students to picket my house until I agreed to let them dig it up again. Saying yes was the path of least resistance to an inevitable conclusion.

I felt the icy wind blow against the back of my neck again, twisting its way around my torso as if I wore no coat at all. "Make it quick, okay?"

Sophie nodded and met my eyes, understanding the reasons for my reluctance. But not enough to ignore the fact that I had a veritable treasure trove of history buried in my garden.

"I got your voice mail, by the way," she said. "I've got to take a group of my students to Pompian Hill Chapel of Ease tomorrow to do some grave cleaning and to repair a box tomb, but I can meet you at the Pinckney house on Thursday morning. Does eight o'clock work?"

"It does for me. I'll check with my client and get back with you. She doesn't want to go inside, but I think she should. She doesn't like old houses."

Both Sophie and Meghan looked at me as if I'd said something blasphemous. "It happens," I said.

We said good-bye, and then Sophie left with Meghan and Skye. Rich stayed where he was, his hands on his hips, looking down into the pit, the bottom now blackened as the slanting sun scooped out the light. I was wary of what he was about to say. I'd learned in the years we'd been working together that he not only had a second sight but wasn't fully aware of it.

"I don't want to scare you, Miz Trenholm. But there's something not right about this. Something not right at all."

Ignoring his implication, I said, "I don't like a hole in my garden, either, but we'll have to live with it for a little while. Hopefully it won't take too long."

I said good-bye, then walked toward the kitchen door, sensing a set of footsteps following me, and knowing they weren't his.

∽

After feeding the twins and tucking them into their cribs for the night, I sat in the downstairs parlor flipping through the new MLS listings on my laptop and making spreadsheets for my new clients. Nola sat doing homework at the mahogany partner's desk that Jack's mother, Amelia, had found for her through her antiques business, Trenholm Antiques on King, while Jack finally took a shower. He'd claimed he hadn't had time for grooming—or writing—while taking care of the babies. He'd looked so traumatized that I didn't point out that if he'd followed my schedule that I'd helpfully written down for him, and tried to be more organized, he wouldn't look as if he'd been wandering the wilderness for weeks.

A fire crackled in the fireplace beneath the Adams mantel—Sophie's pride and joy. It was a thing of beauty, but it still made my fingers hurt when I looked at it, as if they recalled all the hand-scraping with tiny pieces of sandpaper Sophie had given me to remove about eighty layers of old paint from the intricate scrolls and loops. My manicurist had almost quit during that period, and if I hadn't given her a generous gift certificate to my favorite boutique, the Finicky Filly, I would still be walking around with bloody stubs for fingers.

I found myself sinking back into what felt alarmingly like domestic tranquility. But there was an uneasiness in the air, an energy that crept out of the walls like morning mist. The sense of unseen eyes watching me. I knew, without a doubt, that the lingering dead had managed to find me again, and that my newfound peace was about to end.

The grandfather clock, where Confederate diamonds had once been hidden, chimed eight times, the sound deep and booming in the quiet house, almost obliterating the sound of what I imagined to be the house inhaling, as if in anticipation of something only it could see. General Lee and the puppies, curled into a furry ball at Nola's feet, looked up at me right before a knock sounded on the front door.

The frenzied movement of three dogs rushing toward the door and barking loudly accompanied me to the alcove, where a replacement chandelier—which had cost me three months of commissions—now hung in the same spot the previous one had been in before it mysteriously fell and smashed onto the marble floor, narrowly missing me. One of the tiles had been cracked, but I had strategically hidden it under a rug so Sophie wouldn't notice and then demand that I have marble crafts-men from Italy come to replace the entire floor and I'd be forced to sell one of the children to pay for it. Because that's the sort of thing that happens when one's best friend is a bona fide house hugger.

My mother, Ginette Prioleau Middleton, stood on the piazza wrapped in a black cashmere cape, looking as beautiful now in her mid-sixties as she probably had been during her brief yet stellar career as an opera diva. Her dark hair gleamed in the porch light, her green eyes bright with barely any lines to betray her age. She was tiny but somehow never appeared small—something I'd discovered since our recent reconciliation and our even more recent battles with spirits re-luctant to head toward the light. A shiver that had nothing to do with the cold tiptoed its way down my spine. My mother never came by unannounced. Unless there was a reason.

"Mother," I said, stepping back to allow her inside.

She kissed my cheek, then handed me her cape, keeping her gloves on. She always wore gloves, even in the summer. Her gift—her word, not mine—was the ability to see things by touching objects, sometimes inadvertently. Gloves protected her from being overwhelmed by images and voices bombarding her from as casual a contact as a stair railing or doorknob.

"I'm sorry to come so late. But I was returning from a Library Society meeting and was passing your house, and knew that it couldn't wait until morning."

"What couldn't wait?" I asked, my throat suddenly dry.

She rubbed her hands over her arms. "Can we go someplace warmer? I need to thaw out."

"I've got the fire going in the parlor." I led the way, the dogs rolling and bouncing at my mother's high heels.

Nola rushed over to embrace Ginette. The two had a tight bond, something I was grateful for despite the fact that sometimes I felt they were ganging up on me. Or laughing at me. Jack had maintained a bland expression when I asked if he'd noticed it, and we'd finally agreed that it must be postpartum hormones that made me see things a little skewed.

"Awesome shoes, Ginette," Nola enthused. "Maybe I can borrow them for a date or something?"

Ginette smiled. "Of course—just ask me anytime. My closet is yours."

I looked down at my fluffy pink slippers, trying to ignore my feet that were still throbbing in memory of the beating they'd sustained earlier in the day. "How long did it take for the swelling in your body and feet to subside after you gave birth to me?"

She and Nola exchanged a glance—I was pretty sure that wasn't my hormones imagining it—before my mother turned back to me. "I don't really think I . . . swelled very much. I was wearing my old clothes and shoes by the time you were a month old. But you had twins," she added quickly. "And you are much older than I was, so that changes the equation drastically, I would think."

My mother and Nola nodded in unison, and again I had the subtle feeling that they knew something I didn't.

Nola went back to the desk and I indicated for Ginette to take one of the stuffed armchairs by the fire while I took the other one. "Can I get you anything to eat or drink?"

She shook her head. "No, I'm fine. Your father's waiting for me at home, so I'll be brief. Have you spoken with your cousin Rebecca?"

Nola let out a groan at the mention of Rebecca's name. I remembered the pink slip I'd received that morning at work, and had promptly discarded and forgotten. "She left a message for me, but I didn't call her back. It was a Monday and my first day back at work, and having to talk with Rebecca would have probably sent me over the edge." I leaned forward. "Why?"

"Well, she called me when she couldn't get ahold of you." The fire crackled, and she turned her gaze toward the flames. "She's been having dreams."

I briefly closed my eyes, seeing the orange and yellow flames imprinted on the insides of my eyelids. "Dreams?"

Rebecca, a *very* distant cousin, had also apparently inherited her sixth sense, except her psychic ability exhibited itself in her dreams. She wasn't always accurate with her interpretations, but usually accurate enough to be alarming.

My mother nodded without looking at me. "She sees a young girl in a white nightgown, and she's banging on a wall." She faced me again and I saw the reflection of the fire in her green eyes. "Except she's banging on the inside of the wall."

I sat back and glanced over at Nola, who'd stopped typing on her laptop and wasn't even pretending not to be listening. "Why does Rebecca think it has anything to do with me? If there was something inside one of these walls, I would know about it."

Ginette rubbed her leather-gloved hands together, the sound

unnerving. "Because the girl was calling your name. And it doesn't necessarily mean this house, either."

I looked grimly back at my mother. "I haven't had any experiences in almost a year—so I don't know who that could be. Except . . ." I stopped, remembering the newly exposed cistern and the footsteps following me across the garden.

"Except?" Ginette raised an elegant eyebrow.

"We've discovered a cistern in the backyard. But it's all bricks—no walls. I don't think they're connected. Maybe there's another Melanie."

My mother stared back at me unblinkingly. "Regardless, you should call Rebecca and thank her. I know you don't get along, but she's still family."

Nola made a gagging noise, then pretended to cough.

"I will. And since you're here, I've got some good news to share. I think I've found a nanny. She has to pass inspection with everybody here first, of course, and I'm going to ask Detective Riley for a background check, but I have a good feeling about her. We share the same views on child-rearing at least."

"That's wonderful news! Not that I don't mind babysitting, but it will be nice for you all to have a regular routine and for the children to have consistent caregiving. I'm afraid Amelia and I are too much the doting grandmothers and err on the side of spoiling them."

I didn't protest or attempt to correct her, because she was absolutely right. And that was one of the reasons I needed a nanny. "Yes, well, her name's Jayne Smith and she walked into my office today to ask for my help in selling a house she's inherited and buying a new one, and it just so happens that she's a professional nanny."

"How lucky—for both of you."

"Actually, I was going to call you about her. She's inherited Button Pinckney's house."

Ginette stilled, an odd expression on her face. "Button was a friend of mine. Amelia and I went to her funeral just last month."

"I know. That's what I wanted to ask you about—if she'd ever mentioned Jayne or if you knew if Button had any family. Jayne's from

Birmingham and never even heard of Button until the lawyers found her to tell her she'd inherited the entire estate."

She looked down at her gloves for a long moment. "There was no one. She never married. She did have an older brother—Sumter. He married Anna Chisolm Hasell, another classmate of Amelia's and mine. They had a daughter, I believe, but she was sickly. She died when she was still a child. Anna and Sumter divorced shortly afterward, but Anna remained in the house with Button. She died about ten years later."

"That's so sad. What about Sumter? Did he ever remarry or have more children?"

After a slight pause, she said, "No. He'd always wanted to be a mover and shaker on Wall Street and moved to New York after his divorce. Just a couple of years after I left Charleston to pursue my music career." She sent me an apologetic glance, a brief acknowledgment that when she'd left Charleston, she'd left me behind, too.

"I'm not sure if he ever came back, but Button told me he'd died of a heart attack. He was only fifty-three." She gave me a lopsided smile. "Button adored him. I don't think she ever got over it. That's when she started taking in strays—animals and people alike. She'd pluck them from the streets and give them a room and money for as long as they needed it. I feel she got taken advantage of more often than not, but she said it made her happy to help others. That's probably how she found your Jayne."

"Possibly. Jayne grew up in foster care in Birmingham. Maybe someone who knew Jayne came into contact with Button at some point and that's the connection."

"Could be," she said as she stood. "I must get home—James will be waiting." Her cheeks pinkened and I tried not to think of my parents—recently remarried to each other—as having a healthy romantic relationship that included physical contact, but there it was when she merely mentioned his name. I should have been thrilled that my parents were madly in love with each other after all these years, but I was still their daughter and it made me a little queasy sometimes if I thought too much about it.

She said good night to Nola and I walked her to the door, pausing just for a moment in the alcove to face me. "Why does Jayne want to sell the house?"

"She doesn't like old houses."

She frowned, her eyes meeting mine. "Hopefully you can change her mind. Button wouldn't have left it to her if she didn't mean for her to keep it. Button was a wonderful person. The best kind of person. We should do our best to honor her request. Maybe you should tell Jayne what Mr. Vanderhorst told you."

"It's a piece of history you can hold in your hand," I said softly.

"Yes. And that sometimes the best gifts in life are the unexpected ones. Including old houses."

She put on her cape, then opened the door to allow in a frigid blast of cold air. She kissed my cheek and pulled up her hood. As she tucked her hair inside, I said, "I don't want to lie to her."

"But would you be? Good night, Mellie." She smiled and then walked down the piazza to the front door and let herself out.

The large wrought-iron porch lights on either side of the door behind me grew brighter and brighter, humming with an unseen energy that made the lights pulsate twice before each bulb exploded one by one, leaving me in total darkness.

CHAPTER 4

Two days later when I left the house to go to work, Jack looked a little worried despite his terse assurances that he was fine with watching the children while he finished up his book revisions. I thought there was a trace of panic in his eyes when I told him I might be home a little later because I wasn't sure how long it would take to go through the Pinckney house with Sophie and Jayne. It wasn't the sort of thing that could be rushed, especially if there were any water issues, a fallen ceiling, rotted floors, or restless spirits—any of which could ruin my day.

Despite reassurances from Mrs. Houlihan that she was still taking my dry cleaning to the same cleaners we'd always used, I'd been forced to wear yet another maternity dress, but had broken down the day before and bought several new pairs of heels at Bob Ellis. I'd called Sophie about the possibility of the newly renovated closet giving off fumes that might shrink leather, but there had only been a long silence on the other end of the phone as if she didn't understand my question. Regardless, my new shoes were a full size larger, and I was pleasantly surprised when my toes were able to spread out when I walked.

Still, I had only made it to Broad Street when my feet required me to hail a pedicab to take me to Glazed, the gourmet doughnut shop on Upper King Street. I was meeting Detective Thomas Riley there to discuss the background check on Jayne Smith. Since he was a cop, I thought it appropriate to have our meeting in a doughnut shop. Plus, it would help me avoid the look of disapproval on Ruth's face as she handed over my bag of doughnuts—which she'd only reluctantly done when I brought in the twins the previous day so she could see them and remind me again how much they looked like Jack. When I'd finally opened the bag back at my desk, I realized there was only one doughnut inside, along with one of those horrible healthy wraps, and the dough-nut looked as if it might have been made with wheat flour and baked. It was like eating white chocolate or a vanilla Oreo—completely pointless—and I'd thrown it away after only two bites.

Thomas was already sitting at one of the small tables across from the counter, two coffees and a pink-and-white-striped bag already waiting on the table. He stood as I entered, and gave me a warm hug in greet-ing. "It's been too long," he said as he helped me out of my coat and pulled out my chair for me, making me appreciate Charleston-bred men all over again.

He slid the coffee toward me. "Lots of cream and sugar—and since I got here early, I took the liberty of ordering our doughnuts. There's not a bad doughnut on the menu, so I got two purple goats—berry and goat cheese filling with lavender icing—a tiramisu doughnut, and a maple bacon. I'm rather partial to the maple bacon, but if you want it, it's yours."

I nearly wept with joy as I opened the bag and smelled the lovely aroma of handmade doughnuts and all that wonderful sugar. He started to speak, but I held up my hand and then took a sip of coffee before pulling out a purple doughnut. We both waited in reverent silence for a moment while I took my first bite.

"Thank you. That is simply amazing," I finally managed to say after thoroughly savoring the fluffy pastry, followed by the strangest urge to smoke a cigarette. I met his eyes. "The maple bacon doughnut is yours," I said. "But you're going to have to fight me for the second purple goat."

"Yes, ma'am," he said. "I need all my fingers for my job, so you just take whatever you want."

I took another bite, then settled back into my chair, cradling my coffee and feeling absurdly content.

"You look beautiful," he said. "Motherhood definitely agrees with you."

Coming from any other man besides my husband, I might have felt uncomfortable. Even though I knew Thomas had been interested in me before Jack staked his claim, our relationship was now firmly in the friend zone. He'd even attended our wedding, and I'd promised—with Jack's blessing—to use my sixth sense to help him with any of his cold cases. He'd called a few times in the past year, but I'd been reluctant to disturb the domestic peace I'd fought so hard for, telling him I just wasn't ready. I wondered if this favor from him meant I'd have to reciprocate whether I was ready to or not.

My cheeks flushed. "Thank you. I feel good now that the twins are sleeping through the night and I can get a full night's sleep. I just wish all my clothes hadn't shrunk—I'm a little tired of wearing my maternity clothes."

He choked on his bite of doughnut and I slid a glass of water in his direction. After waiting a full minute before speaking, he said, "I have that information you asked me for about Jayne Smith. I must admit that when you first told me her name I thought it must be some kind of alias, but that seems to be her real name—although she added the Y in her early twenties. There is no birth certificate on file owing to the fact that she was deposited on the steps of a church in Birmingham and turned over to foster care shortly afterward. The creative minds in the child welfare system must have given her the name."

He grimaced and I felt like crying. It seemed the motherhood hormones that had started in the first month of pregnancy liked to linger much longer than nine months. I supposed they were responsible for my desire now to cry during Humane Society commercials or after seeing Facebook posts showing baby animals that Nola liked to show me. I thought of the woman I'd met in my office and couldn't reconcile what I knew about her with the heartbreaking image of a baby being left on church steps.

"That's so sad. So she has no idea who her parents are?" I took a large bite of the purple goat doughnut, hoping it would push down the lump in my throat. My mother had left me when I was six, and I'd been raised by an alcoholic father. For my entire childhood, I'd felt abandoned, but at least I'd known who my people were, had known the house on Legare where generations of my mother's family had lived. And I'd always had my grandmother, who'd loved me unconditionally. It seemed unfathomable to have no history, no prologue to the story of your life.

"No. I did a little digging into Button Pinckney, too, since it wouldn't be out of the realm of possibility that she might have had a baby and secretly gave it up. Lucky for us, Ms. Pinckney was very active in various social clubs, so her photo appears in the society pages pretty much every month during the year Jayne was born—apparently not pregnant and with no gaps in time. In addition, she was her sister-in-law's companion after her niece's long illness and death, and, according to everyone who knew Button, never left her side."

"So she's just a generous philanthropist who decided to give her entire estate to a deserving orphan."

"Apparently. And Jayne certainly fits that description, considering how she started out. It's really incredible that she turned out as well as she did. She was a straight-A student, never got into trouble, and although she had a succession of foster parents, they all had good things to say about her."

"But she was never adopted."

Thomas shook his head. "Sadly, no. She came close several times, but it always fell through."

"Does the paperwork mention why?" I took a long drink of my coffee, unable to forget the image of a small baby abandoned on the steps of a church. I wanted to think that it was because I was a mother now, with my own small babies who needed me. But there was something else, too. Something I couldn't identify.

His eyes met mine. "This is where it really gets interesting. Every single one of the foster families said practically the same thing: that she was a wonderful child but in the end wasn't adoptable because"—he paused and opened a manila folder on the corner of the table to riffle through several pages before pulling one to the top—"things always seemed to happen around her. Little 'disturbances.'" Thomas made little quote marks with his fingers. He looked down at the page and continued reading. "She was never named as the exact cause, but all events seemed to occur when she was in the vicinity, making her guilty by association."

I sat back in my seat. "That's odd."

"Yep. And there's one more thing I think you might find interesting." He paused, drumming his fingers on top of the folder as if trying to decide how much he should say.

"Tell me everything," I said. "If she'll be watching my children, I need to know all of it."

"True." He took a deep breath. "She's afraid of the dark. Has to have all the lights on when she sleeps."

"Many children are. She didn't outgrow it?"

After a brief pause, he said, "Apparently not. I got the references from her last two employers sent over, and it's mentioned in both reports. Which are all glowing, by the way. The first called her 'Mary Poppins' and considered having another baby just to keep her with their family now that their other children are too old for a nanny."

I perked up. "Which is the important part—that she's a good nanny. I'm okay with her keeping the lights on in her room all night. That's pretty minor, really." I took a long sip of my coffee, thinking. "Anything more specific about those 'disturbances'?"

"No, but from everything I read, I've gathered that it was regular occurrences of breakages—lamps, dishes, that kind of thing."

"So she's a little clumsy," I said, feeling relieved. "As long as she's never dropped a child, of course."

"Nope, nothing like that. As I said, her former employers can't say enough good things about her. Heck, just reading these reports makes *me* want to have children just so I can hire her."

He reached for his wallet to place a generous tip on the table before standing and pulling my chair back for me. "How's the real estate business these days?"

"Hopping, I'm happy to say," I said as he helped me into my coat. "Made it easy to step back into my job."

"So no time to help with any cold cases, huh?"

I thought for a moment, recalling how happy I'd been in the last year with no spirits staring back at me in a mirror. No disembodied knocks on my door. "How cold?" I asked.

"Twenty years. A nineteen-year-old College of Charleston student was murdered, and the case was never solved. Her sister recently found something that made her think it would make it worthwhile to reopen the case."

Despite my reluctance, my curiosity was piqued. "What did she find?"

"Half of a gold charm—like those old BFF necklaces where each friend gets half. Except this one had the first letter of the dead sister's sorority, so it looks like the other half had other Greek letters on it. Perhaps spelling out another fraternity or sorority with a coinciding letter, but the other half is missing."

"Why would the woman think it's important?"

"Because she'd never seen it before. She was moving into her parents' home and found her sister's trunk in their attic—the one that had been in her sister's dorm room at the time of her death. It had never been opened since they brought it home. The woman found the charm in the bottom along with a broken chain. She's positive it didn't belong to her sister and could be the lead we needed to finally solve it."

"Even I have to say that's a long shot."

He looked at me steadily without saying anything, as if waiting for me to fill in the blanks.

"Unless someone can talk to the dead girl," I said slowly.

"Yeah, that's pretty much what I was thinking."

I studied my hands as I slowly pulled on my gloves. "I'll think about it and let you know. Life's pretty crazy right now. Maybe after I get this nanny thing sorted out."

"I understand—thank you."

"Thank *you*," I said, "for being so quick with the references. Jack and I appreciate it."

"Anything to help," he said, giving me a devastating grin that might have my knees weakening if it weren't for Jack.

We stood outside the shop on King Street. "Where are you headed—can I give you a lift?" he asked.

"If you could take me to my car on Tradd, I'd appreciate it. I'm driving over to meet Sophie and Jayne at the Pinckney house she inherited and wants to sell. She has absolutely no interest in hanging on to it."

He raised his eyebrows.

"It wouldn't be the first time a virtual stranger left an albatross of a house to an unsuspecting stranger. Selling an unwanted inheritance is always an option."

"Yeah, but still. It's a nice albatross. That house must be worth . . ."

"A lot. Haven't seen the inside yet, so it could be a total gut job." I narrowed my eyes. "What's wrong?"

"I'll have to ask my dad, but there was something bad that happened in that house back in the late seventies or early eighties when he was still a beat cop. I was pretty young, but I remember it because he was pretty shook-up about it—and he's not the kind of guy who gets easily shook-up."

"I'll ask Jack to do a little research. I'll need to know for full disclosure reasons, assuming Jayne will still want to sell it after she's been inside."

"She wants to sell it and she hasn't even seen the whole thing?"

I paused. "She hates old houses."

He stared at me blankly.

"It happens," I said, getting tired of justifying this perfectly rational perspective—one I happened to share for personal reasons but not professional ones, obviously. "You'd be surprised how many people will only consider houses built in the last decade. Most of them are afraid of the maintenance and care an old house requires. Jayne's a single woman who probably just doesn't want to mess with all that, and I can't say I blame her. She can find something nice and brand-new in Isle of Palms or Daniel Island for what she might sell the Pinckney house for if I do my job right."

Thomas walked me to his car and held open the passenger door, then shut it behind me. After he slid behind the steering wheel and buckled his seat belt, he sat staring ahead without speaking for a long moment.

"What is it?" I asked.

"Were you afraid of the dark when you were little?"

I turned to look out the side window and spotted a woman wearing white pants and running shoes and a fanny pack standing in the middle of the street to take a photo down King Street, apparently oblivious of the waiting traffic. "I was. At least until my mother left me. That's when I realized that real life was a lot scarier than whatever might be hiding in the dark."

He nodded sympathetically and then started the engine. "I was, too, but only because I would stay up late to listen to my dad telling my mom about some of his cases. Enough to make a kid's imagination run wild after the lights were switched off." His jaw clenched. "I'm just wondering what would terrify a person so much that she grows into adulthood still being afraid of the dark."

"It probably has something to do with being abandoned as a baby. They say some traumatic experiences stay with us no matter how young we were when they happened."

Thomas turned the steering wheel and pulled away from the curb. "Yeah. That's probably it. Poor kid."

"Poor kid," I repeated. I looked away again, embarrassed to find my eyes moist, and remembered the moment I realized that my mother wasn't coming back and how I'd promised myself then that I'd never be afraid of the dark ever again.

CHAPTER 5

I arrived at the Pinckney house on South Battery after Jayne did, something I always tried to avoid when showing a client a house for the first time. I preferred to curate what they saw initially and took note of, focusing on the positive attributes so they wouldn't notice the cracks in the mortar or wood rot in the window frames. That would happen later, after they'd fallen in love with the old house and were already willing to restore the ancient pile of lumber without a thought to the hole of debt that they were about to step into.

I'd driven my car, finally finding a parking spot four blocks away after circling the area for nearly fifteen minutes. Jayne must have walked, since she was wearing flats and her face appeared windblown. Her blond hair, pulled back into a low ponytail, had begun to frizz around the edges like a frayed rope. After stumbling in my heels for four blocks, I knew I didn't look much better.

She stood on the sidewalk with her back to the house, her arms folded tightly across her chest, her hands in tight fists. I squinted—my glasses left on my desk as usual—thinking she might actually be smiling until I got close enough to see her clearly. The grim set of her jaw called to mind the expression of a condemned prisoner heading up to the scaffold.

"Good morning, Jayne," I said brightly.

It was hard to understand the words that were forced from behind her clenched teeth, but I was pretty sure she'd said "good morning."

As I fumbled in my purse for my lockbox key, I said, "Dr. Wallen-Arasi should be here momentarily—she's always running a few minutes late. If you'd like, we can wait for her outside so she can tell us a little bit about the architecture and history of the house, or we can go ahead inside. . . ."

"I'll wait." Her eyes had taken on a desperate cast. She took a deep breath, letting it out slowly before speaking. "You're probably wondering why I have such an aversion to old houses. I lived in one off and on for a few years when I was around nine until I was fourteen. With a foster family. They said it was a nineteen thirties Craftsman cottage that they'd restored themselves."

"Was it nice?"

Her eyes were bleak when she turned them to me. "Nice enough, I guess. But I hated it. I hated the way the wooden floors creaked, and the way the wind blew under the eaves in the attic. And I really, really hated the front stairs with the thick oak balustrade. They were so proud of it, too—that balustrade. They'd found it in the barn and refurbished it so that it looked as good as new—even paid a carpenter to re-create missing and damaged spindles so you couldn't tell what was new and what was old." She looked behind me, across the street toward the river. "But it was still the same old balustrade. I always thought it would make nice kindling."

I remembered sanding down the intricate mahogany balustrade in my own house and how I'd shared the same thought at the time. "Okay," I said, making mental notes to transcribe later. "In your future house, no Craftsman style, no creaking floors, and a solid attic."

"Just new," Jayne said, turning around to peer through the elaborate garden gate—one I was pretty sure had been crafted by the famed blacksmith Philip Simmons. "And not located near a hospital."

"Because of all the noise from the sirens?"

She didn't respond right away. Tilting her head in my direction, she said, "Yes. The sirens. They can keep a person up at night."

I was about to ask her more, but the car at the curb in front of us pulled out just as Sophie's white Prius appeared and slid neatly into the spot. She and Jack were like parking spot conjurers, something for which I'd yet to forgive either one of them.

I watched in horror and amusement as Sophie stepped from the car, dressed in head-to-toe tie-dye in various hues of green. Even her unruly dark curls were pulled back from her face with a lime green tie-dye elastic headband. Her feet were clad in her ubiquitous Birkenstocks, these in green patent leather, her socks subscribing to the tie-dye theme.

"I hope you're planning on sending Skye to live with me when she's old enough to learn about fashion and the proper use of color and patterns."

Sophie grinned. "Only if you'll send Sarah and JJ to me when you're convalescing from your foot surgery to repair them from the damage your shoes are causing."

"There is nothing wrong with my feet—" I began, but Jayne interrupted by stepping forward with an outstretched hand.

"You must be Dr. Wallen-Arasi. I'm Jayne Smith, and I appreciate you coming out today."

Sophie pumped her hand up and down. "Please call me Sophie. Everybody does."

"For the record," Jayne said, "I like your shoes. I don't think I've ever seen patent leather on a Birkenstock before."

"Remind me later and I'll write down the name of the store."

I was relieved to see panic flash in Jayne's eyes. "Don't worry," I said. "She's been threatening to tell me where she shops for years, but I've yet to be persuaded to join the dark side."

I missed Jayne's reaction because I was watching Sophie, a small pucker between her eyebrows as she studied Jayne. "Have we met before? You look familiar."

"No, I'm pretty sure we haven't. But I get that a lot. I must have one of those faces."

"Yeah, probably." Sophie smiled, then turned back to her car and pulled a folded square of cloth out of the passenger seat. "I brought a housewarming gift." She unfolded it and held it up. "It's an anti–cruise ship flag. Every homeowner in Charleston should display one in protest."

I sighed. "Jayne just got here. Let her assimilate first before she's forced to take a position on such a hot topic, all right?" I took the flag and refolded it, then placed it back in Sophie's car.

Sophie frowned at me, then refocused her attention on the house, sighing as if she'd just witnessed a miracle. "So, this is your inheritance."

"Technically," Jayne said. "I just happen to own it now—but only temporarily."

"I'm sure you'll change your mind when you see what an architectural masterpiece this really is. It's been owned by only two families since it was built, and I've never had the pleasure of going inside before, so this is a real treat." Sophie stepped back to see the facade better. "To the untrained eye, it's just a typical double house of cypress and heart pine above a stout brick basement. But when you study it a little more closely, you'll see that its Georgian simplicity is lightened by dentils under the corona of the eave cornices, the pattern repeated in the bull's-eyed pediment and pillared portico. It's really quite lovely."

I wondered if Jayne's glazed-eye expression matched my own.

"How old is it?" Jayne asked.

"I'm not exactly sure, but definitely pre–Revolutionary War." Sophie headed toward the split staircase under the portico that led from the sidewalk to the front door. "One of my students several years ago included this house in her dissertation. It has a very interesting bell system based on differently toned chimes for each room. Part of the interview process for servants was to make sure they weren't tone-deaf so they'd know where they were needed. I think the bells are still in the house, although I doubt they're still working. But what a piece of history!"

Jayne and I shared a glance behind Sophie's back.

A very fat ebony cat emerged from between the iron slats of the gate, struggling just a little to get its rear end all the way through. It plopped down on the sidewalk and stared up at us with one dark green eye, the other socket covered with a slit of pink, furless skin. It yawned with disinterest and then waddled its way toward the other side of the stairs until it disappeared.

"I hope the house doesn't come with a cat. I'm allergic," Jayne explained.

"Why would you say that?" Sophie asked from the top of the stairs.

"Didn't you see that enormous black cat come from the garden?" I asked. "It was so large I have to assume it's loved by somebody."

Sophie shrugged. "Either that or there are plenty of rodents to keep it busy."

I sent her a warning glance, but she was already studying the moldings at the top of the two portico columns.

I began climbing, only realizing that Jayne wasn't behind me after I'd unlocked the lockbox and then the front door, pushing it open to the familiar smell of dust, mothballs, and old polish. And something else, too. Something I couldn't identify that smelled vaguely medicinal and reminded me of my grandmother.

I looked inside at the high-ceilinged foyer, peering past the dull pine floors into the front parlor. Heavy cornices with wedding-cake ornamentation capped the tall ceilings, the missing chunks resembling the teeth on a jack-o'-lantern. Like silent ghosts, sheet-covered furniture sat around the room suspended in time.

Stepping back onto the portico, I said, "Coast is clear, Jayne. No cats that I can see."

She didn't look convinced and her arms had returned to their crossed position over her chest.

"Oh, my goodness. It's a period mantel—with original Sadler and Green tin-glazed earthenware tiles!" Sophie called from inside the house.

I smiled down at my client. "This is as good a time as any to see the interior, Jayne. Sophie's enthusiasm can be contagious when it's not being annoying."

I was rewarded with a half grin. Reassured that she'd follow, I walked back into the foyer, my heels echoing in the empty house. A sound like fluttering wings came from the room opposite the parlor. I turned my head in time to see a flash of white passing through the thick plaster wall, accompanied by the soft patter of small bare feet.

An icy cold chill began to wrap its way around me as I listened to the sound of approaching feet, heavier than the first set, and definitely wearing shoes. My ears tingled even before I felt the hands gripping my shoulders and shoving me toward the door. I tilted my head to escape from what I knew was coming next—a cold, hollow voice whispering into my ear. The words were soft and feminine, but not enough to make them any less frightening. Frigid air scraped across the side of my head, punctuating each word as if to convince me that the voice wasn't in my imagination. *Go. Away.*

I began singing ABBA's "Dancing Queen" as loudly as I could, my proven remedy to drown out voices I didn't want to hear. It was something I'd learned as a child to escape the disembodied voices and still proved useful—but only when I'd prepared myself. And I hadn't. My mother had been in this house multiple times to visit her friend Button Pinckney before she died, and I'd thought she would have mentioned a few extraneous souls.

Sophie came from the drawing room, staring at me with wide eyes as I began to back out of the front door. My progress was suddenly halted when I bumped into Jayne.

"Is everything all right?" she asked.

The temperature in the room had returned to normal, yet I had the sensation I'd had the day in my office when I met Jayne. That whatever it was was still there, but someone—or some*thing*—was blocking me from seeing it.

"Yes," I said, forcing a smile. "Everything is fine. I sometimes like to check out the acoustics in these old houses for fun." I faced Sophie. "Did somebody leave a window open or crank the AC?"

I noticed Sophie's expression. "You must be coming down with something. I don't think the house has central air, and the only unit I saw from outside was in an upstairs window."

I faked a cough. "Could be."

"Does it get as hot here as it does in Birmingham?" Jayne asked, her words stiffened by her clenched jaw. "I mean, would central air be required for resale?"

Both Sophie and I stared at her for a moment, trying to see if she might be joking. Finally, I said, "It will really depend—you can either have the work done or reduce the price accordingly. Either way, summer in Charleston is like living in a toaster stuck on high. Air-conditioning is generally not considered optional."

I left the front door open, telling myself it was with hopes of crisp, fresh air instead of giving me the option of a quick exit.

Jayne still had her arms crossed, but she was looking at me with an amused expression. "ABBA, huh?"

"You like them?"

She wrinkled her nose. "I didn't say that. They were a little before my time. I saw the movie *Mamma Mia*, though, so I'm familiar with their music."

Sophie began walking toward the staircase. "You didn't hear this from me, but Melanie's a little obsessed. She denies it, but I'm pretty sure she has a white leather fringe jumpsuit in her closet."

I joined Sophie at the staircase, but Jayne remained where she was, her gaze focused at the landing where the stairs took a turn and disappeared from sight. I followed her gaze, then stopped. The fat cat with the missing eye sat on the landing staring disinterestedly down at us. "How'd that get in here?" Jayne asked.

"Must have sneaked in while we were talking. I'll send someone from the office who likes cats to come get it to see if it has a tag."

"And if it belonged to Button Pinckney?"

"I guess it will go to a shelter."

"What cat?" Sophie asked.

"That one," I said, pointing to the empty spot where the cat had been. "Well, he or she was here a moment ago. It's rather chubby, and is missing an eye. I don't know how easy it will be to find it a home, so let's hope it doesn't belong to the house."

I waited at the doorway to the parlor, hoping Jayne would take the hint, but she remained where she stood, her feet planted like a recalcitrant toddler. "There's nothing to worry about," I reassured her. "I promise the cat will be taken care of."

She looked at me for a moment before stiffly nodding. Slowly, she moved inside, her gaze never leaving the top of the stairs. The skin on the back of my neck assured me that we weren't alone in the house, yet the feeling of being barred from seeing anything extrasensory remained.

The stench of decay and a sense of foreboding permeated the space, brightened only by the extraordinary light flooding in from the front windows. It would be even brighter once they were cleaned, but even now I could see how beautiful this house had once been. "The lawyer told me that Miss Pinckney never left her room on the second floor for the last few years of her life. She had a housekeeper and nurse who took care of her. That might explain the neglect of the rest of the house."

"It's old," Jayne said. "And it smells old. And . . ." She shivered, clenching her hands even tighter over her arms. "And I definitely don't want to live here."

She moved toward the door but was called back by Sophie's voice.

"Oh, my gosh—I think it's a William Parker glass chandelier. There's only one other one I know of in Charleston and it's at the Miles Brewton House. It's worth a fortune."

We moved into the drawing room to glance up at the cloudy chandelier that hung crookedly from exposed wires, the plaster medallion that had once encircled the hole now crumbling beneath our feet.

"I don't think I'd pick that up if I drove past it at the curb with the rest of the garbage," Jayne muttered.

"And this wallpaper," Sophie continued. "It's hand-painted silk. You see the vertical lines that show where each strip is? That illustrates that the owners were wealthy enough to buy multiple strips instead of just one long one. They wanted the lines to show to display their wealth and status."

I looked closely but saw only faded wallpaper sagging from the weight of years, weeping at the corners from age and moisture. Where Sophie saw beauty, all I could see was decay. Signs of neglect were everywhere—from the scuffed and unpolished floors, to the mold spots in the wallpaper and the crumbling moldings that were now rapidly turning to dust. I was fairly certain that Jayne felt the same way.

I practically had to drag Jayne with me as we followed Sophie from room to room, listening to Sophie list all the unique, valuable, and historical elements of a house that neither of us could really see or appreciate.

I considered my house on Tradd Street separate from my thoughts on this house and most of the old houses in Charleston, if only because it was now my home and where I was raising my young family. My babies had been born there, and would learn to walk and say their first words there. The wooden floors would be scarred by the wear and tear of small shoes, scooters, and wooden blocks, marking the passage of another generation growing up at 55 Tradd Street. And I had visions of Nola getting married in the outside garden, and Sarah walking down the staircase in a prom dress waiting to greet her date. That particular vision also included Jack holding a rifle and looking menacing, but I shook it off quickly.

The Pinckney house was just brick, wood, and mortar, the longtime residence of a family I'd barely known and had no connection to. I found myself torn on how to advise my client, knowing the mental, physical, and bank-account-draining aspects of restoring a historic home.

I couldn't look at Sophie, who was studying her surroundings as if she'd just found the Holy Grail, King Tut's Tomb, and the Garden of Eden all rolled into one. Telling Jayne to sell it as is would break Sophie's heart. And leave me vulnerable to her unique form of vengeance. The last time I'd advised a client to sell a house outside the protected historic district in dire need of repair and guaranteed to be demolished, Sophie retaliated by distributing flyers with a Photoshopped picture of me in a turban and one of my cell numbers printed on it, advertising free psychic readings. I'd had to change my number.

"Did you hear that?" Jayne asked when we finally made it to the second floor.

It had been a tinny, hollow sound. I would have thought I'd imagined it if Jayne hadn't said anything. "Yes," I said. "I think it's coming from the room at the end of the hallway."

"What noise?" Sophie asked from halfway up the stairs. She was busy studying the cypress wainscoting that had been stained to look like mahogany and ran up the wall on the side of the staircase. There were nicks and chips in the wood, little placeholders in time left by people long gone. Or so we'd like to think.

"It sounded mechanical," Jayne said. "Like one of those old wind-up toys."

I was already walking toward the end of the hall, feeling the odd sensation of being pursued from behind, and a separate, more gentle presence in front guiding me down the dark hall. I still couldn't see, but I could feel both of them, sense them the way a plant follows the light. Whatever it was behind that door at the end of the hall, I needed to get there before Jayne.

I reached toward the round brass knob, but it was already turning, the door pushed open without any assistance from me. Jayne caught up to me in the doorway, apparently unaware that the door had opened on its own. We stared inside, taking in the large mahogany dresser covered in perfume bottles and tarnished silver frames filled with old photographs. A small end table was covered with an assortment of pill bottles and an empty water glass sitting on a lace doily. An enormous rice-poster bed held court next to it, the silk bedspread and pillows neatly placed on top. I thought of the housekeeper who'd taken care of the deceased owner, thinking she'd made the bed as her last duty to the old woman.

A cold breeze greeted us and I watched as Jayne shivered, wondering if she'd noticed the temperature drop in the already chilly room. I wanted to stamp my foot in frustration at my inability to see whoever it was. It wasn't that I *wanted* to see them. But if I knew they were there, I'd rather see them than just feel them. It made it harder for them to sneak up on me and surprise me when I least expected it.

"This must have been Miss Pinckney's room," Jayne whispered, as if the old woman were still there, sleeping in the giant bed.

"You're probably right," Sophie said from behind us. "It's the only room where the furniture isn't covered. And there's an air conditioner in one of the windows." She crossed the room to a rocking chair in the corner near the window unit, an elegant piece of furniture with slender spindles and delicate rockers on the bottom. A small chest sat beside it, a stack of books teetering on its wooden surface. Sophie picked up the book from the top of the pile. "Apparently, either she or her nurse really liked Harlen Coben and Stephen King."

"Too scary for me," I said, not overlooking the irony. I began walking around the room and pulling open the heavy curtains to let in light, feeling oddly compelled to do so. Almost as if somebody were telling me to do it. Yet each time I grabbed a drapery panel to open it, I felt an opposing force trying to stop me. Jayne watched me with a furrowed brow as I wrestled with each window covering. "They seem to be stuck on something," I explained, yanking one across the rod. "Don't feel obligated to keep these."

Sophie frowned at me. "I disagree. Those are Scalamandre, if I'm not mistaken. An exquisite reproduction of the originals, I would bet. Made to last, unlike so many things these days."

"Was this Miss Pinckney?" Jayne asked. She stood by the dressing table, a large oval frame in her hands.

Peering over her shoulder, I saw a photograph of a beautiful young woman with a bouffant hairdo and thick black eyeliner, placing her in the late sixties or early seventies. She wore a white gown and gloves, and stood next to a young man only slighter older than she was. He resembled a young Robert Wagner—one of my mother's old flames—and looked even more dashing in his white tie and tails.

"Yes, that's her. And I'm thinking this was taken at her debut. She, my mother, and my mother-in-law, Amelia, made their debuts at the same time. She said that Button's brother escorted her, since their father had died when they were little."

"I'm pretty sure I never met her." Jayne paused for a moment before carefully replacing it and picking up another, this one of three girls in Ashley Hall uniforms. Jayne pointed to the tall, thin girl in the middle, her bright blond hair held back by a headband, the edges of her shoulder-length hair flipped up. "I think this is her, too."

I took the frame from her, noticing how faded the photograph was, the years leaching color from the paper and the images. I smiled. "And that's my mother and mother-in-law on each side."

"They look so happy," Jayne said, replacing the frame.

"They were best friends, according to my mother."

"Who's this, do you think?"

Jayne held up another photograph of a girl about ten years old, more recent than the ones of Button. The colors were sharper and the television in the background looked as though it could have been early to mid-eighties. The girl bore a striking resemblance to Button, the same light hair and large, almond-shaped blue eyes.

"I'm not sure," I said. "But it could be her niece. Her brother had a child."

Jayne looked at me with surprise. "Then why didn't she inherit everything?"

I glanced over at Sophie for help, but she was busy studying something in the rocking chair. "She didn't survive childhood. My mother remembers that she was . . . sickly."

The frame fell heavily onto the tabletop, almost as if it had been wrenched out of Jayne's hand and thrown down.

"Sorry," Jayne said. "I'm so clumsy."

My phone began to ring in my purse, the ring tone one I didn't recognize. My hand froze on the purse clasp, willing it to stop ringing.

"You can answer that," Jayne said. "I don't mind."

"It's not important," I said, keeping the tremor out of my voice. "I'll just silence it so we can focus." I reached into my purse and flicked the button on the side of the phone without looking at the screen, knowing it would be the same unidentified number as before.

I picked up the frame, the clips on the back apparently loosened in the fall and allowing the glass and photograph to slip out. I turned the picture over to see if there was any writing on the back. There, in faded blue ink and in a feminine hand, was written the single name *Hasell*.

"Is that a misspelling of Hazel?" Jayne asked.

I shook my head. "It's actually an old Charleston family name—there's a street by that name that runs from King Street past East Bay. It's pronounced like Hazel but spelled with an S. My mother told me that Button's brother, Sumter, married a Hasell, which would explain why they used it for their only child."

As I replaced the photograph and glass back in the frame, I studied it more closely, seeing now the dark circles under the child's eyes, the pale translucence of her skin, the faint blue veins that bracketed her temples. I thought of the robust cheeks and bright eyes of my own children, and I felt a stab of loss for this girl I'd never known. I couldn't take my gaze away from the image, noticing now something familiar in the shape of the chin and the delicate arch of the eyebrows.

I was about to pick up the photo of Button to compare the faces when I heard that odd, metallic sound again that Jayne and I had heard earlier. We both turned toward Sophie, who was holding something up in her hands, a look of surprise and wonder on her face.

"That's hideous and bordering on creepy," I said, staring at the old china-faced doll in her hands, noticing that Jayne had stepped behind me as if for protection. The doll's straggly brown hair made a cloud over its expressionless face, the two large dark eyes staring unblinkingly back at us. I suppressed a shudder.

"The vibration of our footsteps on the stairs must have shifted it in the chair to make that sound. If this is what I think it is, it could be worth a small fortune." Sophie smiled widely as if unaware of the terrifying object she was holding.

"What is that?" I asked, staying where I was. Like with clowns and dollhouses, there was something inherently disturbing about antique dolls. Certainly the stuff that childhood nightmares were made of.

Sophie looked protectively at the doll. "I'm pretty sure this is a Thomas Edison doll—the first talking doll. There are only a handful left, and even fewer are intact, which makes them so valuable. They have these little tin phonograph cylinders inside their torsos—all recorded more than one hundred years ago. They're all nursery rhymes that are kind of hard to understand, and one in particular—'Now I Lay Me Down to Sleep'—is a little scary because it sounds like a woman shouting under duress. For some reason they didn't sell and they halted production after only a month."

"For some reason?" I repeated. "I can't imagine parents disliking their child enough to gift them with such a thing unless they were being punished for something serious like vandalism. Or murder."

"Does this mean that it belongs to me now?" Jayne asked. She didn't sound as excited as Sophie probably expected her to.

"Yes," Sophie said brightly. "I'd have to take it to an antique doll expert who's a friend of mine to verify, but I'm pretty sure that's what this is." She flipped it around to show an opening through a hole in the back of the doll's white linen dress. "The cylinder is so delicate that if I tried to make the doll talk, it would break. There's new technology that can digitally convert the sound from the cylinder so you can hear the original recording, which might be cool to hear."

Both Jayne and I were shaking our heads. "That won't be necessary," Jayne said. "Let's let your expert friend assign a value so that I can sell it as quickly as possible."

"Let me talk with my friend first to see what our first course of action should be. We'll leave it here for now, where it's safe." As Sophie was distracted replacing the doll in the rocking chair, I gave a thumbs-up at Jayne to let her know that at least on this subject, I was in full agreement.

"I think I've seen enough," Jayne said, turning toward the door.

I followed closely behind her. "This is a huge decision, and something that involves a lot of thought. I want you to mull it over for a couple of days, and then we'll talk."

She stopped and faced me. "I don't like old houses, and seeing this hasn't really changed my mind. I'm ready to list it as is."

I could feel Sophie's gaze boring into the back of my head. "I know, and I understand your point of view. I really do. I just want you to consider Button Pinckney. She entrusted this house to your care for whatever reason, but I'm sure she didn't make her decision lightly. That's something you need time to think about."

Her narrow shoulders sagged. "Fine. I'll think about it. But I can tell you I won't change my mind."

We headed toward the stairway and once again I had the sensation of being pursued and another of being pulled back. I stared straight ahead, trying to see but still aware of the wall that was apparently interfering with—if not totally blocking—my sixth sense.

Halfway down the stairs, I heard the sound again, something tinny and metallic, but this time it sounded more like words. Neither Jayne nor Sophie appeared to have heard it, so I kept heading toward the door, almost as eager as Jayne to close the door behind us.

It wasn't until I was relocking the key in the lockbox that I realized that the doll had spoken, but it wasn't a nursery rhyme. It had been the unmistakable two words that I was unfortunately growing accustomed to. *Go away.*

CHAPTER 6

"Are you ready?" Jack asked as he opened the door to the nursery, where I'd been dressing the twins in preparation for our meeting with Jayne.

"Almost. If you can put on JJ's shoes, that would be helpful. I've already put them on twice and he keeps taking them off."

Jack approached us where we sat on the floor and leaned down to kiss me and squeeze Sarah's cheek before hoisting his son in his arms. "Hello there, big man." He frowned at the miniature loafers. "I don't blame him for not wanting to wear those things. His feet are round blobs with toes. How about those awesome soft high-tops I bought him?"

"They don't go with his outfit," I protested, watching as Jack opened the closet door as if I hadn't said anything.

"Do you remember where you put them?" he asked, his voice muffled.

I bit my lip, wondering if I should tell him that I didn't know. But I was familiar with where every sock, hair bow, and diaper cover was kept—thanks to a spreadsheet I'd developed—and Jack would know I was lying. I sighed. "They're still in the box, on the top left shelf underneath the mini Van Halen T-shirt and faded baby jeans."

"Well, no wonder you forget to put these on him if they're tucked way out of the way. I'll put them in the front so you can't miss them."

I refocused my attention on placing two red bows in Sarah's hair. It was unfair that she should have thicker and prettier hair at one year than I had ever had, but I knew it was from her father's DNA. Even as he was approaching forty, Jack's hair was as thick and abundant as it had been when he was a teenager. I'd probably go bald before he lost a single strand.

Sarah sat with a straight back and her small, plump hands resting in her lap as she stared up at me with her big blue eyes. Sarah was so much easier to dress than JJ, actually enjoying it when I brushed her hair or put on a new pair of shoes or a dress. JJ was lucky he wore more than just a diaper, as dressing him was like wrestling with an octopus. Being a perpetual charmer, he always made sure to give me a hug and a kiss when I'd reached my limit so that I quickly forgot how annoyed I was.

JJ gurgled happily as Jack fastened the Velcro of the high-tops on his small feet, kicking out his legs twice to show his pleasure. "See? He loves them," Jack beamed as JJ began his litany of *dadadadadada*. His other favorite word was "car," which he helpfully pointed out whenever he saw one. He'd yet to say "mama," but I still held out hope. Sarah, in the meantime, had mastered both parents, as well as the names of every family member and all three dogs. The only name she appeared to get stuck on was that of my cousin Rebecca, preferring to stare mutely or burp.

Jack frowned. "Matching outfits again?"

I finished with the little elastic band on the hair bow and stood, Sarah in my arms, admiring her smocked dress with the white Peter Pan collar that I knew would remain pristine until we removed the dress at bedtime. It matched the cute short suit her brother wore, right down to the collar that would be hopelessly stained if not completely torn off by the end of the day. "They were until you switched JJ's shoes." I thought for a moment. "Maybe I should put Sarah's tennis outfit on her, since apparently we're now going with a sports theme."

Jack firmly grabbed my elbow and led me from the room. "They're fine, Mellie. They're perfect."

He stopped in the doorway and leaned in to kiss me, making me forget whatever it was that we'd been discussing. The doorbell rang and he lifted his head. "We'll continue this later. Right now let's all be on our best behavior so we make a good impression."

"Shouldn't she be trying to impress us?" I asked as we made our way down the stairs.

"We've passed that point, Mellie, don't you think?" His voice held a note of desperation. "The doorbell's working again at least, so I'll take that as a good sign," he said optimistically.

Mrs. Houlihan, with the two puppies nipping at her heels, had already opened the door and was taking Jayne's coat by the time we reached the foyer. Jayne hung back in the vestibule, looking smaller than I remembered, her face showing her uncertainty. She wore a pale blue sweater and neatly pressed navy pants, her only concession to fashion a pair of pearl earrings.

I handed Sarah to Jack, who easily balanced a child in each arm, then held out my hands to the visitor. "Jayne," I said. "I hope you found us all right."

She took my hands and nodded, looking around her with wide eyes. "I did, thank you. I didn't realize . . . I mean, you said you'd inherited your house. I guess I just didn't realize it was so . . ."

"Old?" I completed for her.

She have me a half grin. "Yeah. Something like that."

Mrs. Houlihan picked up Porgy and Bess and retreated to the kitchen while General Lee made his grand entrance by strolling sedately from the drawing room. I watched with surprise as he sat at Jayne's feet and licked the top of her shoe, something he never did with strangers. "Come in," I said, pulling her forward. "As you can see, we have a pretty full house."

As soon as she caught sight of the children, her entire demeanor changed from jittery awkwardness to what looked a lot like pure joy. "Oh, this must be JJ and Sarah."

Before I could introduce her to Jack and the babies, JJ grinned and held his arms out to her. He was never shy around strangers—especially women—but this was the first time I'd seen him choose *anyone* over his father.

Jack looked as surprised as I was and quickly relinquished the little boy. Sarah, never one to be left out, reached for Jayne, too, and was soon happily ensconced in Jayne's other arm.

"I guess they like you," I said. "Come into the drawing room, where you can sit down. Their weight seems to double every five minutes."

She sat down on the sofa I indicated, placing each child on a knee, and immediately began a slow bounce, not fast enough to jiggle plump cheeks, but just enough motion to keep them happy. Ignoring me, General Lee snuggled up against Jayne's feet.

"This is my husband, Jack Trenholm," I said after everyone was settled. I half expected Jack to desert me, too, and find an available corner of the couch near Jayne.

"It's a pleasure to finally meet you," Jayne said, her earlier nervousness replaced with a sure confidence that I found promising.

"It's good to meet you, too." A small frown furrowed his brow. "You look vaguely familiar. Have we met before?"

She smiled patiently. "No. I just have one of those faces, so I get that all the time."

He nodded, but I could tell he wasn't completely convinced. "Must be. So." He clamped his hands over his kneecaps in what I'd come to recognize as his serious stance. "You're a professional nanny looking for a job."

"Yes, I am. I'm new to Charleston and I would like to continue with being a nanny. It's something I really like, and it's something I'm good at. I've always enjoyed the company of children—of all ages."

"And you had a lot of practice growing up in foster care."

I shot him a warning glance, wondering why he'd chosen to bring up her childhood. We'd already gone over the questions we were going to ask, as well as topics to be covered. Her childhood wasn't one of them.

"That's correct. I made the choice to find a way to be happy in what could have been very unhappy circumstances. Besides taking care of the physical needs of my charges, I try to instill that philosophy in them. That there's always a way to look past the bad to see the good."

"That's very optimistic of you."

Her cheeks flushed, and I noticed for the first time how pretty she was.

Jack nodded. "You have some very glowing references from previous employers. Very impressive. But we have a few questions that weren't covered." He cleared his voice and I had the distinct impression that he was deliberately avoiding my gaze. "How do you feel about lists and schedules in terms of child-raising?"

I sat up, not having anticipated this question.

"They're very effective," Jayne said.

I sent Jack a smug smile.

"When they make sense," Jayne continued. "If it's nap time, but the children are engrossed in a book, or a puzzle, or studying butterflies in the garden—really, anything that absorbs their little minds—it makes sense to adjust the schedule. They'll be ready to give their minds a rest and sleep better if I let them play a little longer."

"But—" I started.

"What about clothing? What is your theory on dressing small children?"

Jayne smiled warmly at the toddlers on her knees, their dark heads resting contentedly against her chest. "Sarah and JJ look adorable—I especially love JJ's high-tops. Their outfits today are certainly appropriate for parties, or church, or any special occasion. Of course I will defer to the children's parents, but my own philosophy is clothing that is comfortable and stretchy—and easy to get in and out of. Not to mention cleans up well."

"But—" I started again.

"When can you start?" Jack interrupted. "We'll pay you fifteen percent more than your last employer, and that will include room and board until your permanent living arrangements are decided. We'll give you a generous vacation schedule, as well as most holidays off unless you choose to work."

I stood suddenly, startling the dog and both babies so they all stared at me with the same wide-eyed look of surprise. "Actually, we have a few more questions, don't we, Jack? And I think we should discuss further before we make any firm arrangements. . . ."

Jack stood, too, then gently took my arm. "Will you excuse us for a moment?"

He pulled me out to the foyer and set both hands on my shoulders. "We have Mary flippin' Poppins sitting in there, and I'm afraid if we let her leave this house without a job offer she can't refuse, somebody else will snap her up. She's perfect—she's qualified, has great references, you like her, and I like her. Heck, the kids already like her and did you see General Lee? When does he ever act like that with strangers? I trust his judgment on people more than I trust my own."

"He likes Rebecca," I said.

"Yeah, well, that's because she's related. He feels obligated."

"Jack. These are our children. Shouldn't we at least interview more people?"

"We could, but you and I both know we will never find as good a candidate as Jayne. I think she might even last more than a month."

"But what about her comments about schedules and clothing? I don't think . . ."

He put his finger to my lips, silencing me. "She seems solid and sensible, and very accommodating. I'm sure we can compromise. But please, Mellie. Let's restore order to this household. Because if I don't get these revisions done before the next century, there might not be another book."

I stole a glance toward the drawing room. "Are you sure?"

"Almost as sure as I was when I decided I loved you."

He was using his blue eyes to his advantage, but I enjoyed it too much to care. "Really?"

"Really," he said, sealing the deal with a soft kiss on my mouth.

"All right, then. Let's go hire a nanny."

We started back, but Jack paused when his phone vibrated. "I've got to take this—it's my agent. I shouldn't be long."

"Good news?" I asked. Things had been touchy since Rebecca's husband, Marc Longo, stole Jack's book idea—the story of a disappearance and murder that had happened in the twenties in *my* house—and made it into a runaway bestseller and Jack was dropped by his publisher as a result.

"I have no idea. I'll let you know."

I nodded, then returned to the drawing room. JJ was sound asleep on Jayne's shoulder, softly snoring and drooling on her blue sweater, while Jayne, Sarah, and General Lee were all staring at the corner of the room. I turned my gaze to see what it was, praying it wasn't another palmetto bug lying in wait to torment me or Nola.

The air shimmied, like fish scales right under the water's surface, undulating and sparkling. I held my breath, watching as it faded quickly, almost as if it had never been. I would have thought it was my imagination if not for the lingering scent of roses.

I turned back to Jayne, who was reaching down to scratch General Lee behind the ears, something else he never allowed strangers to do. "There must be a bug or something in the corner. I couldn't see what it was, but I don't have my glasses on. I'm squeamish about bugs or else I would have gone in for a closer look." She grimaced.

My gaze settled on Sarah, who was now frowning at the corner, looking as if somebody had just taken away her favorite toy. "I'll tell Jack to pull back the curtains. We have an exterminator, but sometimes bugs will get in anyway—even in January."

Sarah reached for me and I lifted her, pressing my nose into her soft hair and holding her close, thinking of every other reason in the world for her interest in the far corner of the room than what I was afraid it could be.

"I'm sorry to just walk in, but the doorbell's not working again and nobody heard me knock."

I looked up to see my mother, looking as beautiful and elegant as ever. She'd already removed her coat, but her gloves remained on her hands. "Hello, Mother," I said as I approached to kiss her cheek. Sarah, recognizing the woman who spoiled her without censure, immediately leaned into Ginette's arms.

"Come meet our new nanny," I said, leading her to Jayne, who was trying to stand without jostling the sleeping baby. "Assuming she's agreed to take the position, that is."

Jayne smiled. "Yes, of course. You're more than generous. And your children are just darling." Her gaze traveled behind me, and her smile faltered.

"This is my mother, Ginette Middleton. Mother, this is Jayne Smith, our new nanny."

Jayne extended her hand to shake and Ginette hesitated just for a moment before grasping the hand with her gloved fingers. "It's nice to meet you. I apologize for the gloves, but I have a condition where my hands are always icy cold. I rarely remove my gloves, even in the summer."

"Please, no need to apologize. And it's a pleasure meeting you."

My mother was still smiling, but her expression seemed strained. Jayne must have noticed it, too, because she said, "I have one of those faces. People always think they've seen it before. But I don't believe we've ever met."

Ginette's expression relaxed. "Yes, that must be it. Are you from Charleston?"

"Birmingham. This is my first time here."

Ginette moved into the drawing room and sat down in my vacated seat. Sarah's attention was immediately focused on her grandmother's jet-black onyx necklace. It had been a birthday gift from my father and had a stunning gold clasp in the shape of a sweetgrass basket. As soon as Sarah's small fingers wrapped themselves around the strands, her face broke out in a rapturous smile, almost as if the joy of the gift had transferred itself into her small fingers.

"Melanie told me that you've inherited Button Pinckney's house."

JJ began to squirm and I took him from Jayne. She settled back onto the sofa while I remained standing, swaying gently. I tried to ignore the grandfather clock because then I'd know we were far off our nap schedule.

"Yes. And I'm sure she's told you that I have no idea why. Unless it was to punish me for something I'm not aware I did." She gave a halfhearted laugh. "It's in really bad shape. I doubt I have the energy or interest in restoring it. I'll probably take a loss and sell it as is."

"Because you don't like old houses."

Jayne looked up at her sharply. "No. I don't."

Ginette regarded her for a long moment, making Jayne glance away. "I should get going." She stood. "When would you like me to start?"

"Would two days work? That should give you time to check out of your hotel and settle in here. I'll have Mrs. Houlihan get your room ready. Would you like to see it?"

She shook her head, almost before I'd finished speaking. "I'll see it when I move in. I just have a suitcase, but I have more in storage. I can have that sent over whenever I figure out where I'll be permanently."

"We do need to move ahead," I said gently. "Sophie is dying to get her hands on your house, and has already started making phone calls to people who restored the Villa Margherita right down the street."

"I really think I can give you an answer now, but I'm afraid it might not be the answer you want to hear."

"I just want my clients to end up where they're supposed to be. I can handle Sophie's disappointment." I tried to wipe the image of me in a turban on a flyer out of my mind.

My mother stood and approached us, Sarah still focused on the beads of the necklace. "Jayne, we've only just met, so I don't know you. But I did know Button very well, for a long time. I know she loved that house. Loved how she could touch the same banister and walk across the same floors as her ancestors had ever since the Revolution." She placed her hand on Jayne's arm. "It was more than a house to her. It became the child she never had, and the only part of her family to survive. She would not have left it to you without serious thought or reason. I just want you to consider that before you make your decision. Maybe the time spent restoring the house will give you the time you need to find out why."

Jayne took one long, slow breath. "Maybe I don't want to know."

"What do you mean?" I asked.

She shrugged. "It just seems that digging into her reasons would be ungrateful. And . . ."

I raised my eyebrows.

"And sometimes the answer you find to a question is something you wish you'd never learned." She was silent for a moment as she watched Sarah's fascination with my mother's necklace. "But I appreciate your insight, Mrs. Middleton, and I promise to give this deep consideration." Turning to me, she said, "I'll let you know when I arrive for work the day after tomorrow. Please tell your husband good-bye for me."

"I will. And he's very intrigued by your story. As I mentioned, he'd be a good research resource."

"Yes, thank you. I'll let you know." She said good-bye to my mother and the children, then headed for the vestibule to put on her coat. I followed her to the door, waiting as she buttoned her serviceable navy wool peacoat.

I opened the front door, and she paused. "There's one more thing," she said.

"Yes?"

"I'll need a night-light shining in the hallway. I have one for my bedroom, but I need one for outside my door."

"All right," I said. "That won't be a problem."

"Good. And thanks again." She said good-bye and walked onto the piazza and then out through the garden gate. I watched her leave, listening as her footsteps disappeared down the sidewalk, trying to think of all the reasons why a grown woman would still be afraid of the dark.

CHAPTER 7

As was typical in Charleston, bitingly cold winter days were often followed by much balmier weather that had us replacing our heavy coats
with cotton sweaters. It was as if Mother Nature were teasing us, making
us dream with an almost feverish anticipation of the upcoming season.
Spring in Charleston was something out of a fairy tale, with every garden,
window box, and planter spilling out with fragrant blooms in every shape,
size, and color. The streets that were merely picturesque during the other
three seasons became works of art in the spring—assuming one liked row
upon row of old houses and couldn't see the shadows hidden behind their
windows. But even I could almost forgive the hoards of tourists who
flocked here for the spring tour of homes and gardens.

As I waited for Jayne's arrival, I sat in the back garden pushing JJ and
Sarah in the little baby swings Rich Kobylt had made for them—
including safety harnesses—and then strung from a low branch of the
ancient oak tree that had probably been just a sapling when the house
was built in 1848. Jack hadn't found it alarming that our contractor/
plumber/handyman was considered a member of our family now and
that he was making swings for our children. And helping himself to
coffee in our kitchen and teaching tricks to our puppies. Porgy and Bess

knew how to roll over, shake a paw, and play dead. I wondered if all that time spent had been billable hours, but Jack wouldn't let me ask.

I was remembering my fortieth birthday party that had been set in this very garden, and humming the song "Fernando," wondering if I was just imagining the children wincing when I tried to hit the higher notes. Whoever said that small children were accepting of our failings must not have actually known any.

Meghan Black, Sophie's grad student, had shown up each day to dig in the hole that had appeared in my garden. Sometimes she'd bring other students, but today she was by herself. She'd spread out a sheet on the grass onto which she'd place anything found in the hole, right next to a floral Lily Pulitzer insulated mug with a tea tag dangling from it. It sat next to a bag from Glazed Donuts on King, which I had to force myself from looking at because it made me salivate. She wore the pearls again, and a pear-colored Jackie O cardigan, but these were paired with jeans and Hunter boots in deference to the digging she'd be doing. Sophie had questioned the practicality of Meghan's clothing choices, but I had to admit that I liked this girl's style.

I stared uneasily at the hole. There was something there, something that hadn't been unearthed yet. But it would be. I felt it. There was just nothing I could do to stop it. It was like the sky before a storm, how you knew it would be a bad one, but you just weren't sure when you needed to seek shelter.

Barking from the three dogs came from the kitchen—the dogs being barred from the back garden until the hole had been filled in—followed by the sound of a shutting car door. I looked at my watch, seeing that it was time for my carpool partner to be dropping off Nola. I turned my head at the sound of giggling and spotted Nola, her best friend, Alston Ravenel, and a girl I hadn't met before emerging from around the side of the house. They all wore Ashley Hall uniforms and carried book bags, and each had that fresh-scrubbed look of youth and good health, their clear-skinned smiling faces completely alien to my own gawky teenage years. The one good thing about having absent parents during that time of my life was that there was no photographic evidence of my adolescence to haunt me into adulthood.

I waved them over and watched as Sarah smiled and gurgled at her big sister while JJ squirmed and reached for Alston, his girl crush. He had a thing for blond women and had been known to reach forward in his stroller at attractive strangers, pinching his fingers open and closed, demanding that they hold him. I tried to tell him it was cute while he was a baby but probably wouldn't be as tolerated when he got older. He didn't seem to care.

"Hi, girls." I stood. "Did you have a good day at school?"

Nola leaned down to place a kiss on each baby's cheek before taking over the swing pushing. "It was great until pickup. Ashley Martin has her license now, so her parents bought her a Mercedes convertible. She made a big show of blocking our exit from the parking lot by putting the top down. Alston's mom was *so* annoyed. We told her that her SUV was bigger and should just run over Ashley and her stupid car."

"It must be hard being fifteen," I said with a smile. Although not as hard as it was being a fifteen-year-old girl's father. It was about to get interesting around here when it was time for Nola to start driving. And dating. I wondered if I should go ahead and schedule family counseling to make sure there was a spot open for us.

"And this is Lindsey Farrell. She lives over on Queen Street in the yellow Victorian."

She shook my hand and looked me in the eye. "It's nice to meet you, Mrs. Trenholm. My mom says you probably won't remember her, but she went to USC with you. You were in the same art history class, I think."

"What was her maiden name?"

"Veronica Hall. You did a project together on early American painters your senior year."

I thought for a moment, only having a vague memory of the name and that project. "I don't think I remember her, but I still have my yearbooks, so I'll look her up. But tell her I said hello."

"I will." She smiled and I saw how striking she was. She had an almost elfin face surrounded by a cloud of black hair, and dark brown eyes that appeared black. But it was her smile that transformed her face from merely pretty to beautiful. It did nothing to disguise the aura of sadness that seemed to permeate the air around her. I looked away, not wanting to see more than what I was prepared to.

"Hi, Meghan!" Nola shouted. Meghan looked up and waved back. Nola was fascinated with the older girl's passion for her chosen field of study, and hadn't even yawned during a lengthy explanation of the history of cisterns—both their construction and usage. I'd seen her sit at the edge of the hole in perfect silence while watching Meghan work, then taking an inordinate amount of time studying each small artifact that was placed on the sheet. I didn't understand the fascination, seeing it as the equivalent of watching grass grow, but as long as Nola's interest didn't slow down the excavation, I left them alone.

"Mrs. Houlihan baked brownies," I said. "Flourless for you, and then regular ones with taste for the rest of us. They're on the stove if you and your friends want a snack."

"Maybe I should try a flourless one," Alston said as she swayed with a content JJ, his chubby fingers wrapped around strands of her long blond hair.

"Unless you're trying to punish yourself, I wouldn't," I suggested.

She giggled, then carefully put JJ back in his swing. He began snorting his disappointment until Nola gave him a push on the swing and he was back to his burbling self.

"We have an algebra test tomorrow, so we'll bring our snack up to my room to help us study. Try not to disturb us, okay?"

"Okay," I said. "The new nanny will be here soon. Will you have a few minutes to say hi?"

"Sure. Just text me and I'll come down."

She and the girls said good-bye and left before I could ask if I could just knock on the bedroom door. As Lindsey turned to follow the other two girls into the house, I noticed something long and rectangular, like a narrow box, sticking out of her backpack. It looked like a board game, but the bottom was facing me so I couldn't see what it was. Nola wasn't into board games, as I was sure she and most of her generation were more into Facebook, Snapchat, and Twitter. I thought it was nice she and her friends were going a little retro.

JJ began to squeal and kick his feet while his hands opened and closed again in what Jack referred to as his crab imitation. I turned around to see Jayne coming from the side garden.

"Hi," she said. "I took a guess that you'd be back here with the children taking advantage of this gorgeous weather."

"Good guess," I said.

She approached the children with a broad smile as if she really was happy to see them. But when her gaze settled on the hole behind us, she faltered. "What's all that?"

"Nothing you need to worry about—just keep the dogs and children away. It's an old cistern that was buried for a long time, and with all the rain we've had the earth sort of caved in. Sophie is sending some of her students to excavate it to see if there's anything of historical significance in it before I tell my guy to bury it again."

"Oh," she said, her forehead creased. "What are they expecting to find?" She definitely sounded worried, and I wondered if she'd read up on me and the house and its propensity to hide buried bodies.

"Just junk. Our construction guy says the ground is stable around the perimeter of the cistern, but if being out here makes you uncomfortable, we can go inside. I want to give you the tour and show you your room and the nursery and the children's spreadsheets. I purchased a small MacBook for you so that it's easy for us to keep track of their care. We can just send updated spreadsheets back and forth to track their outfits, food consumed, vocabulary word of the day, diapers changed and their contents—that sort of thing. I've also set up a Google calendar for their social lives—which includes birthday parties, trips to the beach, and museum visits."

She didn't say anything for a moment, and it looked as if she was waiting for me to tell her I was kidding. I knew that expression because I got it a lot from family and well-meaning friends who didn't have a clue how to organize their lives or those of small children.

My phone rang and I suppressed a sigh as I recognized Suzy Dorf's number. I ended it and then before I could remember what we'd been talking about, I got a *ping* telling me I had a text message. I looked at it and tried not to squint to read it, despite the fact that I'd made the font as large as it could go. So large, Nola suggested, that my texts could be read from outer space.

Have you heard about the new movie they're filming in Charleston? I have the scoop you might want to hear. And besides, you owe me an interview.

I began to respond with *Why would I owe you anything?* But after three failed attempts to make a capital W for the first word, I gave up. I didn't owe her anything, especially not a response to her ridiculous text. The previous year she'd printed the contents of an anonymous letter she'd received at the paper about buried bodies in my garden. The only thing I owed her was a wish that she'd become one of them.

"Sure. Let's go inside," Jayne said. "I left my stuff on the front porch and can bring it in as soon as I know where to put it."

I picked Sarah out of her swing and watched as Jayne lifted JJ. "Jack can bring your bags in when he gets home. Is it a lot?"

She shook her head. "No—just a regular suitcase. I travel light. Old habit to break, I guess."

There wasn't any note of self-pity in her voice, but it brought back again the image of her as a baby being left on a church doorstep. It made me want to offer to redecorate her room in her favorite colors and furnish it with all the things she loved. Which was silly, really, since I didn't know her, much less her favorite colors. I might have moved around a lot with my military father, but I'd always had my own room that I'd been allowed to decorate, hanging up as many ABBA posters as I wanted. It made me feel sorry for her, for her less-than-perfect childhood that she'd managed to overcome. Maybe because I was now a mother, I saw a need to be a mother for those in need of one.

As we walked toward the back door, each holding a child, I made a mental note to start a spreadsheet to keep track of all the things we could do to make Jayne feel welcome and at home, then made another note to go online to see if I could find any ABBA posters she might want to hang on her walls.

We walked slowly through the house so she'd be familiar with it, pausing for a moment in front of the fireplace in the downstairs drawing room. "Have you had any thoughts on baby-proofing this room yet?" she asked.

"I've purchased all the corner protectors and cabinet locks but haven't had to use them yet. Sarah is very obedient and doesn't do anything once you ask her not to. And JJ prefers to sit and wait for someone to carry him to where he wants to go—preferably his dad, but if Jack's not available, then a female person. I have all the safety paraphernalia in a section of their closet upstairs with everything labeled so you can see what we have."

"Labeled?"

"Yes. And I bought you your own labeling gun just in case I've missed anything. Actually, I haven't labeled the inside of their dresser drawers yet—so that can be your first assignment. You can do it while they're napping—JJ could sleep through a hurricane and Sarah has so much fun babbling to herself in her crib that she won't even notice you're there."

She blinked a couple of times before smiling. "Of course." We turned to leave, but she paused in front of the grandfather clock. "Is it broken?"

The pendulum was swaying back and forth, the familiar ticktock echoing in the room, but the hands of the clock were stopped at ten minutes after four o'clock. I looked at my watch just to make sure that I hadn't somehow lost track of time, something I'd been unfamiliar with until I met Jack. I stared at the time for a moment, something about it jarring my memory. I frowned. "That's weird. It's been working perfectly. I guess I'll have to call somebody."

I showed Jayne the kitchen, where JJ started to clap his hands in anticipation of being fed. "He likes his food," I said. "He'll eat anything and at any time, but prefers somebody else to feed him. Sarah is a good eater, but more selective and much prefers to feed herself."

Jayne nodded. "It's good for them to retain their individual personalities. It's important that they see themselves as separate persons."

I led her out of the kitchen toward the stairs. "They look so much alike that it's amazing to me how different their personalities are."

"Well, they do come from two different parents. Are you and your husband very much alike?"

"Not at all," I said at the same time as I heard Jack behind us say, "Practically identical."

We turned to see him emerging from the music room that had also become his writing office. His mother had helped me find a lovely mahogany writing desk from the early part of the last century, and had moved it in front of the window that overlooked the side garden.

I sent him a reproachful look, quickly forgotten as he bent to kiss me in greeting. He nodded at Jayne, then scooped up Sarah, who was reaching for him. I was used to women turning their heads when Jack walked by, but I'd thought the one I'd given birth to would at least make me her favorite.

I looked over at JJ, who seemed happy with his face buried in Jayne's neck. With a sigh, I said, "Are you done for the day? I was just showing Jayne the house and wanted to introduce her to Nola."

His smile faltered a bit. "Wasn't the most productive day, but maybe that's just my muse telling me to take a break."

He'd been distracted and distant since his phone call with his agent. Although his current project was generating a lot of buzz in-house, the news that Marc Longo's book, *Lust, Greed, and Murder in the Holy City*, was getting a lot of press had Jack irritated and disheartened. The fact that the story idea was centered on our house and had been the impetus to our meeting and the subject of his own book, which had been canceled because of Marc Longo's subterfuge (pretending to be interested in me so he could glean insider information), didn't improve Jack's mood. There was something else, though. Something that had emerged in that phone call that he hadn't yet shared with me.

I was trying to get over my habit of avoiding bad news and confrontation, preferring to think that both were like ghosts and if you ignored them long enough, they'd go away. But, like with pregnancy, I'd learned this wasn't the case. Still, I told myself that if I needed to know, he would tell me.

He faced Jayne, wearing what I referred to as his author back-cover-photo smile, and her cheeks flushed. I made a mental note to ask Jack to turn down the charm a notch the same way he'd had to do with any of Nola's friends who visited. I'd yet to suggest he grow a paunch or lose his hair, but I wouldn't push it beyond the realm of possibility.

"I've been doing a little research on your new house on South Battery. It's considered one of Charleston's treasures—both for its architecture and its history. I've been doing a little digging, too, into Button Pinckney's life. She was an incredible woman—a huge philanthropist and a devoted advocate for animals and children. She was often quoted as saying that the house was like the child she'd never had. Lots of speculation as to what would happen to it when she died."

"And she left it to me." Jayne swayed with JJ in her arms, his eyes slowly drifting closed.

"Yes. To a complete stranger. Being a writer, I'm intrigued. There's definitely a story here. Maybe even enough of a story for a complete book. Button Pinckney was an educated, intelligent, and cultured woman. There was a reason why she chose you. I'd hate to see the house sold before we can find out why."

"Jack," I said, "now's not a good time to discuss this. I'm showing Jayne around right now. I scheduled the talk about the Pinckney house for tomorrow morning at eight fifty-five. I'm sure I put it on your calendar."

Both Jack and Jayne stared at me unblinkingly before Jack turned back to Jayne. "Yes, well, we can certainly wait until eight fifty-five tomorrow. I just wanted to make sure Jayne had all the information before she made her decision. And to let her know that she can be our live-in nanny for as long as she needs, or at least until her house is fully renovated and she can see it in all its glory. Maybe she'll decide she loves it when it doesn't appear to be so old."

Jayne's lips turned up in a half smile. "This is an old house, too, but the feeling here—with the exception of the backyard—gives off a really friendly vibe. Like it's a true family home with a lot of warmth."

"That's because we've already exorcised all its ghosts."

Jack said this with a hearty laugh, but Jayne shot him a sharp look. "Ghosts?"

"Don't worry," I said, guiding her toward the stairs. "All the worst ones are gone. The ones left behind are friendly." I'd said this as an inside joke for Jack, but Jayne continued to frown.

We were halfway up the stairs when we heard a shriek from Nola's room. Despite holding a small child in his arms, Jack sprinted up the stairs and threw open Nola's bedroom door. "Is everything all right?"

Jayne and I moved up behind him, peering into the room. The three girls sat on top of Nola's tall four-poster bed, a Ouija board between them. They turned toward us, each face paler than the next. "It moved by itself," Veronica said.

A new presence hovered around the periphery of the room, something dark and disturbing, like the soft ripples on the water's surface signaling the approach of something big. And invisible. Just as before, I couldn't see it, couldn't speak to it or touch it. It was as if that same curtain had fallen between me and the spirit world, blocking my entrance. For someone who'd spent a lifetime resenting the fact that I *could* interact with spirits, I now found myself resentful that I couldn't. Something was jamming my brain waves, and I think that scared me more than anything else.

Jayne bent down to pick up the triangle-shaped board piece, then dropped it immediately as if it had burned her. "You shouldn't be playing with that," she said, her voice low and in a tone I'd not heard yet. "It's not a toy."

We all turned to look at her in surprise. Feeling all gazes on her, she attempted to smile but failed. "A mother of a family I worked for told me that. She said it wasn't a children's game." Her gaze traveled to a corner of the room. "She said that sometimes it can attract unwanted . . . visitors, and you have no control over whether they're good or bad."

"They're not real," Alston said. "All that ghost stuff isn't real. I think Nola pushed it off the board to scare us." She looked at Nola hopefully.

"Guilty," Nola said with a sidelong glance at me to let me know she was lying. A frisson of fear shot down my neck. Our house was filled with spirits. Most old houses were. They were there in every creak of the floor and tick of the antique clocks. But we'd learned to live in harmony with them, knowing that when they were ready to move on they'd let me know. But even without seeing this new presence, I knew it didn't want to go anywhere.

"Close it up, please, Nola. Jayne's right—it's not a game." I caught a whiff then, of moist earth and dead leaves, and I immediately knew where it had come from. Turning to Jack, I said, "Please make the introductions. I need to step outside for a moment."

He gave me a quizzical look, but I didn't pause as I quickly walked out the door, then ran down the stairs and through the house to the back door. I threw it open and stifled a scream as I nearly ran into Meghan as she clawed desperately to open the back door.

She brushed past me, then closed the door, leaning her back against it. Her skin was unusually pale and her eyes were so wide that I could have sworn I saw the whites all around her irises.

"Are you all right?" I asked as I led her to the kitchen table and pulled out a chair.

She began to nod, then shook her head. When she eventually found her voice, she said, "It was the weirdest thing. . . ."

"What was?" I asked, although I was sure I knew what she was going to say.

"I was digging and I thought I'd found something, so I was really focusing on a small area, and then all of a sudden . . ." She wrinkled her nose and gave an involuntary shudder. "This smell. Like rotting . . . dead stuff. We once had a squirrel die in our chimney and that's how we found it—from the smell. It was like that. And I swear the temperature dropped about thirty degrees, because I could actually see my breath."

"Can I make you some tea? You seem a little shaken up."

She shook her head. "I really just want to get home. Do you mind if I leave my stuff out? I don't really want to go back right now. And I'll leave by the front door if that's all right with you."

"Of course," I said, nodding sympathetically. "Maybe you're coming down with something. It is flu season, after all."

She nodded gratefully as she shakily stood, holding on to the edge of the table. "I guess I should have listened to my mother and gotten that flu shot."

"Probably," I said, gently leading her toward the front door. "I'll pack up your things and put them in the gardening shed in case it rains. They'll be there whenever you're ready to return."

Meghan thanked me and then left. When I walked into the foyer, I saw Jayne and Jack walking down the stairs, a child asleep on each of them. I frowned. "Why do they never do that for me? They're always wide-awake when I'm with them."

"I think children are good at sensing a soothing presence," Jack said with a grin.

Before I could retort, Jayne said, "Or they were just tired. Meeting new people can be exhausting to young children—there's so much new information they have to process."

I smiled at her, her approach to refereeing confirming my decision to hire her. I reached for Sarah and JJ, balancing each child in my arms, feeling them come awake and begin to squirm. So much for a soothing presence. "I'll go feed the children while Jack brings your things up to your room so you can unpack and get settled."

"Thank you," Jayne said.

I began walking toward the kitchen.

"I think I'd like to restore the house on South Battery before I sell it."

I turned around. "Really? I mean, I'm glad to hear it, but it's not what I expected. What made you decide?"

"Oh, a number of things." Her gaze settled on JJ and it seemed as if she was avoiding looking in my eyes. As if she didn't want me to see something.

"Like what?" I asked.

Jayne shrugged. "It has a little to do with what you told me about Button Pinckney and her motives, and how she chose me. That's no small thing. But mostly . . ." She paused. "Mostly it's this house."

I stared at her, not understanding. "My house?"

She nodded. "It's beautiful and historic, but it's *home*. It has a soul, a good vibe, you know? I'm aware this sounds silly, but it's almost as if it knows there's so much love here and reflects that."

She looked at me as if for affirmation, but all I could do was nod.

She continued. "And somehow, I know the Pinckney house is the same way under all that mold and falling plaster and sadness. There must have been a lot of happiness there before that little girl died. It was once a beloved family home, and it's been left in my care." Her eyes finally met mine. "I've been looking for a home to call my own my whole life. Even if this is the last thing I ever expected or wanted, I can't just turn it down out of hand. It would be . . . not right. Like throwing away an opportunity without really giving it a chance."

"There's always a way to look past the bad to see the good," I said, repeating the philosophy she'd gleaned from being in foster care for so many years.

Jayne smiled. "Yeah, pretty much. I guess what I'm saying is that I'm going to give it a chance. Maybe hang on to it at least long enough that we can figure out Button's motives. And see what the house becomes. Maybe once we can get rid of that awful doll and the dark window coverings and old wallpaper, it might make a huge difference. Maybe all the cosmetic reparations will help . . . What did Jack call it?"

"'Excorcise its ghosts,'" I said with a forced smile.

Her own smile wavered. "Yes, exactly. Then I can decide whether or not I want to sell. And hopefully it will be restored by then."

I tried to hide my sigh of relief. "Great. I know Sophie will be thrilled."

She continued to smile, but there was definitely something in her eyes, something that told me I didn't have the whole story and that she had no intention of sharing it with me.

We heard Nola's door open and the sound of girls' voices. Jayne faced me again. "Make sure she gets rid of that game, okay? It's not like I believe in that stuff or anything, but why tempt fate, right?"

"Right," I said uneasily, then headed back toward the kitchen to feed the babies. I was in the middle of cleaning up pureed organic sweet potatoes and tiny cubes of chicken—courtesy of Mrs. Houlihan and Sophie's food processor baby gift—when I began to smell the stench of something rotting mixed with the scent of freshly turned earth.

Pretending I hadn't smelled anything, I finished wiping down JJ— Sarah was a pristine eater and hardly needed a bib—then picked them both up from their high chairs. It was only as I exited the kitchen that I noticed the large clock over the door, the audible sound of ticking confirming that the battery in the clock still worked, despite the hands that were firmly stuck at ten minutes past four o'clock.

CHAPTER 8

"Hello, beautiful."

Just the sound of Jack's voice over the intercom turned my insides to honey, my brain to cheese grits, my thought processes to those of a goldfish. I stared at the intercom on my desk, wanting him to speak again while at the same time wishing he wouldn't. I was supposed to be working, something that was incompatible with Jack's proximity.

Jolly's voice came over the intercom, and I could tell by her wavering tone that she wasn't immune to Jack's charms, either. "I'm sorry, Melanie. Your husband is here. Should I send him back to you?"

"No need," I heard Jack call from outside my office before he opened my door. Even in the days when I'd found him to be as annoying as he was attractive—and that ratio hadn't changed all that much since our marriage—he always seemed to fill a space. There was something in the wattage of his smile and the sheer force of his personality. Not that I would admit it, but I was happy that all three of his children seemed to have inherited this particular character trait. I made a quick mental note to create a list of things the twins had inherited from me, although I was afraid it would be a rather short one.

He came over to my side of the desk and placed a long, lingering kiss on my mouth. When he pulled back, he kept his eyes on me but used a hand to slide papers from the center of my desk to the edge. I knew what that particular glint in his eyes meant—I had the twins to prove it—but my office wasn't the right place no matter how tempting his kisses were.

"Jack—no. I would die if the new receptionist figured out what was going on in here. Can I take a rain check?"

"Can you wait that long?" he asked as he kissed me again.

Just so I could recall a few brain cells, I slid my glance over to my computer screen, where I'd been working on a spreadsheet of houses for a client. Clearing my throat, I said, "So, to what do I owe the pleasure?"

"Jayne was blowing bubbles in the front garden with the babies and puppies—which is a little too adorable, by the way—and they didn't look like they needed my help. I'd just sent in my revisions to my editor in New York and figured everything was under control, so I took advantage of the situation and not only showered and shaved, but put on real clothes, too. I figured I'd take my best girl out to lunch to celebrate."

My stomach growled—a common occurrence now that even Mrs. Houlihan was conspiring against me and not stocking any of my favorite snacks in the kitchen. My only choices were fruit and gluten-free granola bars and absolutely nothing with the words "Hostess" or "Sara Lee" on the box. And instead of doughnuts or cheese grits and bacon for breakfast, she was making me things like egg-white omelets and vegetable frittatas. No wonder I was hungry all the time. All this healthy eating was not only baffling but killing me.

"The Brown Dog Deli?" I suggested eagerly. It was near my office on Broad Street and had the best sandwiches in the world. They served things like hummus and vegan chili dogs, but they also had a lot of real-people options, too.

Jack looked at his watch, my wedding gift to him, engraved with our anniversary date so he'd never have an excuse for missing it. "It's still early, so hopefully it will be quiet enough so we can talk."

I sent him a worried glance as I stood and picked up my purse. "Is everything all right? With Jayne and the children?"

He put his hand on the small of my back as he guided me from my office. "They're perfect. It's just . . . well, we'll talk about it once we get food in your stomach. We both know what you're like when you're hungry." He moved his hand around the elastic waistband of my skirt. "Have you lost weight?"

I stopped to look up at him. I didn't own a scale, having never needed one, the only person ever concerned about my weight being my ob/gyn while I was pregnant. I'd always been on the thin side and able to eat anything I wanted. It was in my genes, and all I had to do was look at my mother to be reassured that any residual lumpiness left over from my pregnancy would work itself out on its own. Until now.

"What do you mean?" I asked. "Do you think I'm fat?"

"Now, Mellie. I was simply commenting on the fact that your skirt seems loose on you. That's all. You know I think you're the most beautiful woman I've ever met." Right before he kissed me I had a stray thought about how he always used a kiss to stop any argument. And how it always worked.

Jolly looked up as we entered the reception area, her eyes brightening as they rested on Jack. I resisted the urge to roll my eyes. "Headed out to lunch?" she asked, and I was pretty sure she'd batted her eyelashes.

"Yes. I'll keep my cell on just in case there's anything urgent. Otherwise please just take a message. I'll be back in about an hour."

Dragonfly earrings dangled from her ears, shimmying as she shook her hair, her gaze not drifting away from Jack. "Can I give you a reading? No charge for the first one."

"A reading?" He looked genuinely confused.

She gave me a reproachful glance before quickly turning back to Jack. "Didn't Melanie tell you? I'm a psychic. I can talk with the dead."

"Can you?" Jack asked, resting his elbows on the reception desk and leaning toward the receptionist. "How fascinating. Do you see anybody around me right now?"

Jolly closed her eyes, revealing a swath of sparkly blue eyeshadow on her lids, and began rubbing her lips together. "Yes. Yes, I do. A man.

An older man with dark hair like yours." Her eyes opened abruptly. "Has your father crossed over?"

"Seeing as I just hung up the phone with him right before I came in here, I'd have to say no. Is there anything else?"

Jolly closed her eyes again and I poked my finger into Jack's ribs, making him grunt softly.

"He's holding up a piece of jewelry—a bracelet, I think. Maybe he's a jeweler?" She opened her eyes again and beamed at Jack, and this time she definitely batted her eyelashes.

"Thank you," Jack said. "I'm sure after I think for a while I'll figure out who that could have been."

"You be sure to let me know, all right?" Jolly wrote something down in the alligator-picture-covered notebook. "I keep a list so I can gauge my accuracy."

"What's your percentage so far?"

Her lips pressed into a tight line. "About five percent. Closer to four, actually. But I'm getting better. I'm taking online classes to hone my skills."

"That's great," I said, tugging on Jack's arm. "I'll see you in an hour." A cool blast of air greeted us as we exited onto Broad Street. "For the record," I said, "I didn't see anybody. Maybe she was seeing you and my next birthday present and just got confused."

He threw back his head and laughed. "Thanks for the reminder that I have five months to prepare."

I tucked my hand into the crook of his elbow. "Maybe Jolly can help you figure out what I'd like."

We were still chuckling as we entered the Brown Dog Deli and were quickly seated in one of the booths against the brightly painted blue wall, liberally adorned with vibrantly colored posters and framed cartoon dog prints. As Jack had predicted, we were ahead of the lunch crowd and our waitress appeared with water glasses and was ready to take our orders as soon as we sat down. I ordered the fried green tomato and pimento cheese sandwich with a side of potato chips while Jack ordered the Pita Frampton. Remembering our earlier conversation about my weight, I changed my side to the fresh fruit mix, lamenting my potato chips as soon as the waitress stepped away from our table.

Jack's left hand with the gold band around his third finger rested on the table. I wanted to reach over and place my hand in his but was afraid that was more a teenager kind of thing to do. I hadn't dated as a teenager, so I had no point of reference, but I'd seen enough young adult movies with Nola, so I had a pretty good idea.

"So," I said before sipping my water through a long straw, "what did you want to talk about?" My old self would never have asked this question, preferring the head-in-the-sand approach—a method that I still returned to more often than not. But this was my marriage—something that would never have even happened if I'd kept my head buried—and I figured it was a good place to start with the new, married version of me.

Jack looked pleasantly surprised that I was the one who'd spoken first, but he made the wise decision not to comment on it. He reached into a pocket and pulled out what looked like a section of newspaper. He unfolded it on the table and I saw it was a clipped article, the edges jagged. I immediately began rummaging through my purse for my emergency bag that held scissors, duct tape, WD-40, toothpaste, and an assortment of other items I might need in any given day.

"What are you doing?" he asked.

My hand stilled. "I'm looking for my scissors. I thought I'd trim that up for you."

"That's probably not necessary. I think all you need to do is read it."

"Right," I said, pulling my hand out of my purse as if it didn't matter. I pulled the paper closer so I could read it, trying not to squint so I wouldn't have to listen to Jack tell me again that I shouldn't be ashamed to wear glasses and that most people over forty did. Since he had yet to reach forty, it was in both our best interests—especially with a pair of sharp scissors nearby—that we refrain from that conversation.

"It's from last Sunday's paper," he said. "The puppies got to it after you pulled out the real estate section but before I could read the rest of it, but your dad brought it over this morning after you left for work to show me. It's from the editorial page."

I felt the first fissure of unease.

"It's from that series the *Post and Courier* is doing about the history of some of the historic houses in Charleston. It wasn't supposed to last this long, but apparently, it's become quite popular, and the staff writer is getting all sorts of social invitations from people hoping that their houses will be the subject of the column."

"Suzy Dorf," I said, not bothering to disguise the sneer in my voice. "She's been trying to reach me. She's actually left several messages and a text on my phone."

He raised his eyebrows, not warranting my comments with a comment of his own.

"She annoys me. I have nothing to say to her—especially after she printed that anonymous letter last year about there being more bodies buried in our garden. I should sue her for libel."

"That might be premature, don't you think? Especially considering that we've just unearthed a cistern in said garden?"

"It doesn't matter. Any dead bodies we find are *our* dead bodies. She needs to mind her own business."

His eyebrows drew together as if he was trying to translate something in his mind. After a brief shake of his head, he said, "She's a reporter. That's what she does." He reached over and slid the clipping closer to me. "Read it."

Trying very hard not to squint, I began to read:

Hollywood is coming to the Holy City! Thankfully, it's not for a far-be-it-from-reality reality series but for a feature film from a major studio. Charleston native Marc Longo's book, *Lust, Greed, and Murder in the Holy City*, hasn't even hit bookstore shelves yet, but there's so much buzz about this book that the rumor mill has reported that the movie rights went to auction for a cool seven figures.

I looked up at Jack, who was valiantly trying to keep his face expressionless. It had been *his* story first, before Marc had stolen it from him and rushed his own version of the story to publication before Jack even had a chance. The murder involved Marc's family, giving him the inside scoop, but the bodies had been found in *our* garden. Jack had already written his own book about how we'd solved the mystery, and he'd signed a publishing deal. It just hadn't been published before Marc got there first. We'd had a small victory when we were able to keep Marc from buying the house out from under us, but only because Nola had lent us the money. It was unfair, and humiliating, and something we'd learned to get past and forget about. Until now.

"Is this what your agent called you about the other day?"

He nodded. "Keep going. It gets better."

I've heard from an anonymous source that the Vanderhorst house at 55 Tradd Street—the setting for the sordid story behind the book—will be used for filming, to give the movie an authentic flair and the all-important nod from the Charleston establishment. And, with the appearance of new yellow caution tape in the back of the property, who knows what else might be discovered and used for fodder for a sequel? The house is supposedly haunted, so this could get interesting. Boo! Stay tuned to this column for further updates.

My hand was shaking as I slid the paper back to Jack. "Well, those Hollywood people have another think coming if they think for one second I'm going to open up the door to my home to let them film a movie about a book my husband *didn't* write. And the *nerve* of that reporter to assume that it will happen, without even asking us!"

Jack cleared his throat as if to remind me that Ms. Dorf had, indeed, tried to talk to me, but I ignored him. "Have you heard from Marc about this?" I drew back, horrified at the direction of my thoughts. "Or Rebecca? She forced us to give them an engagement party. Surely that doesn't give them the right to assume . . ." I stopped when I caught sight of his expression. "Why are you smiling?"

"Because you're so sexy when you're angry."

I blinked a few times. "Stop distracting me. I—*we*—have every right to be angry. Why aren't you taking this as seriously as I am?"

He reached over and took hold of my hand again. "Have you ever considered how long it's going to take for us to get back on our feet financially and pay Nola back? She refuses to call it a loan, but I don't think we've ever considered it anything else."

I stared at him for a long moment, sure I misunderstood. "Jack, surely you can't . . ." I was interrupted by my phone ringing. Jack stared at it, noticing the number without a name, then met my gaze. "Did you change your ring tone? I was kind of getting used to *Mamma Mia*."

I shook my head as I hit the red button to end the call. "No. I have no idea where this ring tone came from. Or who's calling. They've called a bunch of times, but I don't recognize the number and they never leave a message—well, only once. They didn't say anything—just a bunch of odd noises." I gave an involuntary shudder, remembering the sound of prying wood and a tinny note vibrating in the empty air.

"Have you looked up the phone number?"

It was my turn to look confused. "Can you do that?"

He gave me a look that said he thought I might be joking, but he reached over and picked up my phone. "You can do a reverse lookup—just type in the number and . . ." He was silent for a moment as he punched numbers into the phone, then paused. "Oh."

The waitress waited until that moment to deliver our food, and for the first time in a long while, I was less hungry and more interested in what Jack had to say. When she finally walked away, I said, "What is it?"

"Do you know a Caroline B. Pinckney?"

I thought hard for a moment, the smell of the food battling with my memory. I began chasing a grape across my plate, hoping that having food in my stomach might jog something loose.

Jack continued. "Do you happen to know Button Pinckney's real name? Assuming Button was a nickname, of course. In Charleston, there's no guarantee that an odd name isn't the name appearing on the birth certificate. . . ."

I dropped the fork with which I'd been trying to stab a grape and met his eyes. "It was definitely Caroline," I shouted. My voice sounded parched even though I'd just had half a glass of water. "Jayne said her name was Caroline." I swallowed. "Why?"

"Because that phone number is registered to a Caroline B. Pinckney on South Battery Street."

We continued to stare at each other for a long time, neither of us questioning the impossibility of a phone call from a dead person.

CHAPTER 9

I stood in the foyer of the Pinckney house with Detective Riley, watching with part amusement and part affront as he studied the disaster around him. I wondered if I would ever really climb off the figurative fence that had me currently planted in the middle of undecided when it came to old houses. Half the time—thanks to Sophie, although I would never admit it to her—I could actually appreciate the attention to detail, architecture, and craftsmanship these old houses held within their thick walls. Yet at other times, usually right after I paid another repair bill, I could picture lighting the dynamite myself.

"Somebody really lived here, huh?" He was staring at the mildew-speckled wallpaper in the dining room.

"Yes—although Miss Pinckney stayed in her bedroom for the last few years of her life. She didn't have any family—just cats, from what I've learned."

"Cats? That's a bit of a cliché, isn't it?"

I sent him a sidelong glance as I walked past him to examine what looked to be a button in the wall. "Kind of like finding a cop in a doughnut shop, don't you think? There's always a seed of truth in every cliché."

He chuckled behind me. "Guilty as charged. Guess there aren't any stereotypes for psychic Realtors, huh? Don't think there are too many of those around."

I pressed the metal button, pausing for a moment to see if I heard an echoing bell somewhere in the house. All I heard was the passing traffic outside and the rumbling wheels of a horse-drawn carriage. I assumed it was from one of the tourist companies, but I wouldn't have been surprised if I looked outside and saw an eighteen sixties Brougham with the bottom half of its wheels invisible as it traversed a street that was currently below the level of the present one. In my world, there was no such thing as a guarantee that the restless dead would leave me alone long enough to simply look out the window and see what everybody else did.

"Hello?"

Startled, I turned toward the front door to see Jayne peering around it, her hand still on the doorknob. "Sorry; didn't mean to scare you."

"Please don't apologize. It's your house." I studied her closely, wondering when she'd come in and if she'd heard what Thomas had said about psychic Realtors. It wasn't that it was something I hid. It was just something I didn't advertise or tell anybody about. I especially didn't share my "gift" with clients. It was a competitive enough business without making clients run away from me screaming right into the arms of one of my competitors on the grounds that I was insane. It simply wasn't good for business.

"Come in," I said, drawing her into the room. I had to pry her hand from the doorknob so I could close the door. I followed her gaze behind me to where it settled on the black cat crouched low at the bottom of the stairs.

"How did he get in here?" she asked as the cat ran soundlessly up the stairs and out of sight.

"Who, me?" Thomas asked as he approached.

"No. A fat black cat," I explained. "We keep seeing him, but he's very fast. I don't know who he belongs to, but someone must be feeding him, because he's definitely not starving."

Thomas didn't seem to be listening. Instead he was staring at Jayne, a small crease between his eyebrows. Before he could say anything, Jayne said, "I have one of those faces, so you think we've met before. But I know we haven't." She held out her hand to him. "I'm Jayne Smith. Apparently, the new owner of this house."

Thomas smiled, revealing perfect teeth and exaggerating the smile lines on the side of his face, transforming him from simply handsome to devastating. "I'm Detective Thomas Riley. I understand from Melanie here that you think you had an intruder?"

Even though he continued to smile, I could tell that he was still studying Jayne with his detective eyes, wondering if she really just had one of those faces.

"Well, we're not sure. But Melanie's cell phone has had several phone calls from a landline number assigned to this house. It's actually been in service for nearly forty years and has not been reassigned according to the phone company." She bit her lower lip and glanced at me as if for affirmation. "There's just one thing. . . ." There was a long pause, and I wondered if she wanted me to speak. Instead I gave her an encouraging look. This was her house, after all. "When Miss Pinckney died, the telephone service was cut off."

Thomas raised his eyebrows, and I knew he wanted to look at me to get my take on the matter, but dared not. "Maybe the records show that there's no service, but there might have been a paperwork glitch. Have you lifted any of the receivers to check?"

Jayne's eyes widened hopefully. "No—we haven't had a chance. I know I saw an old turquoise phone on the wall in the kitchen." She began walking excitedly to the kitchen, as if the thought of having an intruder in the house making phone calls to my cell was much more palatable—and conceivable—than any other explanation.

We followed her into the kitchen and watched as she picked the handset from the wall and held it to her ear. Her eyes closed briefly before she shook her head, then slowly hung up the phone. "It's dead," she said.

That's not the only thing, I thought, but kept my mouth closed. She'd made her decision about keeping the house—for now—and I didn't want to muddy the waters. Whatever was here could be dealt with or just ignored, depending on how persistent it became. I hoped without Jayne being any the wiser.

Thomas leaned against a kitchen counter, then immediately straightened and brushed at his sleeves as he noticed the dust coating the kitchen table and chairs. "I'll double-check to see if the number's been reassigned and who it's been reassigned to. If it hasn't, well, things get a little more complicated." He didn't look at me, but I could tell he wanted to. Instead he tilted his head slightly to regard Jayne. "Are you sure we haven't met?"

"Positive," Jayne said with a smile. "Because I'm pretty sure I would have remembered meeting you." Her cheeks pinkened as she seemed to notice for the first time that he was an attractive male and not just a police detective. "I mean, well, you're a detective. And tall. With clean fingernails. And I like your shirt."

I rolled my eyes behind her back and tugged on her elbow to get her to stop. She was worse than I'd been when I met Jack. I'd also sounded like a teenager who'd never been on a date before. Which was actually pretty accurate at the time. I supposed that was something else Jayne and I had in common—lonely childhoods that didn't leave a lot of room for a social life or relationships of any kind.

"Thank you," Thomas said with a smile in his voice. "My oldest sister bought me this shirt for my birthday. I'll let her know that I received a compliment on it today."

Jayne was saved from spouting more infantile gibberish by the distinct sound of a ringing bell. She looked at me in surprise. "I thought the servants' bells didn't work."

"I thought so, too," I said, avoiding her gaze. "I guess we were wrong." We turned back to the kitchen.

"They're over here," Jayne said as she walked into the butler's pantry, its glass-covered cabinets full of crystal and china and what looked like a salt-and-pepper-shaker collection. I peered closely at what appeared to be a peanut-shaped ceramic saltshaker with the word "Georgia" painted on its side. I had a sinking feeling that there was a set from all fifty states. I'd have to get Amelia in here to see what was in these cabinets and the rest of the house and let Jayne know whether any of it was valuable. I hoped for Jayne's sake that the china was rare and expensive so she'd have an excuse to sell it and not keep it out of obligation to Button Pinckney. The china was covered in pink roses, with gold-covered scalloped edges. Definitely old, and definitely European. And definitely hideous. I assumed all the Pinckneys had been very slim, since eating off those plates must have diminished appetites.

Jayne pointed to a metal box with a single bell. "That must have been what made the noise."

"I don't think so," Thomas said, using his height to full advantage and getting a closer look. "There's no hammer anymore—or it rusted away. But this dog won't hunt, that's for sure."

I found it odd that nobody asked the obvious question: *Then how did the bell ring?*

After an awkward pause, Jayne said, "It must have been the doorbell," and began marching toward the front door, Thomas and me dutifully following. She opened it and swung the door wide, then stepped out onto the front landing as if to make sure nobody was hiding. Turning around, she pressed her finger into the old doorbell button, her effort rewarded by silence.

"Actually, Jayne," I said, "most doorbells in these old houses rarely operate because of the high humidity and salt in the air."

She walked into the foyer and slowly closed the door. Crossing her arms over her chest, she said, "It must have been a bike from outside, then. So many people on bikes in Charleston, I noticed. I'll have to get one."

A flash of white from the landing flitted across my peripheral vision, but I dared not turn my head. I became aware of my second sight being blocked again, like a hand being held over my eyes, allowing me to see only what it thought I should.

A loud thump and then the sound of scurrying little feet tumbled downstairs. "Help me!" It was the doll's voice, high-pitched and strident, the words seeming to echo in the otherwise silent house. Jayne and I turned around in time to see the black cat race across the landing and disappear up the stairs.

Thomas immediately held out his hand to prevent us from moving forward. "Is there anybody here?" he called up the stairs. Stepping forward, he pulled his gun from his shoulder holster and began climbing. "I'm Detective Thomas Riley from the Charleston Police Department and I'm armed. Please show yourself."

He motioned for us to stay back as he silently climbed the stairs two at a time. We listened as each door was thrown open, then waited as Thomas moved from room to room upstairs searching for an intruder. After several long minutes, he reappeared on the landing, his eyebrows knitted together. "It's all clear. But, well, this is the dangedest thing I've seen in a while."

Jayne and I nearly collided as we raced toward the stairs, then halted as we reached the upper hallway. The Thomas Edison doll, so fragile and valuable, stood by a half-open door at the end of the hallway, one of its arms reaching upward as if trying to grasp the doorknob. Or as if it had already opened the door.

"Those are the stairs to the attic," Thomas provided.

"Do you think somebody's trying to play a prank on me?" Jayne asked with a quavering voice.

Thomas returned his gun to the holster and approached Jayne. "I suppose we need to consider the possibility. It certainly doesn't appear to be a burglary—nothing's been ransacked, anyway. You might want to check with Miss Pinckney's lawyers to see if they have an inventory of the house you can check against what's here." His eyes met mine for a moment over Jayne's head. "Just in case, I would suggest changing the locks and installing a security system—there doesn't seem to already be one. It's an up-front expense, but from what Melanie has told me, there are a lot of valuable items inside the house."

"Including that doll," I said, indicating Chucky posed at the door.

Thomas gave an involuntary shudder. "Really? I'm glad you told me. Otherwise I would have offered to take it with me and toss it in a Dumpster on the way home."

"It talks," I said. "Although it's not supposed to, but Sophie told us that it has to be wound up first and that the mechanism is too delicate for it to work now. And it only recites a single nursery rhyme."

Our eyes met, recalling the two words we'd all heard. *Help me.* That wasn't part of any nursery rhyme I knew. I swallowed. "I'm thinking Sophie got it wrong, but she's arranging for an expert to take a look at it so we at least have an idea of its value."

Jayne's arms remained crossed tightly in front of her, with little half-moons dug into her skin where her fingernails were. "I'm wondering if there might be a secret entrance to the house or something. That might be where the stray cat gets in and out."

Leaving the doll where it was—nobody volunteered to put it back in the rocking chair in Button Pinckney's bedroom—Thomas led us toward the stairs. "I'll walk around the house and give a thorough search for what might look like any hidden openings. Melanie—why don't you call your friend Yvonne at the archives and see if she has any of the old blueprints from this house? You never know what you might find."

You never know what you might find. "I'll do that. Jack and I haven't seen Yvonne in a while, so that will be nice."

I noticed a large two-bell brass carriage clock—the metal splotched in places, giving the surface the appearance of reflected clouds—sitting on a narrow hall table at the top of the stairs. As we passed it, it began to chime. Out of habit I looked at my watch but was surprised to see that it was eleven twenty—not a time that would warrant a chime on any clock. I stopped to look at the face of the clock and stilled. Although it was still chiming, the hands of the clock weren't moving, frozen on a time that was becoming frighteningly familiar. Ten minutes past four.

"Oomph."

My head whipped around in time to see Jayne pitch forward on the stairs. She seemed to roll forward in slow motion, her body hitting the wall of the landing, before momentum flipped her head over heels down the rest of the stairs.

Thomas had already reached the foyer and was quick enough to break Jayne's fall before she could hit the hard floor. I raced down after her, careful to hold on to the bannister, then crouched next to where Thomas had sat her on the bottom step. "Are you all right?"

She was rubbing her ankle. "I think so. But my ankle's hurt."

Thomas carefully removed her shoe and began gently pressing on her ankle. "Doesn't seem to be broken, but I'm taking you to the hospital to be completely checked out. You hit your head pretty hard on the landing wall."

"Really, that's not necessary—"

"Yes, it is. Both professionally and personally. If my mother found out that I witnessed a pretty woman fall down the stairs and didn't take her to the hospital, she'd hit me with a frying pan."

Jayne's cheeks flushed as she lifted her lips in a half smile, then looked back up the stairway. "That was the weirdest thing. . . ."

"What?" I asked uneasily. "How you tripped?" I felt like a liar, knowing full well she hadn't tripped.

Jayne shook her head. "No. I should be more seriously hurt than just a twisted ankle. But it was as if I had a little cushion each time I hit a step or the wall."

"That is weird," I said, shrugging as if that sort of thing happened every day. Which it did in my world, but I didn't want to tell her that. But I'd felt it, too, the softer presence that wasn't afraid of whatever other spirits still lingered between the old walls. There were battling forces in this house, and something was keeping me from seeing the whole picture. But there was one thing I was sure of: I couldn't let Jayne Smith back in the house until I knew what—or who—did not want any guests.

Thomas leaned down and picked Jayne up, her arm sliding around his shoulders, her cheeks a dark scarlet. "Can you grab her purse and shoe? You can toss them into the back of my car."

"I'll go with you . . ." I said as I ran after him.

"I'm off duty and you've got a husband and two babies to get home to. We'll be fine—I'll call you and let you know what's going on."

"Your shampoo smells nice," Jayne said to the side of Thomas's head. "Or is that your deodorant? I'm glad you wear deodorant."

I rolled my eyes as I threw her stuff into the back of Thomas's sedan, then watched as Thomas carefully buckled Jayne's seat belt. She sent me a thumbs-up and I reciprocated, still holding up my thumb as I watched his car pull away.

I realized I hadn't locked up the house and was almost to the front door when it slammed in my face, the rusted key scraping against the decrepit lock from the inside of the house, and leaving me with the distinct impression that I wasn't welcome.

CHAPTER 10

I checked the mailbox on the front gate as I came home for lunch the following day. I always made a point of dumping anything we didn't need into the outside recycling bin before it even made it into the house. Jack was forbidden from getting the mail because it always ended up in a pile on the kitchen counter that would stay there until the next millennium if I didn't take charge. He'd thanked me for taking over this chore with a grin that had showed all his teeth. It was nice to be appreciated.

I stood at the back door, going through the mail piece by piece, dropping all except a bill from Rich Kobylt's business, Hard Rock Foundations—for the restoration of the kitchen window as well as two dining room window frames that had rotted through—and a heavy linen envelope addressed to Mr. and Mrs. Jack Trenholm. It was thick, like a wedding invitation, and before I turned it over to see the return address, I ran through my head anybody I knew who'd be getting married. With the exception of octogenarian librarian Yvonne Craig, I didn't think I knew anybody still single.

The return address was engraved onto the back of the ivory-colored envelope. There was no name, but the address was in New York City.

I opened the back door and smelled something wonderful cooking on the stove, Mrs. Houlihan gently stirring a pot's contents with a wooden spoon. The three dogs were in their individual monogrammed beds. Nola swore they could read and that was why they always ended up in the right bed. I had my doubts—nothing that cute could also be that smart. It worked against the laws of nature.

I gave them each a scratch behind the ears, then turned to Mrs. Houlihan expectantly. "That smells divine. What is it?" I reached to lift the lid from the pot, but the older woman slapped gently at my hand.

"It's a vegan meat sauce for the whole wheat spaghetti you're having for dinner tonight. It's from the cookbook Dr. Wallen-Arasi gave you for Christmas."

"I thought I told you to donate that to Goodwill."

"Did you? I must have forgot. I must say, I've been making some of the recipes at home and my clothes are fitting much more loosely."

I narrowed my eyes at her, wondering if she was trying to say something else, but she busied herself with sorting spices on the rack on the counter.

My interest and appetite having fled, I carefully hung up my coat in the small closet we'd had added to the butler's pantry, checking each pocket carefully and making sure the lapels of all the coats were facing the same way. Nola had learned quickly, but there were two of Jack's coats that I had to fix.

I slid open the kitchen drawer where I kept the letter opener. That was another thing I'd told Jack I'd take care of—the opening of mail. I'd shown him several times the correct use of a letter opener, even shown him where ours was kept, but it was as if he refused my instruction, and if an unopened envelope accidentally fell into his possession, he'd open it like a hungry bear at an overstuffed garbage can.

I carefully slid the letter opener into the corner of the envelope, then gently moved the blade to the other corner, leaving a clean, precise opening the way Mother Nature intended. I pulled out an engraved invitation on heavy cardstock without an envelope or RSVP card—the way etiquette sticklers did it.

I stared at the elegant script, and I suddenly felt light-headed. It wasn't a wedding invitation at all. It was an invitation to a book launch party. I read over it a couple of times just to make sure I wasn't misinterpreting it, then shoved it back into the envelope and when I stacked the mail, I put it under the bill in the hope that Jack would overlook it and I could pretend I'd never seen it. It did occur to me that I could shred it in the paper shredder in Jack's office and no one would be any the wiser. It was what the old me would have done. But I was a mature married woman now, and it would be up to Jack to notice the invitation and respond.

A heavy thump and then the sound of something being dragged upstairs brought me out of the kitchen. I stood at the bottom of the stairs and listened, thinking it was from Nola's room, which at the moment was practically vibrating with loud music that sadly wasn't the ABBA album I'd given her for Christmas.

I heard JJ laugh and I smiled as I took the stairs two at a time to reach the nursery. I opened the door and paused, my own smile quickly fading as I took it all in. Jayne sat in the rocking chair with her foot resting on the ottoman, her ankle wrapped in a bandage. Both of my children sat on her lap holding a brown paper lunch bag—definitely not one of the educational toys that lined the room and the bookshelves—and laughing each time one of them squeezed the bag and made a crinkling noise. Jack, his button-down shirt discarded on the side of Sarah's crib, wore only his sweat-soaked T-shirt. But the most disconcerting sight of the entire scenario was the furniture, all moved into a new position and ignoring the feng shui design created by the interior designer I'd hired to help set up the nursery.

Jack grinned at me as he wiped the sweat from his forehead. "What do you think? Jayne suggested that the room would be more functional this way, with more play room, and I agreed."

Sarah smashed her paper bag between two fists, causing both children to start chortling with glee. I looked down at the beautiful handmade rug that had been a gift from Jack's mother, the primary color design of building blocks with the children's initials on each one, now completely hidden by the bucket of toys upended in the middle of it.

Jack approached to kiss me hello, but I stepped back, citing his sweat as my main reason. "Looks like you've been busy," I said.

"We have," Jayne exclaimed. "Sarah and I were building all sorts of structures with the blocks, and JJ was having a blast knocking them down. That's when I realized that they needed more room, so I asked Jack to help."

I stared pointedly at the wrap on her ankle. "I thought the doctor told you that could come off in a day."

"It hasn't been a full day yet, but Jack said I should rest it as long as I could and to keep it on at least until tomorrow morning. I think he was just looking for an excuse to play with the children."

"Probably," I said, my lips feeling brittle.

"I guess since all the heavy lifting is done I'll go take my shower and then we'll go see Yvonne." Without warning, he kissed me on the cheek and left.

"You forgot your shirt," I called after him.

"I'll put it in the laundry chute," Jayne offered.

Sarah clambered off her lap, then crawled to a corner of the rug where the large, chunky Duplo blocks had been snapped together to make what resembled a house, complete with a roof, two chimneys, and a front porch that looked as if a chubby fist had taken out a chunk. I noticed that she and JJ were in matching outfits—if you considered white onesies and diapers outfits. She picked up a Duplo girl with yellow hair and began to pound it against the side of the house.

I waited for Jayne to tell Sarah that people used doors, but she didn't say anything, preferring to study her as if my daughter were an anthropological experiment. With a frown, I squatted down next to Sarah and looked into her sweet face that at the moment was scowling at me. "Sweetheart, people use doors to go inside the house."

"Uhhh," she grunted as she resumed banging the poor plastic girl against the fluorescent yellow wall.

In a gentle voice, I said, "Sarah, can I please have the little girl?"

She continued to hammer the girl against the house like a weapon, ignoring me. Jayne placed JJ on the floor, then knelt in front of Sarah. "She's been doing this all day—it's like she's made up her mind that girls going through walls is the right way." Jayne held out her hand. "May I please have the girl? I'll put her to bed inside so that she's all rested for tomorrow."

Sarah solemnly dropped the toy into Jayne's outstretched palm. With an apologetic glance at me, Jayne said, "Like I said, we've been doing this all day. She has a very firm belief in the way things should be."

"I wonder where she gets that from," I said, curious as to which branch of Jack's tree that particular trait might have fallen out of. I thought of his parents and figured it had to go further back than that.

Jayne was looking at me oddly. "Yeah. I wonder. So, Melanie, could I ask you something?"

"Sure," I said, hoping she was about to suggest replacing the furniture where it had been.

"I don't want to go back to that house on South Battery until it's fully renovated. I find it . . . unsettling."

I struggled to keep my expression neutral. "All right. I understand. You did tell me that you didn't like old houses, so I'm not surprised. Are you saying you changed your mind about keeping it?"

She shook her head. "No. I agreed to keep the house for now out of respect for Miss Pinckney's wishes and to see if the house's aura changes any with the renovations. But she didn't say I had to live in it. For now, I really have no desire to cross the threshold in the foreseeable future."

I hoped she didn't see my relief. "That's not a problem. I spoke with Sophie today and she'll be happy to lead the restoration, determine if any grants might be available, and if she can use parts of the work as curriculum. She'll figure out the numbers so she can discuss them with you, and any major decisions will have to be signed off by you. I'm sure for the sheer happiness of working on the house she won't mind being in charge."

"What about the doll?"

I shuddered, remembering the doll standing by the opened attic door. "Sophie spoke with her friend the doll expert and he's eager to take a look. He's stopping by tomorrow to pick it up and says it will take a few weeks before he can get back to us."

"Tell him to take as long as he needs."

I smiled. "Will do. Well, then, we'll see you in a couple of hours. Hopefully we'll find something in the archives that will tell us more about the house. Maybe even something about the family."

I kissed the children good-bye, then turned toward the door. Jayne called me back.

"Melanie?"

"Yes?"

"Nola's friend—Lindsey. Do you know her well?"

I shook my head. "I met her the first time when you did. She says her mother and I went to college together—I don't remember her. I need to pull out my yearbook to see if I recognize her. Why?"

JJ reached his arms to be picked up again and Jayne lifted him, her eyes focused on his little face. I couldn't help wondering if she was using him as a reason to avoid eye contact with me.

"I'm not sure," she said. "It's just, well, you know how some people seem . . . haunted?"

"A little," I said, glad her focus was on JJ.

"Well, that's the sense I get from her. As if she's being dogged by something."

"Because she brought the Ouija board?"

"No," Jayne said, finally looking at me. "I think because she reminded me a little of myself when I was that age. All alone, even in a roomful of people."

I nodded, unwilling to admit that I knew exactly what she was talking about. It hadn't been that long ago that I'd felt the same way—before Jack, and before I'd reconciled with my mother and father. There was something about being raised with absent parents that made a permanent scar in a person's psyche.

I pondered my next question for a moment. "Since you're kind of a child-rearing expert, do you think I should limit Nola's association with her?"

Jayne shook her head. "Nola's pretty grounded, which is a tribute to both her own strength and the parental guidance she's received from you and Jack. I think she and Lindsey could be good for each other."

I nodded. "Thanks. And I'm not going back to the office when we return, so you can have the rest of the day and evening off."

"Thank you." She looked up at me. "I'm kind of hoping you don't find anything in the archives."

I raised my eyebrows.

"I don't mean to sound ungrateful. Really, I don't. My lawyers have explained that there's enough money in the estate to do the restorations, which will allow the house to be sold for a pretty hefty sum. I won't have to worry about money after that, which is a nice thing to know." She paused. "It's just . . ."

"It's just . . . ?" I prompted.

"Do you ever think that it's just easier ignoring bad stuff in the hopes that it will go away?"

I thought for a moment, debating whether I should tell her that I'd cut my teeth on that very same philosophy. And remembering the invitation downstairs that I'd tucked beneath a bill, hoping it might get overlooked and forgotten. I decided that as her employer and the mother of two, I needed to come up with a more mature response. "It probably is easier," I said. "But in my experience, the bad stuff isn't like a mosquito bite—you know, leave it alone so it disappears instead of scratching it and making it worse. Usually the things you don't want to deal with get worse the longer you wait."

She contemplated me for a long moment. "Do you believe in . . ." She stopped suddenly, and I wondered if she'd also felt the temperature in the room drop. JJ continued to babble, but Sarah looked up, then stared at the door expectantly.

"Do I believe in what?" I asked, remembering Jayne being pushed down the stairs the previous day. And her opposition to the Ouija board.

Sarah began whimpering and Jayne bent to her eye level, her answer lost as she soothed my daughter and I took the opportunity to look around the room. But all I could sense was that dark curtain again, pulling tightly closed and blocking my view.

I bent to kiss the top of each baby's head, then retreated to the door. "We'll be back soon."

We said good-bye and I closed the door behind me. I walked slowly down the stairs, fairly certain I knew what she'd been about to ask me, and still unsure I knew how to answer.

CHAPTER 11

66**W**as there anything in the mail?" Jack asked, one hand on the steering wheel, the other thrown casually around the back of my seat. The Fireproof Building on Chalmers, where the South Carolina Historical Archives were kept, wasn't that far and Jack had suggested we walk, but my feet were close to bleeding because I'd worn my favorite pre-pregnancy heels all morning. Despite the numb tingling on one side of each foot and the blisters on the other, I'd promised my beautiful shoes that I'd wear them for the rest of the day before I added them to the shrine at the back of my closet.

Jack smelled of shampoo and soap and *Jack*, and I couldn't make myself ask him to remove his arm until he apologized. For what, I wasn't sure. All I knew was that I felt unsettled, and that it had started when I walked into the nursery and saw him and Jayne and our children together. I'd felt somehow superfluous, my old insecurities resurfacing like a rash that hadn't completely faded. Because, deep down, I still believed that capturing Jack's attention had been a fluke, and that one day he'd wake up and really see me as the pathetic, awkward, and insecure teenager I'd once been and was afraid I still was.

"Mellie?"

I realized I'd been staring at his jawline while allowing my thoughts to ramble down a road I didn't want to travel. "Um, I'm sorry, what did you say?"

"Was there anything in the mail?"

Crap. "A couple of things, I think. There's another bill from Rich Kobylt. I didn't look at the amount because I didn't want to start thinking ugly thoughts about hiding a body in cement. I mean, it's not like it hasn't been done before."

"They'd know where to look," Jack said seriously.

"True. And who knows what else they'd dig up while they're looking, and then we're falling down another rabbit hole. So I'll let you deal with the bill."

He seemed to be waiting for me to say something else.

"What?" I asked. "You think I should handle the bill?"

"No. You said there were a couple of things in the mail. What was the second thing?"

I considered throwing myself out of the car while it was still moving. He wasn't going that fast, and I was close enough that I could walk home even if it made me permanently lame.

"Oh," I said, flicking my wrist to show him how unimportant it was. "It was an invitation."

Jack was a true-crime writer, used to digging for details and asking questions. I had no idea why I'd thought he wouldn't notice my evasiveness.

"An invitation?"

I nodded.

He sighed. "An invitation to what?"

I stared longingly at the side of the road, my hand hovering over the door latch. "A party. At Cannon Green."

"A party? Well, that's something. What kind of party? Baby's first birthday? Retirement? Engagement? Celebrating Sophie's new enterprise of handmade grass skirts from Africa?"

"A book-launch party," I said quickly, coughing into my hands in the dim hope that he wouldn't hear and would let it drop.

"A book-launch party?" he repeated, each consonant perfect. "For whom?"

When I didn't answer immediately he glanced at me, a look of incredulity mixed with uncertainty clouding his features. "It couldn't be . . ."

"It's for Marc. For *Lust, Greed, and Murder in the Holy City.* I think it's a big deal—the invitation was sent by his publisher. Maybe that's why we're on the guest list—it's a mistake because they don't know your history with Marc."

"Oh, they know it. And I'm pretty sure Marc made sure we were on that list."

"So we're not going, right?" I asked hopefully. Spending money on an evening gown for a party for Marc Longo was right up there on my priority list alongside doing psychic readings at the Ashley Hall alumnae weekend (as suggested by Nola).

Jack didn't even hesitate. "Of course we're going."

"But why put ourselves through the misery of seeing Marc gloat, and watching people who should know better fawn over him? He *stole* that book from you. And then he tried to steal our house from both of us. Why on earth should we go to a party to celebrate him? Don't forget that Rebecca will be there, too. She'll be wearing some atrocious pink gown, and just the sight of her in it and her smug, self-satisfied expression will probably make me throw up."

Jack grinned, his dimple deepening. "And that alone will be worth it. Just make sure you aim it at her."

I elbowed him. "But seriously, why would you want to put us both through that?"

"Because if we don't show up, it will send the message that we're deeply hurt. By being there, we show them that we don't care. That we can rise above their pettiness and appear at a celebratory party for Marc and his book because we're happy for him and his success. Because we're better than that. We're mature adults who can put bitterness behind us and move on without hard feelings."

"Is that how you really feel?"

"Heck no. I'm mad as hell and I think Marc is a completely dishonest jerk and if this were another century, I would have called him out at dawn for a duel. Sadly, I can't do that. So instead we'll go to his party with smiles on our faces and eat as much caviar as we can. Put some in napkins to bring home if we have to. And make them think that we're up to something."

He studied the road in front of him, and I had the feeling that he was avoiding looking at me for a reason—and not just to avoid the tourist standing in the middle of Broad Street taking a photo of St. Michael's.

"Is this about using our house for the movie? Because we are *not* going to agree to that, right?"

As if even parking spaces in Charleston weren't immune to Jack's charms, one opened up on Meeting Street just as we approached the Fireproof Building. He easily slid the minivan into the spot before turning to me with a smile. "We're here."

"Jack . . ."

But he'd already leaped out of his seat and was opening the passenger door for me. He glanced at his watch. "We're a little late—hurry up. I hate to keep Yvonne waiting."

Grabbing my hand, he led me up the familiar staircase and into the building, then up to the familiar reading room, where Jack and I had spent many hours researching various Charleston historic factoids.

Yvonne was sitting at one of the long wooden tables with several books set out in front of her, little scraps of paper marking spots inside each one. She looked up and smiled before standing, the rhinestones in her cat's-eye glasses sparkling.

She stood on tiptoes to kiss Jack on each cheek, then turned to me. "You look lovely as always, Melanie. Are you keeping Jack in line?"

"Of course," I said at the same time Jack answered, "Not even close."

She winked and then kissed my cheek. "Same ol' Jack," she said with a wistful note in her voice, and I thought, not for the first time, that if she were thirty years younger and he were still single, she would have set her cap for him.

"I like your new glasses," Jack said, eyeing Yvonne. "They frame your face beautifully."

Her cheeks flushed a flattering pink. "Careful, Jack. Flattery will get you everywhere."

"And don't I know it?" he said, squeezing her shoulders and making her flush even more.

Clearing her throat, she turned our attention to the books on the table. "They've moved so many of the archives to the new College of Charleston Library, but happily most of what you were looking for I found here. You might still want to go look there and at the archives at the Charleston Museum for more on the Pinckney family. It's a very old Charleston family—two signers of the Constitution and a governor. My mother was a Pinckney, you know. Different branch from Button and her brother, Sumter, but our family trees touch somewhere. Their mother, Rosalind, was a cousin—many times removed, of course—but we would spend summers together at our family plantation on Edisto. We were of an age, you see."

Jack and I sat down in the hard wooden chairs. "It looks like you've been busy," Jack said. "I know I can always rely on you to find the information I need."

"Glad to hear it," she said. "One would think that by this time I'd have been mentioned in the dedication of one of your books." She stared pointedly at Jack.

I stared at my husband. "I can't believe that you've never done that despite all the help Yvonne has given us. Really, Jack."

"Actually," he said, and I noticed a tic in his jaw, "I was planning on dedicating the book I was working on when I met Mellie to Yvonne. And then the book wasn't published."

"Don't you worry about that, Jack. Despite being a dyed-in-the-wool Episcopalian, I do believe in karma. Mark my words, Marc Longo will get what's coming to him eventually. Hopefully we'll all be lucky enough to witness it in full living color." She grinned, her perfect dentures gleaming.

She turned to the books spread out in front of us. "So, let's take a look at what I found. I was not fortunate enough to find the original blueprints for the Pinckney house on South Battery. However, I think I found something even better." She spun an old leather-bound volume around to face us. "The blueprints for the house that stood there before it was built."

Yvonne folded her arms primly in front of her as we examined the old sketch of a modest dwelling that had once occupied the lot where Jayne Smith's house now stood on South Battery. "As you can see, the property was once fronted with swamp that led out to the Ashley River. Starting in 1909, city leaders had the swamp filled in and the level of the land raised and created Murray Boulevard."

I kept silent, wondering what any of this had to do with anything.

"Let me guess," Jack said. "The man who built it was a sea captain."

Yvonne gave him an appreciative look. "You've been cheating on me and doing your own research."

"Guilty as charged. I thought I'd do some poking around just in case I might find something that could lead to my next book, and I came across the deed to the original plot of land, owned by Captain Stephen Andrews."

Yvonne looked at him expectantly.

"Gentleman Pirate," he added.

"Although it was never proven; nor was he hanged at what is now White Point Gardens with Blackbeard and Stede Bonnett, as he easily could have been. Despite guards watching his house, he managed to escape to Barbados, where he lived out his long life. And had many children with younger and younger wives, into his nineties." She set her mouth in grim disapproval.

I was getting impatient listening to the boring history of someone who'd died a long time ago and didn't even own the house I thought we were investigating. "And the point of all this would be . . ."

Both Yvonne and Jack sent me a blank look, similar to the ones Sophie gave me when I was suggesting a cheaper, more sensible alternative involving replacing anything old in my house.

"Well," Yvonne said patiently, "with Charleston Harbor leading right out to the Atlantic, having a house this near the water made illegal activities such as pirating and smuggling—and perhaps escaping to another country—a lot less complicated than if your house were farther inland."

I sat up. "Like a tunnel or something?"

"Exactly," Jack said. "And even when a house is leveled for whatever reason, and a new one is built over it, any tunnels and staircases leading to them might not have been destroyed."

"But what does that *mean*?" I persisted.

"Nothing yet," Jack said. "It's just a piece in a puzzle. It may mean absolutely nothing, but we won't know until we put all the pieces on the table."

He had the old spark in his eyes and it made me happy to see it, and grateful that he was the writer in the family and I was just the Realtor who saw dead people. Because I found it very difficult to get excited about houses that no longer existed, and even those that still did. Unless I was selling them.

Yvonne slid a manila folder toward us and opened it to reveal several photocopied papers. She picked up the top sheet and put it in front of us. "I did find this write-up from 1930 when the house was renovated by none other than Susan Pringle Frost, the mother of the preservation movement here in Charleston. It was featured in *Architecture* magazine and includes a floor plan you might find helpful."

Jack tapped his fingers on the tabletop while he studied the drawing. I pretended to look at it, too, but without my reading glasses—securely tucked into my nightstand—all I could see were fuzzy black lines.

"And this here?" he asked, pointing to a square drawing of more fuzzy black lines.

"That's the first floor, otherwise known as a basement and only used for storage of nonperishable items, since it was prone to flooding," Yvonne pointed out.

"Or for temporary storage of pirated items until they could be distributed elsewhere," Jack added. "And if there was access to these storage areas during Prohibition, I'm sure they could have been used for contraband alcohol."

"Without a doubt," Yvonne said with her genteel smile as if we were talking about our favorite type of tea. "But from the documentation here, all access points from the house were sealed during the restoration, and the area filled in to reinforce the home's foundation."

Jack sat back, a look of disappointment on his face. "Well, there goes one story idea. I was hoping to go treasure-hunting—with Jayne's permission, of course—in the bowels of the house. But it appears they don't exist anymore."

Yvonne slid the folder closer to him. "When one door closes, another one opens. Take this home—you never know what else you might find."

Glad to have the mind-numbing talk about the house over with, I turned to Yvonne. "I know we can dig up more information on the Pinckneys in the archives, but I was wondering what you knew about them, being family. My mother was a school friend of Button's, but they lost touch after she left Charleston in the early eighties and she just knows vague details. We're really trying to figure out why Jayne Smith, who never met Button, has inherited her entire estate. There has to be a reason other than Miss Pinckney was a philanthropist who liked helping animals and orphans."

Yvonne's eyes sparkled behind her glasses. "Because, as our Jack has told us time and again, there is no such thing as coincidence."

I smiled in agreement, but I wasn't sure if I liked her use of the word "our." Last time I'd checked, our marriage certificate listed only his name and mine. I gave myself a mental shake and wondered when I'd stop being so insecure about Jack. He'd picked *me*, hadn't he? Not that he'd really had a choice, seeing as I'd been expecting his babies. But he loved me. He told me that a dozen times a day. And not only was Yvonne old enough to be his grandmother, but I really liked her and I shouldn't be having thoughts about asking for a meeting in the ladies' room for a private chat about my man. I dug the heels of my hands into my eyes, realizing those were the lyrics to a song I was too old to know about, much less remember.

"You okay, Mellie?" Jack rubbed his hand on my back as every nerve ending in my body responded with a snap to attention.

"Yes, just tired." I gave Yvonne my biggest smile to show her I was truly sorry for my thoughts, making her regard me warily. "I was just hoping you could give us a little insider information about them. Maybe point Jack in a research direction we hadn't considered."

"I can certainly try," she said. "Although when Rosalind died, I'm afraid I lost touch with her children. I just knew that Sumter had moved to New York, leaving his ex-wife in the house with poor Button."

"Why poor Button?" I asked.

Yvonne was thoughtful. "I suppose because as the only girl, she was the one always left behind to be the caretaker. Rosalind, sadly, had an extended period of bad health and Button stayed at home to take care of her despite having aspirations of going to college. She wanted to be a veterinarian—she was always taking in strays, then enjoyed nursing them back to health. When Rosalind finally died, it was too late for Button to go back to school or meet a husband. All the men in her group were already married with families. And besides, she had Anna and Hasell to take care of. Sumter was traveling so much at the time for his work that it was really up to Button to make sure Anna and Hasell had what they needed."

"Anna?" Jack asked.

"Sumter's ex-wife. Poor thing. She doted on sweet Hasell, took such good care of her through her many illnesses. None of the doctors and specialists she saw was ever able to tell her what was making her little girl so sick, but Anna kept up a brave face and told anybody who would listen that whatever it was, she'd find a cure and make her better." Yvonne was silent for a moment, gathering her composure. "Sadly, that never happened. Sweet Hasell died when she was only eleven years old. She was such a lovely child, too. Funny, smart. And so kind. She loved all the homeless animals Button brought into the house. She even worried that her mother was wearing herself out taking care of her." Her eyes clouded for a moment. "That child wasn't even cold before Sumter divorced Anna and moved to New York. It's no wonder Anna couldn't cope with life on her own. So Button took care of her until Anna died in 1993."

Jack's eyes were dark with thought. "I'm assuming Anna must have been around my mother's age, but she was only about thirty-one when she died. Do you remember what happened?"

She looked stricken for a moment, and I had to remember that not only was she a true Charlestonian, which meant she'd been born with a natural reserve, but she was also from a time before the Kardashians and social media, which made nothing private. She delicately cleared her throat. "I'm not really sure. The immediate family closed ranks and there was never any discussion in public. The obituary only read that she'd died at home."

A small shiver swept its way down my spine, like a cold finger slowly tracing its way down each notch of bone. "At home? As in the house on South Battery?"

Yvonne nodded, and I closed my eyes for a moment, remembering the presence of more than one spirit, one tugging on me to stay and the other telling me to go away. And then . . . nothing. Just the knowledge that someone, some *thing* was there that I wasn't being allowed to see.

Jack sat up, his elbows on the table. "Did you go to the funeral?"

"No. I didn't even know when it was. It was over before I even knew that she'd died."

She paused, as if considering whether to tell us more.

Jack leaned forward and took her hands in his. "I'm sorry if we've brought up a sad memory."

Yvonne smiled appreciatively up at Jack. "That's very sweet of you, Jack. But really, what I think you've done is made me aware that something was amiss. That something went unmentioned because it wasn't seemly."

Jack held on to her hand without saying anything, and it seemed to be the encouragement she needed.

"There was one thing. . . ."

Their eyes met, and I found myself holding my breath.

"Anna wasn't buried at Magnolia Cemetery next to her husband and daughter. They buried her in her family's cemetery in Aiken. As Button was the only remaining close family relative, that would have been her decision."

"That's very interesting," Jack said.

"Yes, it is, isn't it?" Yvonne leaned closer. "And I trust you to use this information with the strictest discretion."

"You know I never kiss and tell, Yvonne."

She flushed as she slid her hands from his. "I'm sure I wouldn't know." He quickly stood and moved around the table to pull out her chair, leaving me to my own devices.

I picked up the folder. "Thank you, Yvonne, for your help. I'm not sure if any of this means anything that can help Jayne, but at the very least maybe it will get Jack started on his next book." I leaned over and kissed her cheek, smelling baby powder and Aqua Net and being reminded of my grandmother.

"You are very welcome, Melanie. You know I enjoy these puzzles Jack likes to throw my way. Keeps me young. Well, that and Zumba."

My eyes widened in surprise but I didn't comment. We said our good-byes, then left, Jack's hand protectively on the small of my back as we walked down the front steps, both of us deep in thought.

When we got down to the sidewalk, I looked up at Jack, his brow furrowed. "What's bothering you?"

"I'm not sure. It's either the reason Button decided that Anna Pinckney wasn't to be buried with her husband and child or the visual of Yvonne Craig doing Zumba." He smiled, and I could have sworn my heart skipped a beat. "I think I need to find out more. I'm going to head to the Charleston Museum now to visit the archives and see what I can dig up."

"Don't you need an appointment?"

He raised an eyebrow. "Not always."

I put my hand on his arm. "Just promise that you'll let me know anything you find before you tell Jayne. She told me that sometimes the answers you find can be something you wish you never knew. Like she's been down this road before and was disappointed. Like she's tried to find her parents time and again and can't stand to hit another dead end."

"And you don't want her to be disappointed because then you might lose a nanny?"

I shook my head. "No. I think it's because I like Jayne, and I think she's had a difficult life so far." *And because she reminds me a little bit of me.* "I don't want to be the cause of any more bumps for her."

"Deal," he said, bending down to kiss me lightly on the lips. He handed me the car keys. "I can walk. I'll see you at home." Something about the way he said that sent goose bumps all over my body.

"See you there," I said, turning toward the minivan, Yvonne's words twirling in my head. *"She died at home."* I needed to go back to Jayne's house, but not alone. If there was a presence in the house that wanted me to go away, there was only one person I knew who could help me overpower it. Or at least help me determine who or what it was, since my abilities seemed to have deserted me, and it was really starting to make me mad. I hit the speed dial on my phone and waited for my mother to pick up, remembering again Yvonne's words, and wondering why Anna had been buried far away from her husband and only child.

CHAPTER 12

The warmer weather had returned, waking up all the dormant gardens Charlestonians took such pride in. Although it was only the beginning of February, flowers were sprouting from window boxes and planters—both easily removed to the indoors for the unexpected frost that was bound to descend before the official start of spring. It was how those native to the city could distinguish who was "from off." The newly arrived residents started planting their annuals at the first waft of warm air, then were spotted weeping from their piazzas at the sight of browned and withered plants when the mercury plummeted below thirty the following week.

I walked the few short blocks to my mother's house on Legare Street, wearing the sneakers and yoga clothes she'd purchased for me. She'd said they were a gift to herself, as she'd decided to begin a walking regimen to stay fit and healthy. She had the stamina and figure of a twenty-year-old, so I had no idea why this obsession had suddenly taken hold of her, but she didn't want to walk alone and I was the most likely candidate for a partner. My father preferred gardening to walking, although I think he might have found power-walking to be too much of a threat to his masculinity—as if gardening weren't mostly a female-dominated hobby. But he seemed to enjoy his status as one of the few males in his gardening club.

That was why I had aqua blue sneakers on my feet (the ones I'd worn during pregnancy were too stretched out to be worn by anyone except perhaps a baby elephant) and was wearing yoga pants in public—something I had actually seen Sophie doing more than once. I wondered whether the end of the world might be near, seeing as how Sophie and I were now wearing similar outfits.

I paused outside the gates of the house I'd lived in for the first six years of my life with my grandmother. I always felt her presence, but it was stronger here. I wondered sometimes if it was the memories of her I felt, or if she still hung out here to make sure I didn't do anything stupid. She still called me on the phone from time to time, so it was probably the latter, but being in this house always made me happy.

My father had a flower box sitting on a wrought-iron garden table and was humming to himself as he placed lemon yellow petunias and gold gerbera daisies in the moist dirt. "Good morning, sweet pea," he said as I kissed his cheek. "I know winter isn't over, but I couldn't resist planting something while the weather's so nice."

"They're beautiful," I said, admiring the colors and placement. He had a real gift for gardening, which I was just beginning to appreciate. I knew what roses looked and smelled like, so that was a start.

"Here for your walk with your mother?"

"Yes," I said. "I thought she'd be outside waiting."

He pursed his lips. "She had an early appointment, but she should be wrapping things up by now."

"An appointment?"

He gave me a terse nod so that I'd know exactly what kind of "appointment" she had. Unlike me, my mother had no problem advertising her psychic abilities. My father preferred not to acknowledge it one way or the other. I guessed that was one thing I'd inherited from him.

I sighed. "Where are they?"

"In the downstairs drawing room." He saw my dubious expression and then said, "Don't worry—you won't be interrupting anything important. Besides, she's been here awhile already."

"Thanks, Dad," I said, wondering if I should be insulted he didn't take our abilities seriously. It had been an ongoing battle between him and my mother, and had been partially responsible for their divorce when I was a little girl. Despite being exposed to several apparitions and paranormal events, he was the Doubting Thomas of the psychic world. He was very good at seeing and understanding only what he wanted to, a confirmation that I was, indeed, his daughter.

I pushed open the front door, pausing at the contraption in front of me. It looked like one of those double jogging strollers that I saw young, fit, and perky mothers running behind down Charleston's neighborhood streets, their jaunty ponytails bouncing happily through holes in baseball caps. I wondered if the client my mother was meeting with had brought it, because I couldn't think of any other reason why it would be sitting in my parents' foyer.

"Mellie? Is that you?"

"Yes, Mother," I said as I made my way to the drawing room. I paused in the threshold for a moment, admiring the play of sunlight through the stained glass window. There was a secret message hidden inside, a mystery that Jack and I had solved, with my mother's help. She'd thought then that the two of us could go public with our abilities, that it was our duty to help others. I was still waiting to be convinced that it wouldn't destroy my career or my reputation.

"Come here," she said, beckoning me to a mahogany game table where it was rumored Lafayette had once played cards. She sat opposite a red-haired woman who appeared to be around my age, the dark circles under her eyes making her seem older. My mother's gloves had been removed and were folded neatly on the side of the table, leaving no doubt that she'd been doing a reading.

"Good morning," I said, leaning down to kiss her cheek, then nodded at her companion. "We're late for our walk, and I have an appointment to show a condo on East Bay at ten."

"Sit down, Mellie. We're just about done here."

I did as I was told, then looked at her with raised eyebrows.

"Veronica, this is my daughter, Melanie Trenholm. Melanie, this is Veronica Farrell. I believe you've met her daughter."

I stared at her with confusion, trying to place the name and the face. "I'm sorry . . ."

"My daughter is Lindsey. She's a friend of your stepdaughter, Nola, and they're in the same year at Ashley Hall."

"Oh, yes. Of course," I said, recalling the girl Nola had brought home. The girl with the Ouija board. There was something else about Lindsey that I had meant to remember but had forgotten. I wish I'd thought to weigh my brain before and after childbirth so I'd have proof that one loses a substantial amount of brain matter with each child.

A small smile lifted her lips and brought a lightness to her pale face. "And I know you from USC. We were in an art history class and worked on a project together."

That was it. I wanted to smack myself on the forehead. "Oh, yes. Lindsey mentioned that to me. I'm afraid that I don't remember much about my college years. I think I've deliberately tried to repress those memories so I won't remember how lonely and socially awkward I was."

She smiled fully now and I saw the resemblance she had to her daughter, despite their different coloring, their delicate, almost fragile bones, their high cheekbones and straight eyebrows. "Patrician" is the word I would have used. I did remember her now, albeit vaguely, and remembered why I'd probably dismissed her from my thoughts as soon as we received our grade on our project. She'd been one of those girls inordinately close with her family. Her mother or sister always called when we were working together, and instead of letting the phone ring she'd answer it, then spend precious work time recounting whatever it had been that had occupied their conversation. I'd found it tedious, although now I could probably admit that in my lonely, parentless state I'd been jealous.

"We got an A if I remember correctly," I said with a smile, as if that might make up for a semester of being dismissive and aloof.

"We did. And well-deserved. You were so committed to getting good grades and it really got me involved. I remember you were very organized, and that was a good influence for me. I think that semester was my highest GPA of my entire college career." Her smile faltered. "My sister visited me while we were working on it. She was staying in my dorm room, trying to decide between USC and the College of Charleston. You met her."

It seemed important to Veronica that I remember. I frowned, trying to sort through my memories like sifting flour and seeing what got stuck. But nothing did. "I'm sorry, I don't remember. Although I do recall that you were close—talking on the phone a lot. Are you still close?"

A shadow fell over her face and I could hear her swallow. I became aware of the scent of a perfume that seemed oddly familiar. The only thing I was sure of was that neither one of my companions was wearing it or I'd have noticed it earlier. I watched as a halo of light appeared and surrounded Veronica, the scent of the odd perfume even more pronounced as the light undulated behind her. My eyes moved to the gilded mirror above a sideboard across the room, revealing the reflection of a young woman in her late teens or early twenties, her hand on Veronica's shoulder, her black-eyed gaze staring directly back at me. I felt relief first—relief that I could still see spirits. And then surprise that whoever this was had been waiting for me.

"She died," Veronica said flatly, as if she was used to keeping the emotion out of her voice when speaking about her sister. "She was murdered her freshman year at the College of Charleston. They never found out who did it."

The light behind her brightened to a clear white, then vanished along with the scent of perfume.

"That's why Veronica came to see me this morning," my mother said gently. "Detective Riley gave her my name and phone number with my permission, hoping that I might be able to help."

I stood to leave. "Since you're obviously not done, I think I'll go walking by myself this morning."

My mother put her bare hand on my arm. "Stay, Mellie. I wouldn't normally ask you to get involved with one of my clients, but because you already have a connection with Veronica, and have met her sister, Adrienne, I think you can help."

I gave my mother a look that I hoped she interpreted as "wait until I get you alone" and resumed my seat. "I'm not sure how I can help. . . ." I got a whiff of the perfume again, recognizing it as the one I wore in college. Vanilla Musk by Coty. It was very popular in the late nineties when Adrienne would have been a freshman.

My mother turned back to Veronica. "You said you had something to show me, something that had belonged to your sister."

Veronica nodded once, then reached into the pocket of her skirt and pulled out a long gold chain with some sort of pendant dangling from it. I bent closer and saw that it had been broken in the middle, the clasp still closed. It was then that I remembered my conversation with Thomas when he'd asked me if I could help him with a cold case. Something about a broken chain found in the dead sister's trunk, discovered in the parents' attic and opened for the first time since the girl had been killed.

I held out my hand and watched as the gold links coiled into my palm like a snake, the broken pendant lying on top. One Greek letter sat at the apex, the second two letters dangling directly beneath lying horizontally, a manufactured jagged tear showing where a matching charm might attach. "I wasn't in a sorority, so I'm afraid this is Greek to me." I hadn't meant it as a joke, but my mother kicked me under the table anyway.

"It's the intersection of Adrienne's sorority, Omega Chi, and another Greek organization with the letter Omega. Could be a sorority or fraternity—without the rest of the charm, we can't be sure. I have no idea where the other half might be."

"Did her boyfriend's fraternity have an Omega in it?" I asked.

"No. She was dating a Kappa Sig, but he had an ironclad alibi and was never considered a suspect." Veronica cleared her throat. "This is newly discovered evidence. Sadly, it was all twenty years ago, so people have moved on, gotten married, forgotten about Adrienne. Even with this pendant pointing to something completely new, Detective Riley doesn't hold out any hope of solving the case. He's been attempting to find and interview sorority and fraternity members from organizations with Omegas in the names from 1996, but nobody remembers Adrienne."

I turned to my mother. "Thomas told me about this case, and I explained that I wasn't ready to do this."

I dropped the necklace onto the surface of the table with a solid and final *thunk*. The girl was still there. I couldn't see her in the mirror, but I felt her presence. Smelled her perfume. I shoved the necklace away from me, not wanting her to follow me home. "I'm sorry, Veronica. I truly am. I'd like to help you, I would. But I've got two babies at home, a career I'm trying to resurrect, a hole in my backyard, rotting windows, and a host of other issues I'm having to deal with right now. I'm afraid I just can't get involved—"

My mother reached out with her bare hand and grabbed the necklace, her elegant fingers folding around it as her head jerked back and her eyes closed. We were completely still for a long moment, and then her head began to shake back and forth as if to say *no*. And then, as if pulled from the ether, a man's voice came from my mother's throat, thrust from the depths along with the stench of mold.

"Don't!" the voice screamed. "You. Don't. Want. To. Know. The. Truth." Spit foamed on my mother's lips, flecks of dirt appearing on her chin.

Veronica stood so fast her chair toppled backward onto the floor with a bang.

I reached over and grabbed the chain from Ginette's hand, and a small fizz of air left her lungs as her head slumped to the table. I stood, breathing heavily as if I'd been the one communicating with whoever or *what*ever that had been. "You should go," I said to Veronica. "We can't help you."

"I'm sorry," she said, picking up her chair and sliding the chain and pendant into her pocket. "I'm so sorry."

I heard her footsteps heading toward the foyer and then the front door opening and closing as I bent to my mother to check her breathing. Her pulse was steady, but she felt clammy to the touch. I helped her stand, then led her to the couch to lie down. Her eyes remained closed as I sat next to her, listening to her breathe, her hand in mine.

"She needs us," she said finally.

"Her sister has been dead for twenty years and we can't bring her back. And if you do that again, it just might kill you."

We heard my father come in and I quickly helped my mother to a sitting position. He stuck his head in the room. "I thought you were going for your walk."

"I think Mother might be a little under the weather," I began.

"We were just leaving," she said with a smile as she pulled herself up from the couch.

"Really, Mother, I think you should stay home if you're not well."

"Not at all. I think a walk in this beautiful weather is just what I need right now."

She gave my father a slow kiss on the lips, making me look away, then headed toward the foyer, where she paused in front of the contraption I'd spotted earlier. "Sophie said you should have one of these—she uses one to run with Blue Skye and loves it. So I bought one for you as a sort of early birthday gift."

"I don't run," I said, eager to return to our previous conversation.

"I know, but it might be something you'll enjoy doing with the children. Especially during the nice spring weather before it gets too hot."

I frowned dubiously at the contraption on wheels. "I really don't think I need—"

She threw open the front door and stepped outside, and I followed. She breathed in deeply and I was grateful to see the color returning to her cheeks. "Nothing like fresh air to clear the mind."

"Mother," I started, but she had begun walking down Legare. She moved at a slower pace than usual, but she quickly found her strength and began pumping with her arms, making it hard for me to keep up. We walked in the middle of one-way streets to avoid twisting ankles on the uneven and ancient sidewalks, facing traffic so we'd know when to get out of the way.

"You said you needed my help with something," she said with no apparent effort to force out the words.

I was puffing beside her and had to run a little to catch up. "It's the weirdest thing, really. There's a presence in Jayne's house—probably two. Did you ever feel something when you visited Button?"

She shook her head. "No. Just the usual vague sense that we weren't alone, but no more than in any other old house in Charleston."

I frowned. "Well, the thing is, I can feel two strong presences, and both have tried to communicate with me, but every time I'm there, something blocks me from seeing anything."

"Blocks you?"

I nodded, glad for the extra moment to suck air into my lungs. "Like a blackout curtain. I've never had that happen before. I was thinking that maybe it was the pregnancy and childbirth, and that I'd lost my abilities along with my entire wardrobe and shoes."

She sent me a sidelong glance. "Mrs. Houlihan is still shrinking your clothes?"

I kept my chin pointed forward. "It's still under investigation. Anyway, despite that disaster in your drawing room, I found it almost reassuring that I could see Veronica's sister."

Ginette stopped. "You saw Adrienne?"

I nodded, and tried to catch my breath. "Yes. I felt her, and smelled her perfume. And then I saw her reflection in the mirror. She had her hand on Veronica's shoulder." I put my hands on my knees for a moment and looked up at my mother. "That means I can still see dead people, right?"

She nodded. "It would seem so. Have there been any other times when you couldn't see anything but felt the presence of spirits?"

I thought for a moment. "Yes—in Nola's room. Veronica's daughter, Lindsey, brought over a Ouija board and they were playing with it."

Her eyebrows shot up in horror.

"Don't worry—we told them it wasn't a game and not to play with it anymore. But something happened before I got there, and there was defi-nitely something in the room—something that might have come from the cistern in the backyard. I knew it was there, but couldn't see a thing."

"That is odd," she said. We resumed walking. "But you saw Adri-enne clearly, with nothing blocking you?"

I nodded. "It's not that I ever asked for this 'gift,' but I kind of miss it when it's not there." I felt my mother send me another sidelong glance but I ignored her. "Anyway, that's why I need your help. These two spirits seem to be pretty strong—one pushed her down the stairs and the other caught her."

"Did you explain to Jayne what had happened?"

"Of course not. I want her to trust me to handle the sale of her house when the time comes. Making her think I'm crazy by confiding in her that I see ghosts isn't a good way to foster confidence. And she seemed to just brush it off as her clumsiness in falling and her luck in not getting more seriously hurt. I mentioned that to Jack, and he thinks her years of trying to fit in with various foster families have sort of forced her to overlook anything out of the ordinary. Which is a good thing, since she's living with us."

Ginette was silent for a moment, thinking. "And you want me to go inside the house with you to see what I can discover since you can't see it?"

"Correct. I can't in good conscience sell a house with a violent ghost or encourage Jayne to live there without getting rid of it first."

We reached Gibbes Street and crossed it, walking toward South Bat-tery. "We're not far from the house. I'm not going to ask you to touch anything, but just give me a sense of what you might be feeling."

My mother's face was filled with concern. "Do we need to stop?"

"Why?" I puffed.

"Because your face is dark red as if you've just run a marathon in-stead of walked a few blocks, and you're panting like General Lee when I take him for walks in the heat of summer."

I frowned at her but was saved from saying anything when I realized that we were standing in front of Jayne's house. I hadn't planned on it, but my feet seemed to have brought us here without consulting me. A truck from Hard Rock Foundations was parked outside, and a Dumpster sat in the driveway partially filled with debris, with the nineteen sixties–era kitchen appliances sitting next to it as if huddling to discuss their escape. Perched on the lip of the Dumpster was the black cat, its tail swishing slowly back and forth while its one good eye stared directly back at us.

"How did that fat cat get up there?" Ginette asked.

"I have no idea. And I don't know who's feeding it or how it gets into the house, but every time I'm here, there it is. I haven't been able to get close enough to catch it to see if it has a collar, but if I do and I find out it belonged to Button, then I'll have to figure something out. Jayne's allergic to cats."

"Poor thing," my mother said softly. "Button was such an animal person. She once said that the more she got to know people, the more she liked her dogs and cats."

I thought of Marc and Rebecca, and their invitation to rub Jack's defeat in his face. "And sometimes I'd have to agree." I turned back to my mother. "While we're here, we might as well go in. You ready?"

She looked back with a soft smile on her face. "I couldn't do it today, not with what I just went through. I need at least a week to regain my psychic strength. Besides, I don't think I agreed to help you."

"What do you mean? We work well together—remember that 'together we are stronger' mantra you make me say again and again?"

"I do. That's why I asked for your help with Veronica. Because we *are* stronger together."

I focused on the cat, as if it might put the words in my mouth that I needed. "Mother, whatever spirit came through you this morning is not a nice one and I'd be happy if I never heard from it again. I'm only involved with this one because of a real estate client. I didn't go seeking it out."

I took a step toward the house, but she remained where she was, her eyes studying something in an upstairs window. I followed her gaze and saw the image of a young girl in a white nightgown, her long blond hair tucked behind her ears, staring back at us.

"Do you see her?" I asked quietly.

"No. But I sense her." She turned to me with troubled eyes. "But you're seeing her now?"

"Yes," I said with surprise. "I think I've seen glimpses of her nightgown, but this is the first apparition."

"It could be Button's niece," she said. "Hasell. She died at the hospital, but she spent most of her life inside this house. It would make sense that she'd return to it."

"But she's a child. Why would she be sticking around?" Our eyes met.

"Unfinished business. Just because she was a child when she passed doesn't mean that there weren't things left incomplete."

I looked back up, surprised to see the girl still in the window. "Her mother died in the house. Did you know that?"

Ginette shook her head. "No. I'd already left Charleston by then and wasn't in touch with anybody who would have told me."

"And she was buried in Aiken, and not at Magnolia, where Hasell and Hasell's father are buried."

"Sumter," she said, her voice very low. "I remember Sumter. I had such a schoolgirl's crush on him when Button and I were in high school."

"Then help me, Mother. Help me figure this out. Help me to help Hasell."

She faced me again. "That will depend, Mellie. Will you help me with Veronica? I think that would be fair, don't you?"

I looked back up at the window just as a dark shadow appeared behind the girl and an arm grabbed her around the shoulders, pulling her out of sight. I blinked, wondering if I'd imagined it just as I had when I was a little girl and thought I'd seen a caped figure in my closet. I sucked in my breath. "All right. You win. But I'm not going to be the one to tell Dad."

She didn't seem to be listening. I followed her gaze back to the window, where the girl had been but where a cat was now perched on the sill, watching us closely until something startled it from behind and it leaped back, disappearing from sight.

CHAPTER 13

I sat up in bed with General Lee at my feet, my phone in one hand, my laptop on one knee and my iPad on the other, trying to reconcile the various spreadsheets and calendars I used to plan my days. What would normally have been a ten-minute task was taking twice as long because of a certain husband intent on nuzzling my neck.

"Don't you need to work on any to-do lists or plans for tomorrow and the rest of the week?" I asked.

He blew warm air into my ear, making me shudder with anticipation. Without raising his head, he said, "I have an appointment at the Charleston Museum archives tomorrow at ten and then I thought I'd come home and have lunch with the twins and give Jayne a break before heading into my office to work a little bit on my new story idea."

I pulled back to look at him. "I thought you went to the archives this morning."

His tongue began a slow lapping around my ear and I had to practice my Lamaze breathing so that I wouldn't scream at the torture. "I did. But they have a new person in charge now and he's a guy. And apparently somebody who believes in calendars and rules and appointments. You'd probably like him."

"I probably would. Should we invite him to dinner sometime?"

He lifted his head and frowned at me. "No." His gaze traveled to my electronic gadgets, then back up to me. "It's time to turn these off, I think," he said as he reached for my iPhone.

I held it away from him. "Hang on—I'm almost done. You know how boneless I get after we, um, well, you know, so I have to do this now while my brain is still functioning." I squinted down at my laptop. "Either something's wrong here and it's not syncing properly or Jayne isn't being consistent with updating the spreadsheets for the twins."

In a move like a stealthy panther, Jack sprawled across me and reached into my nightstand drawer. "Mellie, didn't your grandmother ever tell you that squinting is going to give you wrinkles?" He dumped my reading glasses into my lap, then returned to his nuzzling. "Maybe this will make you get your work done faster so we can play."

I placed the glasses on my nose and mentally slapped down all my nerve endings and brain cells that were reaching for Jack. "But seriously, what if she's not doing the spreadsheets? And I don't think she's labeled their drawers yet, either."

With a heavy sigh, Jack straightened and plumped a pillow behind his head so he could sit up against the headboard. "Whether she did so or not, she's spent countless hours playing with them, taking them for walks, reading to them, singing to them, making them laugh. The sorts of things we do with them when we're here. I'd rather my children be happy than organized."

The word "blasphemy" came to my tongue, but I bit it back. Because somewhere, deep down, I realized that he might be right. "Still," I said, "I think she should discuss with us if she wants to change something."

"Well, actually . . ."

"Jack! Don't tell me you had a conversation with her about our children's care and didn't consult with me!"

"Well, last Saturday when Jayne had her day off, we happened to leave the house at the same time for our morning run and of course our conversation turned to the children and what she thought of her job so far."

"Jayne runs?"

He shrugged as if he hadn't really considered this before. "Yeah, I guess so. I mean, she had no problem keeping up with me and she looks pretty fit, so maybe she does do it regularly. Anyway, she mentioned how much fun she was having with the children, how bright and sweet and well tempered they are—guess they get that from me, huh?"

I smiled as if I were listening to what he was saying instead of obsessing over his words "she looks pretty fit." Jayne was the nanny. Presumably, she had a body, but Jack wasn't supposed to be noticing it.

"Anyway," he continued, "she was mentioning how much she enjoyed their outings and playtimes but how she was afraid it was cutting into her other chores such as keeping up with the spreadsheets and labeling. So I told her to keep doing what she was doing, because the children are apparently thriving and love her."

"Without consulting me first," I said frostily, immediately regretting my tone. My toes were still tingling from his caresses and I didn't want to disappoint them or the rest of my body if there would be no follow-up because I'd been unreasonable. It was all about control, something I'd had to fight for ever since I was a little girl and was currently having problems relinquishing now that I had more support in my life. It was just really hard giving it up completely.

He sat up straighter. "Now, Mellie, we love our children equally. And you're a great mother. But you and I have different styles of parenting. I'm wondering if maybe the reason why we haven't been able to hang on to any of the previous nannies was that they were stuck in a tug-of-war—"

An earsplitting scream shattered the silence outside our bedroom. Before I could even register what it was, Jack was already leaping from the bed and running toward the door. "Stay here," he said. General Lee looked up and gave a quick bark, then returned his head to the mattress. A quick yip from one of the puppies brought his head back up and then, with ears pulled back, he was racing out the door like a superhero.

"Don't worry," I muttered, sliding from the bed. "I'll be fine." I recognized the sound of someone crying—Jayne?—along with the sounds of General Lee and both puppies barking, Jack asking what was wrong, and Nola making soothing noises to the dogs to quiet them. There was no sound from the nursery—not that I expected any from JJ, and even Sarah, although probably suddenly awakened by the sound, was much too laid-back, like her father, to let things ruffle her. Not willing to remain in the room any longer, I made my way to the door and peered out.

Nola, wearing her father's old college football jersey, stood with a puppy under each arm, staring helplessly at the scene in front of her. Jayne was crouched over something on the hallway carpet runner, sobbing hysterically, and Jack—shirtless, I noticed—had his arm around her, trying to draw her to him.

A tingling on my scalp drew my eyes down the corridor, where a black shadow, human shaped but wider and taller than any human I'd seen, crept along the wall, growing larger as it made its way toward Jayne's open bedroom door.

I gasped, and Jayne jerked her head up in time to see the black mass reach her doorframe, the shadow thrown from the streetlights' shining through the downstairs windows, elongating it over the wallpaper like a vengeful bat.

And then I couldn't see it at all, although I could feel it. Could feel the cool air in the upstairs corridor, could smell the rotting scent of mold. I reached up and flipped the light switch, and all that was left was Jayne with tears streaking down her face and wearing only a thin night-gown, and my shirtless husband with his arms around her trying to offer words of comfort.

"What's wrong?" I asked. There was a lot wrong with this particular scene, but I was pretty sure I was the only one noticing that part of it.

"The night-light," Jayne sobbed. "Somebody pulled it out and smashed it."

I stepped closer and I immediately felt a sharp stab in my big toe. Lifting my leg, I saw what remained of the small, clear lightbulb that had been happily burning in the pretty plastic flower night-light when we went to bed. It was pulverized now, as if a large and heavy shoe had trampled on it, mashing it into the rug.

Stepping back and placing my weight on my heels, I said, "How did that happen?"

I felt Nola and Jack staring at me, but I ignored them, meeting Jayne's gaze instead.

She sniffed. "I might have done it accidentally. I wasn't sure if it was on, so I came out into the dark hallway to check on it. I might have panicked and then somehow knocked it out of the socket and stomped on it. I'm usually pretty controlled, even when I'm scared, but I think it's because this is still a new house to me. . . ." Her voice trailed off as she studied the pulverized bulb and night-light.

"We can get you a new one tomorrow," I said before turning toward the nursery. "I'm going to go check on the babies." And I did want to check on them. There had been something in the upstairs hallway, a dark, foreboding shadow that I was pretty sure had been the same presence I'd sensed the day the girls opened the Ouija board and Meghan Black felt something cold and disturbing in the cistern. But I also needed to step away to regain my composure and confidence that had somehow taken a severe beating at the sight of shirtless Jack with our nanny.

I flipped on the small lamp in the nursery, the one that threw images of pink and blue elephants along the wall, then went to check on the babies. I was confused at first before remembering the new placement of the cribs. It did work better, giving more space in the middle of the floor for toys and blocks. But I hated it right now, if only because it hadn't come from me.

I peered into JJ's crib, where he lay on his back with all four limbs splayed wide, his head to the side so his thumb could rest comfortably against the mattress while he sucked it. He smiled in his sleep and it made my heart squeeze with love for this happy little boy. Amelia had said that when a baby smiled in his sleep, it meant he was talking with the angels. I could certainly believe that, although I wouldn't have been surprised if the angels were joined by others for a big old family reunion.

I pulled the baby blanket over him, knowing he'd soon kick it off, then turned to Sarah's crib.

"Mamamamamama."

Sarah's eyes met mine as I leaned down to pick her up. There was nothing like a sleep-warmed baby in footie pajamas pressed against your chest, your nose buried in downlike hair that smelled of baby shampoo.

"Hello, sweet one," I cooed.

"Mamamamama," she babbled again, and I held her a little tighter. Jack and Jayne had both pointed out that M was an easy consonant for children to say, which was why an M word was usually the first word uttered and that babies as young as JJ and Sarah might not necessarily be referring to me when they said "Mama"—not that JJ had done so, but one assumed it would happen soon.

Still, I liked to think that Sarah knew who I was and was calling me by name. I held her close and started to sway, and even considered singing, but thought twice about it because I was afraid it might make her cry. I spun gently and felt her relax in my arms, until I became aware of the soft scent of roses permeating the room.

Sarah's head jerked back and she seemed to be staring at something behind my shoulder. She reached out her hand, then smiled. "Mama-mamama."

"Louisa?" I whispered to the empty corner, but whatever it was had gone, leaving behind only the lingering aroma of roses and a sense of matronly warmth and safety.

∽

I was wrestling with a produce bag at the Harris Teeter on East Bay the following Saturday when I heard my name being called. Mrs. Houlihan was at a family wedding, which was why I was doing the food shopping, and it was Jayne's day off, which was why I had both children in the buggy. So when I recognized the voice calling me, I cursed both the housekeeper and nanny for leaving me in this predicament. It was a lot harder to escape from a grocery store lugging two small children and a diaper bag than if I'd been by myself. I knew this because in my single days I'd done it more than once to avoid awkward situations.

"Hello, Rebecca," I said without warmth. She wore pink yoga tights and a matching jacket, and she carried her dog, Pucci—General Lee's baby mama—in a little pouch she wore on her chest. "I didn't know they allowed dogs in grocery stores," I said pointedly.

"Oh, they don't. But I can't bear to be separated from my baby, so

I had her certified as an emotional support animal so she can go with me everywhere."

"How lucky for the general population," I said.

She reached over the babies and gave them each a quick pat on the head as if they were animals. Animals that might bite. "Hello there, little children," she said in a way that made me hope she'd stick to dogs and never have actual children of her own.

"Say hello to Cousin Rebecca," I said, trying to be polite. JJ gurgled and reached for her blond hair while Sarah burped. I hadn't trained her to do that, but I was just as proud nonetheless.

"They're so adorable," Rebecca said. "They look just like Jack, don't they? Lucky for them."

I pretended it was meant as a compliment and just smiled. "Well, it was good seeing you, but I only have a small window before JJ wants to be fed. . . ."

"We haven't received your RSVP for the big party yet. I hope it didn't get lost in the mail."

The invitation remained on the kitchen counter as the subject of much conversation—mostly by Mrs. Houlihan, who needed her counter space. I'd told Jack I didn't want to go but would go if it was important to him. He'd have to be the one to pick up the phone and call, however. Which was why it had remained untouched on the counter.

I forced a smile. "Yes, well, we've got such full calendars. We're trying to juggle a few things to create an opening, but we'll let you know."

"Marc's publisher is going all out. There's going to be a live band playing twenties music, and a full bar and great food." She leaned toward me conspiratorially. "We're going to make a *big* announcement and we're really hoping that you and Jack will be there to share the good news with us. Because we're family."

JJ chose that moment to fill his diaper in a loud and malodorous way, making me more proud of him than if he'd graduated from Harvard Law as a baby. Rebecca stepped back, waving her hand in front of her face. Even Pucci gave a little bark of protest.

"Sorry," I said. "I really need to get home. . . ."

Holding her finger under her nose, Rebecca said, "I met your new nanny—Jayne, is it?"

I sighed, knowing she would have left already if she didn't have more on her agenda. "Yes. Jayne Smith. She's really wonderful. The children love her and she seems to be fitting in quite well."

"I'd say so. I saw her and Jack with the children at Waterfront Park last week. They appeared to be having lunch at the fountain and having a grand old time. They looked very cozy," she said, watching me closely.

I smiled my biggest smile. "Yes, like I said, we all love her. She's a great fit."

She didn't take her eyes from me. "I hear she's inherited the old Pinckney mansion on South Battery. I wonder how your mother feels about that."

"What do you mean?" I asked, moving closer to Sarah because JJ's diaper was making my eyes burn. "Because Button Pinckney and my mother were such good friends?"

"Well, that. And the fact that she was madly in love with Sumter Pinckney. My mother said that Ginette expected to marry him and was brokenhearted when he chose Anna Hasell instead."

I waved my hand at her dismissively. "It was more like a schoolgirl crush. Your mother must be remembering incorrectly." Before she could say anything else, I tossed the unopenable plastic produce bag on top of the heirloom tomatoes and began moving my buggy away. "I really need to go now. Please give your mother my best."

"Don't forget to RSVP," she called out after me, but I pretended I hadn't heard.

I left the buggy half-filled with groceries and carried the children out to the car, deciding it wasn't too cold to open the windows in the car for the short drive home. Several times I reached for the Bluetooth button on my steering wheel to call my mother and ask her about Sumter Pinckney, but each time I let my hand drop, not sure if I really wanted to know the answer.

CHAPTER 14

I left for work through the back door on the way to a few showings for a client, belatedly realizing that I'd gotten into the habit of using the front door because of the gaping hole in my backyard and the lingering feeling of unease I sensed whenever I was back there.

I was surprised to find Nola squatting down in front of the hole, wearing her school uniform, her backpack on the ground nearby. As if she could sense me and hear my unasked question, she called over her shoulder as I approached, "Mrs. Ravenel is running a little late, so I thought I'd check with Meghan to see if they've found anything interesting."

I stopped behind her, looking at the hole to see Meghan and another grad student I'd been introduced to earlier, Rachel Flooring, with small shovels gently scraping away dirt from old bricks. Apparently, Meghan didn't like to work in the cistern alone anymore, and always had at least one companion to dig alongside her. "You're here early," I said, noticing her ubiquitous pearls and cardigan sweater.

She smiled brightly up at me. "I know. But there's a sale at J.Crew today that I wanted to get to, so I figured if I started here early I'd have time to get there before lunch."

Of course, I refrained from saying. "Have you found anything new and interesting? I was kind of hoping you would be done by now and I could fill in this eyesore."

Both she and Rachel looked at me as if I'd just suggested throwing a bag of kittens in a well. When Meghan had regained her composure, she said, "We want to be thorough, which is why it's taking so long. But believe me, we're working as fast as we can. We just don't want to damage the bricks, because they have historic significance, and we'll want to analyze them, too."

"Look what they've found," Nola said as she pointed at something on the blanket, where the girls had been placing artifacts—their word, not mine.

I stared at the collection of what appeared to be small animal bones and pottery shards. "Looks like what the plumber pulled from our garbage disposal last week," I said with a grin. It quickly faded as I was met with the collective frowns of all three girls.

Nola straightened, then shouldered her backpack. "I'll do you the favor of not repeating what you just said to Sophie."

I raised my eyebrows.

"Sorry. I meant Dr. Wallen-Arasi. But she told me I could call her Sophie."

"I know, but we're in Charleston," I said, hoping that would explain everything.

We said our good-byes and I followed Nola to the front of the house, where Jayne was tucking a blanket around the children in the jogging stroller my father had brought over to our house. I'd yet to use it, but Jayne apparently enjoyed her morning jog with the children in tow. She wore tight running pants that accentuated her long legs and toned hips, and a close-fitting top that showed off arms that didn't seem to wobble as she bent over the stroller to make sure the children were protected from the cool morning breeze. I quickly looked away when I realized I was frowning. Wrinkles were the last thing I needed right now.

"I like our new nanny," Nola said. "She's really good with the babies and doesn't seem to mind your OCD impulses."

"Excuse me?"

She was already moving toward the front gate. "Oh, nothing." She stopped. "There is one thing. . . ."

"One thing?" I asked, wondering if she was talking about Jayne or about to apologize for the OCD comment.

She shrugged. "It's just that I'm not really blaming her or anything, but ever since Jayne's arrived I can't seem to write any music. I'm sure it's just bad timing, but it's odd, you know?"

"I'm sure it's just a phase. Talk to your dad—he goes through creative dry spells, too. He might be able to guide you through it. But I'm sure it has nothing to do with Jayne."

"I know. You're probably right. It's just so weird. Like a curtain has been pulled over that part of my brain I use for creativity."

I blinked, thinking it odd that she'd used those exact words to describe her artistic block, but was distracted from pondering it further by a familiar sedan pulling up in front of the house and parking at the curb. "It's Detective Riley. I wonder what he's doing here so early."

Nola jerked her chin in Jayne's direction. "I could guess. But she definitely needs some coaching. I overheard her yesterday on the phone talking with him, and I think she actually complimented him on his use of toothpaste and the fact that he had two legs. I mean, who says that stuff to anyone, much less an attractive member of the opposite sex?"

Realizing that her question was most likely rhetorical, I didn't bother to respond that I actually knew someone besides Jayne who was equally as awkward. But the person I had in mind was married now, so it didn't matter.

Alston's mother pulled up next to Thomas with a wave, and with a quick peck on my cheek, Nola ran to the van, waving to Jayne and Thomas as they pulled away.

"Just the two people I needed to see," Thomas said as he and I approached Jayne and the stroller. "I know it's early, but I hoped to catch you before you got into the workday."

He eyed Jayne appreciatively and I watched as her cheeks turned a bright red. "Good morning, Thomas," she said. "I have two children. Here. To run. I mean, they're not mine. But . . ." She closed her eyes as if mentally scolding her tongue. "Good morning," she said again, then forcibly shut her mouth. Nola was right. It *was* painful to witness.

It was clear that Thomas was struggling not to laugh. To hide it he squatted down in front of the jogging stroller so he could be eye level with the children, the way somebody used to small children would do. I knew Thomas was a favorite uncle to a gaggle of nieces and nephews, so it didn't surprise me. He reached over with his thumb and rubbed Sarah's cheek. "Looks like Mommy's already kissed you good-bye."

I was already digging in my purse for the pack of emergency tissues I always carried. "I thought I'd wiped it off."

"No need," he said. "I got it all with my thumb. You must not have been wearing your glasses." He'd said it lightly, but his words stung. I was already feeling old and dowdy next to Jayne, and I didn't need him to highlight that I was quickly headed toward bifocals and a cane.

I looked pointedly at my watch. "I really need to get to work."

He straightened. "Yes, sorry. A couple of things I thought both of you would be interested in. First, I went back to South Battery and really gave a good look around the perimeter to see whether there might be a hidden access point to the house where the cat could be getting inside, but no luck. I'll keep looking."

Jayne had begun to stretch, her forehead pressed against her knees, and Thomas's voice faltered for a moment. I wanted to point out that the only reason she could do that was that she hadn't given birth to two babies.

Refocusing, Thomas said, "And the phone number that had been assigned to the landline at the house is definitely disconnected. It must have been a crossed line coming from another phone, because that's the only thing we could think of that would make sense. Not that crossed lines really happen anymore, either, but that's as good a guess as we could make." His gaze rested briefly on mine. "Just let me know if it happens again. The good news is that it doesn't appear as if an intruder has been in the house. Still, you need an alarm system not just for your own safety, but also to protect all the valuables in the house. I have a contact in the business who can get you a good deal. If you like, I can set up an appointment for you. I'll even be there with you if you want me to be. Not because I don't trust him to give you a fair deal, but because I know you don't like being alone in that house."

"Yes," Jayne said, nodding vigorously. "The house. It has a cat."

I nudged her with my foot. I was beginning to worry that the children would never learn how to carry on regular conversations if this was what they heard all day. I made a mental note to make sure Jack, Nola, and I had lots of normal conversations in the twins' hearing so they would know how nonawkward people spoke.

"Thank you. That would be nice," she said before clamping her mouth shut and sending me a grateful grin.

Thomas continued. "I thought maybe we could use that time to also check the inventory you received from your lawyers just to make sure nothing is missing, and then possibly have dinner together."

He'd said it with a casual tone, but I could tell he was holding his breath, anticipating her answer.

She swallowed and I could almost hear her lining up the words so that they were organized before they came out. "Thank you. That would be nice."

She smiled and we both smiled back, all of us seemingly relieved that she'd managed at least one coherent sentence. JJ began to bounce up and down and vocalize his impatience at being kept still for too long. Jayne rubbed his head, then reciprocated with Sarah so she wouldn't feel left out.

"Do you run?" she asked Thomas before turning abruptly and pushing the stroller into the street, then jogging away from us with a wave.

Thomas raised an eyebrow. "I think she meant to ask me if I was a runner while at the same time explaining that she needed to run. An economy of words. Very impressive."

"I've had some very coherent conversations with her, so I think it's just you," I said.

"Great. Well, hopefully, after we've spent some time together, she'll relax a little." He stared after her for a moment. "I know we've never met before—I'm positive—but I can't help thinking I should know her. Maybe she looks like a celebrity, and that's why she seems familiar, you know?"

"Like one of those women on *The Biggest Loser*?"

He gave me an odd look. "I don't think so. It'll come to me—it always does. I'll let you know."

"Is there anything else? I really need to get to work." I didn't tell him that I had just enough extra minutes to stop by Ruth's Bakery and get my doughnuts and coffee with lots of cream. I happened to know that Ruth was taking a few days off to visit her sister in Charlotte, and a cousin would be in charge and so had planned my day accordingly.

"Yeah," he said, reaching into his pocket and pulling something out. "Veronica came to see me yesterday and gave me this to give to you." Holding out his hand, he let the broken chain with the Greek letter pendant dangle from his fingers. "She told me that your mother had called her to tell her that you would help solve her sister's murder. She understands that you have other things going on in your life right now and she said she could wait. She's waited twenty years already, so a little longer won't matter. But she wanted you to have this just in case you forgot."

Like I could. The memory of my mother speaking in the other-worldly voice was enough to scar me for life. I held out my hand and felt the cool metal fall into my palm. "Okay. I don't know when I'll be ready, but I'll let you know."

"Thank you. I know it's a big thing to ask. And just to clarify, it was Veronica who suggested she go speak with Ginette—she'd heard about her from a friend, and trusted her because she knew you and had read about you recently in the paper when that whole business of who really owned your house came out a year or so ago. I'd never go behind your back. I need you to trust me on that just in case you do decide to work with me on future cold cases."

"I know. I'll keep you posted," I said.

We said good-bye and I made my way to the converted carriage house we used as a garage. I sat in my car for a long moment, feeling the weight of the necklace and broken chain in my hand until on a whim I decided to wrap it around my rearview mirror. The memory of Adrienne's reflection and the grief in Veronica's voice wasn't something I could easily forget.

I watched as Jayne jogged by on the opposite side of the street, heading toward the river with the stroller, her ponytail swinging, her posterior not even shaking in its Lycra prison. She looked as though she belonged in this neighborhood with those children and that house. With a handsome husband who looked just like Jack.

I forced my thoughts away from that train wreck and turned the key in the ignition, something Nola had said niggling at my brain. I was sliding into my parking spot behind Henderson House Realty when I finally remembered what it was. She'd said something about feeling as if a curtain had fallen down inside her brain, blocking the place where her creativity existed. I knew what she'd meant. Because that was exactly what I'd felt the first time I stepped into the Pinckney mansion on South Battery Street.

⁓

My father was in the garden at my Tradd Street house when I came home later that afternoon. The twins were parked in their double stroller, watching him trim the remaining Louisa rosebushes by the fountain, their attention alternating between the snapping of his pruning shears and the splash of water from the peeing statue.

A small Jetta sedan with a Citadel bumper sticker was parked at the curb in front of the house. "Anybody I know?" I asked, indicating the car as I covered the children's faces with kisses and sat on the bench in front of them. They both bounced up and down, so I unbuckled them and put one of them on each knee, jostling them gently as I'd seen Jayne do.

"Oh, yes," my dad said, lowering his shears. "It's that Cooper Ravenel—Alston's older brother. Seems he's come to ask for Jack's permission to take Nola to a Citadel dance."

I raised my eyebrows. "I guess I'll be staying outside for a little bit, then, waiting for the thunder to clear. Did you hide Jack's hunting rifle?"

"Probably should have," he said, glancing back at the house and making me worry.

"Where's Jayne?" I asked.

"Apparently, she's a bit of a cook, and when Jack said he was in the mood for Italian, she asked Mrs. Houlihan if she could help her in the kitchen tonight. I don't know what's going on in there, but it smells wonderful and I don't think tofu is involved at all."

"How nice." There must have been something in my tone of voice, because he sent me a hard stare. Eager to change the subject, I said, "Rebecca told me something interesting the other day that I hoped you might clarify for me. She said that Mother was crazy about Sumter Pinckney, and that she thought they would get married."

He lifted a branch with the tip of the shears and tilted his head each way to analyze it. "Why don't you ask your mother?"

"Because I thought if she wanted me to know, she would have told me. It's just odd, though. I've been practically living and breathing the Pinckney house, and even brought her there, but she never mentioned anything about him other than that she remembered him, and that she had a schoolgirl crush on him. But Rebecca said it was much more than that."

With a sigh, my father put down the pruning shears and sat next to me on the bench. "I met your mother at a Citadel dance when we were both nineteen. She was someone else's date, but that didn't stop me— I've always been one of those people who believes that once you see something you want, you figure out how to get it. That's how it was when I saw Ginny. It was love at first sight for both of us. So even if she had a schoolgirl's crush on a friend's older brother, it was never more than that. She chose me, and I chose her, and we loved each other hard and we loved each other completely so that there wasn't any room for anybody else. And that's all there is to the story."

I didn't mention their divorce or subsequent reconciliation because that would complicate things. They were together now anyway, so none of it really mattered. But I felt reassured, somehow. That despite my rocky early years, their love for each other and for me was real and lasting, even with the bumps in the road we'd navigated to get where we were now. Maybe I just needed to hear it, regardless of what Rebecca might believe and feel the urge to tell me.

"Thanks, Dad. I don't know why I let Rebecca get under my skin like that. Like Mother wouldn't have mentioned it if it were true."

"Exactly." He put his hands on his knees and stood, catching sight of the broken gold necklace and pendant I'd knotted around my neck; I'd meant to bring it into the house instead of leaving it hanging on my car mirror.

"What's that?" he asked.

Before I could answer, Sarah reached for it, the pendant disappearing into her tiny fist. Her eyes popped wide-open and she screamed, her small fingers opening as if they'd been burned. She jerked back from me so fast that she would have fallen from my lap if my father hadn't been there to catch her.

Despite the fact that the roses hadn't begun to bloom yet, the heavy scent of them invaded this corner of the garden, acting as a pacifier for Sarah, who quickly quieted, her gaze focused on something near the fountain.

"She must be hungry," my dad said, stealing the words from my mouth.

"Must be," I said, standing with JJ and reaching for Sarah. I made my way across the garden in my heels, smelling roses and listening to the sound of the fountain, and wondering how far down the road of denial he and I were willing to travel before we ran into the truth.

CHAPTER 15

I took a deep breath as I stood outside Jack's study. I'd just come back from my morning walk with my mother and hadn't showered yet, but I knew I'd better get this over with before I changed my mind. This was all part of the new mature Melanie. It wasn't that I didn't think being open and honest was good for me. It was just that change was hard, like learning to choose vegetables instead of chocolate.

I gave a brief knock on the door, then opened it and stuck my head inside. Nola's grand piano dominated the middle of the room, but looking past it I could see Jack at his desk against the window, wearing the cardigan sweater with elbow patches the twins had given him for Christmas. I'd told him that we'd thought it made him look more writerly and that it—along with the sheepskin-lined moccasin slippers Nola had given him—would help get him over his creative slump. It worried me a little to see him wearing both now.

He didn't seem to notice my presence until I was beside him, as he was apparently absorbed in the folder of papers from Yvonne that were spread over the desktop along with a yellow lined pad on which I could see the scrawl of his writing punctuated with bullet points.

I saw that he must have been propping his head up with his hand, because he had an adorable cowlick in the middle of his forehead. He blinked for a moment as if trying to register who I was and where we were and what time of day it was. Having apparently figured it out, he smiled. "Did you have a good walk?"

I nodded. "Yes—the weather's perfect. Not too hot, and not too cold, and very little humidity. I'm going to try to enjoy it while I can." I pointed to my hair, still smooth despite that morning's exertions. "Look," I said. "No Brillo pad frizz."

"Good for you," he said. "Although I kind of like your bed-head look." He raised a suggestive eyebrow, then lifted his arms the way JJ did when he wanted to be held. "Come sit," he said.

"But I'm all sweaty," I protested.

"Maybe I like you that way. Or are you suggesting we go upstairs and shower?" Without waiting for my response, he pulled me into his lap. "Mmm," he said, burying his nose into my neck and winding his fingers through my hair. "Just what I needed right now."

I smiled and relaxed into his embrace.

"Speaking of frizz," he said, his voice mumbled as he pressed his lips against my neck, "Jayne's trying a new shampoo that she swears by to keep the frizz down when the humidity rises. You might want to ask her about it if you're really worried. Of course, I'd like you bald."

I stiffened, the thought of why Jack and Jayne would be having a conversation about her hair doing its best to block all my nerve endings. He pulled back, a look of concern on his face. "What's wrong?"

"It's nothing. But I did want to have a conversation about something that's been bothering me."

He surprised me by grinning. "Is this the new and improved Mellie you keep warning me about?"

I swatted him on the shoulder. "It's hard enough without you point-ing it out when I'm doing it."

He quickly schooled his features to look more serious. "Got it. So, what did you want to talk about?"

I took a deep breath. "Would you be upset if Sarah had inherited, um, certain abilities from my side of the family?"

He tilted his head, just like General Lee when I told him it wasn't time for a treat. "As in an ability to communicate with the dead?"

"Yes. I see her staring into corners and other places where there's nothing going on but she seems to think there is. Even when I can't see anything—which is happening a lot lately. And then yesterday, in the garden with my dad, she grabbed hold of a necklace that may be a clue to an old murder and it made her scream."

"Like what happens to your mother when she holds an object."

I squeezed my eyes closed and nodded.

He didn't say anything for a long moment and I began to worry. Eventually, I opened my eyes to find him smiling broadly.

"Why are you smiling?" I asked.

"Because you're funny."

"You think this is funny?" I asked, starting to get annoyed.

"Not at all. The subject of our daughter needs to be discussed with serious consideration. What's funny is that you think that something so fundamentally *you* would be a negative thing for our daughter to inherit. I love you, Mellie. I love everything about you—some things more than others. If our Sarah has inherited your psychic abilities, then good for her. We should embrace it and celebrate it. And when the time comes, we can teach her how to manage and deal with it. Maybe it might even help you not to be so uptight about your own skills. I sometimes think that if your father had been more accepting, you wouldn't be this way."

"Uptight? I'm not sure I understand—"

He put his lips on mine and I quickly forgot exactly what I'd been upset about. When he finally pulled away, leaving me limp and boneless and my chin feeling raw from his unshaven bristles, he smiled. "Now, doesn't that feel better?"

I wasn't sure if he was referring to the kiss or the conversation, but either way I was feeling better than when I'd entered the room. I wasn't yet able to formulate words, so I simply nodded.

"Good. I'm glad we're on the same page, and I'm glad you came in here to discuss it with me. Is there anything else you want to get out in the open?"

I had a brief image of Jayne in her running outfit, jogging behind my two children in the stroller, but quickly dismissed it. If I were trying to be a more mature person, I had to take it slowly. I'd save that discussion for another time.

"No," I said, then turned to look at the papers scattered on his desk. "Did you find anything new?"

"I'm not sure yet—I've been going through my notes all morning trying to see if anything jumps out at me, but nothing so far. There is one thing," he said, tapping his finger on the yellow notepad. "The little girl—Hasell. As the only child from that generation, she would have inherited the house when Button died instead of Jayne. Just for interest, I thought I'd look into Hasell's short life. And that's where it gets interesting."

"Why?" I asked, feeling an odd sense of foreboding. "Interesting" to Jack usually meant murder and mayhem. And dead people. That was why he was a writer. To me it only meant more dead people who needed me to solve their problems, since they were no longer here to do it themselves.

"I found her death certificate in the archives. She was almost twelve when she died but weighed only seventy pounds."

"Poor thing," I said. "She must have been really ill. Was it cancer?"

He shook his head. "No. And that's just it—the cause of death on the certificate was simply marked as 'unknown.'"

"Unknown? In this day and age they couldn't figure out what she died from?"

"It's strange, isn't it? I'm going to have to view her medical files."

I frowned. "But those aren't generally open to the public, are they? I mean, unless you're a member of the family."

"I might be able to work around them. I have ways."

I leaned against the desk. "Don't you need to know who her doctor was?"

He slid a photocopy of a newspaper obituary over to me. "That was easy. She died on January third, 1983, attended by Dr. Augustus Gray, family friend, and survived by her aunt Caroline—Button—her father, and her mother. No other relatives were listed."

"So, what next?" I asked.

"I track down Dr. Gray, or his descendants, and find out if he kept records of his own outside the hospital records. With all the new regulations, there's no way I could have access to them through the hospital. But back then, it's completely feasible that her doctor might have kept his own."

"And if he left behind a lonely widow . . ."

Jack grabbed me around my waist and placed me in his lap again. "Mellie, if there is, she's probably rather elderly now. Besides, there will never be another woman for me. You're it. Even if she were young and gorgeous, I wouldn't notice."

I rested my head on his shoulder. "I know, and I'm sorry. It's just that old habits . . ."

"Are hard to break," he finished. "Speaking of which, what on earth is this?" He reached over and pulled out his desk drawer, where ten night-lights of varying designs and colors were lined up inside, all facing the same way, like soldiers. On the other side of the drawer were pieces of paper that had once been strewn all over and had now been organized and stacked. And labeled.

"It's a bunch of night-lights I bought for Jayne in case she keeps breaking them. I'm out of room upstairs, but you had all this wasted space in here. . . ."

"It wasn't wasted, Mellie. I was using it to store my notes, and now I can't find anything."

"But, see, I made it easier. Did you not find that index card on top of the pile that showed you how it was all organized?"

He was smiling, but the look somehow didn't seem genuine. Like the one Sophie had given me when I offered to take her to my hairstylist for her birthday gift. "You are free to organize your own things, and even the children's until they can fight back. But you promised to leave my things alone."

"I know, but when I opened the drawer and saw the mess—"

His lips touched mine, and by the time his tongue had parted my lips, I'd already completely forgotten what we'd been talking about.

❧

My mother picked up what looked like a piece of thread connected to two round pieces of lace from one of the displays at Victoria's Secret on King Street. She held it up as if considering it until I reached over and snatched it out of her hand. "Mother!" I protested.

"Not for me, Mellie. For you. I thought if we were going to be buying you new bras, you should get new underwear, too. Men notice those things, you know."

"Mother," I said in a low voice, looking around to see if anybody had heard, Jayne in particular. I'd been a little embarrassed to run into her at a lingerie store, even though she'd quickly explained that she was looking for new jogging bras. It was her day off, so it would make sense that she'd be running errands. I just wished she'd been running them elsewhere.

"That's not underwear," I whispered loudly. "That's a medieval torture instrument. And it's not going anywhere near my body."

Jayne stuck her head around a rack of athletic bras and panties. "I have to agree with her there. I once heard a story about a woman having to have her thong underwear surgically removed. Apparently, she'd gone to an amusement park and there was some mishap on the log flume."

I made a mental note to have a discussion with Jayne later about what would and would not be appropriate topics of conversation while out on a date.

Ginette, surprisingly, was grinning. "How awful," she said. "But imagine the stories she could tell her grandchildren."

Both she and Jayne dissolved into adolescent giggles, leaving me to stare at them and wonder what I'd missed.

Turning away from them, I said, "I'm going to go look for a bra for Nola. She refuses to come try on anything, so I have to be her personal shopper. I'll just guess on her size, and hopefully it will look good with her dress for the Citadel dance."

"Thirty-two-B," Jayne and my mother said together before looking at each other and laughing again.

"Whatever," I muttered, walking away from them.

"Not yet," my mother said, calling me back. "None of your new clothes are fitting you properly because you're wearing your old bras. You need something with more lift—maybe even a push-up or two. Sweetheart, don't take this the wrong way, but your breasts are sagging."

Jayne had the decency not to look smug, but instead looked genuinely concerned. "It's normal after childbirth and breast-feeding. It comes with age, too." She and Ginette nodded in unison, like a couple of dashboard bobble-heads.

"Thank you, Jayne. I wasn't aware that my body had changed since giving birth to twins at the advanced age of forty."

Her face flushed. "I'm sorry, Melanie. I didn't mean—"

My mother put a gloved hand on her arm. "She knows. She's just sensitive about that subject. She'll be thinking differently once we get her into a few 'wow' bras."

"Oooh, I want one of those," came a voice from behind a hanging rack of silk nightgowns.

I cringed, recognizing Rebecca's voice a split second before she appeared in front of us. She wore Pucci in her little front carrier, and they both had matching pink bows in their hair. I saw my mother eye the dog and pouch.

"She's a certified emotional support dog," I explained, watching with amusement as Ginette rolled her eyes.

"Hello, everyone. What a nice surprise." Rebecca's hands were full of little hangers with various bras dangling from them. "I'm just having the devil of a time finding the right bra for my dress for the big launch party. There's going to be a lot of press, so I have to look just right." She eyed me carefully. "I'm hoping you've already started looking for a dress. I imagine it will be hard to find something now that you're, well, between sizes."

For the first time in my life, I found myself sucking in my stomach. "Actually, I haven't given it much thought. When is the party again? Jack called to RSVP and he might have neglected to put it on my calendar. I hope he thought to check to make sure I was free."

Rebecca's lips formed a straight line. "On the twenty-seventh. You RSVP'd, so you have to come."

"Do you think I could wear these together?" Jayne appeared from behind my mother, holding up a bright floral athletic top with striped running pants.

"Only if you're planning on running away with the circus," Rebecca said before noticing to whom she was speaking. "Oh, it's Jayne, isn't it? We met at the park—you were with Jack and the children having lunch, I believe. Although I've run into you since then, haven't I?" She pretended to think for a moment, a pink-painted nail tapping against her chin. "Oh, right—running around Colonial Lake. You were with Jack again and the twins were in that adorable jogging stroller. You looked like the perfect Charleston family. Actually, I've been meaning to ask you what type of jog bra you were wearing—you're pretty chesty, but I noticed it was holding you high and firm."

Jayne turned beet red as she opened her mouth to say something, but her lips kept on moving as if unable to find the correct words and failing.

"We're so happy to have Jayne as a member of our household," my mother said, her tone reminiscent of the opera diva she'd once been. "I hope you were there for some exercise, too." She let her gaze slowly roam up and down Rebecca. With a frosty smile, she said, "It's been lovely seeing you, Rebecca. Please give my best to your mother. Tell her that it's been too long and we must have lunch together soon."

"I'll do that. Actually, I might want to come, too. I've been following my friend and former colleague Suzy Dorf's column on the history of some of these wonderful houses we have here in Charleston—kind of obsessed, really, which makes sense, since the story of Melanie's house will be making my husband famous—so of course I'm fascinated with Jayne's story of how she acquired the Pinckney house. My mother swears that she thought you and Sumter Pinckney were a serious item, but Melanie says I was mistaken. Just imagine—that it could have been yours if that were true. It's just such a fun coincidence that Melanie's nanny now owns that same house!"

She smiled and I was happy to see a smudge of pink lipstick on her front teeth. None of us mentioned it.

"Anyway, Mama said she could be mistaken—that she was probably just thinking about when you moved up to New York to start singing and then Sumter moved there a couple of years later. She said my daddy—who knew Sumter from their days at Porter-Gaud—ran into you together when he was up there on business."

Only the flare of my mother's nostrils showed any indication of how annoyed she was. "Of course I saw Sumter when I was in New York. He was my best friend's older brother and he was kind enough to take me to dinner a few times so I wouldn't feel lonely. We might even have seen a play or two until my career took over my life. They were a lovely family. Now, if you will excuse me . . ." She turned her back on Rebecca and walked to the back of the store, where bins of underwear were sorted by color, none of which was white.

"Yes," I said. "We have a lot of shopping to do before the twins wake from their nap. . . ."

Jayne, having finally found her composure, looked at Rebecca. "You have lipstick on your teeth. But you might want to leave it there so people will have something else to look at besides that silly contraption on your chest. And whether you know it or not, you're giving a bad name to people who really need a support animal. Think about that the next time you strap your little marshmallow dog into a baby carrier."

Realizing there really wasn't anything else to say, I gave Rebecca a small smile and wave, then followed Jayne to the back of the store to join my mother. When I was sure we were out of Rebecca's sight, I gave Jayne a high five, and not just because she'd put Rebecca in her place, but also because I was gratified to know that she could, in fact, speak in coherent and well-thought-out sentences.

I was in a better mood as we continued the search for padded bras that also lifted and smoothed, but there was something Rebecca had said that kept pecking at my brain like a moth around a lightbulb. Something about coincidence, and how Jack was a firm believer that there was no such thing.

CHAPTER 16

I laced up my sneakers and slid on my sunglasses just in case anybody recognized me during my first attempt at running. Sophie had volunteered to come with me, but I'd declined, saying I was a big girl and could do it myself. The truth was that I was going to do something I'd seen on the Internet—interval training, a mixture between running and walking. Or what I liked to call survival. I'd skimmed over most of the article with its boring mentions of how many minutes should be spent doing each, deciding I would just stop when I got tired and walk until I felt like running again.

As a last thought, I grabbed General Lee's leash, rationalizing that if I gave out from pure exhaustion, I could blame him and stagger home. I thought about bringing Porgy and Bess instead because they would have more energy, but quickly dismissed that idea because walking them was an exercise in gymnastics and frustration, since they appeared to be allergic to walking in a straight line and also seemed hell-bent on either crippling or killing me by constantly crossing their leashes and running in opposite directions.

General Lee gave me a look of apprehension as I began moving my legs at a pace that was slightly faster than a walk, but much slower than what others would refer to as a run unless one was a turtle. He soon caught hold of the idea and kicked up his speed, his short furry legs practically prancing. He actually appeared to be smiling. I had no idea how old General Lee was, since I'd inherited him with the house, but he was way too old to be outpacing me as I struggled to keep up. A couple of coeds with College of Charleston shirts darted past us, ponytails flying, making me feel like another reptile entirely—one that was related to the turtle but now extinct.

By the time I reached South Battery, I was convinced I would drop dead of a heart attack, and stopped, planning to turn around and go back home, feeling I'd done enough exercising for the day. But when I started walking in the direction from which we'd just come, General Lee yanked suddenly on the leash, yapping frantically. I turned to see what he was barking at and spotted a large, fat cat perched on the garden wall of the house opposite. Without my glasses, it was hard to tell, but as I approached, General Lee now in full attack mode, I could see the flap of skin that covered the empty eye socket, and the one green eye staring at us intently, the tail teasing us with its long, leisurely sway.

Just as we reached the curb in front of it, it jumped to the ground and ran down the sidewalk away from us. General Lee yanked on his leash so hard that it slipped from my hand, and he began chasing the cat. It was still early enough that there wasn't a lot of traffic on the street, but my dog couldn't be trusted off-leash. If it were diagnosable in dogs, I was pretty sure he had ADD; his ability to be distracted by pretty much anything that moved or made a noise was enough proof for me.

"General Lee, stop!" I shouted to no effect. "Come," I tried, as if in his entire life he'd ever actually heard and listened to that word. "Treat!" I said instead, knowing that was the one word that might actually register. It didn't. I had a sharp pain in my side before I realized we were heading to the Pinckney mansion.

I watched the cat run up the outside steps and disappear through the open front door, General Lee close on its heels. I stopped at the foot of the driveway, bent over double, and dug my fingers into my side in a futile attempt to get the pain to stop.

"Melanie?"

I opened my eyes at the sound of Sophie's voice, but I lacked the energy and the oxygen required to straighten. I saw Birkenstocks and the bottom of a purple gauzy skirt with rainbow-colored elephant heads splattered like vomit all over the fabric. I let my gaze slide behind her to the Dumpster, where I spotted the backside of a man leaning over to lift something, his jeans slipping far past where they should be. I clenched my eyes shut again. "Is that Rich Kobylt?"

"He's helping me remove the cast-iron tubs from all the bathrooms. What are you doing here?"

I straightened slowly, the pain gradually lessening. "I was running after General Lee, who just ran inside the house chasing that black cat."

She looked confused. "I didn't see a cat, but I did see General Lee, who was running a lot faster than I've ever seen him move."

"Yes, well, the cat is apparently a lot faster than he is." I looked behind her to where I saw Rich and another man lifting a claw-foot tub up a ramp that led into the back of his pickup truck, another three tubs waiting next to it. "Why aren't those going into the Dumpster?"

Sophie looked as if I'd struck her. "Because these can be refinished. They're solid cast iron! Do you know how much those would cost today? Besides, you're the first one to admit that all the buyers these days are looking for old stuff that looks new—and with the modern bathrooms we're putting in this house, these will be perfect."

I looked at the tubs, with so much of their porcelain paint chipped off that they looked like brown-and-white cows. "I'll have to trust you on that one."

Rich noticed me and walked over, pulling up his pants as he approached. I wondered if I left an anonymous gift of a belt on his driver's seat, whether he'd wear it. "Good morning, Rich."

"Mornin', Miz Trenholm." He jerked his chin toward the house. "Your dog's gonna have some trouble catching that cat. I've tried a bunch of times, but he's a fast 'un. None of my team can, either. Course, they claim they didn't see him, but that's only because they don't want to be bothered. They'll be bothered all right when that cat dies somewhere in the walls and starts to stink. Ever smelled that before?"

I almost said that I had, and worse, too, but chose instead to focus on his bumper sticker, which had the numbers 0.0 in a white oval. "What does that mean?"

"It means I'm more sensible than my wife and value my knees more than she does. She's a marathon runner and has a sticker that says 26.2. So I had to get my own."

I had a vision of him running, his pants falling down to his ankles and making him trip, and I figured it was a good thing he wasn't a runner.

I also wanted to high-five him and ask where I could get a sticker, but I caught Sophie frowning. "I guess I should go find my dog," I said.

We left Rich to deal with the tubs and I followed Sophie inside. If possible, the interior was an even bigger mess than it had been when I was last inside. Crumbled plaster and strips of moldy wallpaper lay in piles along the walls, the furniture moved to the centers of the rooms and covered in tarps, the paintings removed from the walls.

Sophie's eyes became moist as she looked around. "Sadly, even with a nice restoration budget, we've had to get rid of more interior elements than we'd like." She brightened. "Happily, that article Yvonne found regarding the renovations in 1930 was extremely helpful. The architectural firm that was used and mentioned in the article still had the files that contained all the wallpaper and fabric patterns, as well as pen and pencil drawings of many of the ceiling medallions and other architectural elements in the house. It was like a gold mine, really. It's certainly going to take away a lot of the guesswork as well as save time. Although . . ."

"Although what?" I prompted.

"I feel sort of guilty making all these decisions. I mean, I bring stuff to Jayne for her approval and she just agrees to everything. She refuses to come see any of the work we're doing. She says she has dust allergies, and I get that, but I could give her a mask."

I shrugged. "She really doesn't care. I don't think she plans on living here, so her goal is to make it as appealing to buyers as possible, in as short a period of time as possible."

Sophie shook her head. "It's sad, really. Most people would give their left arm to be in her position. Myself included. If I didn't know about her background, I'd say some people have all the luck."

"Yeah, well, not everybody thinks inheriting an old home is a gift. Some might even view it as a punishment." Before she could argue, I said, "I've been meaning to ask you—what's going on with the cistern in my backyard?"

"Oh, yes. That. Well, there's been a bit of a delay."

I wanted to scare her with my narrowed-eye stare, but she busied herself picking through the piles of debris in front of us. "Yes, well, Meghan Black—my research assistant who's been doing much of the work while I've been focusing my efforts here—had a little accident with the XRF machine."

"The what?"

"It's an X-ray machine we use to analyze bricks to determine what rivers they came from, which allows us to figure out the origins of the bricks. Since cisterns were usually made from old bricks from various places, this could be fascinating."

"Fascinating." I repeated the word, but I made my inflection different from Sophie's, hoping she'd take the hint. She didn't.

"Sadly, Meghan dropped it on her foot and broke it. I hate to say it, but at least her foot broke the fall, so the machine is okay. But she's in no shape to crawl in and out of a cistern for a while. And my other grad students are too busy working on their theses or helping me here. We'll just have to wait until she's up and about for the excavation to continue." She said this last with her nose practically pressed against the wall, studying something I couldn't and didn't care to see.

"That's lovely. Hopefully it will all be done before the children graduate from high school. I'd hate for one of them to fall in."

She was relieved from saying anything by her phone ringing out "Imagine" by John Lennon. I couldn't hear the other person, but from the horrified look on her face and furtive glances in my direction, I knew two things: It was something that involved me, and it wasn't good news.

"I'll call you back," she said before hanging up the phone and looking at me with wide eyes.

"What's wrong?"

"I'm not sure. Remember my friend John Nolan—the antique toy expert who knows a lot about the Edison dolls?"

"Yes. He came and picked up the doll last week. Does he have good news?"

She clamped her lips shut and shook her head. "I'm afraid not. The doll appears to be missing."

"Missing? As in he misplaced it?"

"He's not sure. He's positive he brought it to his office and locked it in the safe he has there for valuable items like that. He remembers very clearly doing it. But it's gone."

"Maybe a coworker took it. Or he put it somewhere else and doesn't remember."

She shook her head again. "He told me that he noticed it missing yesterday and has spent the last twenty-four hours looking for it and asking people who might have seen it. Apparently, he's the only one who knows the combination to the safe, and it was still locked when he went to go check on the doll."

Our gazes met for a long moment, as if each of us was daring the other person to speak first.

A man's shout followed by a loud thump, as if something heavy had been dropped on the floor above us, jerked our heads toward the stairs. A flash of white flitted past my field of vision, disappearing around the corner by the landing.

"Did you see that?" I asked quietly.

"See what?"

I felt what I could only call relief. I had seen an apparition, and it hadn't been blocked—but neither had the dark, oppressive feeling that weighed down my shoulders now, pressing my feet into the floor and making them hard to move.

"Everything all right up there?" Sophie called.

When there was no answer, she headed up the stairs and I followed, not because I wanted to but because I didn't want to be left alone. We paused near the top of the stairs, trying to gauge the situation.

A workman wearing a white Hard Rock Foundations T-shirt stood in the hallway, his back pressed against the wall, a hammer lying in the middle of the floor. The color of his face matched his shirt. As if afraid to lift his hand from the wall, he pointed to the end of the hallway with his chin. "It wasn't there ten minutes ago when I went down to the kitchen to get my hammer. But I know the door was closed, because it was locked and I figured I'd have to jimmy it with my hammer."

I knew what I'd see even before I turned my head and caught sight of what had alarmed the workman. The Edison doll, its face blank and its eyes as wide and staring as before, stood inside the door on the bottom step that led to the attic, its head facing us with unblinking creepiness.

The high trills of a little girl's laughter echoed around the hallway, its origins unclear. The dark presence I'd felt downstairs was behind us now, passing through us toward the open door. We all shivered, but only I knew why. "I'll get the doll," I said, my voice cracked and dry.

General Lee barked and then came bounding down the attic stairs without the cat, and sat at my feet watching the progression of the cold mass of air moving toward the door and the steps. He stayed where he was, the little coward, when I moved forward. I strained to make out the shape of the dark stain of air that seemed to stretch and shrink in front of me. The stench was unbearable, like the smell of rotting meat, reminding me of my conversation with Rich Kobylt about the cat.

It surged ahead of me, up the attic stairs, hovering halfway up. Without taking my eyes off it, I took another step forward within grabbing distance of the doll. I reached out my hand, ready to snatch the hair and yank it toward me regardless of how valuable and rare it was. The doll didn't belong on those stairs, and I resented it thinking that it did. My fingers brushed only air, falling short of the doll's head, and before I could try again, the door slammed in front of me, narrowly missing my hand.

Sophie uttered a small expletive completely out of character for her, and I was sure the workman would have said even worse if he'd not already run downstairs, leaving his hammer behind and a promise that he would never come back.

Without taking my eyes off the door, I reached down and picked up General Lee, feeling his little body quivering in my arms. A loud meow came from the other side of the door, making the three of us jump.

A vigorous scratching began in earnest, causing General Lee to whimper and struggle in my arms. "We can't leave it in there," Sophie said.

"We can't?"

Sophie frowned at me. "No. It could damage the doll. And it would be inhumane," she added hastily. She was horribly allergic to animal hair and had never been a pet person—which was why my dogs liked to sit on her lap when she visited. "One of us has to open the door and let it out."

"Let me guess," I said. "You're volunteering the one of us who's had more experience with unexplained things like doors slamming with nobody there."

Her eyes widened innocently. "You said it, not me."

I unceremoniously dumped the dog in her arms, then faced the door again. "Is there anything up there?"

She sneezed, and I felt partially gratified. "It's the little girl's bedroom, I think—although why one would put a child in a hot attic is beyond me. I don't think it's been touched since she died. Well, except for water damage from the leaking roof. Didn't you show it to Jayne?"

I shook my head. "We assumed it was just the attic with the usual collection of attic junk."

"Jayne needs to come take a look, decide what to do with it. The girl's nightgown is still at the foot of the bed."

I was sure my look of horror matched her own. The sound of vigorous scratching was louder now, but that was not what propelled me forward. I felt the other presence, too, the one I associated with the flash of white that I'd seen several times on my visits to the house, a presence that was light and without malice. I could almost feel gentle hands moving me toward the door. It opened as I neared, revealing a bright ray of sunlight streaming down the stairs from the attic window, illuminating the doll and the cat sitting next to it. The other presence was mercifully gone.

With a loud screech, the cat leaped past me and then down the stairs, General Lee barking his annoyance at being held back.

"Did you get it?" Sophie asked.

I turned to her with the doll in my arms. "Yeah, I have it."

"No. I meant the cat. Did you find it or did it run back up the stairs?"

"It ran past you—didn't you see it?"

She shook her head. "I must have been too busy trying to restrain Cujo here when it slipped by. As long as it's not trapped in the attic."

"Yeah," I said. "What a relief."

She put down the dog and handed me the leash and I happily relinquished the doll. "I have no idea how this got here, but I suggest you plant it in your friend's office so that he thinks he's merely going insane instead of giving him proof."

We walked quietly down the stairs and were surprised to find Rich Kobylt standing in the middle of the foyer, his Clemson hat off as he scratched the back of his head.

"Anything wrong?" I asked, trying to pretend I hadn't seen one of his workers run from the house like a bat out of hell.

"Can I be honest with you?"

Both Sophie and I nodded.

With a lowered voice, he said, "I don't want to scare you or nothin', but I think this house might be haunted."

We stared back at him with carefully neutral expressions.

"But don't you worry. I'm a little sensitive to this stuff, and I'll let you know if I think there's any danger." His eyes drifted to the doll and I saw him shudder violently. "Good Lord, what is that?"

"Not to worry—we're taking it out of the house. One less thing to haunt it."

"Thanks, Miz Trenholm. Back to those tubs now. I'll keep you posted."

As soon as he was outside, a door slammed upstairs just as a whirring and popping began deep inside the doll's chest, and then subsided. We held our breaths for a long minute, waiting to see if it would speak. With a sigh of relief, Sophie carried it across the foyer and had almost reached the door when the high tinny voice that brought to mind raw fingernails scratching at the inside lid of a coffin screeched out at us. *Help. Me.*

CHAPTER 17

I sat on one of the gliders in the nursery with Sarah on my lap as I dried her chubby little toes and smelled her sweet fresh-from-the-bath baby scent. I needed to find a way to bottle that so I could whip it out and sniff it to calm me down when I was feeling stressed. Like now. I had yet to grow used to the furniture rearrangement, and now, adding to the chaos, there were upended bins of primary-colored plastic toys that didn't match the décor at all. The carefully stacked and labeled bins of blocks and educational toys that I'd spent hours creating and organizing were untouched in their spots on the shelves against the walls.

I had to turn my head away from the mismatched outfits Jayne had laid out on the changing tables. It was too much for me. Instead I closed my eyes and inhaled the sweet scent of my baby. Even JJ's cries of protest about being removed from the bathtub didn't faze me.

Jayne emerged from the children's bathroom with JJ swaddled in a baby towel and his head covered by a hood with panda bear ears. It was cute and made of organic and self-sustaining cotton—a gift from Sophie—but it didn't match the one I'd used for Sarah. I closed my eyes again and took a big sniff of Sarah's damp, dark hair.

I didn't need to be in the office until one o'clock, so I'd offered to help Jayne with the twins' bath time. I had it on the children's spread-sheet to be done at night before bedtime, but JJ had upended his bowl of oatmeal over his head at breakfast. It was just easier to keep them both on the same schedule whether Sarah also needed a bath or not.

I'd wanted an opportunity to speak with Jayne about going back to the Pinckney house. I was meeting Jack's mother, Amelia, there at ten o'clock to look at some of the decorative items and furnishings to de-termine value. Whether Jayne sold the house or not, she'd have to make a choice about what to do with everything inside it. Neither Sophie nor I was willing to make those decisions for her.

"Jayne," I started at the same time she said, "Melanie . . ."

"You first," I said, happy to wait a little longer.

She sat down on the other glider with JJ on her lap and began drying him gently with the towel. His eyes closed halfway as she rubbed his scalp and dried behind his ears, JJ looking remarkably like Jack when I massaged his shoulders after a long day of writing.

"It's not like I'm going to go or anything, but I just wanted to let you know so that if she asks why I'm not there, you'll know what to say."

I stared at her, blinking, trying to unravel her words to make sense of them, but couldn't. "Excuse me?"

She moved down to JJ's toes, making him arch his back and squeal with delight. Sarah frowned at him. "Sorry. When I'm nervous or un-comfortable, I tend to babble and not make sense."

"Yeah, I noticed."

She glanced up at me with a small flush in her cheeks. "You're talking about Detective Riley, aren't you? We're supposed to have din-ner on Friday night, but I'm thinking about canceling. I mean, I'd probably choke on my own tongue."

"He's a police detective," I pointed out. "I bet he knows the Heim-lich maneuver."

She grimaced. "Point taken. We were supposed to go to dinner after reviewing the inventory of the house after what we thought was the break-in, but I couldn't stand the thought of going back inside, so I gave it to Sophie to check and then canceled dinner. But then he called and asked again, so I'm stuck."

"And you wanted me to tell you what I think?"

"Oh, no," she said, standing to take JJ to his changing table and expertly fastening a disposable diaper onto him. "I mean, I'd love your opinion if you'd like to give it, but that's not what I was trying to say. It's about that party." She wrinkled her nose. "I got an invitation, too."

I opened my eyes wide, her words suddenly sinking in. "The book launch? They invited you?"

"I know—weird, right? But don't worry—I won't go. You need me to stay here with the children anyway."

I carried Sarah over to her changing table and pulled out a clean diaper, weighing my words. I had a good idea of why Rebecca had invited Jayne, but I would never say it out loud. "I do agree it's odd, but please don't decline unless you really don't want to go. I'm sure I could get Jack's parents or my parents or even Nola to babysit."

"The invitation was addressed to me and a guest. I could ask Detective Riley. Assuming I went."

I snapped the white onesie with more concentration than it required. "Really, Jayne, if you want to go, then go. And I'm sure Thomas would love to be your guest." I bit my lower lip hard enough to make it bleed. My cousin was a meddler, loving to create drama and to irritate me. Or maybe that was just her personality and she couldn't help it.

"Well, if you're sure. I don't have many chances to dress up, so it could be fun. But only if you can find a sitter. If you can't, just tell me and I'll stay home with the twins." She hoisted a fully dressed JJ on her hip and he smiled at her. She looked at me while I was fumbling on my third attempt to snap the one hundred or so buttons on the front of Sarah's one-piece outfit, just realizing now that I was nearing the end that I'd missed the third button and would need to start all over. Or leave it as it was and let people think she'd dressed herself.

"Why don't we trade?" Jayne suggested.

I nodded with resignation and reached out for JJ, then switched places with Jayne. "We'd better let the expert handle this, I guess."

"No," said Jayne. "I'm not the expert. I'm the nanny and you're the mother. I wouldn't call either one of us an expert, but that's not what we're going for, is it?"

"I guess not," I said with an unforced smile.

Jayne focused on refastening Sarah's outfit while I watched her. I knew from Thomas's background check that she was about ten years younger than I was, yet she seemed so much older. Or more mature, I thought. She was a great nanny, terrific with the children and dogs, Nola, and just about anybody we put in her path. Except maybe Thomas, but he didn't count. She was kind, and funny, and—remembering her set-down of Rebecca at the lingerie shop—very astute and not the kind of person to be walked over. I liked her, I supposed. *Really* liked her, although it was hard to admit even to myself. I wondered if my own insecurities would ever stop interfering with my relationships.

"It's your turn," she said, lifting a fully dressed Sarah. I glanced over at the little hairbrush and untouched bows on the dresser, torn between putting them in myself and waiting for Jayne to do it. Sarah hated them, but I kept telling Jack that it was just a matter of Sarah getting used to them. He'd said that the more I pushed, the more she'd resist, having inherited a certain amount of stubbornness from her mother. I hadn't spoken to him for the rest of the day, not because I thought he was completely off base, but because I was afraid he was right.

I sat down again, bouncing JJ on my knee and enjoying listening to him chortle. "I'm meeting Jack's mother, Amelia, at the Pinckney house later this morning. She owns an antiques store on King Street and knows quite a bit about old furniture and decorative accessories. I suggested she come look and see what's there, to give you a general idea of value. To maybe even help you decide what you might want to keep, or even auction separately. You'll get more that way than if you sell the contents with the house."

"You don't need me for that, do you?" Her eyes were round and wary and oddly familiar to me.

"No, I suppose not. Although it would make things go faster if you could tell her right off the bat what you don't want to keep. Like that hideous rose china set in the butler's pantry."

"How did you know I hated that?"

"Didn't you say so?" I shrugged. "Maybe it's just because I thought it was ugly that I couldn't imagine you not agreeing." I looked at her for a moment. "And there's another thing, too. Sophie thinks you should come look at the attic. Apparently, it was the bedroom for the little girl who died—Button's niece. According to Sophie, it's rather . . . extraordinary. She doesn't think she should be the one to determine what to do with it."

"Have you seen it?"

I shook my head, remembering the screaming doll and the slamming door. "I was in a rush last time I was there and didn't have the chance. But I thought today would be a good time for us to head over there. Jack's home and said he'd be happy to watch the children. I think he's procrastinating—I think that's what writers do with most of their time anyway, so it's not like we'll be taking him away from his work."

She smoothed Sarah's hair behind her ears, the bows apparently forgotten. I closed my eyes and sniffed JJ's head until the irritation passed.

"How long do you think it would take?" she asked.

"I wouldn't think more than an hour. I'll treat you to a pastry from Ruth's Bakery afterward as a reward."

She worried her lower lip between her teeth. "I do love her bacon and chocolate cupcakes."

I swallowed at the thought, embarrassed to find myself salivating. It had been too long since I'd had anything that resembled sugar. "I haven't tried those yet. I'll split one with you."

She frowned.

"Or we could each get our own," I added hastily.

An almost imperceptible shudder went through her. "Okay—you win. I can stand anything for an hour, right?"

I pretended to be busy nibbling on JJ's neck so I wouldn't have to answer, remembering my last visit to the house with Sophie when fifteen minutes had seemed more like an eternity.

ঌ৹

Amelia's Jaguar was parked in the driveway when we arrived. Standing at the bottom of the outside steps, I'd thought for a minute that I'd have to hold Jayne's hand and drag her with me. I hadn't seen the cat, nor did I feel any presence, sinister or otherwise. So far so good. Maybe whatever it had been was still too exhausted from terrifying us the last time. Jayne took a deep breath and followed me inside.

Scaffolding had been constructed in the downstairs rooms, where most of the water damage and crumbling moldings had been, and a few of Sophie's students and hired conservation experts were busy with the laborious job of removing most of the damaged cornices and medallions bit by bit. As Sophie had explained it, they had been removed so they could be restored and the missing pieces reconstructed while the roof and ceilings were being repaired. I refrained from mentioning to Sophie that a huge sander would do the job in a fraction of the time and that there wasn't really anything wrong with a smooth ceiling. I suppose I treasured our friendship too much.

"Melanie, is that you?" Amelia called from the dining room.

Jayne and I found her next to the large breakfront between the windows. There was even more of the hideous rose china in there, along with more crystal than I'd seen in one place outside Vieuxtemps on King Street. There were also, I was disappointed to see, even more of those salt-and-pepper sets, giving the intricately carved antique breakfront an almost clownish appearance. If it could express itself, I was sure it would have cried at the injustice.

"Hello, Amelia," I said, kissing each cheek as was her custom. Perfectly turned out in a Chanel suit and pearls, her blond hair in a tight French twist, she appeared tiny and reserved, but I knew her to be a lovely, warm person who adored her grandchildren and was known to crawl on her hands and knees just to make the babies laugh, or to lie on the floor to create a barrier for the children to clamber over.

"And this is Jayne Smith, our nanny."

They shook hands and I saw the look I'd grown accustomed to when introducing Jayne. "She has one of those faces," I explained. "So that you think you've met but you haven't."

But Amelia didn't laugh or step back. Instead she continued to hold on to Jayne's hand and stare into her face. "It's just the oddest thing. . . ." She stopped and then smiled, finally dropping Jayne's hand. "I'm sorry. I know we haven't met. But for a moment there, I could have sworn you were someone else. Wrong age entirely, which brought me to my senses. They say we all have a doppelgänger—perhaps not in the same generation." She laughed, but the sound seemed forced.

"So you're the marvelous nanny Jack has told us so much about. I thought that you might have a halo and wings the way he carries on."

Jayne blushed and I laughed, although I didn't find it funny at all. Not the image of Jayne as an angel, but the fact that Jack talked about her to other people. But she was our *nanny*. Of course he talked about her. Other people with nannies talked about them, too, didn't they? I didn't know anyone with a nanny, so I'd have to take that as a probably.

"We have no idea how we'd get on without her," I said.

Amelia smiled at Jayne, but there was something behind the look I couldn't translate. "I got here a little early and one of the nice workmen let me in. I hope you don't mind, but I took the liberty of walking around and jotting down some notes. You have some very valuable and sought-after furniture here. Several pieces by famed cabinetmaker Thomas Elf as well as a few from Chippendale. And you have quite a collection of Royal Albert bone china—I believe I counted place settings for at least seventy, with plenty of serving pieces."

"Are those the rose-patterned dishes?" Jayne asked.

"Yes. Is that something you would like to keep?" Amelia asked.

"No," Jayne and I answered in unison.

Amelia laughed and then wrote something on the notepad she carried with her. "Got it. It's not my taste, either, but there are a lot of people who love that pattern. I think I could get a very good price for the entire lot." She led us from the dining room, through the kitchen, and into the butler's pantry. "As you can see, there's even more china here. But there's also a very large collection of salt and pepper shakers." She arched her elegant eyebrows. "I happen to know that Button collected these, but only after she visited each state. There are fifty sets, all in pristine condition."

"Are they worth anything?" I asked.

Amelia gave me a rueful smile. "Only sentimental value, I'm afraid. Although there is this one set." She put down her notepad and pen, then gently pulled open one of the glass-paned doors. Reaching over a yellow triangular set meant to look like cheese with eyeballs and with the words "Wis" and "Consin" written on each one, she carefully lifted a pair from behind them.

They were shaped like fluffy white cotton balls, the words "Lake Jasper, Alabama" painted in black on each one. She held them in the flat of her hand. "It's been a while, but I'm pretty sure that this is where Button's family had their lake house back in the day."

"They're cute," Jayne said generously. "Is there something special about them?"

"I'm not sure. I don't usually carry this sort of thing in my shop, so I really have no idea. But I noticed on the bottom of these that someone had painted something." Flipping them over, she showed us where someone had added on each shaker *May 30, 1984*. "I'll ask Jack to research it, find out if the date has any significance. Perhaps they were souvenirs for a Woodstock type of event. That might up the value a little but not a lot, I wouldn't think."

"That would be great," Jayne said. "Thanks. And no, I really don't have any plans to hang on to this collection, as lovely as it is."

"You're very diplomatic," Amelia said, carefully closing the cabinet doors. "It's probably one of the reasons why you're such a good nanny." She led us back into the foyer. "I'll give you a complete list of what I find and approximate values. You don't have to do anything with it right now—take your time. But you really should get an alarm system. There are a lot of priceless things in this house."

I frowned at Jayne. "I thought you were working with Thomas to get one installed."

"Yes, I was. I mean, I am. He's very tall."

Amelia raised her eyebrows.

Jayne shook her head. "I mean, yes, he's tall, but that doesn't have anything to do with the alarm system." She swallowed and took a moment to regain her composure. "What I meant to say is that we're working on it. We just need to set up an appointment."

"We work with a wonderful company at the shop," Amelia said. "If you'd like, I could ask him to come look around here and give you an estimate. Would that work?"

Jayne nodded vigorously. "Yes, that would. Thank you. And I'll tell Detective Riley that he doesn't need to worry." She seemed almost relieved.

"Have you seen the attic?" I asked Amelia.

"Yes, although I had been up there before, with Button. When sweet Hasell was still alive."

"So you met her?" I asked.

She nodded. "Yes. A few times when I was visiting Button, she asked me to come say hello. That poor little girl was so lonely, and so desperate to see people. Her mother was afraid of germs, you see, and kept Hasell pretty isolated. I was only allowed up when Anna wasn't home."

"What about my mother?" I asked. "Did she ever come visit Hasell?" I found myself holding my breath, not wanting her to say yes. Because then I'd have to wonder why my mother hadn't mentioned it to me.

Amelia tilted her head. "No, I'm afraid not. She wanted to, but she and Anna were not friends. Anna probably knew about me and a few others being sneaked into the sickroom, but if she'd found out that Button had let Ginette up to see her daughter, there would have been hell to pay."

"Really? Is it because my mother was in love with Anna's husband, Sumter?"

"She told you that?" Amelia asked with a raised eyebrow.

"No. She just said that she had a schoolgirl crush on him when she was in high school. And that she and Sumter were in New York at the same time and that he was kind to her. But that would have been after Hasell's death and his divorce. My cousin Rebecca intimated that there was more, but I should know better than to believe her."

Amelia was thoughtful for a moment. "Yes, well, Anna was very possessive. I'm not even sure why she tolerated me. She seemed to believe that every woman was competition for the affection of her daughter and husband and therefore couldn't be trusted. I think she only tolerated her sister-in-law because Button was so kind and gentle, and a good friend to all who knew her."

Amelia began leading us up the stairs. As I put my foot on the bottom step, I felt a quiver in the air around me, the way I imagined a bear opening its eyes after a long hibernation. I shivered, not sure if it was because the temperature had dropped or because we were heading upstairs toward the attic.

Amelia paused on the landing and rubbed her hands over her arms. "I suppose the air-conditioning must be on up here, because it's definitely colder than downstairs."

"Probably," I said, remembering the window unit in Button's room and praying that was what it was. I turned to look at Jayne and saw her chilled breath rising from her opened mouth.

Amelia resumed climbing. "I never really blamed Anna for being the way she was. She was an only child, left behind with staff so her parents could travel the world without her. Her father owned an architecture and construction company, so they were very wealthy, and they made sure she had the best of everything, except themselves. She was always starving for affection. I think that's why she was never really one of our crowd. Button, Ginette, and I were good friends and would have welcomed her into our circle, but Anna didn't know how to share her affections."

I paused on the landing, feeling the warring between two separate and distinct entities, the push and pull that I had quickly begun to associate with being in this house. I slowly climbed each step, feeling like a woman being led to the scaffold, Jayne close behind me.

I half expected to see that doll again by the attic door, but I hadn't received a panicked phone call from Sophie, so I was hoping it was still locked up in the safe in her friend's office. Behind a pile of bricks. And a Catholic priest with holy water.

A door shut behind us, and I jumped. "That's Button's room," I said. "It must be the air conditioner," I added hopefully, praying that my companions wouldn't point out that the door would have been blown open, not closed.

"Good," Amelia said. "Leave it closed and let's give the upstairs a few minutes to warm up." She headed toward the attic door, seemingly unaware of the pulsating air that shimmered around us, or the putrid smell of rotting flesh.

She turned the doorknob and I held my breath in the split second after I realized that I didn't need to. The curtain had come down again inside my head with an almost audible *pop*. The air had settled, the smell gone, leaving only the fresh scent of sawdust and new plaster.

I drew in a deep breath as she pushed the door open. I glanced back at Jayne, who seemed completely unaware that something had just happened. I was relieved, not wanting to relive the scene of her being pushed down the stairs.

We began to climb another set of steps to the attic, well lit from the window at the top.

"Why would they put a sickly child up in the attic?" Jayne asked.

Amelia reached the top of the stairs and turned to look at us. "It was Hasell's choice. She always wanted to travel the world but couldn't. So she satisfied her longing by being able to see the water and the boats and ships passing by. She would make up stories of the great adventures she imagined the passengers were having, and a lot of other really creative stories of her own imaginary world. She actually wrote them down in a large notebook, always saying that one day she'd like to have them published. Not that she ever had the chance, of course. I actually looked for the notebook earlier, but it must have been removed at some point."

Jayne was humming something to herself as we both stepped into the attic, the sound immediately stopping as we took it all in. Despite the peaked ceiling and an exposed rafter bisecting the middle, it would not have been apparent that this room was an attic. There was water damage evident on one entire wall, but the rest of the room, although musty, was mostly unscathed.

The four walls had been painted a bright, azure blue, with vivid depictions of sea and sky and foreign lands. In one small section a replica of the house had been painted on a spit of land next to what was labeled the Ashley River, and there were other bits of land throughout the mural showing the Eiffel Tower and the British houses of Parliament and other known landmarks from around the world.

"This is amazing," Jayne said with awe in her voice. "Who painted this?"

"Her father—Sumter," Amelia said. "He was very artistic—although you'd never guess it from his choice of profession. And he loved his daughter. Button once told me that he was glad they had this huge house so that he would have room for the dozen or so children he planned to have."

I walked toward the bed, a hulking ghost beneath white sheets draped over four posts, one edge having slipped to reveal a delicate white eyelet nightgown draped at the foot of the bed, its color faded yellow with age. "Could Anna not have any more children after Hasell?"

Amelia turned on the ceiling fan, stirring up dust but moving the still, heavy air. "She didn't want to. Hasell needed all her attention, and Anna didn't think it would be fair to any siblings not to give them the attention they deserved. I don't think it ever occurred to her or to Sumter that Hasell might not live to adulthood."

Jayne gasped and I turned around in time to see the black cat running down the steps, then disappearing into the hallway.

"What's wrong?" Amelia asked.

"That cat," I said. "We have no idea how it gets inside the house. I hate to think there's a hole somewhere—who knows what else might be crawling inside?"

Amelia frowned. "I do hope you find out where it's gaining access. Maybe when the security people come to wire the house they'll find it."

I was only half listening. A reflection of sunlight had refocused my attention on a corner étagère that had been covered by a dust sheet that must have come loose and slipped to the floor. It had to have been recently, because there was very little dust on the shelves or on what appeared to be hundreds of snow globes in all sizes covering all the available surfaces.

"Oh, yes, Hasell's snow globe collection," Amelia said as she approached. "Whenever Sumter had to travel on business, he'd bring one back for Hasell. But a lot of these places he visited only because Hasell wanted to go there. I think that sometimes he went out of his way to make a stopover just to pick up a snow globe." She picked up one that had a giant sun wearing sunglasses floating in water tinted blue by the painted background, the word "MIAMI" spelled out in bright orange on the base. Amelia gave it a shake and we watched specks of sparkling sand erupt from the bottom like a sudden typhoon and rain on the sun, blocking its smile for a moment.

Amelia replaced the snow globe. "That's why I wanted you to see all this. Of course you can decide to donate it all to Goodwill or some other worthy organization. Or keep it here, or even store it somewhere. I just didn't think it was something that should be left up to somebody else. You didn't know Button, but she entrusted you with the care of this house and everything in it."

Jayne had gone very pale, her skin and lips appearing almost bloodless. "I need to be alone for a moment—do you mind? I'll meet you downstairs."

"You don't look well at all," Amelia said kindly, approaching with her hand outstretched.

Jayne shook her head rigorously. "No, I'm fine. You two go on. I'll be down in just a minute."

"Are you sure?" I asked, feeling the temperature drop again, and the familiar sensation of skin prickling on my scalp and neck.

"Yes," she said shortly. "Just go."

With a quick glance back at Jayne, Amelia and I climbed down both sets of stairs and stopped in the downstairs foyer. "You go on," I told Amelia. "I'll wait here and make sure she's all right."

She nodded, a delicate fold in the skin over her nose. "There's something about her. . . ." She paused.

"She reminds you of somebody?"

Amelia shook her head. "It's more than that. It's not even that I think I might have met her before. There's just something so . . . familiar." She smiled. "Never mind." She kissed me on both cheeks and then headed for the door. "Let me know that she's all right."

"I will." We said good-bye and I stood in the dining room watching the workers painstakingly chiseling away a small patch of rotten woodwork, something that would have tempted me to whip out an ax and make firewood.

A door slammed, and I looked up the stairs to find Jayne walking quickly down them, clutching tightly to the banister as if remembering the last time she'd descended them. When she reached the bottom, a loud meow brought our attention to the landing behind her, where the cat sat, licking its chops as if it had just eaten. I looked at Jayne, eager to talk with her, but she avoided my eyes.

"Stupid cat—I think it scratched me," she said, and walked past me, pulling up the neck of her T-shirt, but not before I saw the unmistakable red welts that could only have been caused by fingernails raking across the pale skin of her neck.

CHAPTER 18

I looked out the front window to see if anybody had arrived yet for the predance party, then held up a tray of canapés to Jack. He shook his head, taking a sip from his glass of Coke instead, making the ice cubes clink. I turned my back and quickly shoved a Brie and prosciutto wrap in my mouth, taking my time replacing the tray and rearranging the other appetizers on the sideboard. I glanced up, noticing that the grandfather clock had once again stopped at ten minutes past four, and the food stuck in my throat.

I took a sip of wine to make sure the food was all washed down before speaking. "Jack—didn't you have this clock fixed?"

He turned to it with a frown. "It wasn't broken. I just wound it and set the time and it seemed fine. Has it stopped again?"

"Yes. At the same time as the clock at the Pinckney house and in the kitchen. I'm thinking that can't be a coincidence."

He sent me a knowing look, then took another sip of his Coke, and I knew he was wishing it were Scotch.

"Really, Jack, it's just a dance. And we know Cooper is a very nice young man. Besides, they're just going as friends. His sister will be there, as well as their friend Lindsey, with a couple of Cooper's friends.

Yes, there's the age difference, but nobody's on a date here—it's just a group thing."

"He's nineteen years old, Mellie. I remember what being a nineteen-year-old boy is like. Very little brain matter and a lot of hormones." He drained his glass and walked over to the bar to pour another one.

"Cooper is not you, Jack. I'm not saying he doesn't have a roaring libido, but he's a Citadel cadet. Surely they teach them how to restrain certain urges. Besides, you know how Nola feels about alcohol. She's already told Cooper that if she sees anything that might resemble un-derage drinking, she's calling you. Same goes for any of what you refer to as 'hanky-panky.' That should put the fear of God in them. They're even renting a limo so they will all be together the entire time, and leave together, so no backseat shenanigans—to use your word, not mine."

"Should I wait on the front porch cleaning my rifle just to send the right message?"

I started to laugh but then realized he might actually be serious. "No, please don't. I don't know what the other parents might think."

"Daddy?" Nola appeared in the doorway looking beautiful and stunning and completely like her father's daughter. I'd helped her select her dress, a pretty purple satin swing dress that was very retro but not too mini, so it wouldn't make Jack's blood pressure hit alarmingly high levels. I'd helped her with her hair—a small bouffant ponytail worn over the full length of her thick, dark hair that was flipped out at the ends.

Jack smiled, his worry erased from his face as he looked at his older daughter. Of all the things I loved about Jack, I thought it was his love for his children that I treasured the most, and that made my heart squeeze. Even when he was acting like a caveman.

He embraced her carefully, not wanting to mess up her hair or makeup, and kissed her gently on the forehead. "You look lovely," he said. His smile slowly morphed into a thoughtful frown. "Did you put that Mace I gave you in your pocketbook?"

She rolled her eyes. "No, Dad. And nobody calls it a pocketbook anymore, either. Unless you're old."

The doorbell rang. Jack put down his drink and smoothed his tie. "I'll get it. And if I don't like the looks of any of those boys, I'm sending them home with a warning."

"Daddy!" Nola called out with alarm.

"He's only kidding," I said to reassure her, although I wasn't quite certain that was true.

The three young men with their uniforms and short-cropped hair looked exceptionally handsome. They were tall, and fit, and had perfect manners. The more I liked them, the more I saw Jack's brow lower.

We already knew Alston and her parents, Cecily and Cal Ravenel, and Cooper, and introductions were made for Lindsey's father, Michael Farrell. I knew Veronica, of course, and had met her again at my mother's house but hadn't spoken to her since Thomas gave me her sister's necklace. I introduced them to Jack, who was friendly and polite, but it was clear his attention was on his daughter and Cooper.

Mrs. Houlihan had stayed to help with the little party, and was busy passing around the trays of food and napkins while Jack tended the bar, making a point of giving the boys glasses of ice water even if they asked for a Coke or lemonade, as if caffeine and sugar might affect their judgment.

Nola had forbidden me from taking photos, but this would have been unnecessary anyway, judging by the number of cell phone photos and selfies that were being snapped. I'd ask Nola to curate hers and forward them on to me. When I'd realized that she didn't have any baby or early childhood photos, it had become my mission to document every moment of her life since she'd come to live with us, as if that could make up for all her early years. I was hoping to give her a scrapbook album as part of her high school graduation gift. It was my little secret, which was hard to keep when Jack and Nola both teased me for my excessive photo taking at every family and school event.

I found myself standing alone with Michael, Lindsey's father. He didn't strike me as being overly shy, but I saw that he kept to himself, smiling and nodding while in a group, then slowly extricating himself with an excuse for food or drink. He never rejoined the people he'd been speaking with, preferring instead to stand by himself, wearing what I would almost call a look of smug satisfaction. He seemed to have an excessive fascination with the furniture and artwork in the room. He'd paused by the grandfather clock when I joined him.

"These old clocks never work, do they?" he said dismissively.

"Actually, this clock has been keeping perfect time for almost two centuries. It's only recently that we've begun to have issues with it." I wanted to tell him that it also had an ingenious hidden compartment where Confederate diamonds had once been hidden, but I had the perverse need to deprive him of the knowledge.

He looked doubtful, as if I were lying to him. "I can hear it ticking, and the pendulum is moving, but the hands are stuck. Seems like a permanent disability to me."

"It's not," I said, smiling, wondering why this man seemed to rub me the wrong way.

As if sensing this, he smiled back. "Look, I'm sorry. Antiques are my wife's thing. I was raised in a small town by a hairdresser and a mechanic. We didn't live in a trailer home, but our house wasn't much bigger or sturdier. And we couldn't drive it anywhere." He laughed a little and I joined in to be polite.

"Anyway, let's just say the only antique we had was a sofa my mother got at a garage sale that looked awful and smelled even worse. So when I married into Veronica's family . . ." He shrugged as if that explained everything.

And in a way, it did. They lived in a big, beautiful Victorian mansion on Queen Street, and I imagined it had been in Veronica's family for a while. "So you don't like antiques?"

"Hate them. Who wants stuff that other people have touched and used before? I swear the house is more like a shrine to dead family members than a house for those of us still living."

Despite my earlier impression, I was starting to like this man. "Some people say that these old houses and the things that remain inside are our touchstones to the past. A way of keeping history alive."

He snorted. "More like living in the past so we have an excuse not to move forward. We've only lived there a year—we moved her parents to an assisted-living facility last Christmas and Veronica inherited it—and I'm just amazed at what people are willing to adjust to so they can live in a historic house. I mean, we freeze to death in the winter because to add a whole new HVAC system to the house would ruin its historical integrity. And to get it done 'the right way'"—he said these last three words using air quotes—"according to Veronica, which would mean getting an architect involved as well as somebody who knows something about historic preservation, would cost a fortune. I say just do it the cheapest way so that we're not wearing our winter coats inside three months out of the year, and to hell with the Board of Architectural Review."

In the not-so-distant past, I probably would have high-fived Michael. But I'd suddenly had a vision of what my house might look like now without Sophie's careful attention to its historical integrity, and it made me a little sad. Not as sad as when I imagined how healthy my bank account would look if I *didn't* listen to her, but sad nonetheless.

"True," I said. "But they do serve a purpose, even if they are annoying. The BAR makes sure that our historic district is preserved and not stripped of all its character. Then we'd just be another Atlanta."

"Is that so bad?" he asked, using his index finger to flick a tassel that hung from the casement key on the clock.

I would *not* tell Sophie that I'd actually uttered words from my own mouth that I'd heard her say time and time again to me. These were usually accepted by me with great derision followed by remarks of how if we became another Atlanta we wouldn't have to deal with the throngs of tourists. Or cruise ships. "I'm not sure," I hedged. "I think one could make an argument for both sides."

I smiled, eager to change the subject before I really dug myself into a hole. I was intrigued by something he'd said about his wife's home. "Speaking of your wife's family, I met your late sister-in-law once, so when you mentioned that your house had become a shrine, is that who you were referring to?"

His demeanor shifted to the way he'd been when I first spotted him at the clock, aloof and dismissive. "Partly. There are oil paintings and old photos of pretty much every family member who ever had their likeness captured. It's ridiculous; it makes those of us who married into the family feel like permanent outsiders. But Adrienne's room . . ."

He almost seemed angry and I was ready to change the subject again, but he didn't seem to want to. "They haven't changed a thing. Even her makeup is still on the dressing table along with her hairbrush that still has her hair in it. Can you imagine? Her clothes are hanging in her closet, and her rain boots are still in the mudroom. I mean, to lose a child is horrible, but it's like living with a dead person."

You have no idea. "I can imagine how difficult that might be for you. But surely you and Veronica will want to redecorate now that you're living in her family home."

Michael blew out a puff of air. "You'd think. And actually, that's what we'd started doing when we discovered Adrienne's college trunk in the attic. Ever since, Veronica refuses to let anything be changed in case we disturb any lingering evidence. Like there would be after twenty years! I'm getting close to fed up, I guess, which is sort of feeding my dislike of antiques." He shook his head. "Sorry—it's just a raw spot for me right now. Didn't mean to drag you into it." His smile was ingratiating again, and I found myself warming to him, wondering if we had more in common than he thought.

Veronica approached and tucked her hand into the crook of Michael's arm and I wondered if I'd imagined him stiffening at her touch. Of course, if there was a long-term argument regarding their current living situation simmering between them, I couldn't blame him.

"I hope you're not monopolizing our hostess," she said, squeezing his arm in either affection or warning, I wasn't sure.

"Not at all," I said. "We were just discussing the merits of history and old houses and their places in our lives. Not to mention the costs associated with renovating a historic house. Trust me, I could write a book, but it would have to be shelved with the horror novels." I'd said it as a joke, but neither one of them laughed.

"Melanie has agreed to help us with Adrienne's case."

Michael pulled away. "I thought you said you were consulting a psychic medium." He looked at me suspiciously.

I sent Veronica a look of warning. "Actually, she consulted with my mother. I happened to be there at the time."

"Yes, well, just for the record, I don't believe in that mumbo jumbo. If you don't mind, the less said about it in front of my daughter would be greatly appreciated."

"You are certainly not alone in that assessment," I said, thinking of my own father. "And I have no intention of dragging Lindsey into any sort of paranormal investigation my mother may be doing."

Veronica frowned at me but didn't say anything.

"Please tell me you don't believe in that stuff, too?" he asked, his voice wavering with a tinge of belligerence.

"Let's just say I prefer to keep an open mind."

He shook his head. "Even if by coincidence something did turn up because of what a psychic medium said, that stuff's not admissible in a court of law, right?"

"I'm not sure how it works in the legal system, but evidence is still evidence."

"But there *isn't* any," he said through gritted teeth, and I stepped back, wondering when the conversation had gotten so out of hand.

Veronica must have thought the same thing, because she pulled on his arm. "I'm sure Melanie has heard more than enough of our issues, Michael. Let's allow her to mingle with her other guests."

I watched them walk away and saw Veronica shoot me a questioning glance over her shoulder.

I joined Jack in a group with Cooper and his parents. I was relieved that the conversation wasn't about blood-alcohol levels or the importance of safe sex—not that Jack would be a role model for either topic—but on the much safer subject of golf. Apparently, both Cecily and Cal were avid golfers, as were their children. When Cal suggested I make up a foursome on Sunday, I saw the horror in Jack's eyes. I had the coordination and athletic grace of a bear and had nearly permanently blinded and crippled Jack on our first—and only—visit to the driving range.

"I don't play," I said, hoping to end the conversation.

"Nola said that Jayne is a pretty good golfer," Cooper interjected. "She apparently used to work for a golf pro and she taught Jayne how to play. Her employer said she was a natural and that if Jayne devoted herself to golf, she could be giving the other pros a run for their money."

Cecily laughed and took a sip of her wine. "Well, now I'm intrigued. I'm not a bad golfer myself and would like to know how I measure up." She faced me. "I'm sure the nanny gets days off. You wouldn't mind her taking your spot, would you, Melanie?"

I thought my cheeks would crack from holding my frozen smile in place. "Wow, of course not—that sounds like so much fun! I'd be happy to watch the children so she could go golfing with my husband."

Jack sent me an odd look.

"I meant my husband and friends. I mean, what's wrong with that?" I was starting to sound like Jayne, so I took a sip from my own wineglass just so I couldn't speak anymore.

Cooper looked at his watch. "Excuse us, but I think it's time to head out."

The girls ran upstairs to refresh their makeup and giggle, then returned to gather their evening bags and wraps. I surreptitiously checked Nola's bag to make sure her father hadn't sneaked in a small can of Mace, and handed it to her.

We ushered the young adults out onto the piazza and forced them all to stand in a group so I could get one picture that wasn't a selfie. As they headed out to the street, where the limo waited, Nola hung back. Giving her a hug, I said, "You look beautiful. Have fun tonight."

"I will. Just please tell Dad to chill out. He kept giving those looks to Cooper all night. I'm afraid he won't even dance with me now. I mean, Dad should trust me. Especially because I have never given him a reason not to."

I glanced back at Jack, who stood on the piazza at the railing and was nursing another Coke on the rocks. He was doing a great impression of a vulture hovering over an unlucky roadkill victim that wasn't quite dead. "I will, and I know. Just please understand that you're his daughter, and he's being protective because he adores you. And I know Sarah appreciates you smoothing the way for her." I squeezed her again and gave her a light peck on the cheek.

She smiled, then sent another uncertain look behind her. "You don't think he'll be waiting on the porch when we get back, do you?"

"Of course not," I said, not completely sure how I'd keep him inside. Maybe I could slip Benadryl into his Coke and knock him out.

Cooper held out his arm to Nola and she took it, allowing him to escort her down the piazza steps into the garden. A cool breeze swept from around the fountain, gently moving her hair and dress, and bringing with it the scent of roses that were at least a month away from blooming.

"Why are you smiling?" Jack said as he put his arm around me.

I looked up at him. "Oh, I don't know. Just a feeling I have that we're being watched over."

Nola was already tucked into the limo with the other two girls and their dates, leaving Cooper by the back door to turn around and wave good-bye. I watched in horror as Jack made a V with his two fingers, pointed at his eyes with them, and then turned them toward Cooper.

I knocked his hand down and waved back at Cooper, whose smile had vanished. "Don't mind him," I called out. "Have fun!"

The limo pulled away and the parents left shortly afterward, leaving a tense Jack and me alone. "Nola asked me to help you chill out. We do have four empty hours to fill." I stood on my toes and kissed him.

"Hold that thought," he said, taking my hand and leading me to his study. "I've been dying to share this with you all day. After several postponements, I finally went into the family archives today at the Charleston Museum, and I think I might have found something interesting."

He flipped on the banker's lamp on the corner of his desk and began to riffle through sheets of photocopied papers strewn over its surface. I closed my eyes, wishing I had a baby to sniff to help with the rising blood pressure. "Apparently, Rosalind—Button's mother—left all her correspondence to the museum, including her son Sumter's. I don't know if there's anything significant in that collection, but I figured I'd go through it just in case, so I made copies. The donation was made after Anna's death, probably a posthumous request made by Rosalind so as not to offend the living. Anyway, I've just had a chance to thumb through it so far, but I did find this. I'm assuming Button cut this from the *Post and Courier* when Anna died, and put it with her brother's papers."

I squinted to read the small, typed print, amazed as I usually was how newspapers could condense stories of giant proportions into a small square of text. I read it twice, just to make sure I was reading it correctly. I met Jack's gaze. "Anna killed herself. How horrible."

"She hanged herself in her daughter's attic bedroom," Jack added.

My eyes widened as I remembered the horrible presence in the house, the push and pull of two warring entities, and I couldn't help wondering if I'd just discovered the identity of at least one of them.

"She must have been so distraught over Hasell's death," I said. "But if she's the very unhappy ghost we've sensed in the house, we need to find out why, and why she's still here." I frowned. "Unfortunately, when only a dead person knows the answer, there's only one way to find out what that is."

CHAPTER 19

I huffed next to Sophie as we walked along one of the paths at Cannon Park, its asphalt edge bordered by an outrageously colorful flower bed full of plantings my dad would lust over but I couldn't name. I pushed the jogging stroller with the twins, and Sophie carried Blue Skye in a carrier not unlike the one Rebecca used for her dog, Pucci.

Cannon Park was near Ashley Hall on Rutledge, so I'd suggested meeting Sophie after carpool drop-off to catch up. I missed seeing her as often as I had when we were both single and before children and spouses had taken up most of our lives. Not that I wanted her to read my tarot cards or tell me again why old windows were far superior to what was being made today, but I missed her company. There was something to be said for a friend who told you the truth about everything, even when you didn't want to hear it. Even if that friend dressed like a *Sesame Street* character, and had suggested underwater birthing as a viable alternative to a normal hospital birth.

"Why are you walking so fast?" I panted, struggling to keep up.

"Why are you struggling? I thought you'd been walking with your mother, and you have a jogging stroller. I assumed that you could keep up." She began pumping her arms and walking even faster.

"No fair—I've got two and you've only got the one. And besides, Jayne uses the jogging stroller just about every day, so I pretty much consider it hers now."

She sent me an odd look but kept up her grueling pace without comment.

We had reached the tall, stately columns and front steps of the former museum building that had burned in 1981, leaving only the columns, all in a perfect semicircle, as a reminder of what had once stood there.

"Do you smell fire?" I asked, putting my hand over my nose because of the choking fumes.

"No," Sophie said matter-of-factly. "You say that every time we're here. You're just smelling a fire that's more than thirty years old."

I brightened. "But I *can* smell it! That's good to know. My psychic abilities seem to be fading in and out on me these days, for no apparent reason. There are times, like right now, when they're as strong as ever, and then other times when I'm completely blocked out."

"That is weird. I'd say it was hormones, but when you were pregnant it went away completely and didn't come and go."

"Maybe it's postpartum hormones."

Sophie finally slowed down so she could look at me. "Seriously? It's been almost a year. They should have settled down by now and your mind and body gone back to the way they were."

"That's not true," I said. "Some people take longer than others to bounce back." I took a quick bite of my slightly squished doughnut from Ruth's Bakery that I'd smuggled into the house. I'd bought a dozen when Ruth was visiting her sister for a couple of days and I'd taken advantage of her substitute. I'd kept them hidden in the back of the freezer, constantly checking to make sure Mrs. Houlihan hadn't rearranged anything and discovered my stash, smuggling one in the waistband of my yoga pants whenever I left the house to exercise. I didn't want to pass out because I didn't have the sustaining fuel I needed.

"Yes, but I'd guess that had more to do with bad habits than hormones."

I looked through the space between the columns, seeing the specter of a giant whale skeleton floating from an invisible ceiling. "Sophie, do you see . . . ?"

"No, I don't see the whale skeleton, either. It was moved to the new museum location before the fire. It's not here anymore."

"But I do see it," I said with a relieved smile. "And that's good. At least until I'm looking into a mirror and see somebody behind me. Then I might change my mind again."

Baby Skye began kicking her legs and grunting, her feet as usual clad in tiny Birkenstocks, bouncing up and down as we passed the playground. Sophie stopped and took the baby from her carrier so she could hold her and look at the baby face-to-face. "Use your hands, Blue Skye. Use your hands to tell Mommy what you want."

The baby stopped bouncing and stared solemnly into her mother's face. And then, as if she'd actually understood what Sophie had said, Blue Skye opened and closed her fists, thrusting them in the direction of the playground.

"You want to go on the swings?"

Blue Skye made the same motion with her hands.

"Do you mind if we stop?" Sophie asked. "She loves it when I push her on the swing."

"Um, sure," I said. "And what was that?"

"It's baby sign language. It's a way for babies to communicate without crying. I highly recommend it."

I wanted to ask her if it would just be easier to teach the child to actually speak, but I knew I'd get a response that would further confuse me. I parked the stroller, then reached into the outside pocket of the diaper bag I'd slung over the handles and pulled out a baggie filled with antibacterial baby wipes and began approaching the swings.

"What are those for?" Sophie asked.

"To rub down the swing before you put Skye in it. She might touch it."

"Exactly," she said, pulling Skye out of her pouch and walking past me before settling her into the little swing. "It's good for them to be exposed to germs. You know, children in the jungles of Africa are healthier than our kids here because they've been allowed to develop immunities. With our constant disinfecting and bleaching, we are really making ourselves and our children vulnerable."

I inwardly shuddered as I watched Skye clasp the sides of the swing and then immediately put her fingers into her mouth. "Please don't tell me you don't believe in vaccinations, either."

She put a hand on her hip. "That would be stupid. Of course I believe in vaccinations. Why on earth would you think that I wouldn't?"

I shrugged. "Well, you wear Birkenstocks. And you're a vegetarian."

She stared at me for a long moment. "Do you ever listen to yourself? Seriously, Melanie. Remind me again why we're friends."

I pretended to think. "Because you desperately need my fashion advice, and I like giving it."

She grinned. "Right. Well, I'm not the one wearing yoga pants with a hidden compartment for doughnuts." She shook her head as she gave the baby swing a gentle push.

I eventually got tired of watching her while I held a baby on each hip, and put the twins in two adjacent swings. When Sophie wasn't looking, I used the hem of my shirt to wipe the places on the swings where the babies might touch them and then tried not to hyperventilate each time they brought their fingers to their mouths.

We chatted about work, children, husbands, and the joys of yoga—Sophie did all the talking about the latter—until the conversation settled on the Pinckney house. "I've never been given such a carte blanche on a restoration," Sophie admitted. "And neither has the restoration company I'm working with. It's a great feeling, knowing I'm not going to be nickel-and-dimed, or second-guessed, or yelled at when something new and unexpected comes up."

"I've never yelled at you," I protested.

"No, but I can tell when you want to, and that's almost as bad. Anyway, it's been really easy working with Jayne on this project."

"Has she told you what she wants to do with the attic and its contents?" I asked, trying not to cringe as JJ leaned over and began mouthing the safety bar in front of him.

"No, not yet. And we really need to start working on the roof. A tarp only goes so far. I can't repair the ceilings on the second floor until we've got the roof issue addressed. I've been up to the attic with my restoration toys and have measured the moisture in the walls and I have to say it's not good. We'll probably have to rip everything back to the studs—and I hate doing that because you never know what you might find. I'm just hoping we won't discover black mold, because that's a whole different ball game. If you could talk to Jayne soon to get an answer, that would be great. I suppose we could just move everything to another room on the second story, but everything there was just so . . . personal. Every time I go up there, I'm left thinking that Button wanted Jayne to take care of that stuff. Otherwise why didn't she just get rid of it all after Hasell and Anna died?"

I stopped pushing, Sophie's words resonating with me. Why had Button left Hasell's room untouched all those years, almost as a shrine, and then left the disposal of it to a perfect stranger?

"Why are you letting him do that?" Sophie asked, watching JJ gnaw on the metal safety bar.

"You said we should let our children touch things so they're exposed to germs."

She reached over and gently lifted JJ's head. "Within reason. That's metal. Why are you letting your baby chew on metal?"

I whipped out a cloth diaper from the diaper bag—Jayne kept it well stocked according to my checklist I kept next to it in the mudroom. At least that was *one* thing she did according to my instructions. While Sophie was busy hoisting Skye up in the swing to keep her from slipping out one of the leg holes, I knotted the clean and bleached diaper around the safety bar just in case JJ felt like chewing on it again.

We resumed pushing, enjoying the quiet morning in the park and watching off-leash dogs running in circles as if they couldn't believe their luck at being set free. I'd brought General Lee, Porgy, and Bess here once, but the puppies had been insistent on running in opposite directions, and General Lee was torn among trying to supervise them, and barking them into submission, and chasing something—or someone—that only he could see. I'd been more exhausted than they had when we returned home, and I'd sworn to never do that again.

"So, how's Jayne working out as a nanny?" Sophie asked. She had opted to share parenting duties with her husband, Chad, an art history professor at the college, instead of hiring a nanny, and the two of them took turns wearing baby Skye while they taught classes. I had no idea what they planned to do once the baby was big enough to walk, but I was sure it would be as unappealing to me as wearing my baby to work.

"All in all, pretty great," I said, remembering the broken night-light, the rearranged nursery, and the incomplete spreadsheets. "The children really respond to her and seem to love her, so that's all good." I could see her preparing to ask a more pointed question, so—always one to avoid conflict—I said, "And Jack says she has the patience of Job dealing with the twins." He'd added "and you," but I refrained from mentioning that part to Sophie.

"It doesn't bother you that she's so attractive?" Sophie managed to squeeze in.

There. She'd said it. The way Sophie could read my mind was pretty close to psychic. It was why she was my best friend. Because she and I both knew that I could never avoid the ugly truth when she was around. But that didn't mean that I wasn't going to try.

"Is she?" I said. "I guess she's pretty, in an all-American athletic kind of way. I don't think blond is her natural hair color, so she's probably closer to average when she wears her hair naturally."

Sophie responded with raised eyebrows.

"Come on, Sophie. She's the nanny. So what if she's attractive?"

She sighed. "I think I should read your tarot cards again."

"Why?"

"Because I think there are certain . . . undertones . . . in your life that you should be aware of. I just get these weird vibes from Jayne. It doesn't mean anything, probably, and most likely it's just because she looks so darn familiar, but I can't place it. That's probably what's so unsettling to me, not that I think there's something going on."

I stopped pushing. "Going on?"

She waved her hand in the air. "That didn't come out right, either. What I meant is that Jayne's uncertain background and the way she looks so familiar just give me pause. I think I'll be happier than even she will be if and when Jack figures out why Button Pinckney left her the house. And I'm sure that what I saw was exactly what they said it was."

"Excuse me?"

"That didn't come out the right way. I swear I'm morphing into Rebecca here. What I meant to say is that a couple of days ago I dropped by to say hello to you and to ask Jayne a question about the new kitchen we're putting in—if she wanted to keep the servants' bells as a piece of artwork. She and Jack were, oh, there's really no better way to put this, but they had their arms around each other standing right there in the middle of the foyer—I let myself in because the doorbell wasn't working again. They were each holding a golf club, and there were plastic cups and golf balls all over the place. Jack said she was teaching him a trick shot."

"A trick?"

"Look, Melanie, I'm sure it's exactly as they said. Jack loves you, and would never do anything to compromise that. But she *is* attractive and she's living under your roof. Don't get me wrong—I like her, too. There's just something . . . uncanny about her." She shrugged. "I just wanted to let you know."

I felt ill all of a sudden. "I think I should go home. I need to take a shower before work, and it takes forever these days to find something in my closet that fits." I turned away, embarrassed to find myself so close to tears.

Sophie lifted out Blue Skye and tucked her into her front carrier. "I'm here anytime for a tarot reading. Just let me know."

"Yeah, thanks," I said, strapping the babies back into the stroller. "I'll call you."

After transferring the babies and stroller into the Volvo, I drove home slowly, my thoughts warring between anger and tears before eventually settling somewhere between rational thought and incredulity. I was a big girl now. The new, mature Melanie. I could discuss anything with Jack because I trusted him. We were married. Life partners. I wasn't the same insecure Melanie Middleton he'd first met, the woman who'd fake a foreign accent just so she could pretend to be somebody else on the other end of the phone.

With renewed confidence, I parked the car in the carriage house and hoisted each child in my arms, entering the house through the kitchen. I heard them laughing from somewhere inside the house, the sound of a golf ball being struck as loud as a firecracker in my ears. I listened to all three dogs barking and scampering after what sounded like a ball rolling across the hard floor, followed by a shout of laughter from Jack. Then there was a silence so loud and pregnant that I couldn't move, could barely breathe. A silence that seemed to go on and on. Even my heartbeats seemed leaden. The children watched me in absolute silence, as if they, too, wondered what was happening on the other side of the kitchen door.

I forgot all about the new Melanie, leaving her on her knees panting in the dust. Quietly, I stepped back through the kitchen and let myself out the door, closing it softly behind us.

CHAPTER 20

I glanced up at the sound of a car door slamming and saw my mother's car parked behind mine in the driveway at the Pinckney mansion on South Battery. It was a Sunday, so the workmen's trucks were gone, although the overflowing Dumpster still monopolized most of the driveway.

She wore a long and drapey red sweater over a black blouse and cigarette pants, with small, dainty kitten heels on her feet. Red leather gloves covered her hands up over her wrists. She looked beautiful as always, and way too young to be my mother. The only thing marring her features as she approached me was the small crease in her brow caused by her expression of concern when she regarded me.

She sat down next to me on the brick steps, unaware or uncaring of their dusty nature. "Are you all right, Mellie?"

I sniffed. "Just a spring cold," I said, adding a cough just in case the sniffing wasn't enough to convince her.

"You told me it was allergies on the phone," she said.

"Yeah, well, I think it might be both."

She frowned at me. "What's wrong, Mellie? Did you and Jack have a fight?"

Maybe it was the last twenty-four hours of misery and lack of sleep, but like a hairline crack in a dam during a flood, that nudge of compassion immediately destroyed all my composure, allowing every self-pitying fiber in my body to spill out onto my mother's shoulder.

She held me tightly and patted my back the way I did to JJ when I tried to tell him that he couldn't eat dirt. "Now, now, Mellie. It can't be as bad as all that. Why don't you tell me about it so we can figure this out together?"

"It's Jack," I sobbed. "And Jayne."

She drew back and for a moment I thought she was upset about the makeup and tears saturating her sweater. "What about Jack and Jayne?"

"When I came home on Friday after walking in the park with Sophie and the babies, he and Jayne were in the foyer." I stopped, hoping she would use her psychic abilities so I wouldn't have to finish the story.

"Okay. They were in the foyer. And then what happened?"

I sighed. Why did this psychic gift never work when I needed it to? "I heard them. I think they were practicing golf swings or something—"

"In the house?" she interrupted. "You'd better not let Sophie know. She'd have a fit and probably plaster them both up in a wall."

Fresh tears sprang to my eyes as I imagined Jack and Jayne stuck together for all eternity.

Ginette resumed patting my back. "I'm sorry, sweetheart. I was just trying to lighten the mood. So what happened next?"

"Well," I sniffed, "I heard the sound of a club hitting a ball and then the ball rolling. Jack laughed at something and then . . ."

"And then?" She leaned forward.

"Nothing. Not a sound. Not a word or another laugh. Nothing. Silence."

"And when you walked into the foyer, what was going on?"

I stared at my mother, stricken. "What do you mean? I didn't want to walk in on them!"

She stared back at me for a long moment, blinking. "You didn't go in to see what was going on?"

I shook my head. "I couldn't. I didn't want to see them . . ."

"See them what, Mellie?"

I shrugged, not wanting to put my fears into words. "You know."

Ginette sat back and took a deep breath. "Actually, I don't. Because you didn't go in to see for yourself and instead allowed your imagination to fill in the blanks."

"But what else could they be doing besides . . . besides . . . hanky-panky?" I spat out, using Jack's words that suddenly sounded worse than if I'd used the word "fornication."

"Oh, I don't know," she said, pretending to think. "Practicing their putting, maybe? Admiring a painting? Or maybe they'd walked into another room and you couldn't hear them. There are dozens of things they could have been doing that could never be called 'hanky-panky.'" She gave me a settling look. "So, what did Jack say when you asked him about it?"

I became suddenly very interested in studying my cuticles.

As if following my train of thought, she gently took hold of my chin with her thumb and index finger and forced me to look at her. "What did Jack say, Mellie? It's been almost two days. Surely you've talked to him by now."

I shook my head, dislodging a drip from the end of my nose. "I couldn't. I've been hiding out in the guest room pretending I have the flu and sneaking into the nursery when Jayne isn't around so I can see the children."

She put her fingers on her temples and I was encouraged, thinking she was channeling somebody to help me. Instead she just shook her head. "This is worse than I thought. Mellie, sweetheart, what happened to your resolution to be a better version of yourself? You're a wife and mother now. You need to be more open and honest in all your relationships—especially your marriage. You deserve it, and—more important—your children deserve it. Jack loves you, Mellie. I have never for a single moment doubted that, and I don't believe you do, either. Regardless of what was going on in that foyer, you owe it to yourself, your marriage, and your children to find out and deal with it."

She reached over and took both my hands in her gloved ones.

"Promise me that you'll deal with this tonight? That you'll talk with Jack and get this all sorted out?" Her lips twitched into a small smile. "I must say makeup sex is always the best sex."

I pulled away, thoroughly disgusted. "Ew, Mother. Please don't ever use the word 'sex' in my hearing—especially when I know you're referring to you and Dad. It's just . . . wrong."

"I have no idea why you think that way, Mellie. After all, how else do you think you got here?"

I shuddered again and she laughed. "All right. I'll try not to say it again in your hearing. But promise me you'll talk to Jack? Tonight. Don't let this fester any longer."

"But what if—"

She put her finger on my lips to silence me. "Just find out. I'm sure it's not anything near as dire as you think. You'll never know until you talk it out with Jack. I know you prefer the head-in-the-sand approach that you apply to most ghosts, but I don't think that's worked out very well for you, either, has it?"

"No, but . . ."

She gave me a look that made me stop what I was about to say.

I made no move to go inside, and not just because of the waves of energy beyond the door in the house behind us, the pulsing against the weather-beaten wood and peeling paint like little fists.

"Mother, can I ask you a question?"

"Of course. Anything. I hope you realize how desperate I am to make up for all those absent years when a girl needs her mother most."

I blinked at her, my eyes prickling with moisture. "Am I fat?"

"What?" She actually leaned away from me, as if I'd uttered a really bad expletive.

"Am I fat? I need you to be honest with me."

She took a deep breath and settled back into her place next to me. "No, Mellie. You're not fat by anyone's definition. You've definitely filled out more since your pregnancy, but it suits you. You might have been a little too thin before—although I have no idea how you managed that, since I've never seen a person eat that much junk food and not be the size of a house—but with the added pounds you have female curves in all the right places."

"So you're saying you can tell that I've gained weight?"

"Sweetheart, your body has just created two of the most precious children—you should honor it by adoring it and treating it well. Most important, you need to realize that dress size is only a number. A woman can be beautiful in any size, as long as she conducts herself with self-confidence. That alone is worth all the makeup and expensive clothes in the world."

I leaned into her. "Where were you when I was sixteen and really needed to hear this?"

"Yes, well, that's part of your problem, I'm afraid. But we'll work through this together, all right?"

I nodded, then sniffed. "Jayne has the body I used to have, doesn't she?"

"Yes, she does. Well, except for the bust. You never had a bust like that. But you're not Jayne. And Jack picked you. Never forget that."

"Thank you," I said. "If it means anything to you, I'd say you've more than made up for lost time. It seems a shame that all your wisdom is wasted on just one child."

A shadow passed over her face, and I looked up, surprised to find a bright blue and cloudless sky. She smiled, casting aside any hint of clouds or shadows. "Yes, well, that's what grandchildren are for. And because of you, I now have three whom I adore. So really I should be thanking *you* for making my old age not nearly as bleak as I once imagined it might be."

Without a tissue I resorted to wiping my nose with the back of my hand while my mother pretended not to notice. "So," I said as I stood, "you ready to fight some ghosts?"

My mother stood, too, delicately wiping the seat of her pants as we turned to look up at the house. "As ready as ever. I got a good night's sleep and I'm well hydrated—and I'm prepared for what's coming. I think that could have been the problem when we met with Veronica.

I was completely taken off guard. This won't be easy, and it will probably weaken me, but I'll be ready for it. And you'll be here to hold my hand so we can be stronger together."

"Deal," I said, unlocking the door and leading her into the foyer. "Why did you suggest we come in the middle of the day? I thought you said that the spirits were always more active at night."

"They are. There are fewer electrical disturbances at night, so they have more energy then. I thought it best that I first meet them when I'm not the one at a disadvantage."

"Good idea," I said as I closed the door behind me. The house was an even bigger mess than the last time I'd been there because, I was sure, of Jayne's reluctance to decide what she wanted to do with all the furniture. So it had to be moved and stacked in a different room as the renovations progressed. The only rooms Sophie had marked as out-of-bounds were the attic room and Button's room because of their personal nature. But, as she'd mentioned, the roof repair wasn't going to wait much longer and something would need to be done sooner rather than later. As long as she promised not to move any of it to my house for safekeeping until Jayne decided, I didn't really care what happened to it.

Ginette lifted the hair off the back of her neck, a sheen of perspiration already making her face dewy. "It's cool outside, but my body can't seem to regulate its temperature, so I'm either burning up or freezing all the time. I guess that comes with age."

"It's cooler upstairs with the window unit—assuming they remembered to keep Button's door open."

"I think it's about to get a lot colder." Her gaze met mine. "Do you feel it?" Her voice was barely louder than a hush.

I nodded. "I hear lots of voices, but I think that's just because we're both here and we're acting as a portal for lost spirits. But there are two strong presences—although there might be more. It's just that they're overshadowed by these other two."

My mother nodded and stared at the staircase just as a flash of white disappeared around the corner of the landing, followed by the very faint sound of running feet. Very slowly and deliberately, Ginette began to remove her gloves finger by finger. "I feel them. One is gentle; almost sweet, I think." She turned to me, her eyes wide. "She wants to show us something. She's the one who wants our help."

I nodded. "I think I just saw her. Running up the stairs."

"You can see now?"

"Yes," I said with some relief. "Like I said, it comes and goes. But nothing's blocking me now."

Her lips pressed together in a grim line. "Button loved this house. It's so sad to see it this way." She spun around, taking in the holes in the plaster and the warped wooden floor planks. "I guess it was more than she could handle as she got older." Her forehead creased. "I wonder why she didn't leave the lake house to Jayne instead of this one."

"The lake house? Amelia mentioned Button's family had one, but I assumed it was sold or something, because it wasn't part of the estate as far as I know."

She nodded, her head tilted back to see the gaping hole where a Baccarat chandelier had been removed and now sat in a corner covered with an oilcloth. "Well, the Pinckney family owned a house on a lake, not too far from Birmingham—that's where Jayne's from, right? Lake Jasper, I believe. In Alabama. I used to go up there for weeks at a time during the summers with Button and her family. The house had actually been designed and constructed by Anna's father's company. That's how the families met, I believe." She smiled to herself, her expression blurred with memories. "The Pinckneys must have let it go at some point. It's a shame, really. It wasn't as grand as this place, but it was cozy and beautiful, and right on the lake. We spent many happy times there. Jayne might have found it easier to be at home there instead of in a place like this."

"Unless it's as old as this place," I said, only half joking. "I'll ask Jayne—maybe her lawyers mentioned it. If not, we'll just have to assume that it was sold years ago."

I led the way upstairs, feeling someone watching us, someone waiting. For what, I wasn't sure. All I knew was that *it* knew we could sense it, could tell that we knew it was coiled and waiting to spring. Probably knew that I was petrified and on edge. And for a brief moment, I wondered why I'd thought that losing my psychic abilities would be such a bad thing.

We paused in the upstairs hallway, my mother looking down the hall toward a closed door. "Can I go see Button's room? I don't think I've been in there since we graduated from Ashley Hall."

I nodded, saddened to think Button had spent the last years of her life in this bedroom, and her whole life in this house, unable to live a life beyond it. She had stayed behind to take care of her mother, and then her sister-in-law, and then had died here, alone.

I pushed open the door, half expecting to see the doll sitting in the rocking chair, then let out a breath when I saw it was empty. The room had an almost tangible occupied air. Although it was vacant, it was almost as if someone had just made the bed, or brushed her hair, and then left, expecting to return shortly. And maybe she had.

"Oh, look at this," Ginette said. She stood by the dresser, where the tarnished silver frames held photos of loved ones who now stared out into the empty room.

I moved to stand next to her. "You probably know a lot of these people."

She nodded, then pointed to the one of her with Amelia and Button in their Ashley Hall uniforms, careful not to touch it. "I can't believe she kept this. I probably have the same photo somewhere—most likely in the bottom of a shoe box."

I looked at the photo of Button with the handsome young man beside her at her debut. "Is this Sumter?"

A sad, almost painful expression crossed her face. "Yes. He was so good-looking, wasn't he? And so funny, too. Not to mention charming. Jack reminds me a little of him, actually." She sighed. "I never expected this house to be empty, without Button, or Sumter, or at least their children. We can't always plan our lives, can we?"

I shook my head. "No, we can't." I pointed at the photo of the young girl. "And that's Hasell. The first time I saw it, I thought she looked a lot like Button. Now I'm not so sure. There's something about her chin. . . ."

My mother moved over to the nightstand, where a smaller frame sat, one I hadn't noticed before. It was a photo of Sumter and Button, although only Button was smiling into the camera. Sumter was also smiling, but his face was turned toward the unseen person at his side. The siblings were both still young and handsome, but it was clear that this photo had been taken several years after the other photos. It wasn't that the two of them were gray and wrinkled—they weren't—but it was more that they wore the years in between on their faces. I wondered if it had been taken after Hasell's death, and around the time of Sumter's divorce from Anna. That would account for the looks of stress around their eyes and mouths.

Sumter wore a dark suit and striped tie; Button had on a simple summer dress with a sweetheart neckline, a single strand of pearls at her neck, and a large, perfect pearl in each ear. There was another person on the other side of Sumter, a woman with a bare arm linked into the crook of his elbow. But she had been cut from the photograph, apparently to fit it into the frame, so only her arm and hand were visible in the picture.

I thought Ginette was going to pick it up, forgetting that she'd already removed her gloves. Instead she stood looking at it for a long moment before quietly saying, "Rest in peace, dear friend."

After a moment, I said, "You ready to go up to the attic? It's Hasell's bedroom."

She nodded. "Yes, I know. I remember Amelia telling me that, and how I thought it was a horrible place to put a child. Amelia found the bed for her, you know. She didn't own the shop back then, but she was working for another dealer and found a bed that could be broken apart and easily moved up the narrow attic stairs."

She followed me out of the room and I left the door open. "Amelia said that you never visited Hasell because Anna didn't like you and didn't want you in the house."

Her narrow shoulders lifted in a shrug. "I suppose that was one of the reasons. But I was also married by then, and had a little girl. Your father and I were having problems and I was too preoccupied to notice that Button might have needed my friendship regardless of whether or not Anna wanted me in her house. It was Button's house, too, but she allowed people to take advantage of her."

I paused outside the door to the attic, as much to steel myself as to find out more about Button's story. "Even after you retired and returned to Charleston and reconnected with Amelia and with me—and eventually Dad—you never called her?"

She looked down, her lashes shielding her eyes from me. "No. I didn't. I really regret that now. She'd been so kind to me. . . ." Looking up, she smiled. "Well, that's all in the past. Let's see about that ghost of yours."

As if conjured, an icy wind blew down the corridor toward us, making the door shake in its frame. My mother looked at me and I nodded to confirm that we weren't alone. "This is where Anna hanged herself, so be prepared. It could get rough."

"I'm expecting it," she said with a grim smile.

Another cold breeze whooshed down the hallway toward us, the door vibrating so hard it felt as if someone was on the other side yanking on the doorknob. I grabbed hold of it with one hand, and my mother took my other hand in her own. I twisted the brass knob, the door pulling from my grasp and slamming against the wall with a loud bang.

A screech pierced the quiet, and then the black cat was leaping from the bottom step and scampering between our feet to run down the hallway and disappear into Button's room. I turned to look back into the attic, willing my heart to stop its heavy thumping.

The first thing I became aware of was the loud buzzing of flies, hundreds of winged black bodies hurtling themselves through the air, the short splatting sound as they hit the walls and window somehow amplified. My mother tightened her hand around mine as we both looked up the attic steps. And screamed.

CHAPTER 21

My mouth was open, but the scream wasn't coming from me. Or my mother. The high-pitched ringing came from the doll that stood fully erect at the top of the steps. The window behind it cast it at an unnatural angle, creating a grotesquely swollen version of itself, and one much more terrifying.

My mother squeezed my hand so tightly that I thought she might have broken one of my fingers, but it would take a lot more than that to get me to relinquish her grasp. The screaming went on and on and on as if the disc inside the doll had become stuck. But that noise wasn't coming from a mechanical disc. It was coming from farther away, from a place where I had no desire to visit.

I tried to back out of the doorway, but my mother blocked me. "We can't leave now, Mellie. It's asking for help."

The shrieking stopped as soon as she'd spoken, the silence now punctuated by the sporadic splats of a dwindling number of flies. My eardrums took a moment to adjust, the piercing scream continuing to echo in them, and the words "help me" buried somewhere in that cacophony.

"I'm not going up there," I said, meaning it.

"Yes, you are. And I'm going with you." She put her foot on the first step and dragged me up beside her.

Immediately, I felt the cold rush of wind on my back, smelled the putrid scent of something rotting. I turned my head to the wall by the side of the stairwell, where the stench saturated the air. "Do you smell that?"

She nodded once. "I think even the dead could smell that."

"Not funny," I muttered. I looked up at the doll that still loomed ahead of us on the top step but had blessedly stopped making any noise at all. "If you want me to go up there, you're going first."

"Fine." Without letting go of my hand, she began leading me up the stairs one at a time, the air now frigid in the attic despite the warmth of the air outside. "Don't let go of my hand, no matter what."

"Don't worry. I have no intention of letting go."

We stopped in front of the doll, my mother face-to-face with it. "She's here," Ginette said. "The little girl. Can you feel her?"

I nodded, aware now of a new sound behind me, a scratching sound like bone against bone. "I can't see her, though, because she's hiding. But I don't think it's from me."

One of the snow globes slid across the shelf, then splintered and shattered in the middle of the room, glitter and water staining the floor beneath the exposed rafter. The plastic smiley-faced orange lay face-down in the puddle like a victim in a crime scene. I looked above the mess and saw a bedsheet, knotted into what looked like a noose, swinging gently from the exposed rafter.

"The two spirits are here now," my mother said softly. "One of them wants me to touch the doll." She stepped into the attic and reached for the doll, but I blocked her.

"But which one, Mother? That might not be a good idea until you know for sure."

The sound of something heavy being slid across wood warned us to duck before the next snow globe was thrown across the room, smashing into the wall behind us.

"Anna?" she called. "Is that you? We're here to help you."

Her request was met with an almost deafening silence, like what I imagined would be at the eye of a tornado, broken only by the ceaseless scratching noise. And then a soft swishing noise, like the twisting of fabric, brought our attention back up to the ceiling, where the noose was unraveling by itself, then slowly slipping from the beam to land on my mother's shoulders. She left it there, her eyes wary.

"Hasell?" she said, her voice calm and quiet. "Are you here?"

The whirring began inside the doll's chest, the popping and grinding noise I now recognized. It went on for several long minutes, the doll's mouth opening and closing but not saying anything until it finally wound down to a stop. I was left with the impression that it had tried but had been stopped by another force.

"Hasell?" my mother tried again. "You're trapped here. Tell us what you need so you can move on to the light. There is a better place for you, and we can help you get there."

I shivered from the cold, watching now as the entire shelf of snow globes bounced and vibrated; then I pushed my mother out of the way before another one shot across the room, hitting one of the posts of the bed and slithering to the floor.

"I'm going to touch the doll now, Mellie."

Once again Ginette reached for it, but the doll tumbled backward as my mother was yanked back by the sheet that was now wound tightly around her neck by unseen hands. She let go of my hand to reach for the fabric at her throat, and I felt my strength diminish like a plug being wrenched out of an electric socket. She tugged on it with the desperation of a drowning man grasping at a watery wave.

I leaped for her, digging my fingers into the taut fabric, aware suddenly of a new smell, faint yet spicy, like pipe tobacco. And just as quickly as it appeared, it was gone, as was the tension on the sheet, allowing it to slip free. My mother fell to her knees, rubbing her neck, which wore red welts striped across it. It was again warm in the attic, and sweat beaded on my forehead, dripping into my eyes.

I helped my mother to her feet, examining the marks on her neck more closely. "You're going to have a fun time trying to explain that to Dad," I said.

"That's what scarves are for," she replied almost absentmindedly as she studied the doll, now on its back, staring at the place the sheet had been draped around the beam. "The doll was Hasell's," she said. "I do remember that. Button gave it to her, not as a toy to play with—it's too fragile and valuable for that—but as a companion. Hasell wasn't allowed any friends because they might have germs."

"Are you going to touch it now?"

She shook her head. "Not today, I'm afraid. I'm a bit drained from that little episode. I don't think I need to right now anyway. I'm fairly confident that Anna is still here—and just as unhappy as she was in life. And poor Hasell, still trapped up here and looking for a way out." Her eyes met mine and I wondered if I looked as weary as she did. "We must help them, Mellie. We can't leave them trapped up here forever. Especially if Jayne moves in."

I began picking up the shattered remains of the three snow globes, stacking their plastic bases in a single pile on a dresser, then piling the glass and larger chunks in another. "I'll let Sophie know where to find the doll. You can have access to it at another time."

She didn't seem to hear me. "Did you smell something while we were getting the sheet off my neck?"

"Like pipe smoke?"

"Yes." A soft smile lifted her mouth. "I think it might have been Sumter."

"So what do we do now?"

Ginette shrugged. "We wait for Jack to turn up something new, to help us understand why Hasell and Anna are still here. Sometimes, when a death is unexpected, the person is confused and doesn't realize she's dead. I don't think that's the case here. I think they're both here for a reason, and I know for sure that at least one of them doesn't want us to know what that reason is. And when we think we know what that is, we come back. At night."

She seemed unsteady on her feet, so I took hold of her elbow and led her to the stairs. We were halfway down before I saw what all that scratching had been. The stairwell wall had been covered from ceiling to floor with what looked like childish writing drawn in pencil. I had to look at it for a long time to realize that the words were written backward, as if from the other side of the wall. I jerked back when I realized what it said.

"Help me," my mother read out loud, meeting my gaze.

We looked back at the marked wall, staring at it for a long moment before heading down the stairs. I was getting ready to close the door, locking in the doll and whatever else was up there, when I heard the unmistakable sound of a mewling cat, coming from inside the stairwell wall.

～

I lay in bed next to Jack, listening to the steady sound of his breathing. I'd feigned exhaustion and had skipped dinner, then gone to bed early, pretending to be asleep when Jack crawled into the bed and kissed me gently on the cheek.

I wouldn't have been able to go to sleep even if the neon lights on the bedside clock hadn't continued to flash the time of ten minutes after four. I'd reset it three times already, but it always reverted to four ten if I made the mistake of looking away or allowing my eyes to close. Not that they closed very often. I'd promised my mother that I would talk to Jack, bring my fears out into the open, be the new Melanie I was trying to be. But it was so much easier to promise something than to actually *do* it.

A cell phone rang shrilly and it took me a moment to realize it was mine, the unfamiliar tone throwing me off as I struggled to sit up and reach for the phone at the same time. I might have fallen out of the bed if Jack's strong arm hadn't reached over to pull me back, nestling me into the curve of his body.

"Hello?" I finally managed, holding the phone close to my ear. As before, there was nobody there, just the odd prying noise that seemed to echo from a long way away. I glanced at the number, knowing it was Button's even before I registered all ten digits.

"Hello?" I said again. I looked at the time on my phone. Four ten. I hit the end button and threw the phone back on the nightstand, then waited for Jack to go back to sleep before I moved.

"Mellie?" he whispered into my neck.

"Umm?"

"Who was that?"

"Button Pinckney."

"Hmm."

Either it didn't register or he wasn't concerned that I was still receiving calls from the house of a dead woman.

"Mellie?"

"Umm?"

"Are we going to talk about what's been bothering you, or are you going to pretend to be sick for the rest of the year?"

I considered faking my death and just lying there, but I realized at some point he'd figure it out. Instead I pushed back the covers and sat up on the edge of the bed, my back to him. It was dark in the room, but the moonlight from the windows granted a blue glow across the bed and onto our framed wedding portrait over my dressing table. It had been taken in the garden of the house, less than a year ago. Next to the birth of our children, it was the happiest day of my life. *"You owe it to your marriage and your children."* It was almost as if my mother were sitting next to me, whispering in my ear.

Remembering how my grandmother used to tell me it was easier to yank out a loose tooth than to let it wobble, I took a deep breath and said, "Are you having an affair with Jayne?"

There was a stunned silence, and then, "Jayne as in Jayne the nanny?"

I glanced over my shoulder. "Yes, of course. Unless you know any other Jayne you might be having an affair with."

I felt him move up behind me, but he was smart enough not to touch me. "There is no affair, Mellie. With Jayne or anyone else. Why would you even think that?" He sounded genuinely surprised.

"Because the other day when I took the kids to the park, we came back to the house and were in the kitchen. We heard you and Jayne in the foyer, practicing golf, and you were laughing. And then it was . . . quiet." It was hard for me to say that last word.

There was a long moment of silence, and my heart sank. I dipped my chin, then glanced back at him. His teeth gleamed in the moonlight and I realized he was grinning, a big, wide, open grin that he only did when he was really amused.

"Oh, Mellie. Sometimes I wonder why I'm the writer and not you, because you have one heck of an imagination."

"What do you mean?" I asked, allowing indignation to creep into my voice.

"Well, if you'd just walked a few steps farther into the foyer, you would have found Jayne and me at the bottom of the steps, listening to Nola in her bedroom. She was singing, and plucking something out on her guitar. She said she mentioned to you that she was having a dry spell, and that had me worried. I was just so grateful that she was making music again, and we didn't want to disturb her."

"Was it any good?" I asked, momentarily distracted.

"For other people, maybe, but it wasn't up to her standards. She's having a creative block. I've told her to just keep working through it and she'll eventually get to the other side. That's why I didn't want to bother her."

"I left Jayne to pick up all the golf balls, and I went back to my study to write."

I felt him come up on his knees behind me, placing his hands on my shoulders.

"Mellie, after all we've been through, you're supposed to trust me now. Without trust on both sides, we can't have a strong marriage. You know that, right?"

I nodded, trying to focus on his words instead of the way his hands felt on my bare shoulders. "But she's young, and pretty. And thin. And you were laughing. What was I supposed to think?"

"Anything but what you were thinking. Mellie. You are the most beautiful woman to me, just the way you are. I married you because I want to spend the rest of my life with you, and raise our children together. There is nobody else I want to do that with."

My eyes prickled with unshed tears. "I'm sorry, Jack. I'm so sorry. I just, well, I guess I still have abandonment issues that I'm trying to work out. I'm trying, though. I really am."

I turned to face him, admiring the way the moonlight skipped across the strong bones of his face, making him look like a marble statue. But when I put my hands on his chest, there was nothing cool or marble about him.

"I love you, Mellie. Despite all reason and sanity, I find that I can't live without you. All I ask is that you trust me."

I leaned forward, pressing my body against his. "I do," I whispered against his lips. "Although I think you could have said that in a nicer way."

With a quick movement, startling General Lee enough to make him leap to the relative safety of the floor, Jack had me pinned on the bed. "Maybe I can convince you in other ways." He bent his head to my neck and began to kiss his way up to my ear.

I grinned. "I'd like to see you try."

My cell phone began to ring again and I grappled for it on the nightstand. Without looking at the number, I turned it off and tossed it across the room, eager to test out my mother's theory about make-up sex.

CHAPTER 22

I waved good-bye to my mother as she dropped me off in front of Henderson House Realty. She'd taken me to Gwyn's in Mt. Pleasant to shop for a dress for Marc's book launch party after she insisted that sewing two old bedspreads together and cutting holes for my head and arms would not be an appropriate gown for the occasion.

I entered the reception area, eager to immerse myself in work so I could forget about the whole episode of trying on dresses, or the reason why I'd been forced into it. Apparently, none of the dresses in my closet actually fit, according to my mother, even if I did manage to get a zipper all the way to the top without any tearing noises. I had no idea when she'd become such a fashion expert, but she seemed to believe that Kim Kardashian–tight was not a good look for me. I wouldn't have minded the comparison if I hadn't caught sight of myself in the mirror from behind and realized that Kim and I had a lot more in common than I ever could have imagined.

"Mamamamama!"

I took off my sunglasses and looked in surprise to where Jack stood in the lobby with the stroller and both children, who were now bouncing excitedly upon seeing me, which did more for my ego than a closet full of great-fitting dresses ever could.

After kissing them both, I turned to Jack, who took his time kissing me hello, and who would probably have extended it if Jolly Thompson hadn't cleared her throat from behind the receptionist's desk.

"Oh, I'm sorry, Jolly. I got . . . distracted." I looked back at Jack. "Was I expecting you?"

"No. And we just got here. Jayne's meeting me here in fifteen minutes to get the children, but I was hoping you had a little bit of time for me to show you something. And then I'm heading to City Lights Café to try to get some work done."

"What's wrong with your office at home? Don't you like the desk your mother and I picked out for you? And your sweater and slippers?"

"I love all of that, I do. I just . . ." He shrugged. "It's like the whole creative side of my brain shuts down whenever I'm in the house— anywhere in the house. I've tried writing in the kitchen, and the dining room. I've even tried writing in the bedroom." He winked. "Although I don't think it's too much of a stretch to figure out why I'm distracted when I'm trying to write in there."

Jolly cleared her throat again and he became serious. "Anyway, I've found that if I write in a café, or a park bench or really anywhere else, I can get into the writing zone pretty easily."

I frowned. "You didn't have this problem before, did you?"

He shook his head. "No. It all started a little over a month ago— which coincided with when I found out about Marc's movie deal, which could have something to do with it."

"Probably." I turned to Jolly. "I don't have any appointments until one, right?"

"That's right." She smiled at the babies. "If you'd like me to keep an eye on them so you can talk without any distractions, I'd be happy to. Everybody's out at lunch, so it's pretty quiet right now."

"That's very nice, thank you," I said, and watched with fascination as she crossed something off one of her lists.

"What was that?" I asked, always interested in other people's methods of organization.

"Every day on my to-do list, I write 'Do something nice for somebody.' So thank *you*."

"You're welcome," I said slowly.

"They've just been fed and diapered, so they should be good to go," Jack said. "They love to be sung to and they're not too particular. Unless you're Mellie—that usually makes them cry."

I sent him a withering glance, but he just smiled back at me because he knew I couldn't argue.

"Will do," she said, coming around the desk and leaning over the stroller. Sarah immediately reached for her sparkling dragonfly earrings, and JJ reached for her breasts. I quickly diverted their attention by diving into the little toy pouch snapped to the stroller and pulling out two stuffed animals before handing one to each child. "Call us if you need anything, but they're pretty easygoing."

"Don't you worry. I love babies."

Judging by the hours I'd already spent while she showed me pictures of her grandchildren on her phone, I figured she had lots of practice.

Jack followed me back to my office and pressed me against the door as soon as I'd closed it. "Too bad we only have fifteen minutes."

I pushed away from him, too aware that Jolly and our children were only a short hallway away—not to mention any coworkers who might be returning from lunch. "That's what our bed at home is for."

"Is it? Well, just for the record, I intend to keep our marriage spicy. So expect it when you least expect it."

I felt my body flush and wondered if I might be having a hot flash. I extricated myself from his embrace and headed to my desk, where I shed my coat, purse, and briefcase. "So, what did you want to show me?"

"Is that a leading question?"

I sighed. "No, it's a real question." I pointed to his leather satchel he wore over one shoulder. It was vegan leather and stamped with a bright green peace sign, and looked just like the one Sophie's husband, Chad, wore when he was on his bike pedaling to class. It had actually been a wedding gift from the couple—I had a matching one that I hadn't quite found a way to use yet.

Jack lifted it from his shoulder and pulled out a thick ream of paper before slapping it in the middle of my completely bare desk. It was a point of pride that I wouldn't leave the office without all papers, pens, and pencils being put in their proper spots. Only frames containing photos of Jack, Nola, and the babies were allowed.

"What is that?" I asked, wincing at the uneven edges of the stack of paper.

"Hasell's medical records. Took up half a file cabinet."

"Those are the actual records?"

"Yes. Lucky for us, Hasell's multiple hospital visits were pre–HIPAA regulations, so her family's private doctor kept all her records in his office, and when he retired he moved them to the attic of his house. Just as we thought, he passed away a few years ago, but his elderly widow still lives in there. She said I could borrow them. Took some convincing, but she eventually caved." He smiled brightly, and I could only imagine what the poor woman endured in terms of endless charm and flattery. He continued. "I'll probably pull an all-nighter tonight taking notes because I have to return them tomorrow. I've already had a chance to go through them, and it's pretty perplexing."

We both sat down on either side of my desk as he began to flip through the pages. "The records begin when Hasell was only three months old. She got pneumonia and was responding well to antibiotics and was sent home, but then came back with antibiotic-resistant pneumonia and bronchitis. She stopped breathing several times while at the hospital, but was revived because her mother was there and administered CPR."

He turned a page so I could read. "This is a note from a nurse, commenting on how Anna, her mother, refused to leave the girl's side and slept on a cot by her incubator for five months until Hasell could go home."

I thought of my rosy-cheeked babies, full of good health and smiles, and despite what I suspected Anna had done to us in the attic, I felt a stab of sympathy for her. "Did she get better after that?"

Jack replaced the page in the stack and shook his head. "No. Things got worse. She had recurring bouts of respiratory issues, but she also developed problems with her digestion. Couldn't keep solids down until she was about five years old. Her mother had to feed her with a feeding tube. One of the doctors noted it was the worst case of gastroesophageal reflux disease he'd ever seen in a patient. She was so weak she didn't learn to walk until she was three and even then could walk only short distances without tiring out. By the time she died, she was bedridden."

I tried not to think of the room with the beautiful mural and snow globes and of the girl who'd once planned to travel the world but never made it past her bedroom door. "But they don't know what she died from specifically?"

"According to her death certificate, no. But I talked to one of my doctor friends who said that her body just gave out, that her organs simply shut down one by one. Her brain would have been the last organ to go, so she would have been aware that she was dying."

He reached into his back pocket and pulled out a freshly laundered handkerchief and handed it to me. "It's hard to hear."

I touched my face, surprised to find it wet, then dabbed at my eyes with the cloth. "It makes me angry, in a way. That all the advances in medicine couldn't fix what was wrong with her. But that doesn't explain why she's still here."

"Isn't unfinished business usually the reason?"

"Sometimes. But what kind of unfinished business could an eleven-year-old shut-in have? Which makes me think that maybe it's not her ghost up in that attic. I mean, the house is more than two hundred and fifty years old. Lots of people have lived and died in that house. She's just one in a long list of candidates."

His eyes met mine for a moment before returning to the pile of paper. He pulled out a loose sheet from the very bottom and handed it to me. "This might change your mind." It was a photocopy of a South Carolina death certificate that he'd shown me before. "I was looking at this again to see if there was anything I'd missed, and there it was." He pointed his finger to a spot on the form.

I squinted, unable to see the really tiny print.

"Oh, for crying out loud, Mellie." He reached around the desk and pulled out the top drawer. "Just put them on already."

Feeling chastened, I put my reading glasses on and looked down to see the name Hasell Chisolm Pinckney on the top line, and then moved my gaze to the spot he indicated. I put my hand over my lips, unable to speak. The words "Time of Death" were printed above bold, black numbers typed neatly in the little box: 4:10 a.m.

"That would be a little too coincidental if that weren't Hasell's spirit trying to reach you, don't you think?" Jack asked quietly.

"Even if we did believe in coincidences," I said slowly, my mind still trying to wrap itself around what he'd just discovered. I thought back to when my alarm clocks had stopped at ten minutes after four, and the phone call came in from a disconnected number. I remembered it had been the first day back at the office. The day I'd met Jayne and learned she'd inherited the Pinckney house, the same house Hasell had lived and died in. That was when Hasell had first reached out to me; I could guess that much. But I was no closer to understanding *why*.

"Which we don't." Jack was thoughtful for a moment and then began righting the papers, stacking them against the flat top of my desk before returning them to his satchel. "There's something else, too."

I looked at him over my reading glasses before realizing that I probably looked like my first grade teacher, Mrs. Montemurno, who'd worn muumuus over her ample body and lots of gold clanky bracelets over the crease in her arm where her wrists were supposed to be. She'd looked ancient even back then and I remembered how the bags under her eyes were always accentuated when she looked at me from over her glasses. I hastily took them off. "Go ahead," I said.

"You mentioned the Pinckneys had once owned a house on Lake Jasper near Birmingham. I'd never heard of it before, but I wouldn't be a writer if I didn't jump at every loose piece of information, so I did some research. The reason why I'd never heard of it before is probably because it doesn't exist anymore. The lake was enlarged in 1985 by the Army Corps of Engineers and the name changed to another, larger lake that was combined with Lake Jasper."

"So what happened to the Pinckney house?" I asked.

"Oh, it's still there, I'm sure. Just underwater. It happens sometimes—to whole towns, even. It's almost like they're encased in snow globes with the roads, houses, shops, and churches still there, only unreachable unless you like to scuba."

"That's horrible. And not a little creepy. Remind me to never go boating or swimming there. I can't imagine what sort of angry spirits are probably hanging around."

"Yes, well, some people say on Sunday mornings, you can still hear the church bells ringing."

I winced. "That's scary, even to me." I thought for a moment, remembering something he'd said. "And it was flooded in 1985?"

After he nodded, I said, "Your mother found a salt-and-pepper-shaker set as part of a collection in the Pinckney House. It's from Lake Jasper and somebody had painted the date May thirtieth, 1984."

He pulled out his notepad and jotted it down. "Just in case it's important. Regardless, the set might be valuable, seeing as how Lake Jasper doesn't exist anymore. Make sure Jayne is aware so she doesn't dump the whole collection at Goodwill before she knows the value." He replaced the notepad, then glanced at his watch before looking back at me with a wicked grin. "Looks like we have five minutes."

The intercom on my desk buzzed and Jolly's voice was piped in: "The nanny's here."

"Hold that thought," I said as I stood.

The children were squealing with happiness upon seeing Jayne and were too preoccupied to notice Jack or me. At least that was what I told myself. I let Jayne know that I'd added a few things to the children's Google calendar, including their first-year checkup at the pediatrician's. I made sure to let her know that I'd added a note to that event about which matching outfits they should wear. She and Jack, and even Jolly, stared back at me with the same blank expressions, making me wonder, just for a moment, if it was me that wasn't understanding something.

We said good-bye to the children and waved to them and Jayne as they made their way outside to the sidewalk.

"Do you want to know what I think?" Jolly asked, her eyes bright behind her glasses.

"About what?" I asked.

"Your nanny—Jayne, right? I thought I saw it the first time she was here, and now I'm definitely sure."

Uneasily, I asked, "Saw what?"

"An aura. She definitely has an aura. It's how you can tell someone has 'the gift.' That's what my grandmother used to say about me, so that's how I know I can communicate with spirits. They're just taking a little longer to recognize that."

"Really?" I said. "Do I have an aura?"

She shook her head emphatically. "No. Not even a shadow, or I would have told you. Sorry."

"That's all right," I said. "I'm sure it's more of a burden than a blessing most times."

"That's for sure." She began fiddling with the dragonfly-shaped pin on her blouse, staring at Jack.

With a straight face, he said, "Any more dark-haired gentlemen holding up a piece of jewelry?"

She shook her head solemnly. "Sadly, no." Her face became grim. "Actually, I'm not sure, so I don't want to say anything. . . ." Although it was very clear that she was itching to tell us something.

"Go ahead," Jack said. "We can handle it."

"It's a cat. And it's talking to you. I just can't hear what it's saying."

I stared at her for a moment, jolted by her mention of a cat. "What color is it?"

She frowned as if concentrating. "One of those striped tabby cats. With a long tail."

I wondered if I'd sighed audibly. "Okay. We'll be on the lookout for talking striped cats."

She shook her head. "You shouldn't take my messages so literally. I'm still new at this, so I do get things wrong—or a little twisted, I should say. But do think on it—it might become clear to you what the actual message is."

"Will do," I said. Knowing Jolly was watching, I gave Jack a chaste kiss good-bye and watched him walk away, headed toward a café where he could write.

I returned to my office and flipped on my computer and tried to work on a list of planned showings for a family flying in from California. Instead I found myself staring at the screen without really seeing it, imagining instead a house and a town floating underwater as if in a snow globe, and the haunting peal of church bells that hadn't been rung in more than thirty years.

CHAPTER 23

I stood with my mother in her Legare Street bedroom, feeling a little like Ali Baba after the secret cave had been opened. She'd emptied the contents of several jewelry boxes of varying sizes onto her bedspread, in search of a necklace she had in mind that would go perfectly with my dress for the launch party.

"I know it's in here somewhere," came her voice from her vast walk-in closet, where several shelves were designated for her various jewelry containers. I was itching to organize them, but she'd refused my offer of help, claiming that they were organized by her age when she'd worn them and by her memories. Still, when I saw the mismatched earrings and knotted chains, I needed to clasp my hands together so I wouldn't do something we'd both regret.

She emerged with a small leather heart-shaped box. It looked old, the hinged fold cracked and worn. "It must be in here. This is the jewelry I wore when I was in high school, and maybe a few costume pieces from college. I can't imagine why it would be in here, but I can't think where else it could be."

"Strange, that. Seeing that nothing else seems to be where it's supposed to be," I said under my breath. "If you'd just let me organize it . . ."

"Mellie," she said, in that tone of voice that usually only seasoned mothers had. She'd been mothering me for only a few years, but she'd already perfected it.

She opened the box and I peered into the jumbled mess inside, the chains wound around rings and earrings, and even a couple of stray buttons lying haphazardly on top. I bit down hard on my lower lip, and tasted blood. With red-lacquered nails, she drew out a pretty gold ID bracelet, the chain narrow and feminine. "I always thought I'd give this to my daughter when she was at Ashley Hall."

"Sorry to disappoint," I said, squinting to get a better look. On one side *Ginette Prioleau, Class of 1970* had been engraved, and on the other, *Ashley Hall, Charleston, South Carolina.*

"I'm thinking I'll give it to Nola her senior year. She's not interested in a class ring, but she'll consider this vintage, so she might like it." She placed it on her dresser next to a single diamond earring stud that was missing its partner, and an S-link gold chain with a broken clasp. I'd already pointed out that I had no missing or broken pieces of jewelry because my costume jewelry was meticulously organized on labeled hooks and clear bins, and my good jewelry was in a locked safe where each shelf was labeled, so I kept silent.

"What's this?" I asked, pulling out a ring with what looked to be an oval onyx stone, a small diamond at its center.

I dropped it in her outstretched palm, and watched her face soften as she recognized it. "I loved that ring. I don't think I took it off for years." She slid it over the third finger of her right hand, and I tried not to notice how easily it still fit. I'd had to have my wedding rings resized so I could still wear them.

"Who gave it to you?"

She was silent for a moment. "An old friend gave it to me for my sixteenth birthday."

"You're not wearing your gloves," I pointed out. "Aren't you picking up a lot of messages?"

"Sadly, no. It only seems to work when I touch an object that has nothing to do with me. Which is a blessing, really, as I'd have to wear gloves inside my own home, which is something I'd rather not do."

"But then you can't relive the memories that are attached to all this." I looked back at the ring. "It is beautiful," I said, admiring the braided platinum that encircled the finger and surrounded the onyx.

"Here, try it on." She slid it off her finger. "I bet it will fit your middle finger, which I think is where it looks best, since it's so long. And it will look beautiful with your dress."

I did as she asked, then held out my hand to admire it. "You're right—it does look good on the middle finger, and it fits perfectly. Are you sure I can borrow it?"

"Of course. Actually, why don't you keep it? It's not doing me any good sitting in my jewelry box, and I can't see myself wearing it again, so why not give it a new life?"

"Why not?" I said, holding it up to the light. "Thank you."

She was distracted by something at the bottom of the box and quickly upended it on the bedspread. "Here it is!" She drew out a heavy gold chain from which hung a perfectly oval opal surrounded by little diamonds.

"It's stunning," I said. "But I'm wearing a V-neck—won't that dip a little low?"

"Of course it will. That's the point. You've got this wonderful cleavage now—enhanced with your new bra, I might add—and it is the perfect accessory to your black sequined gown. I don't even think you need earrings or a bracelet—just this necklace and the ring and you're all set."

I allowed her to drape the necklace around my neck, noticing how it hit me right between my breasts. "You don't think it might be . . . too much?"

My mother became serious. "Mellie, darling. This is as much Jack's night as it is Marc's. Marc is stuck with that silly Rebecca, who will be dressed up looking like a pink parfait—all empty calories. But you will be there looking like a filet mignon and making Jack proud that you're with him. It's going to be a difficult night. At least walking in, you will already be two points ahead."

I frowned. "I really don't think of it as keeping score, Mother."

"Well, you should," she said, starting to pick up various pieces of jewelry and drop them into the boxes.

"Did you know that Jayne was invited to the party, too?"

She glanced at me over her shoulder. "Yes. She asked me to help her find a dress."

I raised my eyebrows, causing my mother to stop what she was doing and face me. "That poor girl needs a mother in the worst way—even more than you did. Have you noticed how much better she is with children than adults? Anyway, I told her yes. I hope you don't mind."

"Why should I mind?" I asked, trying desperately to keep the pique from my voice.

She sent me a knowing look. "We're going Sunday, her next day off, and you're welcome to come. It might be awkward, but I'd hate for you to think that I picked out a prettier dress for her."

"Really, Mother? I'm not *that* immature."

It was her turn to raise her eyebrows.

"Besides, I'm not the one who says I should be keeping score."

"That's different," she said. "Rebecca's motives are never good. Whereas I really don't think Jayne has a conniving bone in her body."

I pressed my lips together to keep from saying anything, remembering my earlier suspicions, and unwilling to completely let them go regardless of how much I trusted Jack or liked Jayne.

She returned to gathering up the jewelry to put it away. I held out both hands, wanting to stop the haphazard way she was dumping the pieces into random boxes. Sensing my mood, she turned her back to me and started moving quicker as if she were afraid I would give in to my urges and overpower her.

My phone beeped in my purse, and I dug it out to answer the text, eager to be distracted from the horror that was unfolding in front of me. "I've got to go. Sophie said they've found a cat and she needs me to come take a look. She suggested you come, too, if you can."

"I should be able to make it," she said, raising her arm to look at the watch on her wrist, then shaking her hand. "This is so annoying. I've had this watch for years without a single problem, and then about a month ago it begins to stop at the same time no matter how many times I reset it."

I felt my skin tighten along my scalp. "What time does it get stuck on?"

She looked at her watch again. "Ten minutes after four. Isn't that odd?"

"Odder than you think." I placed the necklace and ring in my purse. "Come on. I'll drive and tell you all about it on the way over."

She followed me out of the room. "What should I tell your father?"

"Whatever you'd like. Just as long as you don't mention that we're going to go look at a skeleton that's been boarded up inside an attic wall for about thirty years."

◇

Sophie, Rich Kobylt, and the entire work crew were waiting in the driveway when we pulled up to the Pinckney house, Sophie with a worried expression and Rich looking as if he was about to tell us again that he thought the house was haunted.

"Did you call Jayne?" I asked as Sophie approached.

She nodded. "She's on her way. Mrs. Houlihan already left, so she had to wait for Jack to come home so she could leave the children."

"Afternoon, Miz Trenholm, Miz Middleton," Rich said as he approached. "My guys are a little unsettled and it's already past quitting time, so I'm going to let them go home. But I'll stick around in case you need help moving . . . the remains."

"It's only a cat," I said. "I'm sure we can—"

"Thank you, Rich," my mother said. "We'd appreciate it." She turned her head to me and whispered, "I'm not touching it."

Rich nodded, then returned to his crew, who began loading tools into the beds of their trucks. Jayne joined us, a little out of breath from her walk. "I'm not really sure I need to go in to see it," she said. "I trust your judgment, Sophie. So if you just want to plaster it over . . ."

"Well," Sophie said, drawing out the word, "it's a little more complicated than that. Figured you should see it all yourself before deciding on how to proceed."

Jayne looked up at the empty windows of the house, and I saw an almost imperceptible shudder go through her. She forced a smile. "All right. Let's go, then."

We walked upstairs single file, Sophie in the front. The tingling at the back of my neck that had begun while I stood outside had fled, leaving me with the unsettled feeling of knowing we were being watched, but unable to stare back. It was like being in a fistfight, except I wasn't allowed to throw any punches. It was maddening, and frustrating, and not a little frightening.

I heard humming, and turned around to see Jayne, who seemed to be doing her best to stay calm. She'd told me a dozen times that she hated old houses, and I was sure we were about to expose a reason why so many people shared her opinion.

Heavy dust hung in the air from the recent construction work, where the worst water-saturated walls were being taken down to their studs. They had only gotten as far as the stairwell wall in the attic—although I didn't know if they could have gone much farther with the murals and furniture still untouched in the room above. At least that meant most of the wall with the backward writing had been destroyed and I could pretend it had never been there.

I almost asked Jayne then what she was waiting for. She had yet to make any decision as to the distribution of the house's contents, and I was getting tired of having Sophie bug me about it. It didn't seem likely that some distant family member would contest the will and tell Jayne to go away—that would have happened by now. Maybe Jayne was hoping that by not dealing with it, the problem would just disappear. As a lifetime subscriber to that school of thought, I was tempted to agree. Except I knew from experience that it wouldn't. Still, I found it oddly comforting that I wasn't alone in my rather warped way of thinking. It was, I realized, one of the reasons why I liked Jayne. As if we were partners in a foxhole and our lives were trench warfare.

When we reached the doorway to the attic, Sophie stopped. A

portable lamp had been placed on the steps to shine light into the dark opening of the adjacent wall, helped by the late-afternoon sun that poured in from the attic window.

Everybody seemed reluctant to move forward, so I did, not feeling brave at all but desperate to get this over with before nightfall. The days were still short and I had no intention of being caught in the attic after the sun set. The azure blue–painted walls where the words "Help me" had been scratched were gone, and all that remained were the darkened wood studs that looked like bones of the house with their flesh removed.

And there, between the studs, was a small doorway cut inside them, and beyond that a flight of wooden steps that led down into a dark abyss running almost parallel to the steps we stood on.

"The door was there all along," Sophie said. "With a spring latch so there wasn't a knob, and the seams hidden in the mural."

"So it was there before the mural was painted," I said, thinking out loud.

"Not necessarily." Sophie's face was pensive, and even in her ridiculous clothes she actually looked like the college professor she was. "The stairs are very old—I'm guessing they were part of the original house and these steps led down to a tunnel used for smuggling or other uses one might want to hide from the neighbors." She glanced up as if we were students and she wanted to make sure we were following along.

"According to the copy of the renovation blueprints from 1930 that Jack and Melanie made for me, it doesn't look like anyone was aware that this staircase existed. There's nothing in the drawings, and no mention of it. The original doorway could have been plastered over when the bottom floor was filled in, and this doorway could have been added later, after the staircase was discovered accidentally—like we did." She pointed to the ceiling above us. "From what I can tell, when they redesigned the roofline, they didn't take into consideration rain drainage. My guess is that they've had a steady leak since the new roof was installed in 1930. Even though several patches have been made over the years, it never fixed what is basically a design flaw."

"So what are you saying?" I asked.

"That sometime between 1930 and now, someone was sent up to the attic to check out a roof leak, and discovered the staircase behind the wall, and then decided to hide a little doorway panel that gave access to the old stairwell." She reached inside to the top step and pulled out an old paint can, its lid and handle flaky with rust. "I did find this, which is why I think the mural could have been painted before the door was made, and then the paint touched up with this. It's only the background color, which makes me think the addition wasn't made by the original artist."

"Sumter," I said. "Amelia told me that Sumter painted it for Hasell."

"But why would they need a hidden door?" Jayne asked as we all moved forward to get a better look.

"I have no idea," Sophie said.

My mother, who'd remained silent up to now, said, "Because whoever put it in wanted it to be kept a secret." She stepped forward and stuck her head through the opening. "Is this where you found the cat?"

Rich Kobylt spoke from behind her. "Yes, ma'am—poor thing's at the bottom of the stairs. His skull is crushed—either from falling down the stairs or . . ." He didn't finish, but I knew all of our imaginations were working overtime. "I'm not a fan of cats, but that's a heck of a way to go."

"What else is down there?" she asked.

"Well, that's the interesting thing," Rich said, scratching the back of his head. "When I first went down there, it looked like the stairs ended at a cement wall. That's when I saw the cat, and it about scared the britches off me."

I didn't remark how that wouldn't have been too hard, considering how low they were hanging, and waited for him to continue.

"Anyway, I was about to come back up to get a bag for the cat bones, and that's when I had this odd feeling, like a little voice almost, telling me to press against the wall where it ran alongside the steps. That's how I found it—a little button. And when I pushed it, a door opened into the butler's pantry downstairs. I went through it and closed it, and dang if you can tell it's there even if you know it. Whoever built that really knew what they were doin'."

I met my mother's gaze. *A little voice.* Maybe a little girl's voice. Maybe Hasell had wanted him to find it. Because it meant something.

"Maybe it was made for Hasell," Sophie suggested.

I shook my head. "These steps are even steeper than the other ones. In her physical condition she couldn't have gone up and down by herself. And she was bedridden for the last few years of her life."

I turned back to Rich. "And there's nothing else?" I pressed, wishing this discovery had yielded more information.

He looked a little sheepish. "I didn't really have much chance to look. That cat scairt me a little, so as soon as I popped through that door in the butler's pantry, I came got Dr. Wallen-Arasi. But from the looks of it there's just a bunch of wooden stairs—and be careful on them, too. Some of them are warped from moisture. Easy to catch your foot on one."

As soon as he finished speaking, I realized that Jayne was still humming and hadn't said anything for a while. I faced her, noticing her skin was a washed-out gray, accentuating her dark roots beneath the blond hair. "What's wrong . . ." I started to ask before I followed her gaze behind me.

Clustered around the old doorframe, a thick, moving mass of buzzing flies swelled and swayed, their sound suddenly noticeable. We watched in mute fascination as they formed themselves into a ball, then flew into the stairwell and out of sight.

Sophie reached the opening first and peered down. "They're gone," she said. "I don't know where or how, but they're gone."

A loud thump sounded behind me and I turned to find Jayne sprawled on the floor in a dead faint, her fall broken by a pillow from the bed that I didn't remember seeing there before. I looked toward the window at the setting sun, and felt the cold air on my back just as the rotting smell of dead flesh crept up from the blackened stairway.

CHAPTER 24

I walked slowly down the stairs at my house on Tradd Street, listening to the reassuring ticking of the grandfather clock in the quiet house. I'd just settled a reluctant Jayne into her bed with an Advil PM, and the twins were already tucked into their beds. They were supposed to be asleep, but I heard Sarah babbling. To whom, I wasn't sure. Nola and her friend Lindsey were holed up in Nola's bedroom studying for an AP American history exam the following day.

When I'd gone up to the girls earlier to deliver a plate of sugar-free carob-chip cookies, I surreptitiously checked for any sign of a Ouija board, and had been satisfied that it hadn't been brought back into our house.

Jack was at his desk in the front room, surrounded by haphazard stacks of paper, making my fingertips itch, and jotting notes on his yellow lined notepad. He looked up as I approached. "How is Jayne?"

"Fine. More embarrassed than anything. She thinks she was holding her breath too long, and that's why she fainted. It's funny, though. . . ." My voice trailed away as I thought back to the attic room and the hidden steps.

"What's funny?" Jack prompted.

"Well, not really funny, but odd. She said she was holding her breath because the stench was so bad. But nobody else smelled anything—until my mother and I did right after Jayne fainted."

"She is younger," Jack pointed out.

I gave him a hard stare.

"Well, it's a documented fact that as you grow older, you lose your sense of smell."

"Nothing's wrong with my sense of smell. Or my mother's. We could smell the construction dust and the mildew, but nothing like the putrid scent Jayne said she smelled—and that I smelled the last time I was in the attic with Sophie, and again right after Jayne fainted."

Jack tapped the eraser end of his pencil on the paper. "Maybe it was her imagination. She has a real fear of old houses, so she'd probably already prepared herself for the worst, even to the point of thinking she could smell that cat despite the fact that it's been dead for years."

He pulled me down onto his lap. "I hope Rich wasn't insulted that she wanted me to help her out to the car and bring her home instead of him. I was practically in front of the house with the kids in the car headed to the park when you called, so I wasn't going to say no."

I was silent for a moment as he buried his nose in my hair. "I think she was afraid he'd trip on his pants if both of his hands were occupied," I said. "But I'm glad you had a chance to see the house. You should go back during the daytime. The more Sophie tells me about the work that needs to be done, the more I'm beginning to understand why Button wanted to unload it onto a complete stranger. Any of her friends would have thought they'd made her mad and she was punishing them."

He chuckled, his warm breath caressing the back of my neck. "It was nice of her to allow me to bring back all those photos from Button's room." He indicated the frames now standing on the back edge of his desk. I noticed the heavy dust and tarnish on them and made a mental note to clean them tomorrow. I couldn't ask Mrs. Houlihan, because Jack had asked her never to touch anything on his desk and so she wouldn't. I'd wondered at her devotion and so had asked her to bake me fudge brownies and she'd refused.

"I'm still not sure what you need them for." I tilted my head backward to give him easy access to my throat.

"They're just pieces in a puzzle. Writing a book is like that, you know. Putting together a puzzle. Except sometimes a bunch of pieces are thrown in that don't fit and sometimes you don't figure that out until after you've wasted a lot of time trying to force them into place." He pulled back, his gaze focused on the frames. "When I'm writing about real people and real events, it helps me to keep their photos nearby to remind me what I'm really writing about. Helps me to focus. Although I'm still not sure what this story is."

I picked up the Alabama saltshaker that on a whim Jack had also asked to take with him, my index finger absently tracing the painted date. May 30, 1984. "The only thing I know for sure is that Sumter and Anna Pinckney adored their daughter. Anna especially. She devoted her whole life to Hasell's care. I just can't imagine how hard it would be to see your child wasting away with nobody able to tell you why or what you can do to fix it."

Jack's eyes were dark. "And Anna was basically doing it on her own. From what my mother tells me, Sumter traveled all the time. Maybe he felt as helpless as Anna, and chose to keep busy by spending as much time as he could outside the house. Or . . ." He stopped.

"Or what?"

"Or Anna made him feel superfluous, not needed. That she was the only parent who could nurse Hasell properly."

I peered over at his notes, noticing the words *Hasell Architecture & Construction* that were underlined three times. "What's that?" I asked.

"That's the name of Anna's father's company. She had a degree in architecture from Clemson—did you know that? She worked for him when she was newly married, but then left to care for Hasell full-time."

"Your mother said that Anna's father's company built the Pinckneys' lake house, and that's how the families originally met. Anna and Button practically grew up together—it's no surprise that Anna would eventually marry Button's brother."

Jack sat up, shifting around piles of paper until he found what he was looking for. "This is a letter I found in Rosalind's archives—Button and Sumter's mother, dated November 1960. It's from her husband regarding the house in Alabama—which I'm assuming is the lake house. He said he'd hired a local couple—newlyweds—to act as caretaker, general handyman, and housekeeper. He planned to keep them on full-time. Like they really intended to use the lake house as a second home, and made sure it was always ready for them."

"Interesting," I said to be polite. Old letters from people long-since dead had never had any appeal to me. Especially since I had other, more direct, ways to communicate with them.

He took the saltshaker from my hand and began to roll it in his fingers. "The way somebody painted that date onto the shakers—it must mean *something*. It looks like it might be the only thing that remains from the lake house. And yet, according to these letters to Rosalind, accumulated over several decades, that house was a real haven for her and her family. A very special place that they all looked forward to visiting as often as they could."

"How do you know it's the only remaining piece of the house?"

"My mother. I asked her about it. She told me that she'd offered to have her moving people load everything up at the lake house to either salvage or sell before they flooded the lake, and Button told her it should all stay intact. So that when she remembered it, she'd know it was all still there, just underwater."

Reaching forward, he pulled a photocopied version of a piece of newspaper toward us. "This was after Rosalind's death, so I'm assuming Button must have clipped it out and added it to her mother's drawer full of correspondence for posterity's sake. I've read through it several times, and the one thing that sticks with me is that the families on the lake and in the town knew what was coming a full year in advance. And the Pinckneys even had my mother offering to help them empty the house and take care of the contents. Yet Button and her brother did nothing to save anything from the house. Only a salt-and-pepper-shaker set with that date written on it."

"It could be anything, Jack. Like your mother said, they wanted to keep the house intact, even underwater—that's why they only took the shakers. And maybe that's the date a favorite dog died. Or a first kiss. Who knows? It was with the rest of the collection at the South Battery house where it probably always was—and not salvaged from the lake house at all. I think you're reading more into this than is there."

He continued to thrum the pencil against the pad. "How many years ago was that—thirty-two? That's really not that long ago. Rosalind's husband said he'd hired a local couple—and they were newlyweds in 1960. It's possible they're still alive, and might even still live locally. I'm thinking I need to take a research trip to Alabama and see what I might be able to turn up." He tossed down the pencil and began unbuttoning my blouse. "I certainly can't get any writing done here, so I might as well see if I can be productive someplace else. In the meantime . . ."

He'd just pressed his mouth to the little triangle of skin above my bra when the doorbell rang. Reluctantly, he sat back and began rebuttoning my blouse. "The doorbell always thinks it knows when it should start working again."

"It's probably someone coming for Lindsey. It's almost ten o'clock." As if on cue, the grandfather clock struck four.

Jack came with me to the door and opened it to find Michael Farrell, Lindsey's father. The men shook hands and then Jack excused himself to go get Lindsey. Out of politeness, I asked Michael if he'd like something to drink and he surprised me by saying yes and following me into the kitchen.

I poured him a glass of sweet tea from the pitcher in the fridge, then joined him at the kitchen table, feeling awkward while gradually growing aware that he was trying to find the right way to say something.

"Is everything all right?" I preempted. "Lindsey okay?"

He took a sip of his tea and nodded. "Yes, everybody's good." He regarded me for a long moment. "I'm trying to find the right way to ask you for a favor."

"A favor?" I said, surprised. "A favor to do what?"

"Actually, it would be a favor to ask you *not* to do something."

"I'm afraid I don't know what—"

"I've been doing some research on you and your mother."

"Oh," I said, sitting back in my chair, finally understanding where he was leading.

"Veronica said that she was only hiring your mother, but from what I've read, you also claim to be 'psychic.' I can certainly understand why you would have tried to evade the truth when we talked about it at your party."

I sat up. "I wasn't trying to 'evade' anything, and I certainly have not made any claims about being psychic despite what you may have read."

He crossed his arms and watched me dubiously, his sweet tea forgotten. "Yes, well, when I asked Veronica about it, she admitted that you and your mother have both agreed to help her find out what happened to Adrienne."

When I didn't respond, he said, "I'd like to ask you not to."

"Look, Michael, regardless of what you do or don't believe, don't you want your wife to find some kind of closure about her sister's murder?"

He placed his fingers flat on the surface of the table, and I noticed how his cuticles were ragged and torn as if he chewed on them regularly. He laughed, but it wasn't a humorous tone. "Of course I want my wife to have peace of mind. And Lindsey, too—Adrienne's middle name was Lindsey, did she tell you? Veronica has got Lindsey all hyped up about finding Adrienne's killer, and there's nothing else those two think about anymore. It's not healthy."

"But that's what I'm saying. There's new evidence that might lead to the killer. There *is* hope that the peace they need can be found."

He shook his head. "No! The new evidence means *nothing*. Even Detective Riley agrees with that. Building up their hopes by saying you can use some mumbo jumbo to solve Adrienne's murder is cruel. And I want you to stop." He leaned forward, lowering his voice. "I'm not asking you. I'm telling you."

I stood, feeling more angry than threatened. "I'm sorry you feel that way. But as I mentioned before, your wife is working with my mother. . . ."

He slid back his chair so quickly it almost toppled backward. He wagged his index finger at me. "I've read about you and your 'adventures' finding dead bodies. I've even spoken to that reporter, Suzy Dorf. We had a nice conversation about you, as a matter of fact. And how it's so convenient that dead bodies are always turning up around you. It's easy to pass off as 'psychic powers,' isn't it? Sounds so much better than insider information."

We heard Jack outside the door, and Michael's demeanor immediately softened. "I'm sorry. It's just my whole household is in such turmoil because of all this. And I just want it to . . . go away."

The door opened and Jack poked his head in. "There you are—we were wondering where you'd gone to. Lindsey's ready to go. They both look dead on their feet." He opened the door wide to allow us to pass through.

Michael smiled amenably. "I was parched, and your lovely wife invited me to have a glass of tea."

We found the girls in the foyer, still in their rumpled school uniforms, looking exhausted. I put my arm around Nola's shoulders and she leaned into me. "Want to know about Manifest Destiny and the acquisition of Texas?"

"Sounds fascinating, but not tonight. I think you both need to get to bed. And, Nola, please pick up your room first—Mrs. Houlihan said she'd like to be able to fit a vacuum in there tomorrow."

Nola pushed away from me. "But I'm so tired!" she said, her shoulders and body slumping as if she'd been excavating rocks and moving them uphill all day.

"You should have thought about that when you were dropping your dirty socks on the floor instead of in your laundry basket," Jack said, and I looked at him appreciatively.

We said our good-byes and watched as Nola slowly climbed the stairs, her feet dragging exaggeratedly. "Time to milk the cows, plow the back forty, feed the chickens . . ."

I hid my smile. "I'm just asking you to pick up your room, Nola."

". . . stack hay in the barn, fix the tractor . . ." she continued until we heard her door shut upstairs.

I thought about telling Jack about my conversation with Michael, but then thought better of it. His expression was drawn and thoughtful, a look I recognized when the writing wasn't going well. I knew at least one way to make him feel better.

I tugged on Jack's hands. "You ready to go upstairs?"

"Actually, it's weird, but ever since you came down the stairs after settling Jayne, I'm feeling a little rush of creativity. I haven't written at night in a long time, but with my daylight writing sort of dwindling, I think tonight's a good time to resurrect it." As if anticipating my protests, he put his finger to my lips. "Only temporarily—until I get a good idea where I'm heading with this book. Don't forget, you'll have General Lee if your feet get cold. And there's always the morning." He looked at me suggestively.

"All right," I said, already missing him upstairs in our bed, trying to focus on how General Lee was a much better foot warmer anyway. "Why do you think you're getting this little shot of adrenaline now?"

"I have no idea. Maybe it's the pictures and the saltshaker—maybe I just needed visuals. Which is why I'm now convinced that I need to go to Alabama for a few days. See if I can talk to anybody who remembers Lake Jasper and who might know if May thirtieth, 1984, is significant. I'm probably grasping at straws, but there are so many different loose ends and I'm convinced that there's a real story here somewhere."

I threaded my fingers through his hair. "I'll miss you. I'd go with you if my schedule weren't jam-packed at work—which is a really good thing. We could use the money." I hadn't yet mentioned the wood-boring beetles Sophie had discovered in the dining room floor, and thought I'd save that for later, too.

"It's just for a few nights. And then hopefully I'll get some new material to inspire me and that might actually make a book."

My gaze fell to the hall table. "What's this doing here?" I asked, walking over to pick up the frame that had been on Button's nightstand, the one of her and Sumter at a party. I stared at their smiling faces, barely noticing the anonymous woman neatly clipped from the photo.

Jack came over and took it from me. "I have no idea. It was on my desk last time I looked. Nola must have moved it. Remind me to ask her in the morning."

I looked closely at the photo, noticing for the first time the date in tiny, faded ink on the bottom right of the photo. "March seventeenth, 1984. Must have been a St. Patrick's Day party—that's why her dress is green and he's wearing a green-striped tie."

"Probably," Jack agreed, taking the frame from me.

We kissed good night and then he retired to his study, bringing the frame with him. I slowly climbed the stairs, thinking about my conversation with Michael, and the photo of Sumter and Button on my hallway table. I was halfway up before the grandfather clock struck the hour, four long chimes that echoed in the sleeping house.

CHAPTER 25

I stared out at the spidery cables holding up the Ravenel Bridge from my spot at the beginning of the footpath that ran parallel to the traffic bridge as it crossed the Cooper River. A large semi thundered by, making me take a step back, and then look again at Sophie.

"You want to do what?" I asked, the sun already baking the back of my neck with no hint of shade in sight. She'd driven me to what she referred to as simply "a new place for us to exercise." I hadn't suspected that she was actually trying to kill me.

"I thought we could do the bridge run. It's only ten K—six-point-two miles for those of you who didn't learn metric—and you only have to go one way. It's on April second, so we're too late for this year, but if we start conditioning now we can run it next year."

I stared at her for a few moments, then began walking away. "I'll wait for you in the car. I've got some calls I need to make."

Sophie ran after me and grabbed my elbow. "I'm not suggesting that we run six miles today. I'm saying we do a little bit every week, and build up slowly. It's like restoring a house—you can't do it in just a day."

She smiled brightly, and I wanted to shake her. With my hands on my hips, I stared up at the bridge again. "I don't know, Sophie. . . ."

"Jayne said that she's already registered to run it this year."

That captured my attention. "Is she?" I looked at the various groups of walkers and runners moving on and off the bridge. They appeared to be of all ages and genders, some with well-muscled calves and toned hips in their running gear, and a whole lot of others that, well, looked more like me.

"The great thing about running," Sophie said as almost an after-thought, "is that it burns enough calories that you can splurge on a doughnut once in a while and it won't make the scale tip."

I frowned at her, but when I didn't start running for the car, she went in for the kill. "We can start by walking. I'll set my phone for fifteen minutes and when it beeps we'll head back. No fuss, no muss."

I wasn't sure whether it was the thought of Jayne's running 6.2 miles or my eating a doughnut without censure, but I dropped my arms and walked past Sophie. "Come on, then, let's get this over with. But we're only walk-ing today. I don't think I could handle running up this incline right now."

"Deal," she said, catching up to me and beginning to pump her arms.

Half an hour later we'd returned to our starting spot. Sophie had barely broken a sweat, whereas I was panting like a dog that had just finished the Iditarod and was soaked with enough sweat that an unsus-pecting passerby might assume that I'd just swum across the river. Once I was back in Sophie's Prius and had the air-conditioning blasting on me, I felt a modicum of pride that I had managed *something*.

Sophie turned the key in the ignition. "Before I take you home, do you have a few minutes to drop by the Pinckney house? I found a stack of photo albums in Button's room. I thought we could box them up and you can bring them to Jayne to go through and figure out what she wants to do with them. I'm afraid they'll get damaged if we leave them in the house during the renovation."

I checked my phone and then my watch before checking the clock in the car just to make sure. "I've got a closing at eleven, but I think I can spare about an hour before I have to get ready. Do you think we could get it done by then?"

Sophie stuck out her lower lip as she looked in her rearview mirror and flipped on her signal before pulling out onto East Bay. "Oh, absolutely. I seriously doubt it will take long at all."

I sent her a dubious look but refrained from mentioning that my house was a never-ending construction zone despite her earlier assurances that the renovation would last less than six months. I'd reconciled with both parents, gotten married, had two babies, and added a stepdaughter since we began work and the house still wasn't completely renovated. I simply didn't have enough breath in my lungs, so I kept silent and stuck my face in front of the air-conditioning vent.

I was relieved to see that Rich Kobylt and several workers were at the house when we pulled up. Not that I was convinced the spirits would leave us alone if we outnumbered them, but it bolstered my nerves before I walked up the steps to the front door. I stood in the foyer, listening to the now-familiar sounds of construction in various places in the house—sawing, hammering, the metallic clank and squeak of ladders and scaffolding. It took me a moment to realize that I was listening for something else, too. And then I heard it. Or maybe I *felt* it. I was semirelieved that the curtain had been pulled back so there were no barriers between me and the spirit world, and I knew it would be only a matter of time before it showed itself to me, too.

"Anna?" I whispered, preferring not to be surprised by an appearance. "Hasell?" I said a little louder. The soft tread of bare feet on the floor above us let me know that I'd been heard. *Hasell,* I thought. But she didn't want to be seen, not yet. I could sense the presence of the other spirit, the one I was convinced was poor Anna, and I wondered if she was the one holding Hasell back. And I wondered why.

I followed Sophie up to the second floor, feeling someone watching us as we proceeded down the hallway to Button's bedroom. I held my breath as I walked in and focused my gaze on the thankfully empty chair where the Edison doll had been found.

"Any word on the value of the doll yet?" I asked.

She shook her head. "Not yet. John took it to an antique doll show in Cleveland, which is probably why we haven't heard from her recently. Isn't there some rule about spirits not being able to cross water?"

"I really don't think there are any 'rules.' And if there were, I'm sure there would be one against old dolls dematerializing and then appearing where they're not supposed to be."

"Good point," she said, walking to the tall mirrored armoire and opening it up. "If you'll pull out the albums, I'll go find a box we can load them in."

I almost begged her not to leave me alone and to suggest we stick together, but she'd already left the room. Making sure the bedroom door was wide-open, I knelt on the floor in front of the armoire and peered inside. Stacked neatly together were three columns of dark brown leather albums with gold-embossed years on the spines spanning from 1960 through 1985—the year the lake was flooded. I pulled them out one by one, careful not to tear the bindings, then stacked them in three piles, loosely organized by decade but not by year. I knew Sophie would be expecting me to sort them by year, and it killed me not to, but it would be worse to prove her right.

Sophie returned, lugging two medium-size boxes with the name of a grout compound stamped on the outside. "I made a bet with myself that you'd have them organized by date by the time I came back." She dumped them in the middle of the room. "I win."

"Ha! They're only sorted by decade, not by year. But we probably should before we give them to Jayne so it's easier for her to go through them." I neglected to add that I wouldn't be able to sleep knowing they'd been tossed haphazardly in a box.

Sophie knelt next to me and grabbed the first album. "Did you look inside any of them yet?"

"No," I said sheepishly. "I was too busy organizing them."

She opened the cover of the one from 1960. "It looks like these were all photos taken at the lake house. If they were once kept at the lake, I'm guessing Button decided these albums would be worth saving. It's kind of sad, though, seeing as how there's nobody left who might find these photographs meaningful."

I took the album into my lap and studied the large photograph in the middle of the first page. It was one of the old magnetic albums, not the archival-quality scrapbooks that Sophie made me use for all my own family photographs, and the colors had started to leach from the photos, the faces exiting like souls leaving this world. The photograph showed a Craftsman-style cottage with lots of porches and rocking chairs, and a long dock sticking out into the dark waters of the lake. It was so different from the mansion on South Battery, as if a conscious effort had been made to create a cozy family home without all the frills and ornamentation of their house in the city. A family of four—mother, father, older son, younger sister—stood on the dock with the house in the background, smiling at the photographer. I leaned forward to study the girl, vaguely recognizing her.

"That's Button," Sophie said. "I carefully peeled off the photo to see if anybody had written anything on the back. From my random checking, I figure that most if not all of the photos have been labeled. Sadly, they're all written in blue ink and some of the writing has already started bleeding into the photos." She pointed to a spot on the photograph, a thin blue vein hovering over the mother's head. "This was taken during the Pinckney's first summer at the lake, and it's a picture of the whole family—Rosalind, Sumter Senior and Junior, and Button. She's about eight or nine."

"They look so happy," I said, slowly turning the pages, looking at the sunburned faces and tanned legs of the family and friends having fun on the water and in and around the house in various seasons. I quickly thumbed through all the pages before handing it back to Sophie to place in the box. I rubbed my palms against my pants legs, feeling as if I'd just been caught spying.

Sophie added a few more of the albums to one of the boxes before handing another album to me. "Check this one out."

I flipped it to the spine to read the year—1967. I began turning the pages, seeing more images of faded photos of the same family, older in these photos, as well as a rotating group of visitors. There were picnics on the dock and yard, and lots of photos of various people on a boat and water-skiing, swimming in the lake, lying on the dock.

I stopped suddenly, recognizing my mother. She was in her mid-teens, looking like a swimsuit model with her long limbs and rounded bust. She and Button and another girl all wore bathing caps and relatively modest one-piece bathing suits, and were lying on towels on the dock, sunbathing. "It's a good thing she wasn't around when I was a teenager to tell me to use sunscreen, because I could have used this photo for blackmail." I'd meant it as a joke, but my throat caught. As a teenager I would have given anything to have a mother to make me wear sunscreen, or tell me how to put on makeup, or buy me a well-fitting bra. All those things that I'd had to figure out for myself.

"That's Anna," Sophie said, pointing to the third girl.

The girl was squinting into the camera, her cap hiding her hair and making it difficult to see what she looked like. I tried to see the tragic woman she'd become, the mother of a lost child, in this girl's upturned face, but she was a blank canvas to me. Unreadable.

I thumbed through the rest of the album, seeing more photos of the family, the three girls, and Sumter. He was a dead ringer for a young Robert Wagner, and I imagined it would have been hard for Button's friends to ignore him. Somewhere, though, there'd been a falling-out between Anna and my mother, and despite Ginette's protests, I'd have to guess it was over Sumter Pinckney. As I quickly flipped through all the albums, I noticed there were fewer and fewer photos of my mother, and more of just Anna and Button, and Anna and Sumter. My parents had been married in 1972, so maybe that was what had happened. And then I was born, and my mother left for New York to further her singing career, leaving all of us behind.

"It's sad to think all this is gone," I said. "Not just the house, but most of the people; the memories. It's almost like none of it ever existed."

"It is sad," Sophie said, stacking more albums in one of the boxes. "It's how I feel when I find an abandoned or dilapidated old house. How can a structure that was a family's home for more than a century suddenly become obsolete? Especially when so much is left behind— personal items, even. As if they've simply been erased."

I handed her the last album, catching sight of the year embossed on the spine—1985. "Hang on. I think we skipped one. The last one I gave you was 1983. Where's 1984?"

Sophie began shifting the albums, reading aloud all the years from the spines. "Nineteen eighty-two, eighty-three, eighty-five." She turned to the other box and did the same thing, reading out consecutive years from 1960 through 1979. "It's not here. Hang on." She moved to the armoire and knelt in front just as I had, and stuck her hands in the dark corners to make sure I hadn't missed any. "Empty," she said, frowning. "I wonder what happened to it."

"Maybe it wasn't with the rest when Button brought all of them from the lake house. Which is sad because if it was left behind it's gone forever. Just like that beautiful house."

"Not necessarily," Sophie said as she folded up the box flaps. "The architectural plans still exist, so it's possible it could be rebuilt somewhere else if anybody is so inclined. I was at the Historic Foundation archives with my students working on another project, and decided to see what I could find out about Hasell Architecture and Construction. That hidden staircase and door were not designed by amateurs. I'm curious as to their provenance. Jayne's allowing me to use the restoration as a project for my grad students, and it's an important detail."

She straightened and handed me a box before picking up the other. She led me down the stairs while she spoke. "Most, if not all, of the company's records are there—including blueprints for many of the buildings they designed and restored."

"And?" I said, my muscles straining as I reached the landing, aware again of being watched. There was definitely more than one presence; I could sense the tug-of-war going on along the periphery of my vision. I rested the box on the banister, trying to get an impression of whether it was safe to continue. I took a step and paused, suddenly awash in the awareness that I was being kept safe. From what and by whom, I wasn't sure. I reached the foyer and dropped my box on top of Sophie's, trying to pretend I wasn't out of breath.

"Anyway," Sophie continued, without even a hint that she'd just carried a heavy box down a flight of stairs, "Anna's name was prominent on many of the designs. Meaning it was truly a family business, and her father wasn't pandering to her by putting her name on the letterhead. I mean, she did have an architecture degree, so it makes sense. But that was the early seventies—and design and construction was definitely still very much a man's world."

I worried my lip for a moment, thinking. "So Anna would have had the knowledge needed to design the hidden door in the attic once the staircase was discovered."

Sophie nodded in agreement. "Not to mention the door into the butler's pantry—it's pretty sophisticated the way it opens and closes so that it's seamless. The old steps continue past the cement wall, which makes me believe that they were definitely used to get to the outside once upon a time and the entrance into the butler's pantry was added later."

"Was there an earlier door leading from the attic to the old set of steps?"

"Definitely. It's apparent from looking at the studs that a larger opening once existed and then must have been closed off when the lower level was filled in and the steps didn't lead anywhere anymore. It would make sense that both the new hidden attic door and the butler's pantry access were put in at the same time, and since Anna was in the business, she probably knew a painter who could replicate the mural Sumter had painted so no one was the wiser about the hidden stairway."

"But why go to all that trouble? It's the same number of steps if you take the hidden stairs or the attic stairs."

Her eyes met mine. "Exactly what I was wondering. And the only answer I can come up with is that whoever put them in—and I'm assuming it was Anna or at least on her instructions—did so to keep their comings and goings a secret."

"That makes no sense. Anna was Hasell's mother, in charge of her care, so of course she went up and down from the attic room often."

"Unless . . ." Sohie said, then stopped.

"Unless what?"

"Unless she was trying to hide the comings and goings of somebody else."

I frowned. "But who? It would help if I could speak with either Anna or Hasell. They're both here—now. I feel them. And I think I could see them if they wanted me to—nothing's being blocked like before. But one of them doesn't want to be seen, and the other is protecting me."

"Protecting you?"

I nodded. "I have no idea from what, but I definitely get that feeling."

Sophie nudged the boxes with her foot. "Let's get these to my car."

"I need to use the bathroom first—my bladder hasn't yet recovered from my pregnancy and still seems to be the size of a peanut. Is there one that's usable?"

"Yes—the one adjacent to Button's room. I've tidied it up some, too, since my girl students were complaining that they had to use the Port-O-Lets outside."

"There isn't one down here?"

"Not one that works."

If only I hadn't had the entire water bottle Sophie had made me drink. I looked up at the stairs, weighing my options. I'd already gone up and back without incident, so it made sense that I should be able to do it again. If I was really fast. "I'll be right back," I said, then ran up the stairs, determined to get back downstairs before the unhappy spirit realized I was upstairs again. I walked quickly through Button's room to the bathroom, thinking twice before I decided to leave the door open. There was no window in the small space, and only one bulb flicked on when I hit the switch. Nobody else was upstairs, and I was going to be quick. I just felt the need to be able to see into the bedroom.

I began humming "Dancing Queen" as I reached for the waistband of my yoga pants and then stopped, feeling a definite shift in the air, a sliding together of light and dark. The temperature dropped and I shivered, but not from the cold.

I heard a noise, a slight *tap-tap* on the open door. I stared at the empty space, knowing something was there, knowing if I really wanted to, I could see it. "Anna? Hasell?" I whispered, then waited, my breaths coming out in white, silent puffs.

For several long moments, I stood there without moving, just wait-ing. I wanted to tell them to leave, that nobody wanted them there and that the house now belonged to Jayne. But if I'd learned anything in the years since my mother had returned to my life and we'd sent other restless spirits onto the next step on their journey, I knew it wasn't that simple. Wishing it were would never make it true.

I took a deep breath. "Please let me help you. You don't have to be here anymore. Just let me help."

The door swung shut so fast it grazed the side of my face. I stepped back in surprise, and found myself at the sink staring into an ancient mirror with half of the silvered backing flaked off.

Go away. The words were screamed inside my head, my eardrums ringing from the shrillness. I felt the pain on my neck immediately, the skin raw and stinging like multiple scratches, and I wanted to cry out, but I was already screaming. I had only a moment to register the blond woman with the wild hair and hollow eyes standing behind me, a deep purple welt encircling her neck, before the lightbulb exploded, sending me into complete darkness.

CHAPTER 26

I must have been desperately scratching at the bathroom door, because by the time Sophie turned the knob—she insisted it wasn't locked—and pulled the door open, I had broken three nails and the skin on the back of my neck felt as if it were on fire.

"What happened?" she asked, clutching both of my shoulders after I stumbled into the bedroom. I was grateful for the support, not sure I could have remained standing without it.

"Anna," I gasped. "It was Anna. I saw her—in the mirror. She had . . . bruises." I couldn't say it out loud. Instead I pointed to my throat.

"Bruises on her neck? Like a hanging victim?"

I nodded.

She brushed my hair off my neck. "What happened here?"

I touched the nape of my neck and my hand came back sticky with blood, the salt from my fingertips stinging the wound. "She scratched me. And told me to go away."

Sophie grabbed my arm and began dragging me toward the door. "Let's get you out of here. Can you handle the stairs?"

I paused, testing the air around me to make sure Anna was gone, then nodded. Sophie clutched my arm and walked with me down the stairs, then out of the house to her car. She blasted the air-conditioning and I sat down, catching sight of both boxes that were already in the backseat.

"So, what do you think that was all about?" Sophie asked, her eyes wide, her hair sprouting curly whorls around her head from the humidity.

"I'm not sure, but I do think I know one thing: Anna is the one who doesn't want us there. It must be Hasell who balances her mother's rage. I've heard of possessive spirits who didn't welcome intruders, but Anna seems to have gone a little overboard. And I have no idea why Hasell is still here—unless it's to act as a barrier between her mother and the living."

"I'd be inclined to agree with you, except for this." She reached behind my seat and pulled out a reusable grocery bag—one of several I knew she always kept in her car. She dumped it on my lap, and whatever objects were inside rolled against one another with a light clacking noise.

"Open it," she said.

I did as she instructed, then reached inside and pulled out the base of a broken snow globe, the word SACRAMENTO spelled out in plastic block lettering in bright green. The back two legs of a Pony Express pony stuck to the base, its front hooves broken off. "I found four smashed snow globes when I went up to the attic to instruct the guys where to move everything so we could begin the roof repair. They were in a neat circle, as if they were broken intentionally and for a purpose. I would even go as far as saying that they were broken in such a way as to cause the least damage. Like they were trying to send a message instead of being just destructive."

"When nobody was up there?" I asked, fishing inside the bag. I pulled out two more, one from Indianapolis and another from Kalam-azoo, then carefully let them drop.

"Yeah. Weird, huh? I thought it might mean something, so I picked up all the bases—including the three that were broken when you were up there with Jayne—and had one of my guys use pliers to make sure all the sharp glass was removed. I put them in here for you. Just in case one—or both—of the ghosts is trying to tell us something."

"Thanks," I said, and leaned my head against the seat, closing my eyes for a moment, then opened them immediately when the image of the hollow-eyed Anna flashed against the inside of my eyelids. I made the mistake of touching the back of my neck and I winced.

"Let me get you home," Sophie said. "You'll want to wash those scratches and put something on them. Should I call Jack?"

"He's in Alabama. He's fascinated with the Pinckneys and the whole flooded town and thinks he might be able to find out more about the family, and maybe something about any connection to Jayne. It's a long shot, but he's struggling with this next story idea and really needs a kicker. He's hoping there's more to Jayne's story, and if there is, he's determined to find out."

She started the engine but faced me before putting the car in reverse. "You're kind of pale and still shaking. Do you want me to stay with you? I can ask somebody to take my classes. And I promise not to read your tarot cards."

"No, but thanks. I'm fine. Just glad to be out of that house."

We both stared up at the imposing white house as Sophie backed out of the driveway onto South Battery. As she watched for traffic, I kept my gaze on the attic window, feeling the sense that somebody was there, watching us. Waiting for us to leave. Sophie pulled onto the street and put the car in drive, diverting my attention. I glanced back at the house as she headed north toward Tradd Street, and I caught sight of the black cat sitting on the front portico, staring at me with its one good eye from between two wrought-iron rails, its tail wagging slowly until it disappeared from view.

∽

I sat on the floor of the nursery with the twins, stacking blocks for the babies to knock over again and again. They would dissolve into hysterics each time and I had a strong suspicion that we could do this all night long with two of us not getting tired of the game. It was Jayne's night off and I'd dressed the children in matching pajamas and had taken the time to blow-dry their hair after their baths so it wouldn't look as wild as Sophie's on a humid day. I planned to get into the nursery first thing to put the bows in Sarah's hair and lay out their clothes for the day before Jayne could intervene.

I glanced at the Humpty Dumpty clock and saw it was half an hour before their bedtime. I wondered if it would mess with their sleep schedule if I slept on the floor between their cribs for the next couple of nights. This was the first time Jack and I had slept apart since our wedding, and I could barely stand the thought of sleeping in our bed alone. General Lee didn't count.

There was a brief knock on the door and then Nola came in, followed by the two bouncing puppies and General Lee at a more sedate pace. Porgy and Bess immediately tumbled into the blocks and sitting babies, making Sarah and JJ peal with laughter.

"You should make a video of the babies and puppies and put it on YouTube. You could make a fortune," Nola said dryly. "That's almost a little too much cuteness."

"What's YouTube?" I asked.

She stared at me for a moment as if unsure whether I was joking. "I'll show you sometime." She sat down next to me and drew both babies into her lap while the dogs began tumbling with each other until General Lee gave a disciplinary bark and they settled down in a heap by his side.

"I guess it's Jayne's night off?" she asked. "I can tell by the matching pajamas. Jayne's not as OC . . . um, particular about what they wear, I guess you could say. I mean, it's not like they need uniforms so we can tell they're ours, you know?"

I narrowed my eyes but didn't say anything. I was too tired from all the events of the day, not to mention being attacked by a ghost, and I just didn't have the resources to defend myself or explain why I did the things I did. Probably because I wasn't even sure myself.

"Since Dad's not here, I took the dogs outside already so you don't have to."

"Thanks, Nola. I appreciate that."

She was frowning, which always meant she had more to say, so I remained quiet until she spoke again. "I tried to take them out the back door, but they wouldn't go. It's hard to move twelve locked paws out of a house and down steps, so I took them out the front door."

"I don't blame them," I said. "I avoid the back door, too, and probably for the same reason."

We both raised our eyebrows in mutual understanding.

"Unfortunately, Meghan broke her foot and it's delaying the excavation process. It's going to be a while until they can get back to it."

She frowned in contemplation as Sarah crawled from her lap toward the chest of drawers where I'd placed the bag Sophie had given me. I'd forgotten all about it, having meant to leave it downstairs, but I'd had the handle around my arm when I carried the boxes of albums inside to Jack's study and then had run upstairs to see the children. I'd needed to see them in an almost desperate way. There was something reassuring and stress-relieving about stroking their hair and soft skin, and feeling their little arms hug my neck. Even drool on my cheek was something I looked forward to.

I turned to Nola. "Has your father asked you about the frame that was on his desk downstairs? It suddenly reappeared in the foyer and we were wondering if maybe you had moved it and why."

"Seriously? You think I'd go into my dad's office and move something? I treasure my hands and fingers too much. So, no. I don't even go to his corner of the room. Actually, I haven't been in that room for a while, even to play the piano. My music is still not cooperating—at least not here. If I'm in the park or somewhere not here, I'm fine."

"Must be something in the air, since your dad is having the same issue. I'm sure it's a passing thing. But are you sure you didn't pick up the frame by mistake?"

She sent me a leveling look. "Positive."

I frowned, not sure which was more upsetting—the fact that she was in a creative crisis or that she hadn't moved the frame. And neither had Mrs. Houlihan or Jayne.

Sarah pulled herself up against the chest and banged on it with both hands, looking up. "What's that?" Nola asked, standing with JJ in her arms. He'd be content to stay there for hours if allowed.

"I guess it belongs to Jayne. They're what remain of seven snow globes that were broken in the attic of the Pinckney house. They're part of a collection that belonged to Hasell Pinckney—the young girl who died."

"How'd they get broken?" Nola asked as she carefully pulled them out of the bag with one hand and began placing them in a row on the flat top of the dresser.

"Good question," I said, rising to get Sarah, who was now bouncing up and down with excitement. "The first three were broken to get our attention, I'm guessing, and Sophie seems to think the last four were broken intentionally. She said it looked like they'd been placed deliberately."

Sarah began fretting and reaching for the bases, but I held her back, aware of the sharp edges of glass that might still be on them.

Nola grimaced. "Why would Sophie give them to you?"

"Just in case they were some sort of message, she said. I figured I'd give them to Jayne and let her decide what to do with them."

Sarah was in the throes of a full meltdown and I attempted to give her a pacifier, which she immediately spat out. "She was absolutely fine a minute ago. I have no idea what's got into her," I said, bouncing her on my hip and walking away, but she kept reaching for the remains of the snow globes, throwing herself into a full backward arch.

Nola picked up the gray-painted base with a suspension bridge still crossing a blue-painted ribbon of water, the word *Cincinnati* written with silver plastic lettering on the lip. She held it up to Sarah, just out of her reach, and the baby shook her head, then pushed out her hands in an emphatic no.

"What are you doing?" I asked, wondering if I should take Sarah's temperature.

"Hang on." Nola held up the one from Ottawa and then Sacramento, each receiving the same reaction.

"Nola," I said, struggling to hold on to the squirming baby. "I think that's enough."

"Just one more," she insisted, grabbing the one from Miami and holding it up for Sarah to see.

She immediately calmed down, settling into my arms and laying her head on my shoulder to show me she was tired. She pointed at all that remained of the Miami snow globe, then placed her finger in her mouth with a contented sigh.

My gaze met Nola's. "Miami?"

She shrugged, the movement making JJ laugh. "Maybe she just likes Miami."

"Or there's something about that particular snow globe she's trying to tell us."

"True," Nola said, resting her chin on the top of JJ's head, which had sunk onto her shoulder. "Or something someone *else* is trying to tell us through her."

I'd thought the same thing but hadn't wanted to say it out loud. But now there it was, out in the open, where I couldn't ignore it. "Let's put the babies to bed, and then I'm going to move those things out of here."

"What are you going to tell Jayne?" Nola asked as she gently lowered JJ into his crib and found his pacifier before covering him with a blanket.

"Maybe I'll just give her the bag of broken snow globes and tell her it was an accident. It's pretty close to the truth. Anything closer and I think we might send Jayne screaming into the nearest woods."

I kissed Sarah's forehead and placed her gently in her crib before covering her with a blanket that matched JJ's. Nola held open the door for the dogs to follow her, then waited for me in the hallway as I carefully placed the bases in the bag before joining her.

"Do you really think she would?" Nola asked. "It seems to me that she's a lot more accepting of all the weird stuff that goes on around you than the average person."

I stared at her, remembering Jack and me having this same conversation before agreeing that it was probably because of Jayne's background in foster care, when she'd learned that she couldn't afford to be surprised or disappointed or shocked or risk being labeled a "bad fit." It was what made her such a good nanny. She knew how to absorb the rhythms of a family in a short amount of time, to assimilate and blend seamlessly into family life. At least that was what Jack had said. I'd been so busy trying to hide the weird stuff from her that I'd simply assumed I was doing a good job.

"I don't know," I said. "But I'm not willing to rock the boat and upset her. If I can just figure out how to get rid of the ghosts in her new house, she doesn't need to know anything."

Nola stared at me skeptically. I was saved from having to say more by my phone ringing the familiar tone of "Dancing Queen." I pulled my phone from my pocket and looked at the screen. "It's your dad." I thrust the bag at her. "Put these in a closet or something until I can explain to Jayne what they are. I'm going to take this."

She took the bag and gave me a thumbs-up before heading to her room with the two puppies at her heel, General Lee at mine.

"Hello?" I said, leaning against my closed bedroom door.

"Hey, sexy." Jack's voice on the phone always did shocking things to my system, but tonight the effect seemed amplified, most likely because of his absence and me missing him so much.

"I miss you," I said, trying not to sound too pathetic.

"Not as much as I miss you. How are Nola and the twins?"

"We're all good." I made the snap decision not to tell him about that morning's episode. It would just make him worry, and there wasn't anything he could do about it anyway. "Just missing you. The whole time I was trying to feed Sarah in her high chair, she kept glancing over at the kitchen door as if expecting you to walk through it." I stopped, recalling my earlier conversation with Nola and realizing that there might actually have been other reasons for her to be looking at the back door. "I can't wait for you to get home." I sounded pathetic but didn't care. I *did* miss him. It was hard to believe that I'd been single for the first forty years of my life, living on my own, until Jack Trenholm came into my life and flipped it on its back. Literally.

There was a pause. "Actually, that's why I'm calling. I need to spend another night here before I head back."

I didn't say anything, afraid I'd start crying and embarrass myself.

"Every lead was turning into a dead end and I was thinking I'd probably come back a day early. I was headed out of town when I stopped at the public library that contains the historic archives from the whole county, and also includes the archives of the flooded town."

I could hear the excitement in his voice, so I focused on that instead of my own disappointment. "And what did you find?"

"Well, I was talking to the archivist, a lovely woman named Mabel, and when I told her I was looking for information on the Pinckney family and their house on Lake Jasper, she got all excited. Her older sister was the housekeeper—the one mentioned in Rosalind's letter—at the lake house. Her husband, now deceased, was the caretaker. Her name is Rena Olsen, and Mabel gave me her phone number, so I called her and she told me to come tomorrow. She's in an assisted-living facility in Birmingham, so it's a bit of a drive, but I have a feeling it would be worth it. She said she's been wanting to tell her stories for a long time—just waiting for someone to ask, I guess. She said she took a toaster and a few other items from the house before it was flooded, and feels guilty about it. She probably wants absolution or something. I should find out more tomorrow."

I couldn't share his enthusiasm, as it seemed the old woman was simply looking for someone to talk to. But this was his job, this researching of every avenue even when it might terminate in a dead end. And even when I believed it would be a waste of time. "That's wonderful, Jack. Maybe you can ask her if the city of Miami means anything." I gave him a brief account of Hasell's broken snow globes and Sarah's odd behavior.

"Sounds like an obscure lead, but I hate to leave any stone unturned. I'll definitely ask her. And when I'm done with the interview, I'll head home."

"Will you call me as soon as you're done?" I hated the neediness in my voice, but I was too tired to disguise it.

"Of course. But only if you keep my side of the bed warm for me."

"You know I will. Good night, Jack."

"Good night, Mellie."

"I love you," I said before realizing that he'd already ended the call.

I dropped my phone on top of the bedside table, then leaned against the side of the tall bed to stroke General Lee's ears while I tried to get a handle on my emotions. He rolled over on his back so I could give his undercarriage a good scratch that somehow made both of us feel a little better.

After a few moments I straightened and was headed toward my closet when I heard a strange sound from behind me. I looked back at General Lee, who was now sound asleep with all four paws in the air, but I was fairly certain what I'd heard hadn't been a dog snore. My gaze scanned the room until it came to rest on the dresser across from the bed, where I'd placed my three extra alarm clocks. I held my breath—but not because all the clocks still showed ten minutes after four despite my having changed them multiple times. Someone had nudged the framed photo of Button and Sumter between them, the reflection from the glass whitewashing the picture and replacing it with a long sliver of light that closely resembled a finger.

"Leave me alone," I said, too exhausted to face one more thing. I turned back around and was almost at my closet door when I felt more than heard the frame whip the air behind me and smack the far wall before landing with a soft thud onto the rug.

I continued walking, quickly closing the closet door behind me, happy to pretend that nothing had happened.

CHAPTER 27

I sat on the piazza trying to get a little paperwork done and pretending I was taking advantage of the gorgeous weather instead of pathetically waiting outside to be the first person aware of Jack's return. I was in one of Mr. Vanderhorst's rocking chairs, still trying to understand how people could just sit and stare out at the world. Every once in a while I caught myself doing that, admiring the hanging baskets of garish purple and red blooms that my father had placed at intervals on the piazza, and listening to the fountain that unfortunately made me need to use the restroom. I'd quickly look down at my papers to remind myself that I couldn't afford to just sit on my porch and watch the world go by.

The front door opened behind me and Jayne joined me. "Melanie— do you have a moment?"

"Sure," I said, feeling a fissure of apprehension as I indicated the rocking chair next to me. She'd lasted a week longer than all the previous nannies combined and I'd already made the decision that I wasn't going to give her up easily. I was already preparing a truce about the matching outfits and labeling gun, in addition to a sizable raise if only she would keep her letter of resignation that I was sure was forthcoming.

"JJ and Sarah are down for their naps, so I figured I'd try a recipe for their dinner from the baby food cookbook Sophie gave you."

"Good," I said, biting my tongue before I could remind her that they sold baby food already prepared at the grocery store. She looked uncomfortable and I knew she had more to say. I braced myself, my knees pressed together and my hands gripping the arms of the rocker while I tried to smile.

"But first I wanted to ask you about this." She held up the saltshaker that we'd taken from the Pinckney house that I'd last seen on Jack's desk.

I sat up. "Oh, Jack was just borrowing it. For visuals. I thought he'd asked your permission to take it from the house."

A small furrow formed over her nose. "No—I mean, yes, he did. I just wanted to know why it was on my bedside table this morning."

"It was?" I asked.

She looked confused. "Yes—I'm sure it wasn't there last night, but it was there when I woke up, and I was wondering if maybe you'd put it there."

"Why would you think I did it?"

Jayne shrugged. "I have no idea. I thought maybe because it had the year I was born on it, you might have thought I'd want it as a souvenir. But as I told Jack, he can keep it." She held it up so I could clearly read the date. *May 30, 1984.*

I shook my head. "Wasn't me. Maybe Nola had it in her hand when she went into your room to rescue one of the puppies and accidentally left it behind. They seem to like it in there. We probably need to get the latch fixed, because they have no problem pushing open your door."

"Probably," she said. "I can take care of that—I'm pretty handy." She stood. "I guess I'll just go put this back on Jack's desk. And please don't bother Nola about this. It's an easy thing to forget. I swear those puppies are baby ninjas. I wish I had just a fraction of their energy."

"Me, too." I looked at her placid face, and heard Jack's words in my head. *"She's used to fitting in and not making a stir. To accepting the unacceptable. Because that's what made the difference between staying with a family and being asked to go."*

Her smile broadened as she looked over my head to the street. "Better go put it back now—looks like Jack's home."

She went inside as I carefully placed my papers in a neat stack by the chair and stood, smoothing my hair and clothes. I opened the piazza door and was waiting on the steps as he approached, wondering what it was that was different about him. For once I wished I were wearing my glasses so I could read his expression instead of being left to wonder why his footsteps seemed to slow when he spotted me.

"Mellie," he said, sounding more surprised than excited. He came up the steps to stand beside me, dropping his bag on the floor and sweeping me up in a tight embrace. "I missed you so much," he said in my hair, almost making me forget the moment of worry I'd felt just seconds before.

"Me, too," I said, relaxing into his arms and allowing the relief of him being back home to sweep through me.

He pulled back and looked at me, and I saw lines under his eyes I hadn't noticed before. "You feeling all right?" I asked.

"Just tired. It's been a long few days."

"It has. Did you find out anything new from the housekeeper?"

He embraced me again and I had the stray thought that he did it to avoid meeting my eyes. "A little bit. She wanted to give Jayne the toaster and chair she took from the Pinckneys' house after they abandoned it because she still feels guilty. I did my best to set her mind to rest. And no, Miami meant nothing to her."

I pulled back to look into his eyes, but he was already reaching for his bag. "I'll tell you all about it later. But first I really need a long, hot shower and something to eat."

I watched him head toward the front door and then pause. "Is Jayne home?"

"Yes. Why?"

Jack smiled. "Because I wanted to know if it was safe to walk around naked after my shower. I don't want to scare her."

He bent down to give me one of his mind-emptying kisses that left me with a stupid smile on my face and only a vague memory of what we'd been talking about. I was still smiling as he made his way into the house, the door shutting behind him, my smile doing nothing to convince me that there wasn't something Jack wasn't telling me.

～

I sat in between my mother and Jayne at one of the makeup counters at Cos Bar on King Street, trying on makeup for the book-launch party the following evening. Jayne and I were, anyway. My mother was just trying on makeup for fun, much to the joy of the employee working with us. Ginette's flawless skin was the perfect canvas for makeup, and her years as an opera singer had taught her not to be afraid of looking dramatic—something she was trying to share with Jayne and me with mixed results.

I hadn't gone with my mother and Jayne to look for a dress, if only to prove that I wasn't petty or jealous and didn't care if they selected a dress that was prettier than mine. Jayne was the nanny and was going with Thomas Riley as her date. They actually made a very cute couple, and I thought they might even have a future together if Jayne could just learn to speak like a normal person when she was with him.

I hadn't seen her dress, but I was sure it was lovely, since my mother had helped pick it out, which, if I was forced to admit, hurt a little. Maybe not having had a mother for most of my life made me feel a little possessive. Jayne had grown up without any parents, but at least she hadn't known what she was missing. I had, and had known the pain of it being snatched away from me.

It was these guilty thoughts that made me agree to invite Jayne to pick out makeup for the big night, despite my protests that I shouldn't wear anything except a thick green moisturizing mask to go with my hair that I was planning to wear in pink curlers.

"All three of you have the most amazing eyelashes," Sultana, the beautiful woman with perfect skin and luminous eyes on the other side of the counter, said as she leaned in again with a mascara wand. "This one is a little more expensive, but it will give you the dramatic look you want with your smoky eye."

"A smoky eye? Won't that make them water?" Jayne asked. I shot her a look to see if she was serious. Apparently, she was.

"Let me show you," my mother said, picking up the sample of eye shadows that Sultana had been playing with. With expert precision, Ginette began covering Jayne's eyelids with color. "We're so lucky to all have deep-set eyes—it makes eye shadow application so much easier and so much fun. We can do tons of things that other girls can't because we have a much larger area to work with."

Sultana handed her a wand of black liquid liner and I watched as my mother perfected a cat's-eye on Jayne. Ginette picked up a hand mirror and showed her. "See? You almost look like someone else entirely— which is sort of the point of dressing up and going to a party, isn't it? It's like preparing for your part and your moment onstage."

She smiled at Jayne, but there was something in her expression as she regarded the younger woman. "What's your natural hair color, Jayne?"

"Dark brown," Jayne said with a little hesitation. She looked around for something to compare it to, finally settling on my hair. "Like Melanie's—but maybe a bit darker."

"Melanie's natural color is actually a little darker—she colors it now to hide the gray that's started to come through," my mother said matter-of-factly.

Sultana thrust a lipstick into my hands either to distract me or keep my hands occupied so they wouldn't do any damage. "Try this," she said. "It was all the rage at Charleston Fashion Week. It will look *gorgeous* on you."

As I applied the lipstick, my mother continued. "You look good as a blonde, Jayne, but I think you'd look stunning as a brunette. Don't you think, Mellie?"

"Uh-huh," I said, grateful for the lipstick that prevented me from forming full words. Otherwise I'd just ask my mother to shout to the world that her daughter was old and gray and that the nanny would outshine her if she'd color her hair back to brown. I closed my eyes, much to Sultana's protests that I would mess up my mascara. I just couldn't face myself in the mirror. Jayne might talk like a teenager at times, but I certainly had the inner teenage voice down pat.

Sultana took the opportunity while my eyes were closed to grab a tweezer and begin plucking at errant eyebrow hairs. "You look like a woolly mammoth," she said. "Let me clean these up for you."

I sighed, resigned to my just punishment for my earlier thoughts.

"Melanie?" Jayne asked.

I braced myself, wondering if she wanted to borrow a pair of shoes— we'd recently discovered that we wore the same size. "Yes?"

"I was wondering—did you hide one of Sarah's toys in that hall chest upstairs? She keeps crawling toward it and banging on the bottom drawer. I didn't want to pry, so I didn't look, but she certainly seems determined to get inside."

"Ouch," I said as Sultana ripped out a reluctant eyebrow hair and apparently a chunk of skin, judging by how much it hurt. I'd completely forgotten about the broken snow globes, or Nola telling me where she'd put them until I could tell Jayne. "Those are the remains of seven snow globes from the Pinckney house. They got broken, but Sophie was reluctant to throw them out, so I brought the bag home. Sarah saw them and was pretty fascinated, so I asked Nola to hide them until I could ask you what you wanted to do with them. Sarah must have seen her do it."

"Well, that explains it," Jayne said. "If it's all right with you, I'll take the bag out and show Sarah the empty drawer. Maybe she'll forget about it."

Ginette laughed. "Not likely—Sarah's pretty stubborn. She gets it from her mother. She's small and cute, but she's like a pit bull with a bone when she gets it in her head that she wants something."

I opened my eyes to find both Sultana and my mother studying my face. "Much better," Ginette said, nodding approvingly, then slid her credit card across the counter. "Go ahead and wrap all this up—my treat."

Despite our protests, Ginette insisted (obviously Sarah's genetic disposition toward stubbornness ran deeper than just one generation) and Sultana began sorting our selections to ring up.

Jayne walked behind the counter to the shelves of perfume and picked one up to sniff. "I'm wondering if there's a way she can play with the snow globes that might be safe. I mean, I wouldn't let her handle them or put them in her mouth, but maybe some kind of game I can make up that might make her happy?"

I considered for a moment. "Well, she did show a partiality toward the Miami one—was really vocal about that one being 'the one.' For what, I have no idea, but as soon as I showed that one to her, she was fine and then went to sleep. If you want to whip them out of the bag and lay them on a table for her to let you know when you get it right, go right ahead." I paused. "Just don't leave them in their room when you're done. I wouldn't want them to get hold of one of them, just in case there's still broken glass."

"All right." A frown crossed her brow. "How did they get broken?"

I cleared my throat while my mother unscrewed the lid of a face cream and took her time smelling it. "I'm not really sure. There's so much construction going on, and so many workmen. I asked Amelia if they might be worth anything, and she said no, so at least there's no restitution involved."

"Not that I'd make anybody pay for them anyway, since it's my fault they got broken," Jayne admitted. "I should have had them moved out of the house long before they started all the restoration work. It's just . . . I don't know. I don't feel as if the house is mine, and I'm finding it really difficult to make these decisions because I still think of the house and everything in it as belonging to Button Pinckney."

"That's normal," I said taking my shopping bag from Sultana. "If you work more closely with Sophie, she can help you put your personal stamp on things to make it feel more like yours. Well, assuming they're historically accurate. She's a little fanatical about that kind of stuff." I smiled brightly. "Of course, I can help you work around them. I'm a real expert on that." My smile faded as I remembered a few times when Sophie had discovered my subterfuge, my knees aching at the memory of me being forced to strip floors by hand after a contraband electric sander had been discovered in my possession. "As long as you don't let her know."

Jayne gave me a worried glance. "Okay. That's good to know. But I still wouldn't feel right. Maybe I'm holding out hope that Jack will discover some answers so I can move forward—mentally, anyway." The air behind her shifted, the temperature dropping as if an air conditioner had been switched on behind us, and I watched her shiver. She reached up a hand and brushed at the back of her neck, as if something had touched her, and I was glad for the scarf I wore that hid the scabs from the scratches I'd received in Button's bathroom. I met my mother's gaze, her eyebrows rising in acknowledgment that we weren't alone.

"Thank you, Ginette," Jayne said as she took her bag. "This wasn't necessary, but I do appreciate it. I had fun."

"Me, too," Ginette said, sneaking a glance behind us as she held open the door and we said good-bye to Sultana with promises to return.

Heavy clouds had been forming while we were inside, and a crack of thunder sounded above us as we made a dash down the street, trying to beat the rain. I turned my head to catch our reflection in the window, not surprised to see the pale form of a young girl in a white nightgown standing behind us, staring directly at me. *Help me.* Her lips didn't move, but the words sounded loud in my ear. I turned and ran faster to catch up, the words reverberating over and over until I began to hum loudly to block them out.

CHAPTER 28

I sat at the vanity in front of my bathroom mirror, playing with the makeup we'd purchased the previous day, frowning at my reflection and thinking I looked more like Tammy Faye Bakker than the glamorous appearance I was going for.

Nola sat on the counter, studying me as I'd seen her do at museum exhibits. "Can I do the eyeliner? I'm good at the cat's-eye look, and I don't think I can watch you remove everything and start over one more time. You're going to wear down your eyelid if you're not careful, and then you'll have to put makeup on your bare eyeball."

"Can that really happen?" I asked, not completely sure she was joking.

Instead of answering she jumped off the counter and took the eyeliner from my hand. Relieved, I closed my eyes, happy to have her expertise. "What would I do without you, Nola?"

"Same thing I'd do without you, so I guess that makes us even."

It took me a moment to realize that she'd just said something nice to me, most likely taking advantage of the fact that my eyes were closed and our positions made it difficult for me to hug her. "Thanks," I said.

She responded with a grunt. After a moment, she said, "I wish you'd go talk to Jayne. She thinks her dress is too revealing and wants to bring a sweater to cover her shoulders and cleavage. I'm thinking it's a pretty conservative dress and no sweater is needed. She'll just look ridiculous."

I remembered having the same conversation with my mother about the red dress she'd picked out for me for my fortieth birthday party. Jack had really liked it. I blushed a little at how much he'd liked it, sobering quickly when I remembered it had led to JJ and Sarah.

"If she feels more comfortable in a sweater, then she should bring it. It's still a little chilly at night and she might need it."

I felt Nola pull back. "Open," she commanded. She examined me closely, a small frown on her face. "Close," she said, then leaned toward me again with the eyeliner wand. "As soon as I'm done here, I'll go pack my overnight bag. I just hope Alston and her mom don't get here before Detective Riley. I want to be able to hear Jayne say hello to him."

She pulled back again and I opened my eyes. "Awesome!" She closed the wand and placed it on the vanity. She paused for a moment and then said, "Lindsey is spending the night at Alston's, too."

Nola didn't sound excited. "You like Lindsey, don't you?" I asked.

"Yeah. It's just . . ." She began picking at her cuticles and I had to bite my lip to not tell her to stop, as I'd found that usually made it worse. "It's just that she's always asking me about you. About when you're going to help her mom find out what happened to her aunt."

I remembered the uncomfortable conversation I'd had with Lindsey's father, something I'd only shared with my mother, since it didn't involve Jack and I didn't think he needed more stress. "It's not that easy, Nola. My brain is pretty much fully occupied with the issues at the Pinckney house, not to mention my career and family. I promised my mother that I would help just as soon as I scraped off a little more from my plate."

"Yeah, that's what I keep telling her." Nola paused. "She wants to bring the Ouija board to Alston's house tonight."

I sat up. "Don't, Nola. That's definitely a bad idea. It's like opening a window—you never know what might fly inside."

"I'll tell her." She opened the door to leave.

"Will Cooper be home this weekend?"

Her cheeks flushed. "I'm not sure. Alston acts funny when I ask about him, and I don't want to be the kind of girl always texting a guy to find out where he is. I like to keep him guessing."

"Smart girl. Don't forget to kiss the twins good-bye—especially JJ. He'll keep looking for you if he doesn't know you're gone. My mom and dad should be here in about fifteen minutes to pick them up; if you could, please let Mrs. Houlihan know." I'd asked the housekeeper to watch the babies while we got dressed, knowing that if JJ were let loose we'd have food stains or holes somewhere on our dresses and need to change.

"Will do," she said, then closed the door after a quick wave.

I lifted the lid to my jewelry box and pulled out the necklace my mother had given me and slipped it over my head. I picked up the ring and slid it on the middle finger of my right hand, admiring its shape and glossy black stone. I brought it closer to my face, studying it, a stray memory pinging in my brain. I was pretty sure I'd seen it before. Most likely when I was a little girl and my mother still wore it. I stared at it for a little longer, trying to remember a moment from my childhood, but couldn't. I closed the jewelry box and stood.

I entered my closet and took the black sparkly gown from the padded hanger, wondering not for the first time how I'd let my mother talk me into buying another sexy dress. At least this one wasn't red. I slipped it over my head, then spent about five minutes doing all sorts of yoga poses to get the zipper all the way to the top.

"Can I help?"

I startled at the sound of Jack's voice, then melted into him as he slid his warm hands under the open zipper, caressing bare flesh. "If you wouldn't mind," I managed.

He bent to place a kiss on my bare neck. "You look beautiful in this dress," he whispered in my ear, sending my nerve endings into a stadium-size wave of excitement. "But you'd look even better out of it."

"Hold that thought," I said. "I think I just heard a car pull up and it could be Thomas or my parents."

"Your mother's coming?" Jack pulled back.

I twisted in his arms. "Yes—don't you remember? I told you that the twins were staying with my parents tonight."

He frowned. "Yes, of course. I remember. I guess I was thinking that Jayne would have brought them over earlier or something."

"Jayne had to get dressed—hair, makeup, and all that. I didn't want her to have to pack up the twins and bring them over to my parents', especially since my mother said she'd be happy to do it."

He was still frowning, and I noticed again the lines that seemed to have appeared overnight. I stepped toward him, my palms flat against his chest. "What's wrong, Jack? Is there something you need to tell me? Something's been bothering you ever since you got back from Alabama."

He smiled his Jack smile, which would have reassured me completely if it hadn't been for the fact that his eyes didn't smile, too. "It's just the book. It's not coming along the way I thought it would."

I stood on my tiptoes to kiss him lightly. "It will. It always does. Just give it time."

He nodded, but his eyes remained worried. "Is Jayne driving with us tonight?"

"Yes. Thomas is coming over and we're driving over together."

"Oh." Jack sounded disappointed.

"What's wrong?"

"Nothing. I was just hoping for some time to talk with Jayne. We never get a chance to have a conversation."

I frowned up at him. "She's the nanny, Jack. Why would you need to have a conversation with her unless it involves the children and me?"

He smiled. "Just being friendly, Mellie. And I thought she'd want to know that Rena—the housekeeper at the Pinckneys' lake house— wants to hear it directly from Jayne that she's forgiven about taking some stuff from the house."

"I'm sure that can wait, Jack. I don't think there's much urgency there."

"No, I guess not," he said, kissing the tip of my nose. "Probably just looking for an opportunity to check it off my list."

I smiled up at him, trying to pinpoint exactly what it was in his expression that I found so unsettling.

My parents were already waiting downstairs when Jack and I joined them just as Thomas rang the doorbell. The dogs went crazy with barking until they saw that it wasn't anybody who seemed intent on scalping us all and calmed down, even allowing behind-the-ear scratches from Thomas. My dad was corralling the dogs in the kitchen when Jayne came down the stairs, and I wished that I had gone to the kitchen with him so I didn't have to see the look on Jack's face. It was different from the one on Thomas's face, but still full of admiration and appreciation of the feminine form. But there was something else in Jack's expression, something that looked a lot like familiarity. Or maybe it was recognition? Either way, it made something thick and hard form in the pit of my stomach.

"You look stunning," Thomas said, walking forward and taking her hand. For a minute it didn't look as though she'd relax her arm for him to move her hand to his lips, but at the last moment she allowed him to take it, dropping her sweater in the process.

"Thank you," she said, smiling shyly, making her eyes sparkle and her skin flush becomingly against the pale blue of her chiffon gown. My mother had done a great job of selecting a dress that was not only beautiful, but also cleverly styled to hide the sheer sexiness of it. The material shifted and swayed over Jayne's body, giving a tantalizing glimpse of skin a little at a time. A high slit that started midthigh gave it that little extra oomph.

Thomas bent to pick up her sweater and she took the opportunity to give him the once-over. "You're wearing pants."

His mouth twitched. "Yes, I usually do when I leave the house. But these match my tuxedo jacket, so I figured I'd wear these instead of my khakis."

My mother stepped forward, her hands outstretched. "You look lovely, Jayne. And so do you, Mellie," she said almost as an afterthought. She looked from one of us to the other. "Did you plan to wear your hair the same way?"

We looked at each other with surprise, noticing we'd both gone with the messy-bun look, complete with a rhinestone clip tucked into the left side. "Actually," I said, "it's just a coincidence."

Before Jack could say there was no such thing, Nola came bounding down the stairs with her Vera Bradley overnight bag. It was pink and floral and not to her taste at all, but Amelia had given it to her for Christmas, so she used it. "Picture time!" she said, holding up her iPhone.

"That's not really necessary . . ." I began, but my father was already reaching for the phone.

He gestured for us to all stand at the base of the stairs, and it felt absurdly like the senior prom I'd never had. He and my mother discussed the best poses and positions as he snapped away, taking so many pictures that my face started to hurt from smiling.

"That's enough, Dad," I said, reaching up to grab the phone from him.

Instead he took hold of my hand and turned it so that the ring faced him. He studied it for a long moment before turning to my mother. "You gave this to her?"

Ginette actually flushed. "Well, yes. I certainly wasn't wearing it, and it was just sitting in a jewelry box. It's a lovely ring, and I thought Melanie could get some wear out of it."

He turned to look at it again, his lips pressed together in a hard line. "Can't believe you still hung on to this, considering it was given to you by a previous boyfriend."

I looked back at my mother, who was definitely red. "It was a long time ago, James. I didn't even remember that I still had it until Mellie and I were looking through all my jewelry for a necklace and found it. It has no sentimental value to me anymore, so that's why I gave it to her."

"An old friend gave this to me for my sixteenth birthday." That was what she'd said when she gave the ring to me. I'd thought by "old friend" she'd meant Button and wondered if the confusion had been simply my misunderstanding or a deliberate avoidance on her part of telling the whole truth.

I wanted to ask her more, but Nola's ride appeared and we spent a few moments saying good-bye, and then my parents went upstairs to relieve Mrs. Houlihan and gather the children and their belongings. I thought it was my imagination, but it almost seemed that Jack was avoiding my mother, orchestrating where he stood to be at the farthest spot from her. When I pointed out that we needed to move the car seats from my car to theirs, Jack seemed almost excited to be going outside.

He kissed the babies good-bye, then excused himself to check on the dogs, lingering in the kitchen long enough that he missed my parents' leaving. I allowed him to help me with my shawl, then held back as Thomas and Jayne stepped out on the piazza, using the moment to have a private conversation.

"Are you all right?" I whispered. "You're acting strange."

He smiled, although the gesture was more of a grimace. "Sorry. It's a difficult night for me, remember? We're going to celebrate Marc Longo's greatest achievement, which involves stealing from me, and I have to pretend I'm thrilled and happy for him."

"You're right—I'm sorry. It's just . . ." I paused, then decided to come right out and say it. "Did you have an argument with my mother? You seem to be avoiding her."

His eyes widened in childlike innocence. "An argument? No, of course not. Like I said, my head isn't in the right place tonight."

He made to move forward, but I clutched at his sleeve. "And why are you looking at Jayne like that?"

"Like what?"

I wished it weren't so dark so that I could read his eyes. "Like, I don't know. Like you really know her. Almost like the way you look at me." There. I'd said it. The new mature Melanie was alive and well.

He put both hands on my shoulders and looked squarely in my face. "She's an attractive woman, so of course I'm going to notice. I'm not blind. But I could never, ever, look at a woman the way I look at you, because I will never love another woman the way I love you." He pressed his lips against mine in the slow, lingering way he knew I liked, and I felt all my worries and concerns evaporate, leaving only small crumbs of doubt clinging to my bowl of insecurity.

We rode in Thomas's car, with Jack and me in the back. He reached for my hand and held it between us on the drive down to Spring Street. I'd only been to Cannon Green a couple of times for dinner. Despite their claims of locally grown food and healthy options, I'd adored my eating experiences there each time, finding the food delicious and the service impeccable.

Thomas handed the keys to a valet and then we entered through one of three green doors that faced the street and into the light-filled restaurant. The delicious scents of food and flowers wafted over to us and I felt my stomach grumble—something I was growing used to now that my entire family seemed intent on starving me. I glanced at Jayne, unaware of all the attention she was causing and the heads turning in her direction. She was more focused on the ambience, and Thomas, and looked about as excited as a five-year-old at her first princess birthday party. I found myself smiling at her, despite my earlier thoughts, remembering Jack's words and his hand holding mine in the backseat of the car.

One full side wall of the restaurant contained the facade of a home that had once stood on the site, but it had been emptied of all its history—the front door of the old house was now actually the entrance to the restrooms—so, thankfully, no spirits seemed to be hanging around. Restored wooden tables filled the space, all set for dinner, but we were led to the courtyard out back, passing under a mezzanine. I looked up and then quickly glanced away when I recognized the reporter Suzy Dorf, whom I'd been successfully avoiding for over a month. Rebecca had once worked for the paper, so I shouldn't have been surprised to see her there. But that was the thing about surprises—they always appeared when you least expected them. Or wanted them.

I'd been hoping for rain, or for at least an evening thick with the heavy humidity Charleston was famous for to ruin the party. Instead it was the perfect evening—cool, humidity free, and dry. Even the stars seemed to want to celebrate, each one shining brightly in the sky above us. Dueling reflecting ponds and fountains spraying small arcs of water vied for attention with the vertical garden hanging on the wall. Bright round bulbs were strung across the courtyard, as if the stars above had descended to see what the party was all about.

A large event space built inside an eighteen hundreds warehouse that had once stood on the site dominated the rear of the courtyard. The support beams and, I suspected, most of the brick columns, were original, judging by the number of spirits I saw hovering in the background, surprised as I was to be seen. A string quartet quietly played by the fountain, hardly loud enough to be heard over the well-heeled crowd of what looked to be around 150 people.

"Cousin Melanie and Jack!" Rebecca's grating voice came from behind, giving me time to plaster a smile on my face as Jack and I turned.

She was, as expected, wearing head-to-toe pink, this time in pink shantung, which would have been lovely if she hadn't paired it with a rhinestone tiara and elbow-length pink gloves. Her hand was tucked possessively in Marc's elbow, her pink a contrast to his black tuxedo and dark good looks that I now couldn't look at without thinking he appeared more greasy than sleek.

"And, Jayne, how lovely you look," Rebecca exclaimed, giving air kisses everywhere as the men shook hands and Thomas was introduced. "Who would have thought a nanny could clean up so nicely—am I right, Jack?"

"So glad you all could make it." Marc's expression was what I pictured a palmetto bug's must look like upon the discovery of an uncovered sugar bowl.

"Matt, so good to see you," Jack said, deliberately confusing Marc's name. He'd been doing it ever since they first met, and enjoyed it too much to stop now.

Marc's eyes narrowed, but his smile never dimmed. "Please help yourselves to the open bar and to the food being passed around. The chef has prepared a special menu just for tonight, so enjoy. The champagne toast is at eight, so make sure you grab a flute so you can join us in a toast after our grand announcement."

I felt Jack's muscles tighten under my hand and I gave him a reassuring squeeze. He sent an undecipherable look at Marc that almost looked like a warning. "Wouldn't miss it," Jack said. "Since we're practically family," he added. I wondered if anybody else could detect the poison beneath the dripping sarcasm.

Marc indicated a large table by the fountain piled high with books. "Buxton Books has graciously agreed to sell books tonight, so don't forget to pick up a copy—these are first editions, so grab one now because I know they're already on the third reprint with all the orders coming in. I'll even autograph it for free." He laughed at his own joke while Thomas and Jayne smiled politely and Jack and I just stared back at him.

Thomas recognized someone and excused himself and Jayne. Marc and Jack seemed to be involved in a staring match, each daring the other one to look away first.

Rebecca took my elbow and drew me aside. "I can't believe you let Jayne wear that dress."

"She's my nanny, not my slave. She's free to do what she wants. Besides, my mother helped her pick out the dress and I thought she did a great job." The words stuck in my throat like chalk, but I couldn't let Rebecca know. "And don't forget that she wouldn't be here if you hadn't invited her."

"Well, you're a better woman than I am. If I ever have a nanny, I'll make sure she looks more like Shrek than Cinderella."

I wasn't sure what was more alarming—the idea of Marc and Rebecca having children, or a nanny who looked like a large green troll. A server with a tray of wineglasses appeared and I eagerly grabbed one. I saw Jack eyeing it wistfully and I knew how badly he must be needing a drink right now. I stopped the waiter. "Can you please bring me a glass of seltzer water with lime?"

When I turned back to Rebecca, she was watching me carefully. "I've been having more dreams. Remember the one I told your mother that I was having about the girl in the white nightgown, knocking on the inside of a wall and calling your name?"

I tried to keep my expression neutral. "Vaguely."

"I'm seeing her again, but now she's pointing toward the bottom of a set of wooden steps, as if there's something there she wants me to see."

She looked at me closely. "Sounds like a good story, doesn't it? I sure hope you figure out what it's all about before I do and tell Marc. From what Marc's told me, Jack really needs a great book idea. The early buzz from Marc's agent on the book Jack just turned in says it's not bestseller material. You know how incestuous the whole publishing world is—there aren't many secrets. Marc says the inside scoop is predicting a print run about half that of his last book."

I drained my wineglass, then smiled softly, pretending none of this was news to me. "Yes, well, we're both proud of it and know his fans won't be disappointed."

She took a sip of her own wine, and it was all I could do not to hit the bottom of it and make it spill down the front of her pink dress.

"I never realized how much this 'gift' of ours could help our husbands in their writing careers." She lifted her glass in a mock toast. "May the best man win."

I didn't raise my empty glass, and didn't care if she noticed.

"Well, not to worry," she said. "After tonight's announcement, Marc's book and movie are going to put us all on the map."

I recalled the conversation I'd had with Jack over the newspaper article about the film deal Marc had made, and how it was speculated that the movie would be filmed in Charleston using our house as the setting. The conversation hadn't continued because we hadn't been officially approached, and I'd simply assumed that Jack and I were on the same side of the fence. Which was a very good thing, since it would have to be a very cold day in hell before I would ever agree to it.

I turned toward Jack, needing confirmation, and discovered he was no longer standing nearby. The waitress appeared with his seltzer water and lime and I took it, replacing it with my empty wineglass, thanking her while looking over her shoulder to find out where Jack had gone. I spotted Thomas, talking with a group of people, but Jayne wasn't with him.

The quartet stopped playing and Marc stepped up to a microphone and I noticed all the servers were now passing out flutes of champagne. "Excuse me, please—now's the big moment," Rebecca said as she walked past me to where Marc was standing. Camera flashes popped all around them like paparazzi, and I was left wondering if they were plants paid for by Marc and Rebecca. I certainly wouldn't put it past them.

Someone touched my elbow and I turned to see Suzy Dorf, as diminutive as I remembered, holding a champagne flute. "You're a hard person to reach," she said, taking a sip from her glass.

"I'm very busy," I said, remembering the reams of pink message slips Jolly Thompson had dutifully filled out despite the fact that she knew I threw them all away.

"Well, if you'd bother to return my calls, then you'd already know what the big announcement is."

"I already know about the film—it was in the paper. But it's not being filmed at our house—we haven't agreed to that, nor would we ever."

Her round brown eyes—looking remarkably like buttons—widened. "Really? Because your husband has. Surely you know that."

Something that felt like a hot flame erupted from my core and shot up my throat to my head. I was pretty sure that was what being hit by a meteor would be like. "I'm sorry?"

Marc was tapping the mic, and Suzy indicated him with her chin. "Stick around—you'll hear him make the announcement now."

I thrust the glass of seltzer water at the reporter. "I've got to find Jack—there's been some mistake. Excuse me, please."

She grabbed onto my arm. "I saw him just a few minutes ago, heading back toward the kitchen." She paused, as if debating whether she should say more, then decided not to.

I didn't stop to pry out whatever it was she thought I should know, because whatever it was had to be the least of my worries. If Jack had actually signed that agreement, a blizzard was about to start in hell.

CHAPTER 29

I'd read accounts of soldiers shell-shocked after an explosion, suddenly deaf and blinded, stumbling forward with no idea of how they got where they were or where they were headed. I felt a little like that now, propelling myself with sheer instinct, looking for the door where the waiters were moving in and out and following them into the kitchen as if I were supposed to be there.

The food smells were stronger there, the noise louder and punctuated with orders being barked from one end of the white-tiled room to the other, the sharp clack of knives against cutting boards, the metallic clanking of silverware, and the ping of china plates being stacked. I was only vaguely aware of all this, a sound track to my own personal nightmare as I scoured the space for Jack. A female waiter—I recognized her as the one who'd brought the seltzer—stopped and stared at me for a long moment. Then, with lifted eyebrows and a jerk with her chin toward a door behind me, she allowed her empty tray to be filled with champagne flutes and exited the kitchen.

My first instinct was to follow her, even if it meant listening to Marc make his announcement. It would make a good excuse anyway as to why I hadn't followed Jack into what appeared to be a large storage room. With a closed door. Behind which I could clearly hear a female voice. But I remembered what my mother had said about becoming the new and mature Mellie. The one who faces the truth instead of hiding from it, and asks questions no matter how unpleasant the answers might be. And believes jumping to conclusions shouldn't be on my list of exercises. And I remembered what Jack had said about trust, and how our marriage was based on it. They were both right, of course. I was a forty-one-year-old married mother of three, and it was time to pull up my big-girl panties.

I could hear the faraway amplified voice of Marc Longo. "Jack Trenholm, related by marriage, has generously agreed to allow most of the filming for the movie to be made in his home on Tradd Street, which is where the story takes place." I felt sick and betrayed, but still clung to a shred of hope that I had misunderstood, or that Jack had an explanation that would make it all better. That what my mother had told me about the importance of finding out the truth was true.

With my shoulders pulled back, I hesitated only a moment in front of the closed door and then, without knocking, turned the doorknob and yanked it open. I had a brief recall of my earlier thoughts regarding shell-shocked soldiers, and wondered if it was possible to survive two episodes in quick succession. My first impression was that it was cold, and that I might actually be in a refrigerated storage room. I blinked twice, but not because I couldn't see. The fluorescent lights were on, illuminating everything in an unflattering blue-white light. I blinked again as if somehow the view in front of me might disappear. But it didn't.

I was sure the pantry was lined with metal shelves and they might even have been full of bins of fresh produce and large condiment containers, but I didn't see them. Because all I could see was the beautiful pale blue chiffon of Jayne's gown, half hiding my view of Jack in his black tuxedo, his left hand—the one with the gold wedding band that I'd placed there a little more than a year ago—cradling her head against his chest. His head must have been tilted toward hers until the sound of the door being thrown open made him jerk it back. I was pretty sure they weren't practicing their chip shots.

For a moment we stared at each other as if none of the bustle and noise in the kitchen registered, as if the girl in blue standing between us, her tear-streaked face pale with shock, didn't even exist. And then all the sounds came back with the intensity of a gunshot, and I felt the percussion through my body, the slow movement of a lead slug traveling cleanly through to my heart.

"Mellie," Jack said, stepping toward me as Jayne pulled away.

But I'd already begun to back up, tripping on my dress and feeling the tug of fabric before the sound of it ripping beneath the heel of my shoe set me free.

"Mellie," he said again as he began running toward me. "Please come back. It's not what it looks like—I promise. Please stop. Let me explain."

But desperation and anger and hurt gave me the energy to move faster than I'd ever run. Somewhere between the kitchen and front doors of the restaurant, I'd lost a shoe, the second one coming off in the middle of Spring Street. I'd only run a block before I realized that Jack wasn't following me, the absence of the sound of running footsteps making me stop. I sat on the curb to catch my breath, wondering what was worse—the image of him and Jayne in an intimate embrace, or the fact that he didn't care enough to pursue me.

I wasn't sure how long I sat there, unaware of any passersby or the weather or any critters crawling along the sidewalk, much less the passage of time. I remembered trying to cry but found I couldn't. Like after all those long, sleepless nights with the babies when I'd tried to finally go to sleep and found that I was too tired. It was like that now. My grief and sadness had gone beyond tears.

I'd somehow managed to hang on to my evening purse, the small strap still dangling from my arm. I fished my phone out of my purse, seeing that Jack had left me fifteen text messages and tried to call ten times. I deleted the texts and voice mails and then blocked his number, the new Mellie voice growing fainter and fainter until I couldn't hear it anymore. Then I dialed my mother, and the sound of her voice almost broke the dam of tears that were blocked in my throat.

I wasn't sure what I said, but she promised me that my dad would leave right away and could be here within fifteen minutes. I don't know how fast he drove, or how many red lights and stop signs he must have blown through, but he was there in less than ten. He took one look at me, barefoot and with my dress torn, and he immediately jumped out of his car and practically carried me back to it as if I were a small child.

I know he talked, and asked me questions, but I couldn't speak. Couldn't listen. All I could do was relive those horrifying few moments in the restaurant kitchen. It had to have been less than a minute, but the memory of it made it last for an eternity.

My mother was waiting at the front door of her house on Legare Street, and gathered me in her arms before steering me up the stairs and into the bathroom, where she'd filled the tub with hot, scented water. She unzipped my dress and then gave me privacy while I stepped in the tub, then sat on the closed toilet lid while I soaked in stunned silence as the steam wafted over me. She didn't talk, which made me think she was there as less of a companion and more to make sure I didn't deliberately slip under the bubbles.

Eventually, the water must have grown cold, because she pulled the stopper on the tub, then placed a large fluffy towel and thick robe on the vanity before stepping out of the bathroom. Afterward, she led me to the large four-poster bed in the room where Nola had once stayed before I married Jack, and pulled back the thick duvet.

"Take these," she said, offering me two white pills and a glass of water. "They'll help you sleep. You'll feel better in the morning, and we can talk."

I didn't question her but took the pills and swallowed them before lying down on the pillow and letting my mother cover me. I kept my eyes open, not wanting to be tortured with the image of Jack and Jayne, and waited for the pills to take me to oblivion.

⁕

Two days later I sat on the floor of my mother's drawing room with JJ and Sarah, the sun creating a kaleidoscope of colors through the stained glass window, bathing us in a multihued blanket of light. My mother laughed as the children tried to catch the colors in their chubby fists, but I could only find the energy to smile.

"Mellie, I wish you would talk to him. You can't stay here forever, with so much unresolved between you."

I stared blankly at her, realizing that I had, actually, imagined staying there in my parents' house forever without ever leaving it or having to see anybody ever again.

"Jack's been here about a dozen times."

"Did you tell him I didn't want to talk to him?"

"I didn't have to." She paused. "He just said that he needed to talk to me."

I sat up straighter. "To you? About what?"

"I have no idea, but he said it was important that he speak with me before you and he had a discussion."

"Please tell me you shut the door in his face."

"I was more polite about it than that, but in essence, yes. I told him that he needed to speak with you first. But, Mellie, one of us will have to talk to him sooner or later. And the sooner the better. It's not a good idea to make assumptions without knowing—"

I cut her off. "He had his arms around her! And they were *not* talking about the weather. And I heard Marc's announcement myself, so I know Jack's been going behind my back in more ways than one." I glared at her. "This is all your fault. You were the one who told me I should be a grown-up and find out the truth no matter how uncomfortable it made me. So I did, and look what happened!"

She frowned but didn't defend herself. "He wants to see the babies. You can't keep them away from him. He's their father."

"Their lying, cheating father who's sold out to Marc Longo of all people. And is sleeping with their nanny. It's like an episode of *Jerry Springer* and I just can't believe this is my life." I wiped away the angry tears that spilled down my cheeks.

My mother sat on an ottoman in front of me and handed me a tissue. "Please, Mellie. Let me talk with him, get to the bottom of this. I'm sure once you know the facts, you'll feel differently. I just can't imagine there's not more to this story, despite what you think you saw. That's not like Jack. Or Jayne. And this whole issue of him agreeing to use the house as a film set without discussing it with you." She closed her eyes and gave her head a small shake. "No. I'm not buying it. I'm on your side, Mellie, but this thing can't be left to fester. Let me call him."

I shook my head, feeling like JJ when I tried to feed him strained peas. "No," I said, feeling just as unreasonable. "Just stop answering the door and his phone calls and he'll forget about us."

"Seriously, Mellie? You think this will all just go away and he'll forget about you and his children?"

The doorbell rang, and I turned to her in panic, realizing it was already late afternoon and I was still in my pajamas. I ran my tongue over my teeth and remembered that I hadn't brushed them yet, either. Even if I didn't want to see him, I didn't want him to be glad he couldn't see me.

My mother stood to go to the door. "Don't open it!"

She gave an exasperated sigh. "Let me see who it is first before we make any rash decisions, all right?"

She disappeared into the foyer and I listened to her footsteps cross the floor, then pause, and then came the sound of the doorknob turning and I flinched.

"Nola! It's so good to see you, sweetheart. Come in. I know Mellie will want to see you, too."

She was right—I did want to see Nola. I'd missed her, but even in my darkest moments it never occurred to me to contact her, because it would be like making her pick sides. Despite her unfortunate choice of fathers, I loved her too much to do that to her.

Nola walked tentatively into the drawing room, wearing her school uniform and carrying her backpack and her overnight bag. The children squealed and she immediately dropped the bag, then sat on the floor to hug JJ and Sarah.

"I missed you guys," she said, rumpling their hair.

"They missed you, too," I said. "So did I."

"Yeah, it's been not so great at home. My dad's a mess."

Good, I wanted to say, but couldn't in front of Nola.

"He really misses you, and Sarah and JJ. We all want you to come back home."

"Is that what he sent you to say?" I asked.

She reached behind her and dragged over the overnight bag. "He doesn't know I'm here. I asked Mrs. Ravenel to drop me off here instead of home. I figured you needed some of your stuff." She looked at me closely and frowned. "Like your hairbrush and some clothes and makeup. But not too much—because you need to come home."

"I want to, but I can't. Your dad . . ." I stopped, not sure how much he'd told her.

As if understanding my hesitation, she said, "My dad wouldn't tell me anything, so I asked Jayne what happened. She told me that she couldn't say anything until you and my dad had a talk. She's moved over to the Pinckney house."

I looked at her in surprise, wondering what sort of self-punishment that must be. Sophie had told me that the doll had been verified as a rare Edison doll and returned to the house. I hoped it was busy reacquainting itself with Jayne.

"Was that her choice?" I asked.

Nola shrugged. "It's her house, and it was a little awkward with her staying with us without the babies."

I'd had visions of her moving into my bedroom, so at least that was one thing I could stop torturing myself with.

"The dogs miss you."

I gave her a half smile. "I can't believe I'm saying this, since my official stance is that I'm not a dog lover, but I miss them, too. Maybe you can walk them by the house sometime and knock on the door?"

"I guess." She looked down at her cuticles, and I noticed she'd begun biting her nails, too. "I miss you, too, Melanie. I really want you to come back."

I heard the tears in her voice, and I felt my heart break into one more piece. It must have resembled pulverized glass at that point, each shard representing every disappointment and loss since the night of the launch party.

I lifted my hand to stroke her hair, thick and dark like her father's. "I can't. I don't think I can live with your father after . . ."

"After what? Nobody will tell me anything! How are we supposed to move forward if nobody's talking about what happened?"

"Exactly," my mother said through tight lips. "It's refreshing to hear something mature for a change." She stooped to pick up the babies. "I'm going to settle them down for a nap and come back with a nice after-school snack for Nola. Be back in a few."

Eager to change the subject, I reached for the bag and unzipped it. "What did you bring me? I hope you brought my slippers—my feet have been freezing."

"I did. And your favorite sweater with the deep pockets to hide food."

I looked up at her in surprise, and she grinned. "I'm not blind, Melanie. And the crumbs on your chin are usually a clue."

For the first time in days, I felt both sides of my mouth lift in a smile. I dug through the contents of the bag, amazed at how thorough and accurate her selections were, down to the thick ski socks I liked to sleep in. I was about to zip up the bag when my fingers hit something hard. Pulling it out, I found the framed photo of Button and her brother, Sumter. I held it up, turning it to face Nola. "Why'd you bring this?"

Nola stilled. "I didn't. Last time I saw it, it was on my dad's desk. And I certainly didn't pack it. Maybe it was in your drawer and I just didn't notice when I reached in and grabbed something?"

I shook my head slowly, my focus drawn to the hand linked through Sumter's, the only part visible of the woman cut out of the photo, part of her arm and her hand. It was the hand that drew my attention. It was long and slender, with narrow tapered nails that looked a lot like my own. But what really caught my gaze was the long oval ring on the middle finger that looked like onyx, with a small sparkling diamond in the middle.

"That's the ring you wore to the party," Nola said.

"Yeah, I think you're right."

She took the frame from me and read the date from the front of the photograph. "March seventeenth, 1984. Were you alive back then?"

I knew she was joking, but I was too fixated on watching her flip it onto its back and open the clips that held the picture to the frame. "Look, Melanie—the photograph wasn't cut to fit the frame. It was folded over." She flattened the picture on her knee and looked at it for a long moment, before slowly turning back to me. "I think that's Ginette."

I took the photo and studied the original picture of three people, a stark white demarcation line where it had been folded and tucked inside a frame for three decades. I stared at the newly revealed image of the woman next to Sumter, watching it fade in and out of focus until I blinked. My mother's face, a younger version than the one I knew now, stared out at me from the photograph, her hand now seeming possessive where it rested in the crook of Sumter's arm. But it wasn't just the fuller face, or softer cheeks, or even the absence of gloves that riveted me and made my suddenly dry tongue stick to the roof of my mouth. It was the obvious fact that my mother was very pregnant in this picture, taken almost a full decade after I was born.

A thud sounded behind us, and we twisted to see a small ball rolling on the rug before coming to a stop by my foot. It was the saltshaker from Lake Jasper, the printed date, May 30, 1984, faceup. My eyes met Nola's. "I didn't pack that, either," she said, her voice shaky.

I picked it up and held it in the palm of my hand, the ceramic icy cold to the touch. "I didn't think you did," I said just as all the clocks in my mother's house began to chime four o'clock.

CHAPTER 30

After Nola left, I took a quick shower and changed into yoga pants and my favorite sweater. I even brushed my teeth. I took my time, trying to prepare myself for the conversation I needed to have with my mother. Thankfully, my father was gone all day at a garden show in Savannah, so that at least was one conversation I could postpone or avoid altogether.

Before heading downstairs, I emptied the bag, wanting to mentally prepare myself for a lengthy stay by putting my things away in drawers. At the bottom of the bag I was surprised to find the grocery bag containing the snow globe bottoms. I quickly texted Nola to see if she had actually packed them and was relieved when I received her response saying that she had because they'd become one of Sarah's favorite games and Nola thought she might want them. I shoved them in the back of my dresser drawer where hopefully Sarah would never know they were there, then went slowly down the stairs, carrying the baby monitor with me.

I found my mother in her garden, sipping hot tea and reading a novel, looking elegant and poised. She looked up at me and smiled. "You're looking better, dear. Nothing like what a shower and a fresh change of clothes can do for a person." She indicated the seat next to her and I sat. "Would you like some tea? And I just took some home-made shortbread out of the oven, so it's still warm."

"No, thanks," I said, placing the monitor on the table and making sure the volume was up.

"Something must be really wrong if you're saying no to sugar." Her soft laugh faded quickly when she saw that I hadn't joined her. "What is it, Mellie? Did Nola say something that upset you?"

I shook my head. "No. But this was in the bag she brought over, although she swears she didn't pack it." I took the saltshaker out of the sweater's deep pocket and held it up in front of her to show her the word *Lake Jasper* on one side and the handwritten date on the other. I didn't expect her to touch it without her gloves, and she didn't.

Her face paled slightly when she read the date. As if it meant something to her. "Where did that come from?"

"Button's house. Jack borrowed it, so it was on his desk, and then managed to find its way into the overnight bag that Nola packed for me." I reached into my pocket and pulled out the photograph, sliding it on the table toward her. "And so was this."

She looked down at the photograph, and her hand started to shake. I took the teacup from her fingers and placed it on the saucer. "That's you," I said. It wasn't a question. "In 1984. Which I can't understand because I was always led to believe that I was an only child."

She placed both hands over her mouth and I wanted to tell her it was too late to keep this secret. Clenching her eyes shut, she slowly lowered her hands to her lap. "You are," she said, then opened her eyes. "You are my only child. The baby didn't survive childbirth."

I wasn't prepared for that answer, and a sharp stab of what felt like grief nudged me between my ribs. "Was it a girl or a boy?"

The tears fell freely down her cheeks. "I don't know. They didn't tell me, saying it would be easier for me to forget. As if I ever could. They never even let me see my baby."

"Who? Who wouldn't?"

After only a brief pause, she said, "Button. And the midwife. And a psychiatrist they said they consulted—all agreed that it would be easier for me to get past the trauma if I didn't know. If I couldn't picture the child in my head, or name it. So I didn't. Not that it made it any easier, of course." She pressed a knuckle into her eye to try to block the tears. "It was a very difficult birth—they said I almost died. I was half out of my mind with grief and pain and fear and eventually I stopped asking, and accepted it."

"And the baby?" I asked. "Where was it buried?"

"At the lake house. I agreed to keep it a secret—there were too many people who could be hurt if they knew the truth, including your father. We knew of the plans to flood the lake, so even though I knew it was illegal, I thought it was somehow okay if the grave would soon be under-water. I couldn't go say good-bye—I was so ill and weak, and didn't get out of the bed for two weeks. But I did select the Bible verses I wanted Button to read, and the flowers—lilies—I wanted placed on the grave. And then Button packed my bags and put me on a plane to New York so I could resume my life. When they flooded the lake and covered the grave the following year, it made it easier to pretend that none of it had hap-pened. But I never really forgot. A mother never forgets her children."

I sat back in my chair, trying to digest what I'd just been told. "Sumter . . . ?" The question hung in the air between us.

"He was the father. We'd had a fling in New York. Hasell had just died, and he was recently divorced and trying to find a new life. And I was divorced from your father, and separated from you, and I was look-ing for someone to love." She wiped her face with her fingers, somehow managing to look elegant. "Even if the child had survived, it would never have worked out between Sumter and me. Because I was still in love with your father, and that would never change."

"When was this taken?"

She looked down at the photograph, a soft smile touching her lips. "At the lake house. When I couldn't hide the pregnancy anymore, I told my agent I needed a break and Button brought me down to the lake to wait out my pregnancy and find a midwife. Sumter was traveling so much for work and paid to have the midwife live at the house full-time until the baby was born. That allowed Button to be in Charleston most of the time so Anna wouldn't get suspicious." She closed her eyes for a moment. "Sumter was in London when the baby was born—two weeks early. He didn't get to see our baby, either."

"Why didn't you marry him? You were both free."

She gave a delicate shrug. "Sumter wanted to marry, but I kept putting him off, saying we could decide after the baby was born. I knew he didn't really want to marry again—he had loved Anna, at the beginning at least. Button didn't want us to marry, either."

"But why? You were her best friend. You would be sisters."

"But there was Anna. Button was afraid of what Anna might do to me if she knew. And the baby. I have to say I was a little afraid of Anna, too. She'd never liked me, and losing Hasell had sent her over the edge. I can't imagine what she might have been driven to if Sumter brought me and our baby back to Charleston. Even if we moved to New York, we could never have kept it a secret from her."

"And then the decision was taken care of for you."

She looked down at her hands and nodded. "I would have loved another baby, although I was afraid that I'd have the same problem I had when you were a child—how the restless dead found us to be a bright beacon and wouldn't leave you alone. What if the baby had inherited our gift? Would I make that child's life miserable, too? I confided in Button, and she just said we'd wait and see. She was like that, you know. Always seeing the silver lining. Always believing that everything would all work out. She gave me so much confidence that I'd started to secretly plan on how I'd raise this child in New York, where nobody would care that I didn't have a husband." She gave a shuddering sigh. "And then the baby died, and I moved back to New York on my own as if I'd never even been pregnant."

I reached over and took my mother's hands in mine. "I'm sorry, Mother. I'm so sorry. What an awful tragedy for you—and then to have to keep it to yourself all these years. But I'm glad I know now." I squeezed her hands. "I'm assuming Dad doesn't?"

She shook her head. "What would be the point? The truth is that I never stopped loving him, despite evidence to the contrary. If he knew I'd ever been pregnant with Sumter's child, he'd always doubt it."

I sat back. "You should tell him," I said softly. "That's what you'd tell me."

She lifted her chin and pulled her shoulders back. "I probably would."

I tapped the saltshaker. "Is there any significance to this date? It's two months after the photograph was taken."

She took a shuddering breath. "May thirtieth was the baby's birthday—I'm assuming Button painted that on there, because I know I didn't. And the photograph was taken the last time I saw Sumter. He came down for a week in March, and we had a St. Patrick's Day party— just the three of us. Button organized it, saying I was lonely and needed a little party, even if we kept it small. Sumter surprised me—just showed up out of the blue. We had a lovely time—mostly reminiscing about the happy times we'd spent on the lake when we were younger." She paused for a moment, lost in thought. "When I let my memories take me back, I never allow them to go past that week."

I was listening to every word, but I was also focusing on the salt-shaker and the photograph. They'd been put in the bag on purpose, to show me something. When she'd finished speaking, I asked, "Who do you think put these in my bag?"

She studied the saltshaker for a moment. "I've been wondering the same thing. I'm thinking it was Hasell, since the baby would have been her half brother or sister."

"Maybe that's her unfinished business," I said. "She wanted to get the secret out in the open before she moved on."

My mother looked doubtful. "That could be it—at least part of it, anyway. It would even follow why Anna would want to obstruct that knowledge. Her hatred of me and jealousy over Sumter would not have gone away in death. But the intensity of emotions in that house doesn't match the circumstances. There's something else. Something connected to me. Something bigger."

Sarah's shrieking on the monitor jerked me out of my seat. I ran into the house and up the stairs, my mother close behind, the shrieks getting louder and louder as we approached the nursery.

The door was shut, just as I'd left it. But the bag of snow globes, which I knew I'd shoved in the back of a drawer in my room, was in the middle of the nursery floor. Sarah was pointing at it and shrieking with what I could now tell was impatience and not fright while she bounced up and down holding to the side of her crib. JJ remained sound asleep on his back, arms and legs splayed, a soft smile curving his lips and looking so much like Jack I wanted to cry.

I picked Sarah out of the crib and smoothed her hair from her forehead. She twisted in my arms so she could see the bag and continued to point. "Mmmmmmmm. Mmmmmmmm."

"What's in there?" my mother asked.

"The broken snow globes from the Pinckneys' attic. Sarah's fascinated with them. She's not allowed to touch them, but she doesn't seem to want to. She likes to play a little guessing game with them. Personally, I try to avoid any contact with them at all, but Jayne or Nola keeps taking them out for her."

As if in agreement, Sarah began bouncing up and down. "Mmmmmmmmm. Mmmmmmmmmm."

"Here," Ginette said, reaching her arms toward Sarah. "Why don't you show me?"

I approached the bag with caution, carefully opening the top until I was satisfied that it held only the bases of seven broken snow globes. I stuck my hand inside and pulled one out at random and held it up. It was the Sacramento base.

Sarah thrust both of her small hands away from her, her head violently shaking from side to side.

"That would be a no," I said.

She began pointing again at the bag, so I dropped the Sacramento base back inside and pulled out another, this one from Orlando.

She made the same gesture as before, and repeated it two more times until I pulled out the Miami base. She put her head down on my mother's shoulder and smiled, only growing agitated when I tried to put it back in the bag.

"I don't think she's done," Ginette said. "Put it up on the dresser and try another one."

We went through the same steps two more times until I once again pulled out Orlando, but this time it met with Sarah's approval, even eliciting a smile. I put Orlando next to Miami and tried to close up the bag, but Sarah made it clear she still wasn't through. We continued through all seven bases while my mother and I gradually become aware that this wasn't just a game. She—or someone—was trying to tell us something. I found it more than a little unnerving that they were communicating through my daughter.

Sarah relaxed only when we had all seven bases laid out in a row in the order she'd approved: Miami, Orlando, Memphis, Sacramento, Indianapolis, Cincinnati, and Kalamazoo.

"What on earth is this all about?" My mother approached the bases with Sarah, but the little girl had completely lost interest in the snow globes and seemed more focused on Ginette's black beaded necklace.

I took my phone from my pocket and snapped a picture and was about to text it to Jack when I remembered that I was pretending he didn't exist. And that I didn't care what happened to Jayne or her house and its ghosts, and had even already passed off the listing to my co-worker Wendy Wax.

I slid the phone back into my pocket. "Can you watch the children for a little bit?" I began shoving the bases back into the bag, listening to them clank against one another as I dropped each one. "I'm going to put these in Jayne's mailbox. They belong to her and I don't want anything to do with them."

"We can't leave things the way they are, Mellie. Jayne won't know what to do."

"Well, then, she can ask Jack for help, can't she?"

My mother's cell phone rang out, her ring tone of Puccini's "Nessun dorma" appropriate but not as wonderful as my ABBA one. She glanced at the screen, then up at me. "It's Jack. Please let me take this."

"Do what you think best, Mother. Just let him know that you aren't interested in talking to him. And if he asks about me, tell him I died. Or moved to Siberia." My eyes settled on Sarah, looking up at me with Jack's eyes, and my heart squeezed. "If he wants to see the children, tell him to send Nola over with the dogs and she can bring the children back with her for an afternoon. As long as Jayne's not there."

She sighed, letting the phone go to voice mail. "I'll just text him. He's very insistent on talking with me, and it's hard to tell him no."

"Welcome to my world," I muttered. I nestled the bag handles into the crook of my elbow. "I won't be long." I glanced at the still-sleeping JJ, then kissed Sarah's cheek as I left the room, the bag bumping against my leg as I ran down the stairs, each brush and clattering noise a re-criminating nudge, reminding me that despite promises to change, I was still the old Melanie—uncertain, fragile, and pathetic.

CHAPTER 31

I slowly jogged down Broad Street the following morning, paying more attention to the uneven sidewalks than to who or what was in front of me. I had enough going on in my life that I didn't need a twisted ankle, too. I preferred to run down the small side streets south of Broad, but I'd had to change my running route to avoid South Battery and any chance of seeing Jayne or her house.

Sophie ran next to me, her breathing easy and her gait just a little faster than mine to keep me motivated. Not that I needed the motivation. I eagerly approached our little runs with enthusiasm now, if only because my struggle for a deep breath took all my concentration so that for at least half an hour I didn't have to think what a mess my life was in.

We passed Henderson House Realty, and I was glad for the darkened front reception room. I still went in to the office each day, but usually very early in the morning or very late at night when nobody else was there. I didn't want to take the chance of Jack stopping by and catching me. I'd do some paperwork, take anything I'd need to work from my mother's house, and go through the pink message slips Jolly left on my desk. Most of them were from Jack and Suzy Dorf, with a few from Rebecca. I didn't read any of them, taking unusual pleasure in the sound of their being crumpled in my fist before I dropped them in the wastebasket.

We were almost at East Bay when Sophie slowed her pace. I glanced over at her to see what was wrong, then followed her gaze toward the next block as she stopped completely. Rebecca, in a different pink jogging suit than I'd seen before, was approaching us, Pucci in her pouch on her chest, pink bows in her ears. It was hard to judge which one of them looked more idiotic.

I began to turn around but Sophie grabbed my elbow. "She wants to talk to you."

I tried to pull away, but she held tight. "Am I being ambushed?"

"I'm sorry, Melanie, but I can't stand to see you so unhappy. Ignoring people will *not* make your problems go away. Rebecca called me yesterday and told me she'd been trying to reach you but couldn't get past your mother or father or the receptionist where you work. She's desperate to talk with you, so I said I'd help."

"Oh, great. So you're the missing link."

She wrinkled her nose. "I think you mean 'weakest link,' but yeah, that would be right."

Rebecca drew closer and Sophie's grip tightened. "You're going to leave a bruise if you don't let go."

Sophie narrowed her eyes at me. "Only if you promise not to bolt."

"Fine. But I won't promise I'll actually speak with her." She let go and I folded my arms over my chest, prepared for battle.

"Good morning," Rebecca said. She at least had the decency to look chagrined.

"It was," I said, staring pointedly at her.

"I guess I deserve that. And I don't blame you for being angry. That's why I needed to talk to you. Not only to apologize, but also to help you."

"How can you possibly help me?"

"I've been having more dreams. More specific dreams, and I know they have something to do with Jayne's house."

I started to back away. "I have no further connection with the

Pinckney mansion, so you might want to save your breath and go find Jayne to let her know."

"They involve your mother."

I stopped and looked at her. "What do you mean?"

"The girl in the white nightgown keeps showing me a staircase with no door, and when she gets to the bottom step, she pulls up a board and pulls something out."

"Like what?" I asked.

"I don't know. She won't show me."

"But what does that have to do with my mother?"

"I hope this means more to you than it does to me, but she keeps saying that Button did the right thing, and that your mother should forgive her."

I stepped back. "What did Button do?"

Rebecca shrugged. "I don't know. The little girl is very faint when she comes through, and I don't always hear her clearly—like she's being blocked."

"Well, if that's all . . ." I said, unimpressed and impatient to get away from Rebecca.

"One last thing. She also said that you should listen to Sarah."

"Sarah?" Sophie said in surprise before I could. "As in her little girl Sarah?"

"Unless you know another one," Rebecca said. "I'm guessing she's inherited the family gift. Is that right, Melanie?"

I kept my face expressionless, not wanting that little nugget of information to be confirmed and used relentlessly as Sarah got older. Whatever had gone wrong between my mother and me when I was little was not going to happen with Sarah and me. It was the only thing I was sure of right now.

Eager to change the subject, I said, "You mentioned something about an apology."

She looked down at Pucci's head and began playing with the pink bows clipped onto the furry ears. I wondered if Pucci liked wearing them any better than Sarah did and realized suddenly that they were the same bows I put in Sarah's hair. I made a vow right then and there that I would never put them on her again.

Without looking up, Rebecca said, "I know I'm partially responsible for this thing between Marc and Jack—"

"It's not a 'thing,'" I interrupted. "It was Jack's idea, his book, and his career that Marc stole from him—with your help, I might add." As angry and hurt as Jack had made me, the whole scenario still burned.

"I know. That's why I'm here. Because I know something that Marc doesn't that I believe will help you and Jack."

I sent her a skeptical look. "Why would you tell me, Rebecca? And expect me to trust you?"

"Because we're family, Melanie, even though sometimes I know I don't act like it. And we share this gift, or whatever you want to call it, and feel no need to question when we talk about dreams and seeing dead people. I love my husband, but Marc can never understand that part of me."

I met her gaze, wanting to tell her that Jack did understand. That he wasn't even disappointed to know that his daughter had inherited the same gift. Instead I said, "So, what do you know that Marc doesn't?"

"Marc knows that Jack is having money issues and that his next book isn't going to help. When Marc first approached Jack about using your house to film the movie, Jack said absolutely not, even after Marc told him some of the inside juice he'd received from his agent about how word in the publishing world is that Jack's career is on the way out."

I swallowed, wondering why Jack hadn't mentioned it to me. Wondering if he'd been trying to protect me from an unpleasant truth.

"But the second time Marc approached Jack, he knew Jack was getting a little more desperate. Jack had made the mistake of telling another writer that his publisher wasn't thrilled with the book he just turned in, and even if they don't cancel the next book in the contract, they probably won't take the option book, and the news got back to Marc. That's how Marc knew he might be more willing to listen."

I swallowed, wishing the lump in the middle of my throat would dislodge itself. "Is that when Jack agreed?"

She shook her head. "No. That's the thing. He never officially agreed. But he did tell Marc that he was in the middle of researching a new book idea, and that it would blow everybody out of the water. That his agent was excited about it and had already approached several big publishers who were interested—assuming his current publisher drops him. The only problem was that the story could hurt people he knew and loved, and he needed to talk to them to get their permission. And if they said no, then he'd have no other option except to sign the agreement to use your house for filming our movie—for a lot of money, I might add. But only if you signed it, too. It was never his intention to do it behind your back."

"So what was that announcement about at the launch party?" Sophie took a step forward, her hands on her hips.

I put a restraining hand on her arm, secretly pleased to have her on my side. Despite her New Age hippiness and her uninformed choices in apparel, she was the best friend I could ever hope to have.

Rebecca sent a worried glance at Sophie. "Marc got a little ahead of himself. Since Jack wasn't returning his phone calls, Marc assumed that Jack's hoped-for book deal wasn't going to happen and that he was free to make the filming location official. Getting you to agree was going to be Jack's problem, not his. The big announcement at the party was supposed to be that two Hollywood A-listers have signed on for the movie to play Louisa Vanderhorst and Joseph Longo. That's it—I swear. I was as surprised as anybody that Marc said what he did."

I stared at Rebecca, torn between hugging her and slapping her and then deciding to do neither. Jack wasn't worth it. He might not have intended to enter into an agreement without me, but he was still an unfaithful jerk who'd broken my heart. "Thank you for telling me. It's all a little too late, but I'm glad I know now."

She gave me a tentative smile. "I hope this doesn't come between us or ruin our relationship."

I heard Sophie shift beside me, knowing she was thinking exactly what I was. *Really? What relationship?*

"Of course not," I said truthfully. "But next time—if there is a next time—please tell me sooner rather than later. It would have saved us all a lot of grief. Especially you, who will have to tell Marc and the film people that I would dye my hair purple and restore another old house before I would *ever* allow that film to be made in my home."

"So you're still thinking about it?"

I felt Sophie move beside me and I held her back before it turned physical. "No. There's no more thinking. There never was. My answer is no. Not maybe, but no."

She frowned as if not understanding and then stepped forward as if to hug me. I stepped back and she recovered nicely, but not before I saw her embarrassment. I had no idea how I could be related to someone so clueless about human relationships.

"Yes, well, I guess I'll be seeing you later. Maybe we can all go out sometime—you, too, Sophie. Have a little date night with just us couples. Wouldn't that be fun?"

"I could straighten my hair and wear a Lily Pulitzer sundress. And heels," Sophie managed to say with a straight face.

Rebecca's smile dimmed for a moment, leaving me to wonder if she really did want some sort of relationship with me. We were connected by more than blood, after all.

Sophie took my arm and began leading me away. We called back a hasty good-bye and then headed in the opposite direction. Sophie spoke first. "So, what are you going to do now? Talk with Jack?"

I shook my head. "What's the point? He's always talking to me about sharing my problems and telling him things, and yet it's clear he's been hiding a lot of stuff from me."

"True, but he was doing it to protect you."

"Yes, well, when I ignore stuff it's usually to protect me, too, so I guess that makes us even." I frowned. "He could have told me we were having financial issues. I turned over the household expenses when the kids were babies because I was so overwhelmed and I haven't been involved since because I was terrible at balancing the checkbook. I could never get the numbers to work out and Jack said it was too painful to watch. But I never would have done that if I'd known he wouldn't have felt like he couldn't come to me with any problems. It's not like I don't know how to cut expenses, or would even resent it if I had to. I thought that's what marriages were all about—sharing everything."

Sophie stopped to look at me and I flinched as I recognized her professor-about-to-lecture mode. "Sometimes you can be a little self-absorbed, Melanie. You're a new mother of twins, you're resurrecting a career, and you're also dealing with body issues. Jack probably didn't want to burden you. And let's not forget the male ego here—his career and ability to be a breadwinner is very closely linked to his self-identity. It would be difficult to admit that to you."

"Body issues? What body issues?"

"Really, Melanie? Is that all you heard?"

"Of course not," I said, resuming walking while scanning my brain for whatever came after the words "body issues." "Trust me, there doesn't seem to be anything wrong with Jack's male ego. I found him in a pantry embracing another woman—our children's *nanny*, for crying out loud."

We walked in silence, our jog long forgotten, until Sophie spoke again. "Is there any chance you might have misread the situation? You're not really known to use patience to analyze a situation, so I was thinking that maybe—"

I stopped abruptly in the middle of the sidewalk, staring at my soon-to-be-former best friend. "Et tu, Brute? And besides, weren't you the friend who warned me about how attractive Jayne might be to Jack? Remember that—when we were walking in the park?"

"Yes, and I'm sorry about that. I didn't really know Jayne that well at that point, and I think I misread the situation and jumped to conclusions I shouldn't have. Maybe you're rubbing off on me." She tried to smile but failed. "But what I do know for sure is that you love Jack and he loves you, and I'm just asking that you think back really hard. To maybe consider that there was more to the situation than what you thought you saw."

"I know what I saw," I said, feeling the anger rise. "It's kind of hard to miss your husband embracing another woman."

"Were they kissing?"

I started to say yes, then stopped. "Not when I saw them. But his head was turned toward hers, like he was about to. Or he'd just finished."

"So you didn't see them kissing."

I slowed my pace. "No. But—"

"Do you hug your children?"

"Yes, of course I do. But—"

"And Nola? And your parents?"

I stopped again in the middle of the sidewalk and faced her, an elderly man walking his dog nearly colliding with us. "Yes, you know I do. What has this got to do with Jack fooling around with our nanny?"

Sophie looked up at the sky as if searching for divine intervention, a look I was growing familiar with. "There are many reasons why we embrace people—and not all of them have to do with lust. I'm sure seeing the two of them together like that would make you want to assume that what you saw wasn't an innocent embrace. But what if it was? What if he was, I don't know, comforting her? Trying to make her feel better? Because that's the Jack I know—a really nice guy who cares about others and who also happens to be crazy in love with his wife."

I wanted to argue with her, remind her of the times when Jayne and Jack were practicing their putting in the foyer. And when the two of them had a picnic in the park with the children. When he comforted her in the hallway after the night-light got broken and he wasn't wearing a shirt. But I stopped before I made a complete idiot of myself. Because I had the sneaking suspicion that she might be right.

I'd once asked Thomas to explain circumstantial evidence, and I'd have to agree that all those instances with Jayne and Jack that kept smacking me in the head could only be called circumstantial. Yet I'd convicted them without a trial and with a jury of one. Worse, at the first sign of trouble, I'd reverted to the old Mellie who'd always found it easier to prove that her world was falling apart instead of really looking and seeing how good it truly was.

"I don't know what to do," I said. I blinked twice, wondering why she was so blurry. Grabbing my arm, she pulled me off Broad and onto Church Street. The store on the corner wasn't open yet and there was very little pedestrian traffic, which made it easy for me to press my forehead against the cool stone of the building, pushing against it until my head hurt.

"Well, you have a few options—all of which involve you talking with Jack and getting all this out in the open. And don't forget about the rest of the stuff Rebecca told you—about Button and your mother forgiving her, and the thing Hasell showed her was hidden in the steps. And listening to Sarah."

I turned around, recalling something else, too. "She said that Jack had a great book idea, but that he couldn't do anything until he'd spoken with the people involved. That it might hurt people he loved." I stuck my hair behind my ears with agitation. "Jack's been trying to talk with my mother, but I wouldn't let him." I stared at her in horror. "What if I've been making everything worse?"

She smiled ruefully. "That certainly wouldn't be the first time. And I doubt it will be the last. But as long as you're willing, it's always fixable."

"Are you sure?"

She put her arm around my shoulder and squeezed. "Just as sure as I know we will never have a date night with Rebecca and Marc."

CHAPTER 32

I listened to my phone call go directly to Jack's voice mail for about the fifth time that day. Despite it being nearly six o'clock and growing dark outside, I had yet to get anything accomplished at work even though I hadn't left my desk all day. The air sat heavy and full, unrelated to the torrential downpour and accompanying thunder and lightning. Or the dark clouds that added another layer of gloom to an already charged atmosphere.

I dialed again, listening to it ring and then cut off with Jack's voice telling me that he'd get back to me as soon as he could. I was sure it was my imagination, but there was something in the dial tone that didn't sound authentic. As if something were mimicking it but falling short of an accurate imitation. Like listening to a favorite song sung by a cover band.

I called Nola and she picked up on the second ring. "Hi, Melanie."

"I'm glad you picked up—I thought something was wrong with my phone. Is your dad home?" I held my breath.

"No. And I'm beginning to get worried. He's usually home by now, but I haven't heard from him. Mrs. Houlihan hasn't heard from him, either."

"Have you tried calling him?"

"It goes straight to voice mail." She paused. "It sounded weird. And my phone is showing the wrong time."

I stilled. "Ten minutes after four?"

"Yeah—how did you know?"

I pulled the phone from my ear and looked at the screen before speaking again. "Because my phone is doing the same thing. We shouldn't be on our cell phones during a storm, so I'm going to hang up. But please have your dad call me when he gets home. Tell him I'll pick up and that I unblocked his number."

"You blocked his number?"

"I know, I know. Please don't say anything, Nola. I don't think I could handle being scolded by a fifteen-year-old right now."

"Sure."

I was about to say good-bye when she spoke again. "Melanie?"

"Yes?"

"Why did you text that photo of the broken snow globes?"

"Excuse me?"

"You sent me a photo of the broken snow globes laid out in a line on the nursery's dresser. I was wondering if it was some sort of code you wanted me to figure out or something."

I placed my hand on the back of my neck, feeling pinpricks of fear beginning to sprout. "I didn't. I'd actually forgotten that I had it on my phone. I meant to send it to your dad."

There was a slight pause before she spoke. "Maybe you hit my name instead so it was sent to me."

I almost agreed with her. Because that would have been the easiest thing, to pretend that there was an obvious explanation to everything. But we both knew there wasn't.

"No," I said. "I know I didn't."

"Then who did?"

"Hasell." I said the name without thinking. It was probably because her time of death was frozen on both our phones that made me jump to the most obvious conclusion. "Maybe she's trying to tell us something."

"I guess that would be weird coming from anybody else but you." Even though her voice trembled a little, I thought I could hear her smile, too. "Do you want me to play with it a little? See if I can make some sense of it?"

"Yes—that would be great. And I'll do the same as soon as I feed the babies and put them to bed. Call me if you figure anything out."

"Okay. And you do the same."

We said our good-byes and I quickly packed up my briefcase to leave. My mother had convinced me that it made sense to bring comfortable walking shoes so I could walk to and from work on days when I didn't have to drive clients anywhere. I slipped on the pair of flats she'd bought for me, and headed toward the lobby.

"Good night, Melanie."

I looked up in surprise at Jolly, who still sat behind the reception desk, smiling brightly. "What are you still doing here?"

"Just cleaning up some things. Making my lists for tomorrow." She stood and came from around her desk, holding what looked like a large photo album. "And your husband dropped this off for you about an hour ago."

"Jack was here? And you didn't come get me?"

"You told me that if he stopped by to tell him that you were out with clients. And with your car being gone, he didn't even have to ask."

"Oh," I said weakly, reaching out to take the album, recognizing it as one of Button's albums Sophie and I had brought over to the house on Tradd Street for Jack. "Did he say why he wanted me to have this?"

"He just said to call him when you were ready to look at it. He's been trying to reach you, but he says you blocked his number so he couldn't." She sent me a reproachful look. "You didn't really, did you? Of all the—"

"Thanks, Jolly. Good night."

"You'll want this," she said, digging into her large purse and pulling out an empty plastic garbage bag. "Otherwise the album will get wet and ruin the photos inside. You don't have your car, remember? Or you could call Jack and see if he could come pick you up. It will give you time to clear the air before you get home to the family. And you can apologize for blocking his number."

She ignored my glare, focusing on putting the album in the bag, while I tried to call Jack again, hanging up before it could go to voice mail. The windows rattled from a series of thunder cracks, the sky letting loose with bullets of rain. "It's not that far," I said, pulling up the hood of my raincoat and tucking in my hair. The wind howled, letting me know that an umbrella would be useless.

Jolly moved to the door to open it. "Hurry up before the streets flood again and you have to swim home. I'd come with you to help, but I'm heading in the opposite direction." As I neared, she sniffed the air. "I like your perfume. Smells like roses."

"I'm not wearing any." I didn't add that I didn't smell roses, either. "Maybe my housekeeper is using a new detergent."

"Or you have a guardian angel," she said with a small laugh.

I took a step toward the door, but she didn't move, preferring to stand staring at me, a frown forming deep creases along the sides of her mouth. "Tell Jayne to be careful." She began rubbing her neck as if it were raw with bruises. "And your mother. At least I'm thinking it's your mother. She looks just like you but is thinner and has a bigger chest. I'm getting bad vibes."

I forced myself to breathe in and breathe out, my mind trying to work its way through what Jolly had just told me. "Bad vibes?"

She nodded. "Yes, I just learned that last night in my online class. It's when you pay attention to your instincts and allow them to take you deep down to your real feelings. It's my first time doing it, so you'll have to let me know if I was accurate."

"Sure," I said through stiff lips. "Good night, Jolly. See you tomorrow." She opened the door for me, and with my briefcase and wrapped album held tightly against me, I headed out into the pouring rain.

∽

My mother greeted me at the door, taking my coat after I'd dropped my load on the kitchen floor by the door. "You look like a drowned rat, Mellie. It's a good thing the dogs aren't here or they'd probably chase you."

"Thanks, Mother," I said, kissing her cheek and then those of the babies who were sitting on a blanket on the floor. Their little arms and feet were busy batting at various toys dangling in front of them from a toy mobile on a stand, and I was apparently not enough of a distraction to make them want to stop. "Where's Dad?"

"He's staying an extra night at the gardening show because of the weather. He'll be back tomorrow. Are you hungry? I made some minestrone if you'd like some."

I suddenly realized I was starving, not to mention chilled to the bone. "That would be great. Just give me fifteen minutes to take a hot shower and to change." I thought briefly of the album lying in its plastic bag on the floor, then remembered Jack's instructions to call him before I looked at it. I grabbed my phone and ran upstairs, dialing Jack's number again, and listening as it went to voice mail before trying again.

I was on my way back down to the kitchen and dialing again when a crash of thunder shook the air, vibrating the pictures on the walls. The lights flickered and went off, and I had a terrifying flashback of my time in Button's bathroom with Anna. I'd crouched down on one of the stairs when the lights mercifully came back on again. There was definitely something in the atmosphere tonight. Something that had nothing to do with barometer readings or burned ions.

"Have you heard from Jack?" I asked as I entered the kitchen.

My mother was ladling soup from a large pot on the stove into two shallow bowls. "No. As a matter of fact, he hasn't called me at all today, which is a first."

"Can you try to call from your phone? I can't seem to get through to him on mine."

She raised her eyebrow at my sudden change of heart, but didn't say anything as she picked her phone off the counter and dialed. I heard a piercing *ping* from across the room and watched as she held the phone away from her ear. "I must have dialed it incorrectly." She tried again, and received the same result.

We sat at the table with the soup in front of us, neither one of us reaching for a spoon. "There's something wrong," I said.

She nodded. "I can feel it, too. Nothing we can do until we know more, so we might as well eat to keep up our strength. I have a feeling we're going to need it."

As we slowly ate, I told her about my talk with Rebecca. "She said that Hasell wanted you to know that Button did the right thing, and that you should forgive her. Do you know what that means?"

A crease formed between Ginette's delicate eyebrows. "No. When I went back to New York, Button and I left on good terms. There was no blame between us, no recrimination or acrimony. Only friendship. I remember telling her how thankful I was that she had been there during that dark time when I'd lost the baby, and that she'd sat by my side until I was well. There is nothing she did that I needed to forgive."

I nodded, my appetite gone. My gaze fell on my phone, and I picked it up. I was in the middle of dialing Jack again when the front doorbell rang, making us both jump. We each scooped up a baby, then went together to answer the door, surprised to find Nola with her school bag, an overnight bag, and all three dogs. She turned around to wave at a car at the curb and I recognized Mrs. Houlihan, who waved back at us.

We ushered Nola and her entourage inside, waiting for her to shed her raincoat before we could hug her. "Daddy isn't back yet and we couldn't get hold of him. Mrs. Houlihan didn't want to leave me by myself on a night like tonight, so she drove me over. We tried to call first, but your cells kept going straight to voice mail."

We returned to the kitchen and my mother put a bowl of soup in front of Nola. I settled the babies in the playpen my mother had set up by the table to keep them from chewing on the puppies and vice versa. She picked up her spoon but seemed distracted, glancing over at her backpack as if to make sure it was still there.

"What is it, Nola?" my mother finally asked. "Is it your father?"

"Yeah, but there's something else, too." Minestrone forgotten, she scraped back her chair and retrieved her backpack. After rummaging through the outside compartment, she pulled out an envelope with a folded piece of notepaper inside. "I've been playing with that photo that appeared on my phone."

"The one of the snow globes?" I asked.

"Uh-huh. I finished my homework early and I was trying to distract myself from worrying about Dad. So I enlarged the photo and printed it out, then got a notebook and started playing with the letters."

Rebecca's words came back to me in a rush. *"You should listen to Sarah."* "Did you use the order Sarah wanted them in?"

"Of course. I mean, we'd have to be pretty clueless not to know she's got the gift or whatever you want to call it." Ginette and I exchanged smiles. "Anyway, you know those word puzzles where you take a letter from each word and form a new word? Well, I did it with each letter of all seven city names in the order they were lined up, using the first letters of each and then the second and so on, and there was only one that made any sense at all." She opened the notepaper and flipped it around to show us. "The first letters made two words when strung together. All of the other ones were pretty much gibberish."

I stared at the page in front of me, with the various lines of letters written in Nola's clear, precise hand, then focused on the first line comprising the first letters. *MOMSICK.*

"Mom sick," Ginette said quietly, repeating the two words that echoed in my own head.

"Weird, huh?" Nola said. "Considering it was Hasell who was sick, and we were pretty sure this was sent by Hasell."

"Unless Anna was ill?" I turned toward my mother.

"No. And I know that for a fact. Her good health was a point of pride for her. She was always saying it was a blessing she was so healthy so she could take care of Hasell."

I put a spoonful of minestrone in my mouth, not tasting it as thoughts twirled around my brain, stray thoughts bouncing around but none settling long enough to make sense. "Of course, there're more kinds of illnesses and they're not all physical."

The house phone rang, and we all turned to look at the desk phone on the counter. "Nobody calls that number anymore."

Ginette stood and seemed to walk with trepidation as she went to answer it.

"Hello?" She glanced at me. "Yes, Jack. She's here. So is Nola. We've been trying to reach . . ." She stopped, listening, while both Nola and I half rose in our chairs. "We can be there in ten minutes. Are you sure . . . ?"

We watched as her hand tightened on the receiver before slowly lowering it into the cradle. She looked up at us, her eyes dark saucers. "We were disconnected."

"Where is he?" I asked. "Is he all right?"

"I'm not sure," she said. "The line was really bad. He said his cell phone had died, so he was using the landline in Button's kitchen."

"But it's not in service anymore."

She raised her eyebrows. "Exactly. He says Jayne needs our help, and he wants us over at the Pinckney house as soon as we can get there."

I bristled. "He's with Jayne?"

"Yes. Rebecca called him to tell him that she'd seen you, and told him everything she'd told you this morning. Including something about the attic stairs." She frowned. "What about the attic stairs?"

"Rebecca dreamed she saw Hasell pulling up a board and lifting something from the bottom step."

My mother paled. "He can't go into the attic. Not by himself, and not with just Jayne."

"You're scaring me," I said, standing. "You stay here with Nola and the babies and I'll go."

"No. He was very specific. He said he needed both of us." She faced Nola. "Are you okay staying here with the babies? They need to be fed, but you can skip the baths because of the storm. Bedtime at eight, all right?"

Nola nodded.

Turning to me, Ginette said, "You can borrow one of my coats, since yours is soaked. And he said to bring the album."

I didn't have to ask which album he'd meant. "Why?"

"He was cut off before he could tell me. But he said it was important, that he would explain everything when he saw us."

She threw on her raincoat and pulled on her gloves while I gave the babies quick kisses and hugged Nola. "You call Sophie if you need anything, all right? At any time."

She nodded. "Be careful."

I forced a smile, then picked up the still-wrapped album and followed my mother out into the storm, knowing with certainty that bad weather was going to be the least of our problems.

CHAPTER 33

We drove my Volvo station wagon, believing it to be the safest option available. The streets already sloshed with standing water, forcing me to drive in the middle of the street. This might have been more alarming if there had been any other traffic, but it seemed everyone else south of Broad was too sensible to head out in a storm like this.

What would have been a five-minute walk turned into a fifteen-minute drive as I inched down Legare toward South Battery. The unlit Pinckney house stood like a dark omen against an almost completely black sky, illuminated only by the flashes of lightning that forked through the sky with an uncomfortable frequency.

As I pulled into the driveway, my headlights passed over Jack's minivan. It wasn't until I'd stopped behind it that I realized the interior lights were on, and the driver's-side door wide-open. I must have let out a cry or a shout because my mother was handing me a portable umbrella and telling me to go. I barely remembered to put my car in park and turn off the ignition before I jumped out and ran toward the open door to look inside.

To my disappointment, it appeared empty. But even more alarming was the fact that the key was still in the ignition, the car running as if

Jack had exited in such a hurry that turning off the car and shutting the door were the least of his worries.

I reached over to turn the key, spotting a photograph facedown on the floor of the passenger seat. Holding the umbrella so I wouldn't drip more rain onto the interior, I reached down to pick it up carefully along the edges. To avoid ruining it with my wet fingers, I placed it on the seat before flipping it over. It was an old Polaroid like so many of the photos we'd found in Button's albums, making me believe that this one might have slipped out of one of them. Probably the album Jack had brought to me at the office, because it would have been in his car. It was a photo of a baby, a newborn. The baby was small, but plump and ruddy-cheeked. Healthy. It was wrapped in a blanket and sported a dark fringe of hair swirling around the top of her nearly bald head, a tiny bow made from yarn clinging to a few wisps. On the white border at the bottom of the photo was a single date written in fading blue ink: *May 30, 1984.*

I dropped the photo back on the floor and jerked back as if I'd been caught doing something I shouldn't. I knew that date—it had been written on the saltshaker from Lake Jasper. I recalled the conversation I'd had with my mother when I asked her about it. *May thirtieth was the baby's birthday.* But that baby had died and been secretly buried. I looked again at the baby's face in the photo, her pink rosebud lips wet with saliva, her eyes wide and curious. She looked very much alive.

A loud meow erupted from the back of the van, followed by a black blur as the cat flew past me and out the door into the rain. I stumbled backward, dropping the umbrella. Leaving it where it was, I slammed the van door, then ran toward the front door of the house, my mother following behind me with the wrapped album tucked beneath her arm.

We stood for a moment under the portico, dripping water and breathing heavily.

"Where did the cat come from?" my mother asked.

"From inside the van. I didn't see it, and I probably didn't hear it because of the rain pelting the roof of the van. I don't know about that cat, but if I had nine lives, it just scared away one of them."

My mother reached behind me and grabbed the large brass knocker and banged it against the wooden door two times. It vibrated inside the empty house, but although we waited for a full minute, there was no sound of approaching footsteps from inside. She reached behind me and rapped again, but I was already searching inside my purse for the house key Jayne had given me.

Before I could find it, the door flung open, ripping the knocker from my mother's grasp, and slamming against the inside wall of the inky black foyer. The wind howled, sending slashing rain into our faces, pushing at our backs until we stumbled into the house, the door slamming closed behind us.

It was still and quiet inside, like being inside a cocoon, the rain and thunder oddly muted. I slid my hand toward where I knew the light switches were and flipped them all, but nothing happened. "The electricity's out," I said.

I sensed we weren't alone, but the curtain had been pulled down again, blocking me from seeing. Whatever had been here opening and slamming doors was gone. I only knew that for certain because the hair on the back of my neck had settled, the gooseflesh on my arms gone.

"Jack?" I called out, my voice eerily reed-thin, as if it had been whispered through a metal pipe. We held our breath for a moment and then I pulled out my phone, not surprised to find *No Service* in the top left corner of the screen.

"At least the flashlight on my phone works," I said with forced cheerfulness as I pressed the app button and flooded the space with light.

"That means I have one, too, right?" my mother asked as she began to fish through her raincoat pocket, the album hampering her movements. "Why on earth did Jack want us to bring this tonight? I hope he has a good reason."

"I'm sure he does," I said, reaching for the bag. She let go just a second before I had a good grasp on it, and the album slid from the bag and onto the floor, its splayed binding facing up, its position like that of a dead bird crashed to earth.

She guided her light to help as I knelt down to pick up the album and

gather anything that might have fallen from it. The flashlight glinted off
the gold-embossed number of the year on the spine and my hand froze—
1984. The missing album. Slowly, I picked it up and turned it over, relieved to see that nothing had shaken loose. I closed it quickly, but not
before I saw two pages filled with photographs of a small baby with a
bow in her hair and swaddled in a blanket. I stood to face my mother.

"Jack said he'd visited the housekeeper of the lake house in Alabama,
who admitted to taking a few things from the house before it flooded."
I placed the album on the hall table. "I think this is one of them."

My mother's eyes were lost in shadow. "So Button would have left
this album in the house and brought the other ones here. Knowing it
would be destroyed. But why?"

I nodded, seeing the date again written on the photograph I'd found
in the van. *May 30, 1984.* I remembered talking with Jayne after she'd
found the saltshaker in her room and wanting to know if I'd been the
one who put it there. "*I thought maybe because it had the year I was born on
it. You thought I might want it as a souvenir.*"

My thoughts spun and bounced, refusing to settle in the obvious
place. I thought of Jack initially avoiding my mother after his return
from Alabama, and then the fiasco with Jayne at the party where, if I
now admitted to myself, it had looked more as if he was comforting her
than anything else. And then Jack's attempts to speak with my mother,
and Rebecca telling me that Jack had found an incredible story idea but
couldn't move forward with it because it could hurt people he knew
and loved.

A loud crack of thunder rent the air. I threw back my head and
shouted, "Jack! Jayne! Where are you?" I wondered if it was my imagination or if I had really heard a muffled voice.

"The cat," Ginette said, pointing toward the stairs with her flashlight. "I think it wants us to follow it."

Feeling like a stupid heroine in a horror movie who runs up the
darkened stairs in a spooky house, I followed the cat, with my mother
close behind me. My flashlight caught the flash of the fluffy end of a
tail and we dashed after it around the landing and then up to the second

floor, then down the hallway to Button's bedroom and through the partially opened door.

"Jack? Jayne?" I yelled again.

"In here!" It was Jack's voice, coming from the bathroom—the same one I'd been trapped in. Where I'd seen Anna's reflection in the mirror, with hollowed-out eye sockets and bruising on her neck.

I might have hesitated, but Jack was inside. *My* Jack. And I wasn't going to leave him there. "We're here, Jack. We'll get you out."

I saw the doorknob twist, and then heard the door shake as he pulled on the knob. "Hang on," I said, looking for a key or something to tear down the door. I thought back to my own ordeal, and how Sophie had simply turned the knob. I held the cool brass knob in my hand for a moment before I gave it a gentle twist.

The door opened easily and I tumbled inside as Jack simultaneously pulled on the door. His familiar arms wrapped around me and I felt his kisses in my hair. "Oh, Mellie. There's so much I have to tell you."

"I've been trying to reach you all day. I'm sorry I jumped to conclusions when I saw you and Jayne. And then when I heard Marc's announcement—"

"Shh. We'll talk about it all later. We need to find Jayne first."

Ginette shone her flashlight in our faces. "Where is she?"

"I'm not sure. We were in the secret staircase and we found Hasell's notebook, and a whole lot of partially filled medicine bottles and empty syringes. It was the proof I needed that her mother slowly poisoned her. That's why Anna had the secret stairs put in—so she'd have access to Hasell without anybody else knowing."

MOM SICK. I must have said it out loud, because Jack looked at me. "It was a message from Hasell. She was trying to tell us that her mother was sick."

The house shuddered around us like a giant awakening, the air inside suddenly electrified.

"That's when the lights went out," Jack continued. "A pair of hands shoved me out the hidden door and it slammed shut behind me. Jayne told me not to worry, that she knew how to fight Anna. It was pitch-dark and I couldn't see her, and she didn't answer when I called her name. I went to the kitchen to call you, and on the way back up the stairs I thought I heard a child asking for help, and it seemed to be coming from this bedroom. When I didn't see anyone, I stepped inside the bathroom and the door slammed shut behind me."

"Did you see Anna?" I whispered.

"No. But before I went into the bathroom, I did see that." He directed my hand to turn the flashlight beam across the room to the rocking chair and the talking doll that sat staring at us, its eyes dark and glassy. I stepped back as the whirring mechanical sounds began, screeching and scratching louder and louder. *"Now I lay me down to sleep."* It stopped abruptly, which was a good thing because I would have thrown it against a wall to make it stop. Or asked Jack to do it because I didn't think I could have touched it.

The cat jumped off the bed and looked up at us. "I think the cat wants us to follow it again," I said.

"What cat?" Jack asked, staring at the exact spot where I'd trained the flashlight.

"The black one standing right in front of us," I said, wiggling the flashlight. I noticed that the cat's fur appeared completely dry despite having been outside in the pouring rain. And there hadn't been any wet paw prints on the floor, either.

"I can't see it." He looked at me with confusion.

Ginette moved closer. "It's right here," she said, pointing a gloved finger at the cat, sitting in the middle of the circle of light.

"No, it's not," Jack insisted.

I opened my mouth to argue but shut it as memories and impressions began to shift in my head, of all the times I'd spotted the cat on the property, and who I'd been with. My mother and I saw the cat, and so did Rich Kobylt. Even General Lee. But Sophie and the other workmen hadn't seen it, and neither had Jack. But Jayne did. Every time I'd been here, and seen the cat, she'd seen it, too.

My mother's eyes met mine, but before she could say anything, the cat took off, pausing at the door as if to make sure we were following, then ran toward the attic door, neatly disappearing through the wood just as we reached it.

I pounded on the attic door with the flat of my hand. "Jayne? Are you in there?" I turned to Jack, frantic. "We've got to get her out of there. If Anna knows who she is, she's in terrible danger."

Ginette pulled on my arm. "What do you mean? Who is Jayne?"

I banged on the door, searching for some reassurance that Jayne was in the attic, and that we weren't too late. "Jayne? Are you in there?"

My mother jerked harder on my arm, pulling me to face her. "Mellie, who is Jayne?"

Jack placed a hand on her shoulder. "She's your daughter, Ginette. The one you gave birth to at the lake house, and believed died."

She paced her gloved hand over her mouth. "How did you . . . ?"

Jack spoke quickly. "I'll tell you more later, but it's all in the album. The pictures of you pregnant, and then the pictures of the baby. The housekeeper told me everything."

I held her elbow as she began to sink, but she straightened on her own. "She can't be alone with Anna. Not if she knows that Jayne is Sumter's daughter." She pushed forward and began hammering on the door. "Open the door, Anna. Open the door!" She tried the doorknob, then pushed on the door several more times before stopping.

"I'll go see if I can open the hidden door from the butler's pantry— Rich Kobylt showed me the little button in the wainscoting," Jack said. "I couldn't open it before, but that might not mean anything. You two stay here. You're stronger together. And if Anna is distracted, that might give you the chance to get through this door and find Jayne."

"And if we have Jayne, we'll be unbeatable," my mother said as she grasped my hand.

Four loud crashes vibrated the attic floor above us as my mother tightened her grasp. "Snow globes," I whispered.

My mother nodded. "Hasell's up there. She must know they're half sisters." Her voice held an edge of surprise. "She'll protect Jayne, but she's not as strong as Anna. Hurry—we must hurry!"

I handed Jack my phone so he'd have a flashlight, then gave him a fast kiss before he ran down the hallway, his footsteps echoing on the stairway long after his shadow disappeared.

The storm continued to batter the roof and structure of the old mansion, matching the barometric pressure dropping inside, the walls creaking and swelling with the stress. An unholy tremor shook the foundation, shoving me into my mother's side. I pretended it was an accident so she wouldn't know how petrified I was.

I swallowed, trying to gain control of my voice. "I hope that means Jack managed to open the door. Let's trust he was right about the diversion." I turned the knob and watched with surprise as the attic door easily opened inward, but I resisted moving forward. "Why can't ghosts hide out in bright sunrooms in the middle of the day?"

Ginette tugged on my hand and, with her phone flashlight guiding the way, led us up the stairs.

The frigid air blew into my lungs, stinging my eyes and skin, and for a moment I couldn't breathe. "Anna's here," I whispered, mostly to make sure my voice still worked.

"Jayne?" Ginette called out.

A groan came from the bed. Ginette aimed the beam in that direction, illuminating the figure of a woman curled into the fetal position. We took a step toward the bed, stopping when we hit a wall of frigid air.

My mother's hand trembled. "That's from Jayne—she's blocking everything now, to protect us. But she's growing weak."

An odd yet familiar fluttering rose from the hidden stairs, overwhelming the noise of the storm. It was flies, hundreds and hundreds of flies, hurtling their small, rigid bodies at the walls, swarming in the small space. "Jack?" I yelled into the opening.

"I'm here," he shouted, but it sounded as if he was out of breath. "I can't get out—something's holding me down." He coughed, and I thought of the flies blocking his airways, slowly suffocating him. "The flies are . . . everywhere."

I pulled on my mother's hand to drag her with me to Jack, but she pulled me back. "No. It's a trap. We need to make sure Jayne's all right first." She squeezed my hand. "And then we fight."

I called down the steps, shouting to be heard over the buzzing, "Jack—hang on!"

With rapid, careful steps we moved into the middle of the room. A swishing sound came from above our heads and we looked up. Long strips of sheets swirled from the rafter, undulating like a human form. I grabbed my mother's hand and ran toward the bed and the still figure lying in the middle.

Ginette tossed the phone on the bed near me and began stripping off her gloves, putting her fingers on a vein in Jayne's neck. "Hold the flashlight, and take Jayne's hand. She's weak from fighting, but her pulse is strong. Hold tight, and don't let go no matter what happens."

I sat on the edge of the bed, then watched as she took Jayne's other hand. She grew rigid, like a divining rod finding water. A surge of electricity traveled from my mother's body and through Jayne, tingling across my palms and up through my fingertips. Jayne's body began to tremble, then shake, her fingers slipping from mine.

"Don't let go," Ginette shouted just as the phone slipped from my grasp and fell facedown, leaving us in complete darkness.

I found Jayne's hand again and grabbed, determined not to let it go again.

"Melanie? Are you here?" From the pressure on the bed near where I sat, I was aware of Jayne digging in her heels against the mattress, trying to sit up against the headboard.

"Yes, Melanie's here. And so am I," Ginette said, her voice intense. "You've been fighting Anna by yourself. Let's show her now what the three of us can do."

We stood with our hands gripped together tightly, the whir of sheets tumbling in the air and filling the space between raindrops and thunderclaps.

My mother's voice was quiet at first, and then seemed to gain strength from some unknown source. I felt the power through our clasped hands, the untapped strength of this delicate-looking woman. "Anna, release Hasell so she can move on to a better place. To a place where she can rest and find peace. If you ever loved her, let her go."

The darkness around us vibrated with an unknown entity, a dark emotion I'd yet to experience and knew I never wanted to. The sheets above us whipped at the ceiling and the wall, seeking something. Someone.

My mother continued, her fingers icy cold in mine as if she were directing all her energy to communicating with the dead. "We know you didn't mean to kill her, Anna. That it was an accident. Was it your guilt that made you hang yourself in this room? Was it? You can find no forgiveness for what you did. But we forgive you. We know the truth now, and there's no reason to keep Hasell here. We forgive you, so you can move on, too. Move on, Anna. Move on from this house and let Jayne live here. It is her rightful home. Let her be."

A frigid wind whipped past us, a long strip of sheeting wrapping its ends around and around my neck, gradually getting tighter and tighter. I knew my mother was watching, could feel her hold on me tighten. "We are stronger than you," she chanted. "We are stronger than you."

Jayne joined in. "We are stronger than you. We are stronger than you."

I was gasping and choking the words, but I managed to speak them, feeling the strength of my mother and sister surge through me.

"Let her go," my mother shouted. "Move on from this place. You are forgiven. Go seek your judgment."

The sweet, pungent smell of pipe tobacco wafted over us, my brain clinging to the scent as bright bubbles of light popped in front of my eyes while the sheet grew tighter and tighter.

"Sumter's here, Anna. To show you the way. He loved you. It was always you. I know you didn't believe it—couldn't believe it—but it's true. And now he's here. He wants to help you. To guide you. Please, Anna, let him. Give us all peace."

"Let us go," Jayne said. "Don't let your anger bind you to this place of sorrow and regret. Go be with your husband and daughter. Be together again."

Mama. The word wasn't spoken out loud, but I felt it inside my head, and surrounding me. The sheet around my neck loosened slightly and I gulped a lungful of air.

Mama. I love you. Come with us now.

The sheet slipped from my neck as Ginette and Jayne gripped my hands to keep me standing. The entire room crackled with static, my hair lifting and hovering around my head like a halo. A glow formed in the corner where the snow globes had been, a small pinprick of blue-white light growing and expanding until it encompassed the entire room. Before it disappeared completely, I saw three people, a man and a woman with a little girl between them, holding hands. They were facing away from us, but they glanced back once before they disappeared completely.

The lights flickered on and I felt a surge of power as if the entire house had suddenly become alit. My mother and Jayne tried to guide me to a chair to sit down, but I was focused on the doorway to the hidden staircase, only allowing myself to truly breathe when Jack appeared at the top, holding a notebook upon which rested an assortment of small bottles and syringes.

He set it down carefully on a low chest and ran to me. It was only then that I allowed myself to let go, to relax into his arms, and believe that everything was going to be all right.

"Hello? Is anybody up here?"

We all looked in surprise as Detective Riley appeared at the top of the stairs, his head nearly brushing the top of the doorframe as he stepped into the attic. "I know you're going to find this hard to believe, but someone using the landline from this house kept calling my cell and hanging up. I figured I'd better come over and check."

Maybe it was the fear and exhaustion, but I started to laugh hysterically, soon joined by Ginette and Jayne. Thomas looked at us in confusion until Jayne raced over to him and threw her arms around his neck. "You're a sore for sight eyes," she said, burying her face under his chin. She pulled back and shook her head. "I mean, it's good you're not there. You're . . ." She clenched her eyes, her forehead creased in concentration. "Here," she finished.

And before she could say another word, Thomas bent his head and kissed her, and I knew I hadn't imagined the soft sigh of relief from everyone else in the room.

CHAPTER 34

I stood next to Nola, frosting the two small birthday cakes, both with dark chocolate icing. Despite the fact that the twins had inherited just about every characteristic from Jack, their love of chocolate was all mine.

"That's not vegan," I said to Nola, catching her licking a finger.

"Pretend you didn't see that," she said. "Or this." She stuck the knife in the remnants of the frosting still clinging to the glass bowl and licked it.

The doorbell rang. I looked at the kitchen clock, relieved to see it was back to telling the actual time. "It's a little early for guests, isn't it?"

"I'll get it," Nola said, giving her hands a quick wash in the sink. I wondered at her enthusiasm at the early arrivals until I saw her smooth her hair behind her ears. Alston and Cooper were expected to attend the twins' first birthday party, what Nola had dubbed "the social event of the season." I told her to hold that thought until we threw her six-teenth birthday blowout, not to mention Jayne's first birthday party, since she now knew the actual date of her birth. Thomas was already helping me to plan it.

Jack passed her on his way into the kitchen. He smiled and moved in front of me. "You have chocolate icing on your mouth," he said.

He held back the hand I'd started to lift and instead gently licked my lip. "Not as good as vanilla, but it will do."

I locked my hands behind his neck. "Are we good, Jack?"

His eyes darkened as he studied me. "If you mean have we passed our first marital hurdle, I'd say yes. If anything, I think we've learned that we each need to work on trusting the other to share the bad stuff. It's a heck of a lot easier dealing with it up front than being run over by the consequences."

"You're not getting any argument here."

He followed my gaze out the window to where my father was putting the final touches on the back garden, where we were having the party despite the hole and caution tape. Nola had strung helium balloons—donated by a contrite Rich Kobylt for speaking out about the hole instead of simply filling it in—along the length of the tape in an attempt to disguise it as being part of the decorations, and my father had moved all pots and containers along the periphery to keep guests from tumbling inside. The only child guest was Blue Skye and I was sure either Sophie or Chad would be wearing her in a pouch and therefore not likely to be toddling past the barriers.

Jayne, in sensible flats and khakis, worked next to my father, laughing at something he said as he stood and reached for her hand to pull her up. He had not taken the news about Jayne easily, just as Ginette had predicted. My mother had always insisted, and still did, that he was the only man she'd ever loved, although the fact that Jayne even existed seemed proof enough that this wasn't true. I placed my head on Jack's chest, listening to his heartbeat. That was the thing with marriage, I thought. There would always be leaps of faith we'd be expected to make, whether we liked where we were supposed to land or not.

We watched as my mother approached, and I saw the way my father's face brightened, the way his body turned toward hers. She stood on her tiptoes to kiss him, a second too long to be called perfunctory, and Jayne smiled. She had finally found the family she'd always longed for, and in a way she'd probably never expected. But she had a mother and sister, and even a father, two nieces, and a nephew. My dad had asked her to call him Dad if she was comfortable with it, and she'd taken to it surprisingly easily.

I felt a little ping around my heart as I watched my parents put their arms around Jayne, but it wasn't jealousy, exactly. It was more like the feeling of loss. Like that of a firstborn on the day her parents bring a sibling home from the hospital, suddenly dethroned from the halcyon days of only-childom. I'd only just found my parents again, discovered new relationships I'd never had, and it was hard to give it up. As Jack said, I wasn't giving up anything, and accepting the new changes would just take time. Like learning to stop labeling every blessed thing in the house (his words, not mine).

I liked Jayne, and even enjoyed admitting our resemblance to each other, especially since she'd dyed her hair back to brunette. And because people thought we were a lot closer in age than we were. She'd moved back into the house on Tradd Street while the renovations continued on her house—moving faster now that there weren't any more "disturbances," according to Rich Kobylt. He'd actually managed to hold on to the same crew for two weeks without anyone running from the house and not returning, even for their tools.

Jayne had promised to stay on as nanny as long as I needed her, or until I could find a replacement. Jack had made some comment about her blocking off her calendar for the next eighteen years, and they'd both laughed. I hadn't.

Jack kissed the top of my head, and I snuggled into him, realizing anew how precious our relationship was, and how easily we almost let it go. There was no pointing fingers of blame—we were both culpable, each of us holding back the truth for fear of rippling the waters. And in so doing, almost creating waves big enough to capsize the boat.

"How's the writing going?" I asked. It had been a subject I'd avoided, understanding now the precarious situation his career was in. He'd been disappearing into his study on a regular basis for the past week, and I figured that if we were going to keep everything in the open between us, I needed to ask.

"It's going great, actually. And so is Nola's music writing. Your mother thinks it had to do with Jayne putting on a mental block so spirits wouldn't bug her. She's apparently very strong-minded, and her block spilled over into other creative processes. Now that she's aware of it, she's using it more carefully."

He kissed the top of my head. "They've agreed to let me write the book, by the way—both Jayne and your mother. All of it. I'm even allowed to use their names. I think Ginette is hoping for a movie deal so we can show up Marc Longo."

I looked up at him in surprise. "I thought you'd decided not to ask—that we would find another way to get the money to remain solvent."

"I did. And then your mother and Jayne approached me and told me not to be stupid. They both said that they're too old to worry what people think, and they want Hasell's story told. She had a short and tragic life and if it can be used as a lesson to help others, then it needs to be out there.

"And I promised them that I would be gentle with Anna's story. Munchausen-by-proxy is a mental illness, borne out of her own personal abandonment issues brought about by her parents' neglect. She knew it, too. And still blamed herself. I think that's why she hanged herself."

"Poor Anna. Despite what she did, it's hard not to feel compassion for her. Even after she tried to scare the living daylights out of me."

"You should have taken your labeling gun after her—now, that might have scared her away."

I elbowed him in the ribs. "Very funny. Somehow I think it took my mother, Jayne, and me to make her see the light. Literally. She was such an unhappy soul. I hope she's found peace. And poor Button. She must have suspected something. Enough to cause her to do something as drastic as faking a baby's death just so she could keep the baby away from Anna. Knowing Anna as she did, she would have assumed that Anna would have tried to find a way to influence the baby's care, perhaps even insinuating that my mother's abandonment of me meant she was an unfit mother, and perhaps then Jayne's raising would have gone to Anna by default."

"Such a sad, sad story." Jack kissed the top of my head. "Why do you think Anna stayed earthbound? Because she couldn't forgive herself?"

"Partly. And also because she didn't want anyone to know what she'd done—that's why she repressed Hasell's spirit, while Hasell stuck around to try to diminish her mother's internal rage that she misdirected toward the rest of the world. And to let everyone know the truth about her death. Not to cast Anna in a bad light, but maybe shine some understanding instead of condemnation for mental illness. I don't know if we would have found the evidence in the stairwell if it hadn't been for Hasell. Or her cat." I shuddered. "I can't believe I didn't know it was a ghost. But because Jayne saw it, it never occurred to me."

Jack kissed my nose. "Don't beat yourself up. Your cluelessness is one of your more endearing attributes."

Mrs. Houlihan bustled into the kitchen, the dogs following behind her, knowing she was bound to drop scraps while she prepared food for the party. "Out you go, you two. Nola and her friends just brought down JJ and Sarah fresh from a nap, and they look sweet enough to eat." She smiled, her round cheeks dimpling, and for a moment I could, indeed, imagine her snacking on my children.

"Let us know when you need us to help bring out trays. The tables are all ready in the garden," I said.

"Will do. But first, if you wouldn't mind, would you please remove that old notebook from the hall table? It's unsightly, and I don't want it to be the first thing guests see when they arrive by the front door."

Jack sent me a quizzical look. "It was in my study. Why is it on the hall table?"

I gave Mrs. Houlihan a thumbs-up as I took Jack's hand and led him to the foyer. "Don't worry—there's no hocus-pocus here," I said, using my father's words for anything resembling psychic activity. "I put it there." Thomas had taken the bottles and syringes for analysis, but had given Hasell's notebook to Jayne, who'd in turn shared it with me.

Hasell had been a gifted artist, her whimsical dreams of exploring the world from the confines of her attic room carefully drawn with colored pencils on alternating pages. She'd used images from the mural and the snow globes, entwining them with those in her vivid imagination, creating a magical world where she could fly among the clouds and visit the four corners of the earth.

On the facing pages her small, childish penmanship told the stories that went with each picture, except they didn't. They were fairy tales, the characters disguised as animals or fairy-tale creatures, their actions exaggerated, their journeys to happily-ever-after convoluted and difficult to follow. It was only after reading it through more than once that one began to read the story she was trying to tell, a story of a loving mother who slipped up a hidden staircase to poison her daughter. It must have been Hasell's way of trying to solicit help from other adults. Maybe it was her isolation that didn't expose her to enough outsiders, with or without her mother's constant presence, or maybe it was the complexities of the stories that allowed those who did read them to dismiss them as the ramblings of a childish, yet creative, mind. We guessed that Anna had hidden the notebook along with her secret stash of bottles after Hasell's death, and then forgotten about them in their secret hiding place.

When Jayne had given me the book, she cried, grieving for the half sister she'd never known who'd led such a short and horrific life, and had known what was being done to her, yet was powerless to stop it. But she'd still found beauty around her, and in her brilliant imagination. I'd hugged Jayne, assuring her that she still had a half sister, and that if she could ever forgive me for thinking she was having an affair with Jack, I'd be the best half sister she could hope for. As Sophie had suggested, the embrace had been one of comfort after Jack had told Jayne the truth about who she was. My insecurities had led me to jump to the wrong conclusion, a mistake for which I'd be beating myself up for a long time to come.

I picked up the notebook and stuck it inside a drawer. "It's for Cooper. He wants to go to medical school, perhaps specialize in psychiatry. He thought this would be an interesting case study." I smiled up at Jack. "Just think, we could have a doctor in the family."

He didn't smile back. "Humph. He'll have to be allowed to date her first, and that's not happening for at least another decade."

We headed for the drawing room, where we could hear the babies chortling, stopping halfway at the sound of a doorbell. I pulled open the door, surprised not only to discover that the doorbell was working consistently, but also to see Meghan Black, leaning on crutches. She had on an amazing necklace and what I was sure was a dress from Anthropologie, and on one foot she wore a beautiful striped espadrille with a grosgrain ribbon encircling her ankle. On the other foot she wore a cast, which explained the crutches.

She smiled, adjusting a bag from Sugar Snap Pea, my favorite children's clothing boutique. "I'm sorry I'm so early, but Nola told me to get here whenever." She held out the shopping bag to me, nearly toppling over in the process. I wondered if clumsiness was a regular thing with her, accounting for the X-ray machine falling on her foot. Jack caught her elbow and she blushed. "Thanks," she said, looking up at Jack and then quickly looking away. I forced myself not to roll my eyes.

"Everybody's with the babies in the parlor. Let's head that way," I said, taking a step in that direction.

She stayed where she was, a frown on her face. "Actually, before we go in, I wanted to give you something." She fumbled with her purse, dropping it twice before she finally got the clasp open. "As part of my assignment, I took a lot of pictures of your backyard, to record the work-in-progress. I was printing them out when I came across an interesting anomaly in one of them."

An ominous prickling sensation crept up my spine. "An anomaly?"

"Well, that's what they call it on that reality haunted house show my mom watches. I don't believe in ghosts or anything like that, but I have to say that this picture kind of weirded me out."

Despite everything that had happened in the last few months, and my giant strides forward in becoming the new Mellie, my first instinct was to run upstairs and pretend I'd never had this conversation. As if reading my mind, Jack grabbed my hand and held tight.

"Can we see?" he asked, holding out his hand toward the small stack of photos she'd pulled out of her purse.

"You can have them—these are copies." She held them out to Jack, then somehow managed to drop them on the floor before they reached Jack's hand. "Sorry," she said, attempting to hold the crutches with one hand while bending down to get the pictures, knocking Jack in the head as he bent to do the same thing.

"You two stay where you are, and I'll get them," I said, kneeling to pick up the four photographs. I stood, holding them out so we could all see them, but far enough away from Meghan that she couldn't knock them out of my hands.

"See how in the first ones it's bright and clear?" she said. "You can see the sunshine and a bit of blue sky through the trees?"

I looked at my poor damaged garden, the toppled rosebushes, and the sunken earth. The photos were all taken on the far side of the cistern, facing the house. I flipped through the first three, all relatively the same, then stopped when I got to the fourth. She didn't have to point out the anomaly—my gaze went right to it. It was a full figure of a man standing on the edge of the cistern. If I hadn't been looking for something, I might have at first dismissed it as a wisp of smoke, but when I looked closely I could see his nineteenth-century jacket and cravat, his dark hair and mustache. The apparition was looking right at the camera, its eyes dark and hollow. But what truly horrified me was what he was holding in his outstretched hand.

"Is that a piece of jewelry?" Jack asked, leaning in to look closer.

It took me two tries to force out the word. "Yes," I said. I met his eyes. "Just like Jolly saw."

"Like I said, you can keep them. I don't think I'll use that weird one in my report, but the other ones are good. I'll probably take more when I come back in a couple of months to finish up."

"A couple of months?" I forced a smile as we finished escorting Meghan toward the drawing room. Nola called to her and stood to help her into a chair, but Jack held me back in the doorway.

"What's wrong?" he asked.

"Besides that man standing by the cistern in our garden who happens to match the description in Jolly's vision?"

"Well, yeah, that's a bit disturbing. But there's something else. Remember—we promised not to keep anything back. I think we've both learned that lesson."

I thought back to the photo I held in my hand, of the odd wispy figure standing by the edge of the cistern. But nobody else had pointed out the dark shadow in the upstairs window, a shapeless *something* looking out at us. From Nola's bedroom. It was one thing to have a spirit hanging out in the backyard. It was quite another to have one lingering around your children's sleeping spaces. I was still so exhausted from the ordeal at the Pinckney mansion. I just needed another week of recovery and then I'd tell him. I'd find an excuse to move Nola out of her bedroom for a week, such as a promise to redecorate it or paint it. Because then I'd be ready to deal with it. Just one more week.

"Nothing to worry about," I said. "Now, let's go celebrate surviving our first year as parents of twins."

He pulled me back into his arms and kissed me soundly. "I love you, Melanie Trenholm."

I met his eyes, feeling the truth of his words. "And I love you, too, Jack Trenholm."

We held hands and walked into the drawing room, feeling the love that surrounded us that almost, but not quite, covered up the sense of foreboding that seemed to lurk beyond the periphery of my vision.

THE GUESTS ON SOUTH BATTERY

KAREN WHITE

QUESTIONS FOR DISCUSSION

1. Melanie Trenholm has psychic abilities that she is reluctant to use in a public way. If you had psychic abilities, would you feel the same as Melanie does and try to hide them from people or would you share them? Why?

2. Melanie is able to see and communicate with ghosts; is this a blessing or a curse? Do you know anyone with similar abilities?

3. The novel is set in Charleston, South Carolina, which is a city that really celebrates its history and is reputed to have many ghost sightings. If you had Melanie's ability to communicate with ghosts, would you choose to live in Charleston and/or work as a Realtor? Why do you think Melanie stays in both her city and her profession when she seems to hate her abilities?

4. Karen White often uses real, existing buildings and locations in her novels. Do you enjoy "seeing" a city through a novel in the way a reader sees Charleston in *The Guests On South Battery*?

5. As a new wife and mother, Melanie still expects to live life according to her detailed plans and schedules, but she is finding it extremely difficult to do so. Why do you think Melanie can't seem to allow for deviation from her plans for her family and life?

6. Do you consider Melanie to be a reliable or unreliable narrator? Why?

7. Melanie has a complicated relationship with her mother, and has to confront her mother's past unexpectedly in the novel. If you discovered your mother had another child whom she never told you about, would it permanently affect your relationship with your her? Do you think Melanie reacted in a realistic way?

8. Jack is the first one to realize who Jayne Smith is; did he do the right thing by not telling Melanie right away? If you were him, would you have told Melanie or kept it a secret?

9. Do you think that Melanie jumped to conclusions prematurely about Jack and Jayne or was she justified in believing they were having an affair? Do you think Melanie should have trusted Jack despite any evidence to the contrary?

Smoky silhouettes of church spires stamped against the bruised skies of a Charleston morning give testament to why it's called the Holy City. The steepled skyline at dawn is a familiar sight for early risers who enjoy a respite from the heat and humidity in summer, as is the beauty of the sunrise through the Cooper River Bridge, and the sounds of chirps and calls of the thousands of birds and insects that populate our corner of the world.

Others, like me, awaken early only to shorten the night, to quiet the secret stirrings of the restless dead who wander during the darkest hours between sunset and sunrise.

I lay on my side, Jack's arm resting protectively around my waist, my own arm thrown around the soft fur of General Lee's belly. The dog's snoring and my husband's soft breathing were the only sounds in the old house, despite its being currently inhabited by two adults, three dogs, a teenage girl, and eighteen-month-old twins. I never counted the myriad spirits who passed peacefully down the house's lofty corridors. Over the past several years I'd extricated the not-so-nice ones and made my peace with the others, who were content to simply exist alongside us.

That's what had awakened me. The quiet. No, that wasn't right. It was more the absence of sound. Like the held breath between the pull of a trigger and the propulsion of the bullet.

Being careful not to awaken Jack or General Lee, I slowly disentangled myself from the bedsheets, watching as General Lee assumed my former spooning position next to Jack. They barely stirred, and I considered for a moment whether I should be insulted. I picked up my iPhone and shut off the alarm, which had been set for five a.m.—noting it was four forty-six—then crossed the room to my old-fashioned alarm clock, which I kept just in case. Jack had made me get rid of the additional two I'd once stationed around the room, accusing me of trying to wake the dead each morning. As if I had to try.

Since I was a little girl, the spirits of the dearly departed had been trying to talk to me, to involve me in their unfinished business. I'd found ways—most often involving singing an ABBA song—to drown out their voices, with some success, but every once in a while one voice was louder than the others. Usually because they were shouting in my ear or trying to shove me down the stairs, making them impossible to ignore, regardless of how much I wanted to.

I stumbled into my bathroom, using the flashlight from my phone, and silently cursed my half sister, Jayne, and my best friend, Dr. Sophie Wallen-Arasi, for being the cause of my predawn ramblings. They had taken it upon themselves to get me fit and healthy after the birth of the twins, JJ—for Jack Junior—and Sarah. This involved feeding me food I wouldn't give my dog—although, actually, I'd tried, and he'd turned up his nose and walked away—and forcing me to go running most mornings.

Although I was more of a jogger than a runner, the excercise required lots of energy that shouldn't be fueled by powdered doughnuts—according to Sophie—and made me sweat more than I thought necessary, especially in the humid summer months, when bending down to tie my shoes caused perspiration to drip down my face and neck.

Barely awake, I pulled on the running pants Nola had given me for my last birthday; she'd told me that they were fashionable *and* functional and had the dual purpose of sucking everything in, making one's back-side look as if the wearer were a lifelong runner. I'd tried to tell Jayne and Sophie that these wonder pants made the actual running part obsolete, but they'd simply stared at me without blinking before return-ing to their conversation regarding reducing their times for the next Bridge Run, which was scheduled for the spring.

I tiptoed back into the bedroom, noticing as I pulled down the hem of my T-shirt that it was on inside out, and paused by the bed to look at my husband of less than two years. My chest did the little contracting thing it had been doing since I'd first met bestselling true-crime-history author Jack Trenholm. I'd thought then that he was too handsome, too charming, too opinionated, and way too annoying to be anything to me other than someone to be admired from afar and kept at arm's length. Luckily for me, he'd disagreed.

My gaze traveled to the video baby monitor we kept on the bedside table. Sarah was sleeping neatly on her side, her stuffed bunny—a gift from Sophie—tucked under her arm, her other stuffed animals arranged around the crib in a specific order that only Sarah and I understood. I'd had to explain to Jack that the animals had been arranged by fur pat-terns and colors, going from lightest to darkest. I'm sure I'd done the same thing when I was a child because, I'd explained, it was important to make order out of the world.

In the adjacent crib JJ slept on his back, with his arms and legs flung out at various angles, his stuffed animals and his favorite kitchen whisk—even I couldn't explain his attachment to this particular kitchen utensil—tossed in disarray around his small body. My fingers twitched, and I had to internally recite the words to "Dancing Queen" backward to keep myself from entering the nursery and lining up the toys in the bed and tucking my little son in a corner of the crib with a blanket over him.

It was a skill I'd learned at Jayne's insistence. She was a professional nanny, which meant—I suppose—that she knew best, and she'd insisted that my need for order was borderline OCD and not necessarily the best influence on the children. There was absolutely nothing wrong with my need for order, as it had helped me survive a childhood with an alcoholic father and an absent mother, but I loved my children too much to dismiss Jayne's concerns completely.

I would not, however, retire my labeling gun and had taken proactive measures by keeping it hidden so it wouldn't "disappear" as my last two had.

Staring at my sweet babies on the monitor, my heart constricted again, leaving me breathless for a moment as I considered how very fortunate I was to have found Jack (or, as he insisted, he'd found me), and then to have these two beautiful children. An added and welcome bonus to the equation was Jack's sixteen-year-old daughter, Nola, whom I loved like my own child despite her insistence on removing my three main food groups—sugar, carbs, and chocolate—from the kitchen.

"Good morning, beautiful," Jack mumbled, his two sleepy dark blue eyes staring up at me: General Lee emitted a snuffling snore. "Going to work?"

Before I was married, I'd always risen before dawn to be the first person in the offices of Henderson House Realty on Broad Street. But now I had a reason to stay in bed and he was lying there looking so much more appealing than a run through the streets of Charleston. Of course, spending the night in the dungeon at the Old Exchange Building was also more appealing than a run, but still.

"Not yet. Meeting Jayne for a run." I stood by the bed and leaned down to place a kiss on Jack's lips, lingering long enough to see if he would give any indication that he wanted me to crawl back into bed. Instead his eyes closed again as he moved General Lee closer to his chest, giving me an odd pang of jealousy.

After quietly closing the bedroom door, I paused in the upstairs hallway, listening. Even the ticking of the old grandfather clock seemed muffled, the sound suffocated by something unseen. Something waiting. The nightlights that lined the hallway—a leftover from when Jayne lived with us, a concession to her crippling fear of the dark and the things that hid within it—gave me a clear view of Nola's closed bedroom door.

She'd been sleeping in the guest room, as I'd decided in March, right after the twins' first birthday party, that her bedroom needed to be redecorated. I felt a tug of guilt as I walked past it to the stairs, remembering the shadowy figure I'd seen in Nola's bedroom window in a photograph taken by one of Sophie's preservation students, Meghan Black. She was excavating the recently discovered cistern in the rear garden and had taken the photograph and shown it to Jack and me. We'd both seen the shadowy figure of a man in old-fashioned clothing, holding what looked to be a piece of jewelry. But I'd been the only one to notice the face in Nola's window.

Having recently dealt with a particularly nasty and vengeful spirit at Jayne's house on South Battery, I hadn't found the strength yet to grapple with another. Despite promises to be open and honest with each other, I hadn't told Jack, having bargained with myself that I'd bring it up as soon as I thought I could mentally prepare myself. That had been seven months ago, and all I'd done was move Nola into the guest room and then interview a succession of decorators.

I stifled a yawn. *Just one more week,* I thought to myself. One more week working every possible hour trying to make my sales quota at Henderson House Realty, of trying to put myself on the leader board once more. I needed it not just for the sense of pride and accomplishment, but also because we needed the money.

Then I'd have enough energy and brain cells to be able to figure out who these new spirits were, and then to make them go away. Preferably without a fight. Then I'd tell Jack what I'd seen and that I'd already taken care of the problem so he wouldn't have to be worried. He had enough on his plate already, working with a new publisher on a book about my family and how Jayne came to own her house on South Battery.

I entered the kitchen, my stomach rumbling as I reached behind the granola and quinoa boxes in the pantry for my secret stash of doughnuts. But instead of grasping the familiar feel of a brown paper bag, I found myself pulling out a box of nutrition bars—no doubt as tasty as the cardboard in which they were packaged. Taped to the front was a note in Nola's handwriting:

Try these instead! They've got chocolate and 9 grams of protein!

Happy visions of running upstairs and pulling Nola from her bed earlier than she'd probably been awake since infancy was the only reason I didn't break down and weep. The grandfather clock chimed, telling me I was already late, so I gave one last-minute look to see whether I could spot my doughnut bag, then left the house through the back door without eating anything. If I passed out from starvation halfway through my run, Nola might feel sorry enough to bring a doughnut.

I stopped on the back steps, suddenly aware that the silence had followed me outside. No birds chirped; no insects hummed. No sounds of street traffic crept into the formerly lush garden my father had painstakingly restored from the original Loutrel Briggs plans. When an ancient cistern had been discovered after the heavy spring rains had swallowed a large section of the garden, Sophie swooped in and declared it an archaeological dig and surrounded it with yellow caution tape. Several months later, we were still staring at a hole behind our house. And I was still feeling the presence of an entity that continued to elude me, but who haunted my peripheral vision. A shadow that disappeared every time I turned a corner, the scent of rot the only hint that it had been there at all.

Walking backward to avoid facing away from the gaping hole, I made my way to the front of the house, tripping only twice on the uneven flagstones that were as much a part of Charleston's South of Broad neighborhood as were wrought-iron gates and palmetto bugs.

"There you are!" shouted a voice from across the street. "I thought you were standing me up."

I squinted at the figure waiting at the curb, and regretted not putting in my contacts. I really didn't need them all the time, and not wearing them when I ran saved me from seeing my reflection without makeup in the bathroom mirror so early in the morning.

"Good morning, Jayne," I grumbled, making sure she was aware of how unhappy I was to be going for a run. Especially when I had a much better alternative waiting for me in my bedroom.

I was already starting to perspire at the thought of the four-mile jog in front of me. Despite its being early November, and although we'd been teased by Mother Nature with days chilly enough that we'd had to pull out our wool sweaters, the mercury had taken another surprise leap, raising both the temperature and the dew point as if summer was returning to torture us for a bit.

Even though Jayne had already jogged several blocks in the heat and humidity from her house on South Battery, she was barely sweating and her breath came slowly and evenly. We'd only recently discovered each other, our shared mother having been led to believe that her second daughter, born eight years after me, had died at birth. Jayne and I had grown close in the past few months, our bond most likely strengthened by the fact that we shared the ability to communicate with the dead, a trait inherited from our mother.

"Which way do you want to go this morning?" she said, jogging in place and looking way too perky.

"Is back inside an option?"

She laughed as if I'd been joking, then began to jog toward East Bay.

I struggled to catch up, pulling alongside her as she ran down the middle of the street. It was easier to dodge traffic at this time of day than to risk a turned ankle on the ancient uneven sidewalks. "Will Detective Riley be joining us this morning?" I panted.

Her cheeks flushed, and I was sure it wasn't from exertion. "I don't know. I haven't spoken to him in a week."

"Did you have a fight?"

"You could say that." Her emotions seemed to fuel her steps and she sprinted ahead. Only when she realized she'd left me behind did she slow down so I could catch up.

"What . . . happened?" I was finding it hard to breathe and talk at the same time, but I needed to know. I'd introduced Jayne to Detective Thomas Riley, and they'd been a couple ever since Jayne, our mother, and I had sent to the light several unsettled spirits who'd been inhabiting her house earlier in the year.

"I told him I wanted to go public with my abilities to help people communicate with loved ones. He said it was a bad idea because there are a lot of crazies out there who'd be knocking on my door."

I looked at her askance. "Funny, he didn't . . . seem to . . . have such qualms . . . when he asked me about some of his . . . unsolved cases." I'd recently agreed to work with Detective Riley on a case involving a coed who'd been missing from her College of Charleston dorm room since 1997.

"That's because you're working incognito. I want to advertise. And Mother said she'd be happy to work alongside me. She thinks you should also go public and work with us." She sprinted ahead again, but this time I was sure it was because she didn't want me to respond. Not that I could have, since my lungs were nearly bursting.

I doggedly pursued her, turning left on East Bay and almost catching up as we neared Queen Street, dodging the fermenting restaurant garbage waiting for pickup on the sidewalk. My feet dragged, the humidity seeming to make them heavier, and my breath came in choking gasps. My stomach rumbled and I quickly did a mental recalculation of my route. In an effort at self-preservation, I took a left on Hasell, not even wondering how long it would take Jayne to notice I was missing. With my destination in mind, I jogged toward King Street and took a right, my steps much lighter now as I headed toward my just reward.

Catching the green light at Calhoun, I nearly sprinted across the street toward Glazed Gourmet Donuts, almost expecting Jayne to show up just as I reached the door and yank me away. Instead I was merely greeted with the heavenly sent of freshly made doughnuts and the delicious smell of coffee gently embracing me and inviting me inside. I stood in the entryway for a moment, inhaling deeply, until I heard a cough from behind me.

I turned to apologize for blocking the doorway, but stopped with my mouth halfway open. Not because the tall, dark-haired man standing behind me was a contender for *People* magazine's sexiest man alive, or because he was smiling at me with more than just casual interest, his dark brown eyes lit with some inner amusement. Nor was it because he wore tight-fitting running clothes that accentuated his muscled chest and was breathing slightly more quickly than the average pedestrian—although, like Jayne, he appeared to be barely perspiring. I stared at him because I'd seen him before. Not just that morning, not just in the doughnut shop, but out on the street several times in the past few weeks as I jogged down the streets of Charleston, or ran errands, or traveled to various house showings in the city.

It hadn't struck me as odd until right at that moment, standing only inches apart. Charleston was a small city, and it was inevitable that I'd run into the same person occasionally. But not every day. I blinked once, wondering what else about him captivated my attention, and realized what it was just as the door opened behind the man and Jayne appeared, looking flustered and not a little bit annoyed.

"I knew I'd find you here," she said, walking past the man to stand in front of me and no doubt try to intimidate me. Which was hard to do, considering we were the exact same height.

I looked at the man again. "Are you related to Marc Longo?" I asked, half hoping he'd say no. Marc was my cousin Rebecca's husband, and Jack's nemesis after having stolen Jack's book idea. We were still trying to recover from the financial and professional setback it had caused Jack's writing career. Marc was also a boil on the behinds of our collective well-being, as he was currently trying to get us to agree to film the movie based on that novel in our house on Tradd Street. Because he was that kind of an insufferable jerk. The fact that I'd once dated him didn't endear him to Jack, either.

"I am," he said, a shadow briefly settling behind his eyes. He held out a slim hand to me. "I'm Anthony Longo, Marc's younger brother. And you're Melanie Middleton."

"Melanie Trenholm now," I corrected. I hesitated for a moment before placing my hand in his.

He grinned. "Don't worry. The only thing my older brother and I share is our last name and our parents."

Turning to Jayne, he said, "And you two beautiful women must be related. Twins?"

I almost smiled at the compliment, but didn't. Because I was certain he already knew exactly who we were. Being in the same family wasn't the only thing Anthony Longo shared with his brother.

Jayne lifted her hand to shake. Her lips worked to form words, and before I could clamp my hand over her mouth, she said, "You have very dark hair. It's brown." She blinked rapidly before dropping her hand. "I mean . . . yes, you have hair. Well, it's nice to meet you." Her face flushed a dark red. Turning to me, she said, "I'm going to get us some coffee and doughnuts."

"Sorry," I said, watching her departing back. "My sister, Jayne, hasn't had a lot of experience with the opposite sex. She seems to get tongue-tied when dealing with attractive men."

He laughed, a deep, chest-rumbling sound. "I accept the compliment, then."

I took a step back, as much to put distance between us as to allow a couple to enter the shop. I was reserving judgment, wanting to hate him on sight, but there was something likable about him. He was charming, like Marc, but without the smarmy self-love that Marc exuded from every pore. I met Anthony's forthright gaze. "Have you been following me?"

His eyes widened, and I wondered if I'd taken him by surprise with my candor or if he was just pretending. Instead of answering, he said, "Why don't we sit so we can chat?" He held out his hand toward an open table, and I led the way.

We sat just as Jayne approached with a bag and two coffees. Marc immediately stood and took the coffees from her while Jayne clutched the doughnut bag close to her. "You don't eat doughnuts?" she said to Marc, then quickly shook her head. "I mean, you don't have doughnuts."

He grinned warmly and I wanted to kick him to tell him being attractive and charming wasn't going to help matters.

"I've got a delicious protein shake waiting for me at home, so I'm good, thanks."

"She won't share," Jayne forced out, clutching the bag even tighter. We were going to have to work harder on dealing with social settings with men. I'd thought that her relationship with Thomas Riley was a good sign that she'd been cured of acute awkwardness, but I'd been wrong. It apparently was on a man-to-man basis.

Anthony's smile faded slightly as he glanced at me, as if needing reassurance that Jayne wouldn't bite.

"She's probably referring to me. I don't share my doughnuts, and if anyone tries, they will lose a finger." I didn't smile, trying to show him that I wasn't joking.

I took a sip from my coffee while eying the bag expectantly, but Jayne kept it clenched to her chest, no doubt planning to hold them for ransom until I finished the run. "So," I said, "why have you been stalking me?"

Anthony quirked an eyebrow. "Stalking? Hardly. More like looking for an opportunity to approach you that wouldn't be noticed by any of your friends, family, or coworkers. It's very hard to do. You're a moving target."

I glanced around, glad we were in a public place and that Jayne was with me. Alarm bells were starting to go off inside my head, the same ones that rang out when Sophie or my handyman, Rich Kobylt, asked to talk to me. It was usually something bad—like wood-boring beetles in the dining room floor—and always something I didn't want to hear, such as the cost of a repair.

"So why did you want to see me?" I asked.

"I'd like to make a deal with you."

"A deal?" Jayne repeated.

Anthony leaned forward. "You may or may not be aware that I own Magnolia Plantation—or, as it's known now, Gallen Hall. It was formerly owned by the Vanderhorst family—the same family who once owned your house on Tradd Street. It was purchased at auction by my grandfather back in the twenties. He was the man found buried beneath your fountain, if you recall."

As if I could forget. I kept still, trying not to remember the menacing ghost of Joseph Longo, or how he came to be buried in my garden along with former owner Louisa Vanderhorst. "Okay," I said, not sure where this was heading but fairly certain I didn't want to go there.

"You may also recall that Marc and I started a winery venture together a few years ago, using the land around the plantation."

"Vaguely." The alarm bells were getting louder now. Jack had recently read to me—somewhat gleefully—an article in the *Post and Courier* about a Longo family member accusing Marc of swindling, and threatening legal action.

"Yes, well, my dear brother knew the land wasn't good for a vineyard—a fact he kept from me when he told me from the goodness of his heart he was going to allow me to buy out his share and give me a good deal." His hands formed themselves into fists. "A good deal on worthless land."

"That wasn't very nice," Jayne said, her tone similar to the one she used when settling disputes between the twins. And Jack and me. She was a nanny, after all.

"You could say that," Anthony said, giving Jayne an appreciative grin. She blushed, then resumed her deliberate breathing.

"So what does that have to do with me? He's married to my cousin, but we're not close."

"I know. Which is why I'm thinking we needed to talk." He leaned very close. "It seems we both have a bone to pick with my brother."

"We do? If you're referring to Jack's career, he just signed a new two-book deal and is hard at work on his new book. Marc gave us a setback, but that's behind us."

"Is it? I thought Marc wanted to film his movie in your house."

"He does. And I believe Jack told him where he could file that idea." Anthony smiled smugly. "I'm sure he did. I've never had the pleasure of meeting your husband, but I've heard Marc rant about him often enough to know they're not friends."

Jayne coughed.

"You could say that," I said. "Which is really why we're putting all of that in the past and moving forward."

"Yes, well, too bad Marc didn't get that memo."

The alarm bells were now clanging so loudly I was sure everyone in the restaurant could hear them. "What do you mean?"

He leaned in a little closer. "Marc has lots of . . . connections. Has a lot of influence, even in the publishing world. Jack's new contract might not be as ironclad as you'd like to think."

"That's ridiculous," I hissed. "He's signed it, and received the advance. He's working on it now and his publisher has big plans for it."

Anthony shook his head slowly. "Doesn't matter to Marc. He has . . . ways to get what he wants."

"And what does he want?"

"Your house."

"My house? We're not selling. Ever. We've gone through quite a lot for that house." I thought of the ghost of Louisa Vanderhorst, who watched over us, the scent of roses alerting us of her presence. Of old Nevin Vanderhorst, who'd left the house to me in his will, knowing long before I did that the house and I were meant to be together for as long as I lived. Or, as Jack had said at our wedding in the back garden, perhaps even longer.

Anthony smiled, but it wasn't friendly. "Tell me, Melanie—would you be financially solvent if it weren't for Jack's income? I'm sure he's getting royalties from his earlier books, but without a new book, sales of his older books peter out, don't they?"

I thought of how we'd had to borrow money from Nola, who had made a few lucrative sales of music she'd written, to keep the house. It was a loan, but we were still working on paying that back.

I started to say no, but Jayne kicked me under the table. "It's none of your business," she said, speaking slowly, as if to make sure the right words came out.

"Right," I agreed. "It's none of your business." I stood, and Jayne stood, too.

Anthony slid his chair back and stood as well, blocking our way to the door. "What if I said I could help you outmaneuver Marc and make a lot of money at the same time?"

"What do you mean?"

"Marc found something that's convinced him there is something valuable hidden in the mausoleum at Gallen Hall cemetery. He can't get access, though."

"Why?" I asked, although with the mention of the mausoleum, I was afraid I knew why.

He inclined his head, his voice very quiet. "I know that you can speak to the dead."

Jayne inhaled quickly, but I kept my eyes on Anthony. "I don't know where you heard that. . . ."

"Rebecca, of course. I know she has premonitions in her dreams—she's even told me of a few she had about me. But she said your powers are much stronger, that you can actually talk to the dead."

"Well, she's mistaken." I slid my chair up to the table so I could inch my way around Anthony to access the door, and saw Jayne do the same thing. "I've got to go. Sorry I can't help you."

We'd made it only a few feet before he said, "I heard about that cistern in your back garden—how several grad students assigned to the excavation refuse to return to the site. I was curious, so I did some digging. Do you know where the bricks came from?"

A cold chill pricked at the base of my neck as I recalled the apparition of the man in the photograph, standing by the edge of the gaping hole and holding what appeared to be a piece of jewelry. And the menacing aura that had pervaded my house and yard ever since the cistern had been discovered. "No," I said, my voice warbling only a little. "And I don't care."

We'd made it to the door when Anthony called out to us, "It's from an older mausoleum in the Gallen Hall cemetery. I thought you'd want to know. Just in case."

I turned to face him. "Just in case what?"

"Just in case you find something . . . unexpected in your cistern."

Jayne pushed the door open, then propelled me into the warm morning air with a gentle shove. I turned around to see whether Anthony would follow us out, and found myself staring at the glass door of the shop. Except instead of seeing my own reflection, I saw the clear specter of a gentleman in what appeared to be an old-fashioned cravat and jacket staring back at me with black, empty sockets.

Photo by Marchet Butler

Karen White is the *New York Times* bestselling author of more than twenty books, including the Tradd Street novels, *Dreams of Falling*, *The Night the Lights Went Out*, *Flight Patterns*, *The Sound of Glass*, *A Long Time Gone*, and *The Time Between*, and the coauthor of *The Forgotten Room* with *New York Times* bestselling authors Beatriz Williams and Lauren Willig. She grew up in London but now lives with her husband and two dogs near Atlanta, Georgia.

KAREN WHITE